DISCOVERY
Book Two of the Discovery Trilogy

F. D. Brant

F. D. Brant

GRESHAM, OREGON

F. D. Brant
PO Box 522
Gresham Or 97030
www.fdbrant.com

Publisher's Note: This is a work of fiction. Names, characters, places, and incidents are a product of the author's imagination. Locales and public names are sometimes used for atmospheric purposes. Any resemblance to actual people, living or dead, or to businesses, companies, events, institutions, or locales is completely coincidental.

Book Layout © 2017 BookDesignTemplates.com

Discovery/ F. D. Brant. -- 1st ed.
ISBN 978-1-946179-21-0

Books Written by F. D. Brant

Science Fiction Adventure

O Gods Strangers and Messengers

Survival Trilogy

Time of Isolation

Desperate to Survive

A Taste of history Past

The Harsh Lands

Post-Apocalyptic

Unexpected Unplanned and into the Unknown

Discovery Trilogy

The Ones Before

Discovery

An Ancient Fire

Contemporary Christian Fiction

The Woman in the Snow

How does one know where their lives may be heading? Fauul thought, *So many changes, so many different directions.* After all, he had been fine in his ignorance going along with his life as a cartographer, working his way up the ladder, single, and because nature had bestowed "good looks", never lacking in female companionship. Yet, now at this very moment, all of that had changed. *Is this change for the better?* Well, if he knew that answer then he probably wouldn't be second guessing himself at this very moment. Back in the township where he was from, life was so different than the one he was leading presently. After all, he was a township whelp, loving that life, but presently he found himself in the middle of the outback, a distance from a remote and very small village. Here, where he presently was living, there were only the beasts, the sister and brother, and the outback.

Yet here he was, and to his surprise, it was by choice. This brought a smile. Who'd have thought that he would do this voluntarily? No him for sure. Personally, he never thought that it would be a female that would influence him this much, and to the point where he wanted to make this change. And he had to admit that was exactly why he was here – because of a female. Lauma, the sister of Lauut, had caught his eye, and even though he had tried, he could not forget her and had returned to discover that it had been no different for her. So, for both, he was here to see if this initial attraction was more than that. Only time would tell. But if the early indicators were accurate, then his future was settled already. And to be honest with the time he had been here the closeness between the two had grown to the point of pursuit. But, as he had learned so far, what one saw in the future was not necessarily what the real future would hold. One way or the other, eventually he would have to return to that township and settle what had been left open when he left. But that again was for a future time, a future completely unwritten, and on those empty blank pages anything could and probably would be written.

* * *

Jllon continued to work the dig site in the desert days east of the small village. While the finds were still coming, so far, none had been as great as what was discovered at the second of the two sites. It was there they had confirmed that the ancients, the *ones before*, were more than myth, and in fact had lived, had existed. Even though, over time, the way the ancients had accomplished things had disappeared, hints, obscure hints of their ways were still here at this dig site. An example of the ways things were observed by the present people, and the way it was really performed, is the myth of flight. As time had passed the stories changed and with those changes they stated that the ancients would fly without any assistance – they were like the flyers. While in reality, they had built devices that allowed them to fly.

Apparently their mode of transportation was vastly different and these ancients had built wide trails and had used some type of substance to make the surface smooth. The nomads of the desert had confirmed that there were other wonders of this construction deep into the desert – including substantial constructions to cross canyons and washes. While in the present world they depended on the beasts to assist them in their many needs, it appeared that it was not so for these ancients. The few items they had discovered, which appeared to have been built for transportation and movement, had no way to attach the beasts. So an alternate power of some kind had to be used. From the initial studies made of one of these devices it appeared they were self-powered – still how this self-power worked, no one knew. Self-powered . . . really?

He had learned, from the wise one of the nomads that the nomads had a verbal history that went back approximately six thousand turns. In that history these trails and constructions across canyons had always been. So he knew conclusively that everything they had uncovered and discovered went farther into prehistory – so far into the past that fact had become myth and legend. So far into the unwritten past that until these discoveries in the desert there had been nothing found to suggest that the *ones before* had really existed and as a result were no more than myth and legend. This left Jllon wondering if the other proposed site far to the west of their present location would be as fruitful. Still, there was much here to keep one on his toes as the discoveries kept coming.

Yes, there was still much to be done, so much to understand, so much to prove . . .

As Fauul continued to learn the ways of the herders he found it was much more complicated than he ever imagined. He had considered the learning of the cartographer craft difficult, and found that this was easily just as difficult, if in another way.

Yet, as he became more and more comfortable with the outback, he felt a growing peace within himself. It was a surprise as he had always considered himself a township kind of male. He loved the energy and chaos and the crush of the people. Still, working here on this property in the outback, he was beginning to appreciate the quiet, the soft breezes, and the open spaces where one would see far off into the distances. The nights were spectacular with the stars seeming to be so close one could reach up and touch them. Sitting on the front porch and enjoying the evening after the day's work had been finished, he was silent and deep in thought about these changes.

"What are you thinking?" Lauma asked, as she snuggled up against him.

Turning and smiling at her he thought. *Just a short time ago I didn't know this female, was single, and had no thought of a mate, and here I am looking at her knowing she is to be my life partner, my mate.* He instead said, "Just thinking about all the changes in my life. You know coming from a township, and only visiting the outback when either work called for it or to travel from one place to another . . . with only me to think about and such."

"Know what you mean really. After all, while not quite the same for me, I was single with no prospects . . . my brother and me, wondering what would happen, as we were the last of our family. There was no male in this village that held any interest for me, and knowing, most likely because of what we had to do here to keep the property working; neither of us could leave for more than a day or two so my prospects were close to zero."

"And yet here we are. Who would have guessed after that first meeting that we would be here together anticipating our accepting each other as life mates?"

Remembering back to the beginning, she smiled and said, "True, I wasn't sure who you and that scout were. We had rumors of a bandit group working the area and they would approach in a similar way. So I needed to be sure."

"Right, and that's why you threw that knife, right?"

Smiling, she said, "Had to get your attention didn't I?"

"You surely did that, and if that did not do it then that dog of yours would have." They broke out and laughed about that rocky start. He continued, "It took a bit for you to even trust us and accept that we were here to purchase some of your pack beasts."

"Yes, all that is true, but then something changed, and I couldn't keep from looking at you, and I could see it was the same for you."

"What me looking at me?" He laughed at the small joke and continued. "Very true, and I think the rest, Doube and your brother, saw it too. But since Doube, and myself of course, would be leaving, I figured I would just get over you and continue on with my life up in that township where I lived."

She smiled saying, "Didn't happen did it."

"No it didn't. And when I showed up at that gather not knowing the situation with you, your reaction was hilarious."

With a bit of puzzlement she asked, "How so?"

"Well when you saw me approaching with your brother I saw all sorts of emotions coming from you. You know, surprise, shock, confusion, and yes even anger. When I saw that anger flash I thought okay now what did I do?"

She laughed lightly saying, "Well, what did you expect? I mean I finally had come to terms that I might never see you again, and then without a note from a runner or anything you show up. Of course I was surprised, and yes even a little angry. It was the last thing I expected."

"I have to admit I tried to get over you, but you are very difficult to get over. Strong willed, and definitely opinionated, one who knows her own mind, and I have to say, one who is not afraid to tell someone if they want to listen, or not."

"Now I'm not that bad, am I?"

Again smiling he said, "Yes you are and it's one of the many things about you that makes me want you."

Blushing a little at that comment she then asked, "How do you mean that?"

Laughing he said, "Any way you want to take it. Anyway do you think we should go back inside and talk with your brother? He's inside all by himself."

"Maybe, but I think he can take care of himself. Maybe we should invite him out here since it is much nicer here."

"Good idea." Standing up and opening the door Fauul yelled, "Lauut why don't you come out and join us. After all it's a great night out here."

"Sound great, but I didn't want to interrupt you two and your private conversation."

Lauma replied saying, "We thank you for that but it wasn't that private. Tell you what I'll go get us some hot beverage to finish out the evening and we can enjoy what's left before we head off to our sleeping spaces." She reluctantly stood up and headed inside.

"Sounds great, will be out there in a moment. In fact since I'm in here let me help you with those beverages. It will be easier with the two of us, and I have the feeling that it won't be long and this old routine that you I and have done for a long, long time will be gone."

"You know something you are probably right." Then somewhat sadly she continued, "I guess things just never stay the same. We have helped each other for so many turns, and I don't think there are siblings around here that are as close as we are."

"Yes, it will be a sad day for me also. Still at the same time a very happy one. You know it's funny how emotions can play both ways over the same event. I mean I will be sad with the loss of our closeness and our working together. And at the same time I will be happy to have you with the one who will be your life mate – which means, by the way, that I gain a brother, something I never had, and you gain your life companion. So we both win, and we both lose."

It surely was true; nothing seemed to remain the same. Even the good seemed to adjust as time continued. All at once something that was comfortable, and very real, suddenly becomes something of a dream, as if it never happened, leaving one to wonder if indeed, did it happen? Lauut wondered how it would be once his sister was part of someone else's life and family. Where he and she had been primary in each other's lives, he would now become secondary. He could see it happening even now. As the two of them grew closer, she seemed to be pulling away from him – a sad thought indeed.

He would be sorry when this part of his life would be gone. They had supported each other through all the difficult times when their sires had died. Then it continued through the better times and lean times. For them it had always been a struggle, and as time went on they found they were a pretty good team. Privately he looked at his sister as she finished preparing the hot beverages, and thought sadly once again, *This familiar scene will soon be gone, and gone forever. Still I cannot deny her. She deserves this so much.*

Lauma seeing her brother in one of his introspective moods didn't say anything. But she was sure she understood what was going on in his mind. Major changes were coming for both of them. After all, for so long it had just been them, and now it was not so. Quietly she said, "Lauut why don't you bring yours out with you. I'll carry out the other two, and when you are ready you can join us. I suspect we won't be much longer anyway. It's been a tough day."

Smiling Lauut replied, "Know what you mean. I'm glad Fauul is here. We sure needed his help today."

Carrying the two cups she went back outside to the sitting area on the porch and handed Fauul his drink.

The night was quiet and it was cooling from the day's heat when Lauma returned, he asked, "What were you two talking about in there? I could hear you but couldn't actually follow the conversation. Of course if it was private you need not tell me."

"Oh Fauul, we were just talking about the changes that are happening with the two of us, you know Lauut and myself. Once you and I met and things have gone in the direction that they have . . . well in the long run it means what Lauut and I had for all these many turns will change."

Thinking before answering Fauul said, "Same for me. It seems that it happens constantly. It seems that no matter how you plan your life, and try to reach those small goals you set for yourself that something always comes along and says that's not the way it will be. Then you're left having to make changes you have never thought you would."

"Yes, I guess that's it. Still both of us had hoped to find a mate someday, and I'm lucky to be the first. But you never think of what type of impact it will make on what you have. It takes being in the situation to fully understand, and now that I am, and I'm seeing it happen right before my eyes. I guess it is just the way of life. There is an old saying that kind of sums it up; it went something like . . . 'before you judge me and what I do, walk the same tracks and trails for a day or two. Follow the path for a while, then when you have seen what I have seen, and done what I have done, only then can you make the call'. I never really understood that until now."

Lauut joined them, sighed and sat down next to his sister, "Really a nice evening here . . . until I sat down I didn't realize how tired I really am. Think when I finish this drink I'm heading off to sleep."

"Sounds wonderful really", she replied, "I believe we will be following you. It's just so nice to let the quiet soak in and stare out there and really see nothing."

"Okay you two" Fauul said, "I've almost finished mine. So I'm ahead of you. I want to walk the yard and think a little, and then I'll head out to my shelter and get some sleep." Finishing his drink Fauul stood up and went inside the main shelter and put his cup in the food prep area and then said good night to both and headed out.

Yes it had been quite a day that was for sure. One of the beasts that was carrying went into birthing pangs. So they, Lauut and Lauma went to see how it was progressing. At first it appeared all was normal, but as time progressed it was obvious that it was going to be a difficult birth and would require both of them full time to save the mother and the whelp. One of them came out of the beast shelter area and told him they would be involved heavily most of the day with this, and he would have to cover for them. So along with his regular work he'd need to cover their work with the herd beasts. All three normally shared this work so it went easily. Now he was going to have to do the work of the three. He wondered how they had coped before he came into their lives. He was sure that this was not the first time they had run into this type of problem.

It probably meant that some things that could be put back for a short period of time would be, and only the minimal would be done for the rest. These beasts were their livelihood, and to advance their lines required thought and adjustments. While they had continued to say they were never as good as their sires, because they had never received all the training from them, it was obvious to Fauul they were very good at this. So, in the end, all three of them had ended up with a very tiring, stressful, day where all were involved with more, and as usual, a longer day of work. So when the birthing was finally successful with both, mother and whelp doing well, they had told him that it had begun as a breech birth, followed by filling him in with the details of what they had to do. After hearing what was involved, he did not know if he could ever do such a thing, let alone want to.

Now that the day was finished he found that he was wiped out, as were the siblings Lauut and Lauma

– they had to be. Still when he reached this level of exhaustion he found that in many ways he could think more clearly. It was like the fog of weariness pushed all the noise and trash away from his ever active mind and he'd think much more deeply. Much had happened to him in the last turn. He, when he looked back, was really surprised. And to find himself here was probably the biggest change and the last he had expected to make. After all, his direction had been strong as a cartographer, and with his skills he would have advanced, of that he was sure. Yet, here he was in this remote small village area, and finding he was actually enjoying it. And that almost made him laugh.

Again he was a township whelp. This was not his life style. Still, he could not but help to admit that it was creeping into his soul. This type of life made one strong, and those who couldn't cope ran back to those townships to hide among the many. He felt that was one of the reasons for the strength in Lauma. Again he realized that only this type of female would be right for him. One who had that inner strength, one who was not afraid to stand up for herself, and any of the rest for that matter. Yes, there definitely was fire in this female, and she knew just what to do and say to put a male in his place, and she was not afraid to do it.

Walking around the beast areas, close to the yard, he leaned over the railing and continued his thinking. He knew that soon he would have to return to the township and to talk with his boss. He had been down here for quite a while and knew that his boss would probably be wondering what was happening. While the one in charge had agreed to an unspecified amount of time, there still was a limit. For a while now, a growing direction of thought had been entering his mind. He realized, due to the isolation of this area that very little had been mapped. He thought that here was a direction of approach he could use. If he could convince him of the need to map this area, and being that he was already here then both problems would be solved. He would be able to continue his primary choice of work, and still be here to help and be with his future mate. It seemed a good solution.

The more he was with Lauma he found that it becoming more difficult to be away from her. It appeared to be the same for her. Still he knew that sooner or later he would have to make the trip back, he really had no choice. So how would he break it to her? He knew the first reaction would be she wanting to go with him, but then realizing almost immediately that she couldn't. He knew that it was probably better that she didn't. While yes he still had the apartment there in the township – he had found a friend to occupy it while he was away; it wasn't something that one would do with a future mate. So that would have been an awkward situation . . . not to mention traveling with an unattached female. This in itself would pose many problems. While it could be done, it was normally accomplished with more than one. He needed to travel rapidly and he needed to tie in with one of the traveling merchant groups for the additional protection it provided. So to bring her along would pose too many difficult and uncomfortable problems and situations.

Enough on this he was really tired and needed the sleep. He found living here you never knew what the morrow would bring. Yet he could not deny the exhilaration he felt when he accomplished something he had never done before. Another thought crossed his mind as he headed for his shelter. He remembered that soon after arriving he had received a letter from his boss delivered by one of the runners. In the correspondence Bihl had mentioned that the Keeper of the Past had wanted to see him. So maybe he could tie this in with this trip, and get that chore out of the way. By the time he was inside his shelter he found that he could barely keep his eyes open. Sitting on the bed he took off his clothes, climbed in, covered up and was almost instantly asleep.

CHAPTER TWO

The work in the desert continued even though, as of yet, there had been no major additional finds to match the flyer and a personal ground transport device. These were the two items that had been crucial in confirming the ancients, the ones known as the *ones before*. The first discoveries had been of an area where these ancients had shelters they lived in. But an intense fire had destroyed them all but completely. Only leaving metal frames, broken dishes and burned out transports. On this first site the work continued and only items that survived the intense heat were being recovered.

When they had uncovered the second site they had been lucky in that it was originally two shelters. The one to the east had collapsed into the other and had, by the way it had fallen, strengthened the western shelter. The first surprise here was the size of these shelters. There was nothing in the present day that could match them. The second was the construction material – it was metal. In the present time such an abundance of metal for use as a construction material was unheard of. What metals that were being used presently were mainly used in axles and rims on the wheels that moved their carts. The amount here would have cost more than any township could afford. Again, in the first site, there seemed to have been much metal used. So either it was cheap back then or these particular ancients were wealthy.

Jllon, once the discoveries were made, had sent a message to the council stating that they had been successful but kept the facts about the *ones before* out of the correspondence. They were now in need of an additional team, and he would personally be before the council in the near future. He knew it was important that he present the information directly to them. The location of their dig had to remain a secret. If word got out, then they would end up with problems of theft, and people digging everywhere to find what they could. Destroying any evidence that lay buried under these sands and destroying the site as proof of their discoveries.

One of the finds inside the one standing shelter was a desk. Again it was made of metal, but the surface was of something different. On top of this surface was a sheet of glass. Again like the necessary space and its looking glass it seemed to be almost perfect. Just how these ancients performed these tasks in making the glass sheet and looking glass was way beyond anything they could do today. While these two discoveries were great, it turned out that once the glass sheet had been cleaned of the centuries of dust there turned out to be things underneath it. What was underneath was one of the biggest finds, and quite a shock to all whom saw it. It was a series of pictures. Yet none like these existed. Even though time had damaged them, and much of what was there had faded, the images still could still be seen quite clearly.

In those images, other than the clothes the ancients wore, it could have been any family from the present. There was a male and a female with a couple of whelps smiling. This image was in the desert, and there were no shelters in view. Still it was obvious that they were their ancestors. Again, looking at the images and all that had been found so far left Jllon wondering what had happened for them to lose all that he saw here. The wonders he had seen so far showed the ancients to be far ahead of them, and yet it was all gone as if had never been.

It made him sad somehow, thinking about what they had lost, and where they might be now if that ability and knowledge had continued. Again this was part of the mystery they were now attempting to solve. Doube, their scout, had shown him a layer of soil that to him spelled a worldwide catastrophe. Doube, whose main field was geology, was in the process of confirming his theory. It would be a while before the correspondence he sent to his counterparts on the other continents checked and confirmed his find. If, in the end, this layer existed everywhere it would confirm the disaster. This meant that even with the suspected advancements that the ancients had, it did not save them. Still enough of them had to have survived or they themselves would not be here, at this time, to uncover these ancient sites. Because the past was his specialty he knew that as a civilization grew it became more complicated. People became specialized and did not need all the skills of previous generations. So maybe that was the way it was then. So, when this disaster fell upon them, the few who had survived probably did not have the necessary skills to start over. This meant that these ancients probably teetered on the brink of extinction.

Still, since they were here now studying this site, some must have survived, and would have re-learned the old skills. This was only guesswork at this time, yet it made sense. He hoped to be able to put more solid answers to the many new questions before he stepped down as the Head Keeper of the Past. He had to admit to having been the leader of the team who had confirmed the old myths was exhilarating. He wondered if there were other greater finds still to be discovered in this desert.

Overall he thought that the ones that were living here wasn't the only way or area that the *ones before* lived. With all the great lands to live on, the running streams, the ocean shores, and the many areas that showed much promise for farming, there had to be other reasons to live here. Yet it was probably because of its remoteness that it had been left alone after it was buried. Lost and forgotten, and off the track or trails of the any whom, in the passing of time, followed. So this area, which was once a place of life, became remote and dead, only to be discovered thousands of turns later.

He would be leaving soon to report back to the council. He would take Doube with him for both his skills as a scout, and as one to put forth his point of view of what they had found. While he was gone he would put Celt Morlen in charge with Payle Evyrs as the second. His mate would continue to be in charge of the females who were here. He hoped to only be gone for a couple of cycles. On this trip speed was necessary. So they would be heading for the coast and picking up a water-craft north. He was hoping the traveling there and back would only be a cycle, with a cycle working in the township. Once there and after informing the ones in charge he would work on getting the second team assembled and while it would be smaller than the first they would continue the work they had started in the desert. Of course this was just tentative, as plans would change as necessary.

Mostly this second team would be here to protect the site. Since, even with the need for secrecy, the word somehow always gets out, and if it were not protected then all of the work would be lost forever. And establishing exactly who the *ones before* really were might be completely lost. Still he was hoping the other area over the mountains and to the west might prove to be just as rich as this site had so far. The ones coming in should be more of the learned with less being simple workers – at least that was the plan – even though half would consist of the ones who would protect the site. The learned would catalog, and attempt to identify what had been found, and of course write up a description before packing it up in preparation of the finds being moved to the Keepers of the Past work area located back in the township. Once there and identified as well as they could, the better ones would be put on display so all who wanted to view these items could.

While in the secondary camp he continued to think about the up and coming journey back to the township when Flar approached excitedly and said, "Jllon! You need to come and look at the image that was just found. We found a second desk and it had glass on top just like the other, but it had a set of different images under it. You're not going to believe one of them."

"What do you mean? It's hard to believe how realistic the ones we've already found are. I don't know what they did to get them so real, but I know we can't do it. Even our best artists cannot come close to that realism."

"All that's true but this one was taken somewhere in the air. And it shows what this place we have been uncovering originally looked like."

"Taken from the air? You mean like from a mountain top or something like that?"

"No, not at all. Literally from somewhere in the air like a flyer that rides the air. Plus unlike the others this one is large, and like the others the detail is unbelievable."

"Then lead on. I have been surprised with what has been found so far, and this one really confirms, if it like you say, that these *ones before* could fly."

Once they reached the large shelter Flar led him into a distant corner that largely had been ignored. With the first cursory investigation, there appeared to have been nothing of interest here. Later as a more thorough search began they found the desk under some rubble. The glass top of this one had been cracked by debris that had fell on it, and it was heavily laden with dirt and fallen debris hiding what lay under it.

With care and not wanting to break the glass sheet any further they cleared the debris, and then carefully cleaned its surface. Then to their surprise, under this glass sheet, was a single image. It covered most of the surface of the desk, and the glass sheet protected it. When they saw what it portrayed Flar left immediately to locate Jllon as he knew that Jllon would want to see this.

When Jllon arrived, Flar led him to the area in the back corner where it was shadowed. Jllon had to wait for his eyes to adjust to the gloom in the area of the desk, which took a few minutes for this to happen. He carefully approached the desk and looked down at its top and he really couldn't believe what he was seeing. It was exactly as if a flyer had been flying over this area and then made this picture. And part of the image showed the tip of what they considered to be wings on the surviving example that had been discovered inside this shelter.

One of the things he immediately noticed, other than the detail of these shelters there next to the trail, he could see that it traveled out of sight off the image in both directions. Here it was like a straight shaft heading out into the desert. It made him wonder, where did it go? And why have such a thing in the desert at all? Then on a second closer inspection he saw outside these shelters more of the ancient's flyers sitting there, plus one that seemed to be just lifting into the air by the shadows on the ground. *So if they had flyers why did they need these trails? Couldn't they just travel in these flyers to wherever they wanted to go?* Again more questions than answers.

Unfortunately the angle of the picture was towards an area where only these shelters and the desert were visible. So if there were additional places for he and the team to dig, this image would not show any of those additional areas. Still in awe over what had been found so far, it began to make him feel very humble. Knowing that sometime in the great past things were vastly different. That part, of course, did not surprise him, but the abilities these ancients possessed were so far ahead of them that it might as well have been magic. Still by having two surviving examples he knew that magic had nothing to do with it. He knew also that these examples would most likely remain a mystery. Age had made them fragile, and any attempt to find out how these items were constructed would, in the end, lead to their destruction. So now what? They had proof, and they had examples, yet in the end, there could be no real advancements for this current generation. Other than the fact that by having them it would spark someone's imagination and maybe in a short time they would be working towards these same kinds of advancements.

Walking back to the camp to continue his reports he found himself slightly depressed. Shaking his head he thought. *Too many questions, just too many. I thought that maybe when the finds started appearing we would have answers. But now I know that was a simplistic point of view.* Instead of solving anything, other than finding the *ones before*, they were left with a hunger to solve the mystery of their disappearance, and the obvious loss of the technology they were seeing here.

Here in the desert they had discovered the find of anyone's lifetime, and yet so far, as great as it had been, it was unsatisfying. He now had tasted, if only slightly, some of what these ancients were able to do, and when he compared it to this present generation, they were found sadly lacking. In fact they were so far behind with what had been found here that they might as well had been the small nesting crawlers looking up at them. And the gulf might actually be greater than that. At least they were aware of their lacking. He was unsure if the crawlers were even aware of them.

Thinking back to when he was a whelp he remembered having been fascinated by their organization. He imagined these crawlers having a society and an actual working order. He would sit for hours at a time, when he could, and watch, fascinated by the work and organization they appeared to have. But as time went by he found that all the different nests he observed these crawlers acted the same. So eventually he lost interest and had come to the conclusion that there was something within in them that made them this way, and it had nothing to do with being intelligent.

Still it would be easy to compare them to the present situation. Thousands of turns had passed, and here they were almost on the same level of those crawlers. What the evidence discovered here was saying that at one time they had so much more advanced, and this paradise had been lost – if indeed it was one. Still why were they so far behind these ancient ones, these *ones before*?

Restless and unable to continue his concentration on the paperwork he got up and headed out into the desert to think. He was finding it difficult to understand what had happened here and probably everywhere else on this world. It seemed that these *ones before* had much and had advanced greatly. Still here they were presently with nothing even close to compare to them. Why had this befell them? He knew not to go too far from the camp. Still he needed to clear his mind. So he wanted an area where he could sit in the quiet and be able to overlook the area. Who knew? Here seemed to be a people who appeared to have accomplished so much, and what, in the end, did it do for them? Apparently nothing, since looking at the present, and now knowing that these ancient people and they were one and the same, with only time separating them. Yet, not the same at all – why the disaster, the death, the destruction, and why were they still here? *Questions, so many questions, with no answers, and probably no way to get any, including the ones that had yet to be asked, or even thought up yet.*

Again shaking his head he thought. *Flight. They actually could fly.* While these flying constructions were not large, it seemed they could carry at least four people. He wondered what it was like to be in the air flying. It must be exhilarating, and the distance one could see had to be great. Kind of like being on top of a mountain and looking into the valleys, he suspected.

Still this seemed to be just part of what these ancients had accomplished. It seemed they worked metals with ease, and built large trails wherever they wanted to go. Then they were able to transverse these trails with carts that required no beasts. It seemed they had been able to do just about anything they pleased.

He found a rock to sit on and the sun felt wonderful on his back as he stared out over the landscape. In his mind's eye he tried to picture what this area must have looked like when the ancients still lived here. But with few references it was impossible. Maybe as more came to light it would be easier. While these shelters represented what the ancients had built, it still lacked what these ancients were like. It did not represent how they lived or felt or what was happening in their lives, or their world for that matter. It was just a point in time with nothing to support it.

What they did with their lives, how they lived, what they did for work, and so many other things wouldn't be answered here. The one and only place they had discovered that had been where these ancients had lived was destroyed by fire. So there was very little that had been recovered and nothing that could have pinpointed a lifestyle. What were their hopes and dreams? Were they much different from theirs here in the present? For any of these and the multitude of questions that had come out of this find he had no answers.

Staring out into the nothingness he finally realized that one of the females was approaching, and subconsciously he knew it was his mate. Funny how it is that one can recognize someone from a distance, before they are close enough to identify, just by the way they walk and move. Knowing it was his mate brought a smile to his face; it was really wonderful to have someone to share life with, a soul mate, as she was to him. He did not know what he would do if something ever happened to her, and it was a place he never wanted to go or think about.

"Saw you leave the camp and head out, and I knew that you were in one of your introspective moods, a little down I suspect."

"Ah, you know me too well. Not that it's a bad thing . . . you're right of course. This site has left me with many more questions than answers – too many really. It bothers me that these ancients do appear to have been our sires from a very distant past. We are just shadows of what they were . . . and I was wondering why."

"Is there enough room on the rock for two?"

"Sure, just give me a moment and I will move over a little." Smiling he continued, "You do know when to comfort an aching soul." Reaching out he took her hand and together they sat quietly. She, patiently waiting for him to continue, as she knew he would.

This was one of the many things that had attracted her to him in the first place. His quieter side and this inward turn he would do now and then. "These *ones before* were so far advanced to us. We would never think of living permanently in a desert, yet here they did. At first I thought that maybe it was not a desert at the time of this place, but those images prove it was. From my view this place should easily be a large township. It makes me wonder – if they could survive here, what were their townships like, especially along the shores, or places with much water. Then you come into more questions, things like, how did they feed themselves, what did they do . . . so many, many things. I just don't know."

"True, but they are not here now, we are. And while it has been shown that they were well ahead of us, that don't mean that the lives they led were any easier, or that there were troubles on a large scale that we have yet to see. While it now has become obvious that they were our sires, something happened back then that changed it all. Otherwise we would be like them with our ways of doing things similar to theirs. So, to me, it seems that even with what they had it did not save them. It makes me wonder if they were really happy. Did they love like we do, and did they dream of what the future might hold for them? Were their families and family lives good or were there many problems? I know from what little we have found so far those questions are unanswerable also."

Smiling, he said, "Thanks a lot. You now added a whole new series of questions to my overly long list." They both laughed as he continued, "Really thank you. As always you have a way of bringing me back from these moods and I really love you for it. I have often thought about what life would be without you and I cannot imagine it. You are that important to me. You help me in so many ways, and you just do it without even thinking about it."

"I guess we do make a great team don't we? I, in many ways, have also looked at our lives, knowing it could be better, but the one thing I would not change is you."

Looking down and then at her he said, "It is the same with me, and I will never understand what drew you to me in the first place, but I am happy that whatever it was did happen and we are mates. Guess we should be heading back so I can finish that paperwork, and you can continue what you were doing . . . we just don't seem to have enough time together."

Smiling she replied, "We have a lifetime. And I know sometime in the future we will be sires and that will complicate our lives more, but it still will be something I look forward to."

They hugged and kissed, got up off the rock and headed back to what they were doing before. He watched her as she headed back to the sifting area as he walked back to camp. Thinking to himself he said softly, "There really isn't anything about her that I don't love, and even though I know she loves me deeply, I will never understand why she chose me." And he knew that no matter what the males thought, in the end it was the female who did the choosing.

She knew that as she left that Jllon was watching her. It was interesting that she always knew when he was thinking of her or was a little down. She turned and waved back to him smiling, a smile that held a promise to him. *I know that other females have always wondered why I chose him, but for me there is no other, and will be no other. There is so much that is right between us, and I do hope it remains so. Still I know the future is beyond me to predict.* She turned back around and went on to where she had been sifting the dirt from the dig site.

CHAPTER THREE

Fauul awoke to the sound of commotion and a bit of chaos coming from the outside. Glancing through the window he saw that dawn was approaching – the skies were beginning to gray. Dressing quickly he headed outside to see both Lauut and Lauma coming out of the main shelter. Looking over to the pens he saw that a couple of wild beasts similar to the dogs were in the pens. Shouting to startle the beasts Lauut and Fauul ran after them to chase them away, while Lauma entered the pens to check on the status of the herd and pack beasts and their whelps. Soon the dogs joined in and between them were able to get these beasts to beat a hasty retreat.

Unfortunately the wild beasts had hurt one of the whelps, and the injuries were severe enough that it was obvious the young one would not survive.

Cursing under his breath Lauut stated, "Why now? With your help we have been making good progress, and to lose even one whelp will cost us heavily."

Not knowing what to say Fauul just stood there helplessly. While he had learned much, he was still so far from understanding all that was involved. And while he knew that a loss was never good, he didn't understand why this was such a setback. Lauma meanwhile was comforting both the dying whelp and the mother who would miss it for a while then continue on with no memory of the loss.

By mid-morn the young one passed on and the mother bawled searching for her missing whelp, not understanding at all what had happened. The three removed the body, and since it was too young to be of use as either food or for its hide, they took up and buried it in the garden area where after the beast had returned to the soil it would help make the soil better.

While all this chaos had been going on they had not found time to eat the morn meal, and now it was late in the morn and all found themselves quite hungry. They went into the main shelter, and prepared themselves a meal. With the lateness it was decided to make it large enough to cover both the morn and zenith meal. Fauul, while the preparations were being completed asked, "What were those things? They looked like your dogs, well sort of."

"Most of the time they don't bother the larger beasts, praying on smaller ones instead, but they are opportunistic. If they feel they can get away with it they will attempt to get a young one now and then. They have always been known as coyotes. Probably somewhere a long time ago the dogs and they were related, but there is no proof of that. Still the similarities are there. They look much like them, they run in packs, and like the dogs are territorial. You've actually heard them at night now and then," Lauut answered. "They are the ones with that high yip."

"Yes I have heard them, but I always assumed it was your dogs out and about. Not a different beast, they were quite similar to the dogs, and were really fast. Have you ever heard if they attack people?"

"Usually they leave us alone. Probably because they see us as their enemy and can do damage to them for which they cannot necessarily defend against. That's why we were able to run them off this morn. They seem to have a natural fear of us, and I for one am happy they do."

"I have heard that there had been attacks a couple of times on some young whelps, but in those cases it appeared that there had been something wrong with the coyote, and in both cases the coyotes were killed," Lauma shrugged before continuing, ". . . And fortunately there had been no harm other than fright."

"Well I'm full grown," Fauul replied, "and they would scare me."

The food was ready and they sat at the eating table and hungrily devoured the prepared meal. After a brief period of time Fauul said, "That's a tough way to be awakened. Going from a deep sleep to wide awake, to out the door on full alert. Does something like this happen often?"

Smiling at him Lauma said, "No, but often enough that it has a tendency to keep one on their toes and ready to go, you know like waiting for the flag to drop when one is in a foot race. Anyway after we finish here and clean up, we will need to go out and cover the blood, and wash the area down. Otherwise the smell of both the blood and coyotes will keep the beasts skittish."

It took the rest of the morn to finish the cleanup, followed by, of course, the normal work assignments that had to be completed. And with as much time that had been lost, the problem now was they only had half the time available. So today they would be working until darkness, and to the point where they couldn't see anymore, only stopping when it would be unsafe to continue. The mid-day meal would be skipped, and then the evening meal would be something quick and easy just before they retired.

Fauul, with how the day went, did not have a chance to broach the subject of his returning to the township and tying up the many loose ends of his life that now existed. He also wanted to see, as they approached the major gather, which would be in 3 cycles, if she would want to go with him back there for a half of a cycle before returning to the property. This would be after the ceremony to unite them, and, of course, the others that would be joined at the same ceremony in the small village. He was absolutely sure that this female was the only one who would interest him, and he was finding it harder and harder to be away from her.

Still he needed to go, and he had always heard that separation makes the heart grow stronger. He never really understood that until now. It was a test, in a way, to find out if they were really meant to be mates. Since the time away would either strengthen their need for each other, or see it fly away like the flyers when flushed from the vegetation. Well the morrow would be just as good a time to talk about it. And with a minor gather approaching he needed to be with any group of the traveling merchants as they left.

His plan was really simple. He would leave at the end of a minor gather, get the necessary business out of the way after the travel, and then come back with another group of traveling merchants as one of the future minor gathers approached. He hoped that there would be at least one more gather before the major one, since he felt he was going to ask Lauma to be his mate. She would need to make the necessary preparations, if she accepted, and so would her brother who would be acting as the family representative.

While he himself had never been involved in one of the ceremonies, he had been to a few, where some of his male friends had joined with their females and had become mates. Of course being without he and his other single friends would tease the one who was joining a female in life. While the ones who were being teased would say that their day would come, and at this point the single males would deny it. He had to admit that he would be one of the loudest. Smiling at himself and shaking his head inwardly, here he was contemplating the very thing himself. Now what would those other single friends be thinking when he told them he would be taking the fall.

Lauut was quite glad when the day ended. It had been rough – losing that young one hurt. It had been a male and quite healthy. Not enough time had passed to see if it would be what they had been hoping for. He and Lauma were attempting to improve the pack beast line with additional strength and stamina, plus an overall gentleness that would allow any to handle them. With the loss it would now be another season before they could attempt it again. "Oh well, just a part of life here on the property," he told himself.

With the problems of the day behind him, he remembered the one bright spot in his life, that being his sister. They were all each other had, and now in a period of time he knew she would no longer be as close to him as in the past. Finally, after all this time, she had found her soul mate. It now seemed like it always had been that way, but he knew that it was an illusion. Fauul had only been with them six cycles, and by observing both of them he knew that they were meant for each other.

Fauul seemed to be kind and considerate. He always appeared to approach something with thought, and it was obvious he was becoming very protective of his sister. She, throughout the day, would watch Fauul whenever it appeared he was unaware of her watching, and he could see that these two were definitely in love.

He had no prospects, and it did not worry him right now. Keeping the property up-and-running was a job enough. There was no time for a female in his life at this moment, except, of course, his sister. He had to admit that he really liked Fauul, and he could see why this male had risen high within his chosen field of work.

His mind continued to drift from one subject to another as the evening wound down and all of them would be turning in soon. He would join both of them out on the porch shortly, but he liked to give the two of them some time alone. Even though they insisted he join them when they went out to relax after the day's work was accomplished. Still he would find some excuse to delay. It was time . . . "Hey you two," he said humorously, "I'm coming out so you can quit talking about me now."

Laughing at his comment Fauul replied, "We sure will, and it was some juicy things your sister was telling me." Fauul laughed once again, "Not really, but it sounded good. We were wondering when you would join us."

"Yeah Lauut," Lauma said, "After all it's been one of our traditions for as long as I can remember, and it seems like something is missing when you are not here."

"Well, it seems you have a male next to you, and I just figured any male would do. So it didn't necessarily have to be me", Lauut said as he came through the door to the porch. "And besides it has been a tough day, and one that has set us back."

"Of course it has to be you. While Fauul here is a newcomer, and of course I do enjoy his company very much, it has been me and you for such a long time."

Sitting down next to them he said, "True, but I really don't want to intrude. I know there is a great chance that Fauul here will be joining the family soon, just as you will be joining his . . . it just kind of changes things. I know that we will always be close just because of our past. Still I knew that someday this day would come when we would not be as we were . . . don't get me wrong here, I really look forward to it. And I do know that someday it will be my time . . . anyway you know what I mean."

Both smiling at his embarrassment, she answered, "Lauut, now come on here. We are all grown up here, and while I am still single I want to have things as close to what we had as possible. When I become a mate, and that isn't here yet, these will be memories for me, my memories, important memories, and good memories they are."

"Besides Lauut, while I have said I will pursue, I haven't committed to anything past that."

Turning around and looking at him Lauma exclaimed, "Now Fauul what do you mean by that statement? I'm not going to be led around just to be left somewhere."

Lauut now smiling at Fauul said, "Now you've done it. I'd duck if I were you. She'd probably throw something at you if she had it."

Looking around at both of them she replied, "Now both of you can stop right there. I know when I'm being teased. Besides I'm outnumbered here . . ."

"She's outnumbered? From what I have seen we would need at least two more males here before she was outnumbered. Don't you think so Lauut?"

"Hey don't bring me into this. But from what I know of my sister you're probably right. She definitely can take care of herself that's for sure."

"Believe me, I am one who should know. That day we met she faced down both me and Doube."

Standing up with hands on her hips she stamped her foot in mock anger and said, "Okay you two enough is enough. I just might sic Sadie on you two just for spite. Then I would have the last laugh here."

"Okay, we have had our fun. Just sit back down and relax. As I remember it, it has been a very tough day. The morrow will be here much quicker than I would like. I know it will be a tough day following this one since we had to miss some of the normal work, which will have to be caught up on the morrow."

Fauul thought maybe he should mention something about leaving, but then thought the better of it. He was tired and didn't want to have to explain for the next couple of hours why it was necessary. He would broach the subject at the zenith meal on the morrow. Looking down Fauul realized his cup was empty, and he wanted another cup. Turning to Lauma he asked, "I'm going in to get a second cup, would you like me to refill yours?"

Looking into hers, she stated, "I have about half a cup left, no I'm fine."

"How about yours Lauut?"

"No I'm good also."

"Okay then, be back in a short time." He got up and entered the shelter.

"So sis, are you still as sure as you were before."

"On what?"

"Oh you know, about Fauul. I'm on the outside here and I can only draw conclusions from what I see."

"Yes, I don't know how to say it, but it's like we can almost anticipate each other. I am finding myself more and more wanting to be with him. It just seems natural – like it is supposed to be this way. There is *a closeness* I have never known coming alive here. Yes, I am very sure he is the one for me."

About this time Fauul returned and sat down next to them. He brought out some snacks, which he passed out. "Saw these and thought it would be a great way to finish the evening here before we head off to sleep."

"Great idea," Lauut said, "this will go well with what I have left to drink."

"Thank you sir," she replied.

"Sir is it? Now what brought that on?"

Looking up at him innocently, she asked, "Aren't you supposed to show respect for your elders?"

That made them all laugh, then Fauul said, "Pow, right in the kisser! Great come back."

They finished the evening drinking the beverage and eating the snacks. With that it was time to head out and sleep. The next day would arrive much too quickly.

As expected the next day did arrive much too fast. It seemed like he had just got to sleep and it was time to start again. Well at least this day was going to be a little more normal than yesterday. Making his trip to the necessary space he took a bath, got dressed and headed over to the main shelter. When he arrived there the morn meal was well on its way. To assist he took the dishes and set them on the table and got the hot beverage pouring them all a healthy portion. If they felt as he did, they all would need it.

While they sat to eat Lauut outlined the day's work. He and Fauul would work the water holes to make sure that all was well with them, and Lauma would work the food garden and pens with the young ones to see how they had fared after the trauma from the previous day. They would all meet back here for the zenith meal before continuing. According to what they had found and accomplished would determine what was to happen for the rest of the day.

After cleaning up the morn dishes they headed out. As they left the area Fauul asked, "So while I know it's not necessarily my business, where did you find those fire starters? Considering the shape they were in they couldn't have come from somewhere where they would have been exposed to the weather."

"True, I really hadn't thought much about it lately – too much going on. With you showing back up, and my sister being the way she was after you left, and then this and that, well you know what I mean."

"Funny how that works. You think that you will have time for this, or have a plan to do something else, and then just because life gets in the way you can't do anything you wanted to. Of course you know that better than I do. I cannot claim to have gone through half of what you and Lauma have. In truth, I don't want to either."

"Still there was no control on that. You find that when such things happen you either let it beat you or you overcome it. It's not something I would want to go through again, but it has been said that whatever does not break you makes you stronger in the end. I can't say if that is the truth. Since I cannot know what I would have been like if our sires had not been killed."

"Many times these trails of life are chosen for us, that's for sure. I know, at times, it would be nice if there were some way to backtrack and go down a different one, but that is one thing we cannot do."

Arriving at their first waterhole they found that there had been some damage to it, and water was being lost. So for half the morn they worked to repair the damage, and watched to see if it would refill. Fortunately it was still early in the turn so water was more abundant. As the turn continued into summer it would not be so. Then what had been stored in both these waterholes and small dams would have to provide until the winter.

Taking a break Fauul said, "You never did answer my question."

"Which one was that?"

"You know, where did you find those fire starters?"

"Oh that. Believe it or not it was underground. Sometime I'll have to show you. Hope you don't have a problem with tight places, because that area can be very tight."

Curious, Fauul asked, "What do you mean by that?"

"Let's just say it was pretty far underground and leave it at that for now. Besides I want to finish this waterhole and then at least inspect another before we head back in for the zenith meal."

"Okay by me. Actually at this point I am wondering why I took a bath this morn. As dirty as this work is I could have skipped it."

Laughing, Lauut said, "Know how you feel. Some of what we do here is really dirty. But at least it's clean dirt."

"Clean dirt? How could there be clean dirt? Are saying there is a difference and there is dirty dirt also?"

"Oh yes, and eventually you will know the difference yourself."

Shaking his head in disbelief he asked, "You're pulling my leg, right? This is a joke, right?"

"No I am quite serious about it really. Anyway we're finished here for now, so let's head on over to the next one to see its condition."

It was after the zenith when they finally got back to the main shelter and washed up for the meal.

Fauul turning to Lauma said, "You know something, I think your brother was trying to put something over on me while we were out there working. You know, me being a township whelp and you two being outback whelps."

"And what might that have been oh great township whelp?"

"Now don't you start."

Smiling, she said, "Well you were the one doing the comparing here. After all I am just a humble uneducated outback whelp."

"That's not what I said . . . anyway your brother stated that there are two types of dirt, clean dirt and dirty dirt. I kind of figured that dirt is dirt, right?"

"No, actually he is right. Time will prove that one to you, and until you see the difference, most likely, you will not believe it anyway. Enough on that, I'm hungry, so let's eat."

"Okay if you say so, not on the eating part, never turned a meal down myself, but on the dirt part."

They entered the main shelter and sat down to eat. Fauul said, "I have something I need to tell both of you."

Alarmed Lauma asked, "Now what?"

Taken back a little by her reaction Fauul hesitated before answering. "Now wait a minute here, don't get too excited . . . it's just that . . . well you know that I took a leave of absence to come down here. And while it was indefinite, I still have to go back and take care . . . you know what I mean, it's necessary to let my boss know what is happening. Plus I have to present to him a plan where I can return here. I am hoping to have this wrapped up in a couple of cycles . . . no more than three anyway. I plan to leave at the end of the next minor gather and head out with one of the traveling merchant groups. Once I have this all worked out, then I want to be back well before the next major gather. Yes, I know that I have helped much around here, and with me gone it will put you two back to working harder, and really it is not my idea to do this.

"Remember when I came back I had no idea if anything would work as I hoped. Fortunately for me it did, and of course I hope for the two of you also. Even though I have communicated by runner, I still must return. It is only right and I owe it to my boss who happens to be a friend. I do not want to have him keep making excuses as to why I'm not there. I know from one of the letters passed on to me that the Head Keeper of the Past wanted to see me, why I don't know. But I suspect it has something to do with those fire starters you found, and then I ended up with one, which was seen by one of the underlings from that department. So I am hoping to tie that one up also."

Silence followed for a short period of time as the sister and brother absorbed all that Fauul had said, Lauut asking, "Are you sure about this? I mean . . . oh I don't know what I mean. You are sure that you must do this?"

"Yes, I have thought about it for a long time now and know it has to be done."

Throughout the whole conversation Lauma was silent, with a shocked look on her face. It was something she hadn't thought about since Fauul had returned. When she had confirmed for herself that he was the only male for her, and now he was leaving, it was a surprise. Yes, she knew it was for a short period of time, but it seemed that even that period of time would be too much. This reaction surprised even her. If one thing she had always prided herself on were her strength and the ability to stand on her own. Now all of sudden it seemed that a rug had been pulled out from under her and she was falling. The confidence that she always had seemed to flee her, and to not see Fauul for even that short period of time seemed almost unbearable. Suddenly she realized that both of them were looking at her, and then she blushed deep red. Trying to hide her confusion and with her emotions giving her away she asked, "What are the two of you staring at? Am I some special object that has to be studied?"

Realizing that indeed they had been staring at her both turned away quickly knowing that once she got herself back under control that they could be asking for it. "I've been meaning to tell you for a while now, and originally I wanted to do that yesterday. Still we all know what happened then and it was not a good time to bring this up. I've been told that separation is a good thing. It can test the ones involved and either prove or disprove their relationship."

"Yeah", Lauma replied. "I've heard that too, but it was something I didn't want to test myself. I have found myself even anticipating your arrival here in the morns for our meal before we go out and work. Then those evenings on the porch have been wonderful. Now you tell me that I won't have any of these comforts for a few cycles. When you first stated this, my first thought was to go with you, but knew immediately that it would not work. This property cannot be worked with just one, and it is not the time of the turn where one could hire someone to replace me, even if we could afford it, which we cannot."

"No, I thought about it myself, but a single female with no chaperone would not be a good thing. Plus, while the bandits do not generally attack small groups of the traveling merchants, adding a female might change that. We all have heard what happens to females who have been captured by bandits, and it is something I do not want to happen to any female, and especially you."

"So when is going to take place . . . that's right you told us. Right after the next minor cycle," Lauut said, "so that you could tie in with a group heading in the direction of the township."

What had started out to be a good quiet meal had turned gloomy as far as Lauma was concerned. She could logically reason it out, but her heart could not bear the separation. Still she had to admit it was something in which he had no choice. That still did not make it any easier. What if something happened to him on this journey? It was always a possibility, and yes he could just as easily have something happen here as well. Suddenly she realized she had no appetite, excused herself and then went to her sleeping space to take some time to think this through.

Fauul rose to follow her, but Lauut shook his head and said, "Don't, she has to think this out, and normally she needs to be alone. Later, possibly tonight when we are all out on the porch, well, we will see then."

Feeling quite helpless and not really wanting to have caused Lauma any stress, he really did not know what to do. This was all new territory for him. Yes, while he had been around females off and on his whole life, none had the impact this one had had. He felt that he needed to comfort her, and to explain that this was just a journey which would initially seem long, but in reality with the work necessary to keep this operation going, the time would just fly and he would be back almost before she would realize it.

The two finished their meal in silence, took the plates into the food prep area and washed them. They left and headed back out to work on a couple of additional waterholes before calling it a day. Fauul lost in thought was not a good companion for conversation, at least initially. Lauut knew his sister best, but even this was a new area for him. To him this was a definite sign she had found her soul mate. No other male had affected her in this way, and it was tough seeing her vulnerable this way. "Females have a way to keep us off balance that's for sure," Lauut said.

"What? Oh, I really didn't think I would get that kind of reaction from just saying that I had to leave for a while. I mean, well, it's not like I am leaving and not coming back. Or leaving and having a great period of time, such as a couple of turns go by before I return. I just really don't understand."

"Not that it is possible to understand the female mind; I do know that she has even said that females don't understand other females, so how can we even come close ourselves? You know we are just simple males here."

"Amen brother. They sure can keep us off balance that's for sure. Maybe that's what they do just naturally. She is one of the strongest females I have ever met. She knows her mind and is not afraid to speak it, but then again there is this side of her that shows how sensitive she is. I just don't know – this is becoming much more complicated than I ever thought."

"Thinking of backing out? After all that's what the pursuit period is all about. At least that is what I was told. It gives the couple time to be closer and to find if indeed it is what they want."

"Me? No, not at all, but this is like being in unexplored or unmapped territory. Everything that is happening for me is a new discovery. No, I am not backing out at all. She, so far, has been everything, and no not perfect, since that would mean I would be looking at this from an immature way. I have my faults and she has hers. Still I can look at no other in the same way. Oh I am a male so when a good-looking female passes by I look, but that is as far as I will go. Yeah I know I even might think or fantasize about the physical part of a relationship, but that's it. Your sister is the one for me no doubt.

"You know I've had friends tell me that there are many females out there that one could love, and probably love deeply. Still, that doesn't mean that you could live with them. I guess the most difficult part is to find that special one that you can both love and live with. I was also told that when the right one comes along you will know. I always thought how trite, how simple. It just cannot be that simple. Yet, here I am having to agree with that statement. By accident we discovered each other, and almost from the beginning I knew – weird huh? Still what can I say? I know that a number of times in the past I thought that maybe one or some other female was the one, and that she was something special, but when it finally happens you realize that these others never even came close."

Listening to what Fauul had just said, Lauut realized that there were some pretty profound statements in this conversation. It was something he had never really considered, yet when he thought about it, what Fauul was saying made good sense. "You know something, I've never heard it stated quite that way, but now that you have said it I can see the truth in it. It kind of makes you see things in a different way. Kind of like learning something that you never knew before, and then seeing something that you had always seen or taken for granted, and realizing that you had never viewed it correctly. Am I making sense here?"

"Well sort of. I guess I would be a great example of that. Let's see if I can give you an example. I am a township whelp, so when I look at the beasts you raise and sell, to me that's exactly what they are. But once I began working on this property I have learned that there are many breeds within breeds and I can no longer just look at a beast without wondering what its lineage is, or that is this or that."

"Yeah, I guess so. At least now with what you just passed on to me, I will not ever look at relationships in the same way again. And I will be more careful. Not that it's easy when some female seems to be interested in you. You know, especially the ones you are trying desperately to stay away from. But I guess you would know that wouldn't you?"

Lauma left and went to the sleeping area and laid down on her bed and began to weep. She didn't really understand her strong response and now the weeping. While this was part of being a female, she had always prided herself on being able to control this part of her most of the time. Still here at this moment she could not keep the tears from flowing. Logically she could rationalize it, knowing that the separation would be only a few cycles and not turns. But for him to leave her that was such a shock. She was finding herself always looking forward to seeing him when he left the workers shelter and heading across the yard to the main shelter. The many small conversations they were having, and the evenings on the porch. These evenings on the porch had always been one of her favorite things to do, and now with him it was even more special.

It seemed to her that all of a sudden she was not whole if he was not somewhere close. She wondered if this was what her sires had had. If so she could so understand now where her mother was and why she could care less that she had apparently mated under her station. She, her mother, seemed to be totally content and involved with her father. So probably for the first time, as a whelp viewing their sires, to now in the present, much more was making sense. Since she now was walking a similar path as her mother, and suspected her mother's mother also. Although probably this time it would be she who would be mating up and not the other way.

How was it that one became this way anyway? After all, even though as a female whelp you always played at the game of the mate life, and dreamed how it would be it was just that – a game. Still nothing had prepared her for what her feelings were doing to her now. Yes, she was aware that the female hormones always played havoc with one's emotions, but this was so . . . so different. This seemed to devour her very soul.

How can one become so dependent on another? It just did not make any sense to her. Yet here she was, the one who's strong willed, and not afraid to put forth her ideas to anyone, crying like a small whelp. Over what? Because a male that interested her, was going away for a period of time? Come on now, this male was just that – a male.

While in her sleeping space she had heard them leave, and thought, *I had better get myself together, there is still work to be done here, and crying and laying here will not get this accomplished.* Still for a while longer she lay there staring up at the ceiling just letting her mind drift, then for a brief time she fell asleep, and awoke with a start, feeling guilty that she had fallen asleep. At least she now felt better and a bit refreshed. She got up went back out and continued her work at the pens. After all, if she didn't then the work wouldn't get done.

CHAPTER FOUR

At the end of the day Jllon called a meeting. He needed to get all the up to date information from the team, and then decide which of the many sketches he wanted to take with him. He also needed a few of the small artifacts they had found. This trip back to the township needed to be quick. The plan was to head north on the inland route and then to the coast to catch a water-craft back. From there, to continue on until they reached the township. Once there he would have to get with his team at the archives and put together a proposal that the council would accept. Plus he needed to have some of the others look over what he was bringing back and get their opinions on what had been discovered. While this was happening he would also need to set up an initial appointment with the council so that he could do an initial presentation.

With the importance of this find, he knew that this would end up before the full council.

Somewhere during this busy time he wanted to contact the mapping division to see if this Fauul had returned yet. Because he, as of yet, had not seen the object that helped launch the dig project they were presently working. Yes, there was much to do there, and way too much to be done once he returned. Once his mission was accomplished, and as quickly as possible, he needed to return with a second team, and bring them up to speed at this site. It seemed to be a bit overwhelming at this moment. How could he, just one male, accomplish all of this in such a short time? He really didn't know, but he needed that second team here by summer.

Summer would be too warm to do any more digging, but the site had to be guarded, and what had been found required further research and cataloging. What had been found so far, at least until they had finished with this site, had to remain a secret – this was imperative. Since this area was large it would be impossible to protect if word got out about the successes they were having.

He wondered if the second area they were interested in, even though he had yet to see it, would be as rich as this one. Still this was in an unknown future. If the second area produced nothing, then it would still be worthwhile. Because this first area in the desert, the last place he would have ever searched or expected to find anything, ended up being the one site, proving the existence of the *ones before*, the ancients of the myths. At least it was the only explanation at this point and time. Plus the evidence found so far had shown that they themselves were the descendants of these ancients.

It was going to be a long night for him, as he would be making final decisions. On the morrow he would pack and with Doube head out in two days. His hope, on the travel portion, was to make good time. There would be enough lost when dealing with the council. While these finds had waited at least many thousand turns to be found, he didn't have that kind of time to recover artifacts. Once the word leaked that the *ones before* had been found to be real, then there would be a frenzy to go find more. This leading to, much more fraud, and many additional fakes, being placed into circulation – plus adding to this the rumors and lies that would be created. These things, the false information and fake artifacts, which would have no basis in fact, would possibly become part of the myths of the *ones before,* further clouding the truths.

It, in his mind, was critical to be able to get as much of the truth uncovered before it became general knowledge. With many of the items found on display for all to view, and records available for any to read, he felt only then would there be a chance to tell the story of their ancestors, their ancient sires, accurately.

He knew that even if the sites were kept a secret until all that could be gained had been revealed – a correct interpretation would be difficult. They presently lived in a different world and from what they had found so far, the ancients' world was one that was vastly different, completely unknown, and to be honest foreign. One of the facts that continually struck him was advancement. These ancients were so far advanced over where they were presently, how could they begin to make a correct interpretation? "Oh well," he said to himself, "time for the meeting so let's see what we have."

Looking over the group he couldn't help but to feel good about all they had accomplished so far. While only pieces had been found, what had been found would be the proof they needed. Still he knew he could neither take the flyer or the ground traveler with him – too heavy and too fragile. They were something that would have to remain here, untouched, where they were. In fact since being re-exposed to the natural air these things had started to deteriorate. He was at a loss on how to prevent it, and no one on the team had any idea either.

"Okay it's time to get this meeting on its way. As you know in two days I'll be heading back to the township. Any of you that have mates and whelps back there can send letters with me, and I will see that they get them. I know the importance of that. I am lucky in the sense that my mate works here so I at least have daily contact with her. I can only take back with me what I can carry in the two packs. The one I have and the one Doube will carry. So I need the best of the artist's works and a number of small objects that I can show the council so that we may get the second team in here, then, if all goes well, we can move on to the other site. So what do you have for me?"

After the meeting he had much to choose from. He really wanted to be able to take messages back so that the team members would have contact with their families. He knew that there was a great chance that he would remain back in the township long enough to receive replies, and then be able to deliver them back to his team on his return. This was such an important part of their society. In the present society family was the most important – everything came after that.

He decided after all that was presented after the meeting, to limit these materials to his pack. Doube would carry the letters to the families, and he would also carry the necessary supplies needed along their journey. While in truth, they would not be on the trail for nearly as long as they had when they traveled to this site, and they would be traveling along the heavily traveled routes, to have some backup was important. He needed to make it as quick as possible, spend the necessary time with the council, organize the second team, or not, and return ahead of them to get things organized on site so they could make the planned move.

Some of what he had decided to bring were some metal disks that had silhouettes of the busts of males on them. Plus there were numbers imprinted, which he suspected, represented a particular turn. Still too much was unknown. He felt that these disks represented some form of financial exchange like the mark system they were presently using. These had been found at the first dig site where fire had ravaged the shelters. They had been uncovered as they had sifted soil and sands from the burned area. He also took a small sample of the metal these shelters had been constructed of. This had been melted by the intense heat of those same fires, and had puddled, then hardened when it cooled.

There were a few miscellaneous items, which were light, he added to his assortment. He felt the drawings and sketches were probably most important. The other items would support these drawings. One in particular he wanted was one of the picture they had found under glass showing an image from the air, confirming the ancients had flight. Of course, the sketches dealing with the two machines that required no apparent outside force to make them move had to be part of the package. Finally he wanted the overall sketches of the two sites, and the shelters they had uncovered at the second dig site. Those by themselves were impressive. There was no way, with the knowledge of the day that they could build such a shelter of such a massive size.

* * *

With everything set and saying goodbye to his team and to his mate, he and Doube headed out just before sunrise. In a short time the areas they were working would no longer be visible to them. He, just before heading around the hillside out of sight, turned around one more time to look. The sun was rising early in the desert, as it normally did, lighting up the large shelter, and then they were around the hillside and all of it was gone. Turning to Doube Jllon asked, "I wonder how long it will be before we see this with our own eyes again?"

"Good question and one I don't have an answer for."

"I know you don't . . . just idle speculation on my part I guess. With this discovery so much has changed for me, and when it is finally revealed I feel it will change our world. I do hope in a good way in the end. Still seeing those images of the ancients we found on that desk haunts me."

"How so?"

"It's simple really. We have a moment in their time captured there, and I know like any of us they had their hopes and dreams . . . I wonder how they fared, whether they survived whatever happened. I guess it is something I will never know . . . still I cannot help but feel for those unknown ones. Even though I know they have been dead for thousands of turns."

"I believe I understand how you feel. We live each day without ever knowing what the next might bring. With the sun's rising we have hope, but when whatever it is struck; did it take that hope away from them? Were they fortunate to have survived as a family? Or did one or all perish in this disaster? It does make one think that's for sure."

"So how does it happen? I mean, you are living your life with the normal everyday problems, probably wondering how some would be solved, then out of nowhere this happens and nothing means anything anymore. The whole world is turned upside down, and I'm sure as the magnitude of this disaster sank in that there was major chaos in the world. I suspect that as society broke down that there was much death caused by the lack of supplies just to sustain life. It really had to be a horrible time in our history."

"True, but somehow we survived. If we had not we would not be here now trying to see that distant past and trying to find out what happened."

"I guess you're right. Still it had to be a dark time, a time of much pain and death. Where the strong ruled whether they deserved it or not. So it leaves one to further wonder how much of how our people, and how our society operates today actually came from those dark times. After all it is our past that leads to where we are now. Just another thought here, and then I will leave it alone for a while. We, at the present, do not have the capability to live in the desert, yet our ancestors did. Apparently we have lost much, and I wonder how long it will take us to at least match them in their apparent abilities."

"Of course I have no answer, and anything I would say would be speculation anyway. Still what we have seen here does make one want to search for more knowledge. I guess if anything comes out of this, other than the proof of the *ones before*, is that it should spur us in right direction, well I hope it is the right direction. If we, in that I mean the people of this time, are careful with the advances we learn from these finds, and then apply them to help each other, I feel that only good can come out of it. Still it would be so easy to try and keep it away out of sight, thinking we are protecting the people. I must admit there is much to think about here, and in the end, I'm glad that it's not I that has to determine the fate of this new knowledge."

"Who would have thought that once the myths were confirmed to be true, that new questions and dilemmas would present themselves? I thought, obviously too simply, that I would have my questions answered." Shaking his head Jllon continued, "Instead I have come away from this with a multitude of additional questions, and presently no way to even begin to answer them. Yet, I have to admit it has been exhilarating to have made such finds, and I can only hope that we continue to do so."

"I've been happy to have scouted on this project. It has allowed me to see so much that I would never have. And to be part of this team that has opened the past has been a privilege – I must say. I know that once we reach the township, that for a period of time I will be free. Please keep in contact I want to continue with you and your team. Plus it will give me a chance to run into Fauul again and renew our friendship. Funny that really this whole thing began when he and I went to purchase those pack beasts from Lauut and Lauma, and of course, the notes we had written about this area. From those humble beginnings the whole world has been changed. Even though it is not aware of these coming changes yet, as we were not."

"Is that not the truth? All of us were so unaware of what was here hidden in the desert, and, as you say, from those humble beginnings great changes are coming. And whether, in the end, they are good changes only our history will know. Yes, I would love to have you continue on the team, and I guess you are right, again, what we have found here will change everything." While they had been talking they found they had made good time, and the weather was cooperating. Jllon hoped this was a good sign that this journey would be a quick one.

* * *

In just a half of a cycle they found themselves entering the township – the journey had been quick. Bidding Doube a good bye, he told him to check in with the department he Jllon worked to keep up to date as to when he planned on returning. The first place Jllon headed was back to his abode to freshen up before heading over to the department that he was in charge of. With the team he worked with here at the archives he hoped to put together a proposal that would be acceptable to the head members of the council. He knew that the full council only met twice a turn. This was at the two major gathers that was common throughout the world.

They had pushed hard to get here. Normally such journeys were at least a cycle, and sometimes up to two. Still by traveling light, and pushing well into the evening and starting before the dawn they had made excellent time. Now he needed to clean up, to rest, and then organize what he brought before presenting it to the workers.

Doube, with time on his hands, and knowing that he probably had at least a cycle before they would head back down to the site, decided to head back home. He had not been on the farm since before the mapping project, and thought that it would be nice to see his family again. While he was not the oldest, he had a sister who was. She, at this point, had remained unattached, and with their sires, continued working the property.

It would take him a quarter of a cycle to reach home, and then he felt he would be able to remain to help for half a cycle before having to return. He wished he could discuss with the family what had been discovered but this was not to be on this trip. Shaking his head he thought. *Too bad really. This is such an important find. Still I understand the reason for silence.* They had barely scratched the surface. Even though much had been revealed, it was not enough to really pin down who these elusive *ones before* really were. Once this was better understood then what was found could be revealed to what would be a surprised world.

Before long he was on the final path leading up to the entrance to the property. This, in itself, brought back many nostalgic memories of growing up here and learning the work. He stopped at the gate leaned on it and allowed his mind to drift as he remembered the many times going through this very gate. He couldn't help but smile as he remembered his first crush he had on a female. Of course it was one way, and she didn't want anything to do with him at all. He wondered what she was doing now these many turns later.

Looking past the gate, in the distance, he saw the many shelters that populated the property. With a sigh he opened the gate and walked on down the path with those many memories flowing. Again, as he got closer, he saw someone out in the yard heading for one of the out-shelters. He thought from the way the person walked that it had to be either his sister or maybe his mother. His sister had taken strongly after her and they did so many things similarly. As he got closer he could see it was his sister and he yelled out, "Hey sis, it's Doube!"

She paused a minute obviously puzzled. It was obvious to Doube that she had not really heard him, but at the same time had recognized something. She turned around looked in the direction the sound had come from and saw someone approaching. Looking closer she recognized her brother. A wave of surprise and joy sweep her face, and she ran to him, saying, "Doube! What the heck are you doing here? We had heard that you'd picked up another assignment and would probably be gone at least a couple of turns. Yet, here you are." With joy she reached out and grabbed him in her arms and they hugged. "So how are our sires?" Doube asked.

"Why don't you come in and find out yourself," she replied

Then hand in hand they headed into the main shelter. Jewlee, entering ahead of Doube, said to their sires, "Look what I found running loose here in the yard."

"Now what . . .? Doube! Wow it's great to see you! What," his father asked, "where did you come from?" Marta come out here our son is home for a visit!"

Doube could hear running feet coming through the shelter and then smiling he saw his mother approaching. She stopped for a moment with a great smile on her face, went up to him and hugged him. "Well, let me look at you," she said. "What are you doing here? Not that I don't appreciate seeing my son. Still we had heard you would be away for at least a couple of turns. I had just spoken with your father about you, and how wonderful it would be to see you again, and here you are." She laughed a delighted laugh and then continued. "Come on let's sit a while and you can fill us in on what has been happening. Oh, I'll get us some hot beverage going. This is so wonderful. You truly know how to surprise someone, and what a wonderful surprise it is."

"Marta, can you give our son a chance to speak? I know it has been a long while, but you're just running on here."

"Am I? Well what do you expect; I haven't seen our son in much too long of a time."

Laughing a little Doube replied, "Now dad you know mom, she just loves to talk. If I remember right you said it was one of the things that drew you to her in the first place. And yes I will sit, and a cup would be wonderful. I can be here for a half of cycle before I will have to return. So I will be able to help around here, and we all can get caught up on what has been happening in each other's lives. It's really is nice to be back here."

They all sat around the eating area catching up on the day-to-day things that had been going on around the farm. Doube said that after the evening chores and meal when they had some additional time he would catch them up completely, but for now hearing about home was great. Once they finished their drink he went out with both his sister and father to assist in the never-ending work that a farm required. Doube went to assist his sister with the farm beasts while Frank went out to the fields to check on the grains that they were growing.

As evening approached they heard the bell ring stating to them that the evening meal was ready. They tied up what they were working on and headed in, first washing up outside to clean off the dirt of the day before entering the shelter. With Doube thinking back to the many times he had done this very thing in the past. In his mind's eye he saw himself growing up here and the trouble a whelp would get into, all the hard work, and of course, all the good times also.

Jewlee, watching him asked, "What are you thinking? You have that faraway look in your eyes."

Smiling at her he said, "Oh just nostalgia I guess. I was kind of looking back on my life here before I left and became what I am today."

With a look of devilment in her eyes she said, "Then you remember that time when you decided that you were going to scare me over there in the beast shelter? You had planned this elaborate trap to get me more than once only to have it backfire on you, and you were the one caught in it."

Both of them started to laugh. "True in the end it got me, but if I remember right, when I sprung it you jumped and started running."

Overhearing part of what the two had been talking about Marta asked, "Okay you two what have you been talking about?"

"Oh we were just reliving some of our whelp and youngling past, and how as whelps we would try different things to get the other in trouble, or such." Doube answered.

"Yes, and how many times with some of the stunts Doube would attempt, that eventually they would come back on him with unknown or unthought-of consequences. Even though I have to admit reluctantly, a few were very successful."

"True, but usually in the end, even though we found some of the things being pulled by you two, and we, as your sires, many times, had to laugh. But," Marta stated, "we still we had to be serious and punish you for them."

That evening after the meal and clean up they retired to the family area and Doube recounted his most recent adventures and the theory he had put forth about the possibility of a worldwide incident that happened thousands of turns in the past. They all discussed the pros and cons, and then Doube said, "Enough on me here. What's really been happening around here?"

While at the present his sister had no prospects, she was quite happy with the way things were. While she was only two turns older, she had taken after her mother in looks so actually looked younger than Doube. Still she had inherited her father's intelligence and had put a number of males in their place. Other than helping around the farm she had no other real plans at this time. So far the sires even though becoming older seemed to be able to continue the work the farm as required. It was good news for Doube. He knew that someday he would be expected to take over the operation. It was something he expected to do and hoped that by the time it took place that much of what he had set out to accomplish would be finished.

* * *

Jllon headed on home. He was tired and dirty and really needed a bath. He knew that Doube would be heading back to the farm to spend time with his sires and sibling before the two of them returned to the site. If the work he was doing took more than a cycle, he would send a runner to the nearest village where Doube was located to let him know he could stay longer if he so desired. If none were received then Doube would be back at the end of the cycle.

Once he entered his apartment he noticed that it seemed to have a stale odor. He immediately propped open the door to let air circulate inside and again noticed that without his mate here it felt empty. He realized that there was no food on the premises, and would have to go out to one of the local eateries to eat. So he took a quick bath, put on some clean clothes and headed back out into the township for a meal. If possible, he would pick up a couple of items for the morn meal. Then in the morn he could do a better job of organizing the materials he had brought back with him before heading over to the department.

Again because of the need of secrecy there would be no one other than the assistant who would see these items. For the rest of the staff he would have to keep things general and vague. This was much too important for it to be leaked before all that could be found and the work was completed. Once there he needed to make the necessary appointments, and once he knew whom he was to see, develop a strategy to approach them. Each member or their staff needed to be approached differently – those on the council. This was one of the things he had learned early after being appointed to the "Head Keeper of the Past" position. Not being a politician himself he had to learn as he went. It was one thing he would never understand, this political world. He had yet to serve his turn in the position. Yet if he had, then maybe these maneuverings would make better sense.

As large as the township was, he knew there was a great possibility that he would never serve – which, in truth, was fine with him. He, originally being from the outback, and the realities that this world presented had ill prepared him for the subtleties of this other world. These many thoughts continued to cross his mind as he took that quick bath, and then rummaged through the dressing area for something to wear. Looking into the reflecting glass he saw a male of average height and weight with nothing that would make him stand out in a crowd. He had dark brown hair that was a bit shaggy right now from not having it cut since they had been on the project, brown eyes, and presently from being out in the sun, highly tanned skin. He wasn't ugly, but he could have never compared himself to Doube who was much better looking than he. And from what Doube said, even though personally he had yet to meet the elusive Fauul, Doube did not come close when compared to Fauul.

He was still so in awe that Nouma had wanted to be his mate. He who was a bit introverted, and not at all comfortable around females, still he had to admit that their relationship was strong, and he knew he depended on her. She definitely was his anchor. Together they had formed a united front against whatever was presented. He complimented her weaknesses with his strengths, and vice versa.

He left to get some food, and realized immediately that the noise of the township was jarring. After coming from the quiet of the desert and back into the crowds, he felt out of place. He would have to get used to the noise and the press of people around him once again even though his time here would be short. *Probably about the time I get used to this again, I will leave. Then when I get back to the project it will seem all too quiet . . . funny how that works, how you adjust to your surroundings and then have to readjust when you move again.*

The next day, after a restless night, he headed out for the morn meal and down to the department. He had the materials with him that he had brought from the dig site. He needed to store them in his office, and begin the work to establish the appointment with the council. Once that process was well on its way he wanted to contact the cartography department and see if Fauul had returned as of yet. He felt that it was still important to both talk with him and to physically see the object that he had sketches of. The one thing he had learned, over time, was that by actually seeing an object one would get a better grasp of what that something was. A sketch or a drawing was nothing more than an artist's interpretation of what he saw, and as such, was not a true representation at all. Plus, through a drawing, one couldn't feel the weight of the object or how solid it was. Nor things, such as the quality of construction, or how the object actually felt in one's hands.

While he was quite happy to have the sketches, since it was one of the two factors that originated this present dig, like what had been found in the desert, of which he had sketches, he knew that these fell far short of the real thing. Still by not having the capability of the ancients it was the best that he or the team could accomplish. He hoped it would be enough.

When he arrived he found that his assistant was not in yet. This didn't surprise him, as he usually arrived before most of the others in this department. This allowed him some time in which to place the materials in a safe place and out of sight. Later he would do a final organization of the items before he presented his case before the council. He sat down and organized his thoughts, and put together his request for a meeting before the council. By having been in this position for three turns he was fully aware of the many steps it would take to finally get to see the council. All he could figure out was that the many layers one had to go through was to weed out what would be considered unimportant. Still he was sure that in the end many things that should be heard by the council never made it that far.

During the time he was working on the draft, his assistant arrived, and was quite surprised to see him there working at his desk. "Sir!" She exclaimed,

"You're the last one I expected to find here today. I really thought you were still on that dig site somewhere down south. Is there a reason you are back? From the information we had received here, it sounded as if you were going to be down there for a much longer time."

Smiling, he said, "I know what you mean. In truth I will be heading back in the near future – will only be here for about a cycle if things go well. Anyway, the word does not need to get around that I'm back. I have to set up a meeting with the council and see if I can get a second team. You see our work down there has been successful. We have found much, but we need to move on to the second prospective site, so I need a second team to continue work and protection on this first site."

"Are you saying that you have found the proof we all were wondering about? You know the *ones before,* as to whether they exist or not, is that what you are saying?"

"Let's just say that we have found something. I cannot say if it is or is not a site of the *ones before.* Still we have uncovered a township in the desert and that is all I can say at this time, and this information can go no further. Now if you would, can you help me with this request to see the council? You are much better at these things than I am. And yes it is important that I wrap this up as quickly as I can."

As they worked through the morn on the draft he showed the assistant some of the small items he had brought back with him. Because the sketches and drawings had the real proof he did not bring these out. He felt that these, plus some of the small disks they had found were the real proof, the hard evidence, and the other items were general enough he could show the latter but not the former. Just before the zenith meal they had finished the draft that was to be sent to the assistants of the council so an appointment could be made. At the same time he put together a quick note to the cartography department and specifically for Bihl Kaetr, Fauul's boss. He wanted a quick meeting with him to find out anything new about Fauul, and at the same time hoping he was back.

They finally broke for the zenith meal, and when he returned he went inside his work space closed the door and continued the work on organizing the materials brought back from the dig site. One of the items he brought back was a piece of something that first appeared to be glass, but wasn't. It was generally transparent like glass, and seemed to be of similar nature. Yet, when one picked it up it was much lighter, and at the same time had a different feel to it. With the thickness of the piece one expected it to be heavy, yet it was not. It also turned out not be fragile like glass. Thick light and strong, whatever it was would be a great item to have now. This material seemed to be used in that flyer they had discovered.

The piece he had come from a stack of broken pieces found in the corner by the second desk that had the large image from the air of the area they were excavating. They had nothing in this present time that came close. Heck even the glass they had presently did not come close to the quality of glass they had found.

He didn't know how to explain it but this glass had a softer feel to it, and the surface seemed to be a bit warmer than glass, and it actually could be scratched. And yes, while glass could be scratched it was much harder to do so, and seemed to have a tendency to break when one did scratch it. While this – what would he call it – special glass did not. So how could it be lighter and thicker than glass yet having the appearance of being much stronger, and less likely to break? Another of those additional questions with no answers . . . well, what did he expect? Actually he had expected to be answering questions, not creating new ones. Still very few of the original questions had been answered, and many, many more had been created. He knew that if an advanced race brought their advancements to a primitive race, to the primitives, all the items the other race would show them would appear to be magic, and this advanced race would be like the gods.

He knew what he was seeing onsite and what he had returned with were not created by magic, but it might as well have been. Since he had no explanation of how any of these items were created. It still left him overwhelmed with what had been found. So much has been lost over time. He wondered if this tearing down of a civilization had happened before. It left him wondering if maybe this had happened many times, and each time they had to start over and learn all over again. These thoughts left him slightly depressed. "Time to move on and away from those thoughts", he said to himself. After all, he had no proof, and it was just a mind game.

Still, realizing where they were presently, in advancing, he realized that when that worldwide disaster had happened that it came close to completely wiping them out. It must have, considering that they were just now rediscovering this world. He realized that in some areas they were advanced in this present, while in others areas were still quite primitive. Were they destined to continue making the same mistakes over and over again? This he did not know, especially with the discoveries they had made in that desert. And what complicated things further, they knew next to nothing about their distant ancestors.

The requested runner showed up in the early after zenith, and took the initial requests to be delivered. Jllon expected to receive a quick answer from Bihl Kaetr, but knew that most likely that it would be a number of days before he received anything back from the assistants to the council. It would probably be a quarter of a cycle before they would see him. Then, who knew how long to move on to the council. Since it was between major cycles he only had to deal with the core group instead of the full council, and he hoped that this was a slow time, giving him a better chance of seeing them quickly. Still there was a chance that the full council would want to be involved with any decisions that had to be made. He hoped not as he really needed to get back and continue the work.

At least by having the expected time before going before the council he'd continue to polish the presentation and hope to convince the council of the importance of this find. Once convinced he would leave the assembly and organization of the new team to his underlings here and head immediately back, again with Doube. At least that was his plan, either way, successful or not, he would head back. He found that he already missed his mate and her assistance when he had to go before the council. She always had great suggestions and ideas to improve what he had developed for presentation. He had to admit that they were a pretty good team overall.

To his surprise, just before the day was complete he received a return message from Bihl Kaetr, stating that Fauul was not back yet, but he could come over on the morrow, say at the zenith meal, and he would fill him in on what he knew. The runner had waited, by the request of Bihl, so that an answer would be received back that evening.

He sent back a quick answer in the affirmative. Bid his assistant a good evening and headed out to one of the local eateries for the evening meal. Once there he ended up sitting in one of the darker corners not wanting any company at this time. He was still being affected by the overall tragedy that had happened so long ago. Where would they be now if this had not happened? That one image of a family from that time still haunted him. They seemed so normal, just a smiling family caught in a moment of time – frozen and out of reach.

It was too bad he was unable to bring that image along, but he knew if they had tried to remove it, most likely, would have been destroyed. So, that image along with the other artifacts that were too fragile to move would remain. Still the metal disks he had were in good condition. Deep in thought he barely tasted the food as he ate and once finished paid the proprietor, and headed back home. Much work still needed to be done on his presentation and he had to approach it as if he would be before the council in the chambers by the end of the morrow.

CHAPTER FIVE

They were silent for a while as both Fauul and Lauut thought about what they had been discussing. They continued to work the small water holes to make sure they were clean and safe for the beasts. This gave both of them time to think about what was happening and how it would affect each one. Fauul said, after some time had passed, "I do agree at times that interest in someone can be misplaced. I guess it can be both ways."

"What? I'm not following here Fauul."

"Oh, sorry. I was just thinking about what you last said, and then realized that it can be both ways. I know personally that I have been attracted to some female, and probably bothered her too much. Since, and if I wanted to be honest, I could see that she was attempting to run away. Still when those romantic feelings arise, it's sometimes difficult to separate reality from the imagination. So if it is that way with me, I am sure it is that way for the females also."

"Oh, you are referring to my comment about having someone interested in you as a possible mate, and you are trying to get as far away from them as possible, right?"

"Exactly. I have found life to be, if nothing else, interesting. We seem to live in the moment – day by day, and then cycles, which becomes turns. While in the immediate moment it's like we don't really notice time going by until one day we look and see and are shocked at how much time has actually passed. We then begin to wonder how it is we are here and what happened to that time, and where did it go? Did we actually live it or was it some dream? Yet, in this moment here we stand looking back." Shaking his head he continued, "It's such a mystery to me, how you live minute by minute and then suddenly a turn is gone."

"So how does that relate to what we were just talking about anyway?"

"Really it kind of just all ties together. I mean take your sister for example, or even yourself. A turn ago all is as you probably remember it. I wasn't in the picture, and in truth as far as I was concerned my path was different. I would have been thinking probably of some of those members of the opposite sex that I wanted to avoid, and going about my life ignorant of what my future held. Yet, now here I am next to you talking about a totally different future and it involving your sister as my mate. Yet, now what we see is the present, and that meeting between all of us is now history, in the past. How quickly it became that, I don't know quite how to say it but now looking back its like this has always been this way, but I know it is not. So how did it go from being a future event to being a past event allowing us to talk about it now, in the present?"

Silent for a moment before answering Lauut said, "That's a lot to take in, I'll have to think about that before I answer."

"True, it is much to think about. But, let's confuse the issue even more. You are what your history says you are. For Lauma and me, our histories started long before we met, and these will have influences on our relationship. Then we will create our own with our relationship. From there we will either look back nostalgically or maybe with no good feelings, all with what is happening at the time. Even with those 'then made' common feelings and events, we will still see them differently. Partly because of our sex, but mostly because of our life histories – this being a part of us individually before we met."

"Okay, I think I am following, so please continue."

"We forget, when we observe the world, that everything that happens, even though it's something outside of ourselves, is being interpreted by ourselves.

What I mean is this; say we look at this mud hole we are cleaning here, and this is a poor example for sure, the way you view it and the way I view the same mud hole is different. Not only because you are there, and I am over here, but because I was raised a township whelp, and you here in the outback. For me this is all new and for you not so new. So the way we see and understand what we do is an inner experience colored by all the past experiences in our lives, so no two individuals will see the same thing in any event. So when I say, for example, that this flower over here is the color yellow, why is it considered so? Because somewhere in our youth it was explained that this was what that color is. Now, there is no way to know if the yellow I see and the yellow you see are the same. It has just been explained somewhere in our past that this is what the color is. Now to my eyes it might actually be blue, but since it was identified as yellow I would always say it's yellow, and then you would figure that it would be that color over there. Since we are not capable of seeing through each other's eyes we cannot say for sure what another is really thinking or seeing or what their reality is.

"Again since everything really is an inner experience even our language has many problems. Again, for example, let's take this conversation, I feel I know what I am trying to convey to you, and I figure I am doing a pretty good job, but because language is so inexact, and the previous experiences of your life color how you will view what I am saying, the meaning could be completely different to you than to me. Then when we agree, both thinking we have it right, in truth we have two completely different views and conclusions. Yet, because we agree we really have no way to confirm that indeed the conclusions were different or even correct."

"Wow that is really deep. I really have never thought about such things. I mean you basically, out here, act and react according to what is being thrown at you at the moment. It keeps one sharp that's for sure, but I really never realized that everything that happens really is an inner experience. Yet, after you just explained it, I can really see it's true. It almost makes one not want to talk at all, or to come up with better ways to explain things."

"Yeah, sometimes you need to be able to explain things in many different ways so that someone else can at least possibly see, again from their perspective, what you are trying to explain to them. Still by not seeing into their mind's eye you really will never know if they have it right."

"You know you're giving me a headache here. You've given me enough to think about for next couple of turns. Look I think we have finished this water hole. From my point of view it is safe and clean for the beasts, and besides it's time to head back anyway. We will need to assist Lauma on the finishing of the work back at the main shelter."

"Fine with me. By the way I usually don't carry on like that, but this incident with Lauma at the zenith meal got me to thinking, I guess out loud, and that meant you had to listen to it. I guess I should apologize to you about that."

"No, no apology needed. It probably did me some good to have heard it. In the long run it will be something to really think about. Besides after working in this mud I am definitely ready for a bath, and I think we both better take one before the evening meal. Otherwise we both will end up on the wrong side of my sister. And I know you've seen that side yourself, and it's one place to stay away from."

Laughing Fauul said, "I can only agree. There is a real toughness in her that one does not want to cross."

With the males gone and with the short nap she had taken Lauma felt somewhat refreshed. Still by being by herself she found herself in an introspective mood. Working more by habit than actually paying attention she kept thinking about the changes that were happening to her. In truth the depth of the emotions she was going through at the present were all new. It was scary.

She thought. *We seem to look for that significant other for most of our lives, and probably never really realize the impact it will have on us when it finally happens. Even all the games I played as a whelp, dreaming about when it would be that way for me never prepared me for this. This male has just turned my world completely on end. He consumes all my thoughts, and I'm so easily distracted. These things were never me, and while on that subject – I feel that I am losing me.*

Looking up at the position of the sun she realized that it was getting late in the day and she was behind in her work, because she had fallen asleep. So she hurried out and went into the food garden and worked it and picked some ripe food for the evening meal. "They are going to have to help close out the beast-pen work that needs to be finished otherwise it will be well past dark before all is done", she said quietly. Again she found her mind drifting towards Fauul, then shaking her head she said loudly, "Distracted – so distracted. If I keep this up I'm going to do something really stupid and hurt myself. There are enough things around here to get hurt on if I'm paying attention, and so many more, if I'm not." Still she couldn't help herself, as she would continue to look out to see if they were returning from the work they were doing. It had become almost an unconscious thing.

Looking back at the conversation at the zenith meal, she knew logically that Fauul had to go back, but it was the surprise of it that had shocked her. She had found herself completely unprepared for that statement and while it really wasn't something that would mean an end to their strengthening relationship, she just hadn't expected it. Then the emotions had taken over and she had just lost it. *I guess that's part of being female.* With a minor gather approaching she knew that she would only have a few more days with him before he had to return to that township that was so far away from her. She still wished that there were a way that she could go with him. It would be a nice break from what she did every day, and she really had never been to a township as large as that one. At the same time she knew all the reasons as to why it was not possible. Shaking her head she said out loud, "I guess I have to be adult about this, I cannot be like an undisciplined whelp and throw a fit just to get my way. Life just does not work that way."

She looked up from her work in the garden and saw, out in the distance, her brother and Fauul coming in. Standing up and pushing a piece of hair out of her eyes she said, "Oh my." Looking at herself, she grabbed the food from the garden and headed inside to clean up a little. She felt that she at least needed to wash her face since she hadn't since her cry earlier in the day.

A short time later Lauut came through the door and Lauma then commented, "You stink! And look at those clothes . . . I thought I was bad."

"Yeah, I know . . . am heading to the bathing space now. It was pretty messy out there, and by the way the other one that was with me is in no better shape so it will be a while before he comes in. Just in case you are interested, which I have a feeling that you are."

"Now what does that mean?" She asked, looking up from the food prep area. Then she saw that he was smiling at her. Then acting mad she made a face at her brother and looked for something to throw at him.

He seeing her intent ran out of the space laughing and headed on into the bathing space. Later Lauut came out clean and helped his sister with the evening meal. After a while he stated, "You know that one is really a great catch for you. We talked quite a bit while we were working out there. And I must say work doesn't bother him at all. Plus he seems eager to learn, which is a plus anywhere you go. Yet, for me, it was what he said that impressed me the most. Fauul thinks things through before acting, and can explain things quite well . . . At least, until we start talking about females, and there, for all of us males, it just breaks down."

"Now are we really that mysterious to you and the rest of the males? After all don't we want the same things in the end? You know a mate, a safe place to live, to be comfortable, and to have family around, these really important things."

"True, but there are things that will never be understood by either sex – about the opposite sex I mean. One of the things that came out of today's conversation for me at least, and I know it wasn't brought up, but is true, is that you females have your hands on eternity."

"How do you mean that?"

"Okay let's look at it this way. It is you who carry both inside you and then outside of you, the next generation. You have a very close and personal investment in them. They are created inside you, and they must depend solely on you for their survival, and in truth many times they can even threaten your survival. Then after much pain of birthing, they continue to look to you for all their support – *while* we males are completely on the outside of this. I know we donate ourselves to the new whelp but it still is a distant thing in comparison to what you females do."

"Wow, I guess you two did talk out there. But, that leads me to a question as to why you males feel that you must be in charge and that we must take a servant roll to you? I see it all the time and this society seems to be set up that way. It's not that I am denying anything you have stated here. What you say is true. It's just that since you now see this, why are things as they are?"

"Sorry, I really don't know, except that I know here we share everything, and I have a feeling it will be much the same with you and Fauul."

Both jumped when Fauul then said, "Sorry you two, I really didn't mean to be listening in, but at the same time I didn't want to interrupt. I think I can partially answer your question Lauma. From what I have seen, this may have come about, and at this time I have no proof, when something or some event in the great past happened. I don't know what, but talking with Doube he felt that sometime in the past a worldwide disaster took place. His feeling is that it came close to completely wiping us out.

"He's right you know, your brother. I believe, at the time when things were finally settling down that there probably was major chaos, raiding, killing, and stealing, and so on. Whatever was before was gone, and I am sure many died from not having the skills needed. Others were outright murdered and what they had taken. Females would have been right in the middle of this. They would have become very important. So much so that they would be protected, and probably at some point became property. And once property would not be considered any differently than the beasts you have out there. Making you, the female, less than what you really are, and in reality nothing more than breeding stock.

Being the weaker in strength, physical strength that is, I doubt that there was much that these females could have done about it. Yet, without them there would be no new generations, no growing of the population. Doube thought it happened thousands of turns ago, and we are just now becoming large enough to know much about our world. So what you see is a shadow of what was. I know from the larger townships that the females are starting to take on more and are not in the subservient roll at all. As usual, it is in the small villages that the change will take place last and most slowly.

"I'm not saying any of this is right, or whether it happened as I just stated, but when you think about it, it probably is pretty close. I myself am quite happy to have not lived through those horrible times. I feel we could have wiped ourselves out just as easily by killing each other to the point of no recovery. Somewhere back then, something finally changed and we, as a race, started rebuilding, and have come to where we are now. I feel we have far to go, and if the *ones before* did exist, then my guess is that we are far from where they were at the time of the disaster."

Both were silent as they absorbed what Fauul had just stated, Lauma saying, "I really never thought about it that way before. If it did happen that way I guess I am glad, being female that I am living now and not then. I don't think I could have survived being property or a slave, since really that's what it would have been."

"Yes, that has many bad connotations, and probably much hopelessness. Since you would have no idea of your future, where you would end up living, and who would be taking you for mating and producing offspring. Again it would have been no different than being one of your breeding beasts out there."

She shuddered; thinking about what had just been stated, saying, "Okay enough on that please. I've had enough shocks for one day, and I must apologize for my reaction earlier today. It was a shock, a surprise, and truthfully I knew that someday you would have to go back for a time, I just didn't think it would be now."

"Believe me I wanted to put this off and give you time to see it coming but it just hasn't worked out that way. The minor gather is only a half a cycle a way and I have to go back then. I have to get everything up there settled. I have an idea to pass by my boss and I think he will go for it."

She was quiet for a bit. She kept thinking about what he said about the past. "Do you really think it was like that? I mean it just seems horrible that it would be that way. I know in the learning centers they do not pass on that kind of ideas about the past."

"There is no real proof, but you can kind of see it when you look at a few things that are around today. Take for example your herd beasts. You know that there are many different herd beasts in the wilds. In those cases it appears that a single male protects and breeds with a large number of females. He is their protection and in exchange he gets sexual favors."

"True, but we are not the beasts of the fields here."

"That's correct, but then if you look at the outcasts and bandit factions that exist today, you can get a hint of how it must have been. The strong control and the females are property to use and throw away. Not a pretty sight by any means. Now let's look at the way our society is presently going. You are beginning to see more specialization instead of general knowledge. This means that the skills that individuals have, as time continues to go, will no longer have the means to survive on their own. It takes a group to survive as each member does their own specialty, supporting the success of the group. In times of disaster one needs all the individual and general skills to survive, and if you don't and do not learn them fast you are dead. It's just that simple. Plus with the breakdown of the system that one lives under, chaos and anarchy is the result.

"Sometimes even having the skills to survive would not be enough as the stronger will come in and take what they want. So after the initial failures of the existing structure, with the weak, old, and unhealthy passing on, then you end up with small tribes of people who look at other tribes with envy, since these others may have something they want. This leads to raiding, lies, and deceit, as one tries to dominate the other. Stealing of females for breeding stock would be common, as would theft of whelps. Anything would be considered okay if it gave you the advantage. I am sure that this led to wars among the people who were alive then.

"Anyway it doesn't take much imagination to see this really. But somewhere along the time line things eventually changed. I really feel that this final change to where we are now probably happened in our near past. That change was the one of finally dropping the tribe mentality and just becoming a people of this world. No, it's not perfect, but I doubt that it will ever be."

"That's a pretty depressing history you just gave. Again it makes me happy, being female that I am alive here and now and not then. What you just presented was something I have never thought about, but when you see it, it does make sense, scary sense, but sense. What do you think Lauut?"

"It's much to absorb. I always felt that we were a noble race, but when you put things in perspective like that it does change ones' view quickly. By the way where did you learn about wild herd beasts anyway? I thought you said that you were a township whelp."

"I did, and I am. But you must remember that I had just about finished a major mapping project in the outback, when I first visited the two of you. The team was in the field a long time, longer than a turn, so I had plenty of time to observe the herd beasts out in the wild. It doesn't take much to come to the conclusions I talked about earlier."

As they continued eating the evening meal they were silent for a while as they allowed their minds to see the ideas that had been presented. Lauma got up from the table and said, "I'm getting some hot beverage would any of you like some while I am up?"

Both of the males nodded, then Fauul said offhandedly, "Before I leave there is just one other thing that I have to take care of, and believe me it is an important one." Getting up he walked over to Lauma and then said, "I have found that the time we have been together from the beginning to be some of the most interesting moments in my life. At this time I find that you are in the center of all of my thoughts, so right now before I take this trip back north I am asking you to be my mate. Obviously because I have found in my mind that you are the right one and I really doubt that I could find another like you. I also want to be able to give you time to prepare. I know that traditionally that the mating ceremony is performed at the major gathers. I know my return will be close to the next. If I asked then, it would leave you with mixed emotions. Partly anger for not giving you the time, partly, I hope, joy because you want this as much as I do."

Again catching her off guard she stared up into his eyes and initially said nothing. Then her brother trying to keep a little light said, "There you did it again Fauul. You have left her speechless. I need to find something so I can write this down.

She then looking over at her brother said, "Enough Lauut, enough . . . Fauul I don't know what to say . . . I mean . . . it's something . . . ah . . ."

"Now that's the sister I know and love!"

Stamping her foot and putting her hands on her hips she turned to her brother and said, "Shut up will you. Here a male has proposed to me and all you can do is make jokes." Turning back to Fauul she then said, "Fauul the answer is yes. I just didn't expect this now. I had hoped that when you returned that I might get an answer one way or the other. You sure know how to keep one off balance that's for sure."

They hugged and kissed each other lightly, and then Lauma said, "You sure know how to turn a depressing subject and evening into one of joy. I can see that we will be having an interesting life together if this keeps up."

"Better interesting than boring, but I'll take boring over dangerous excitement that's for sure." Fauul replied. Then he asked, "Thought you were going for some additional hot beverage were you not, followed by bringing us some too?"

"Was I? I don't know something just distracted me I guess." She smiled and said, "But I will take that distraction anytime."

Lauut shaking his head commented, "Boy, now I will never have any peace here. Plus with her being up in the clouds I guess I will have to do the work for both of us." Then smiling at his sister he said, "Just kidding sis really. With the conversation that he and I had today I did not know that he was going to ask. Well, at least the mystery is over, and with that our lives are once more in for a major change – although this one is much nicer than the last one that's for sure." Then looking at the two of them he wasn't sure they had even heard what he had just stated. Shrugging he just sat there and watched.

Fauul returned to the table and she brought over the beverage and they continued the meal, followed by cleaning up the dirty dishes. Once the cleanup was complete they all headed out to the porch as was the tradition, and sat quietly. Lauma, leaning against Fauul, who had his arms around her shoulders, seemed content.

Looking at the two of them Lauut thought. *It sure looks right those two like that. I know that someday I will find the same in someone. Funny I had always thought that it would be me before my sister. Guess it shows how much I know.*

Looking again he began to feel like an outsider, which was strange, since he and his sister had always been close. He got up excused himself and decided he needed to walk a bit. Fortunately there was a partial moon so it was light enough to see. At least he wouldn't trip over something as he walked the yard. He felt with everything that was said and revealed during this day that he had much to think about. That Fauul turned out to be a deep thinker and probably one who could be a learned. He had such an easy way of explaining things.

Going out to the pens, he leaned on the railing and looked out on the pastures staring and letting his thoughts drift from one thing to the next. It took a few seconds before he realized that his sister was leaning on the railing next to him. Turning he said, "Well sis I guess change is in the air. Not that you didn't already know it. It's hard for me to come to terms that you will be mated soon. I really always felt I would be the first, and being the older one also, wanting to continue to protect you in my way."

"I do know what you mean. This decision is life long and from it everything takes a new branch or turn. It really hasn't quite sunk in completely yet, and probably when it does I will be somewhat scared. After all while most of us have this happen, it is very much different when it is you or your turn. Here I plan on being with a stranger and become intimate with him. That in itself is very scary. He was raised where he was and I where I am, but those worlds are very different. It leaves one wondering how couples ever work it out. And yes I know many do not. Then, of course, it changes our relationship also. Not that you haven't figured that out."

"Yes, I've figured that out, and I have to come to terms with the fact that now I am second in your life. That by this mating, you join his family, and he joins ours. We have had many tough times and maybe with this things are finally heading for better times ahead. I really don't know. I know that I have to think about it a lot, not that I haven't, because it has been on my mind all the time. Still from what I have seen you two are just right for each other, and I couldn't be happier for you. I can only hope that I am as lucky."

"As they say, only time will tell. I know once he has left to go back I will need to get to the village and talk with my two friends and get their help. You will need to contact the village so that we can be included in this next major gather. As if we aren't busy enough trying to keep this place operating, and now I am complicating things by mating. And while on that subject I have heard that there will two others so with mine added there will be three."

"That's right, by being the family's representative I have to inform the village elders so it can be included. You're right, there is much to do adding to the already heavy work we have here."

"I'm going back to Fauul now and leave you alone. I just felt that I needed to talk with you a little to see where you were, and if you were alright with how things have transpired."

"Oh I am quite alright with it. When we were working out there today Fauul passed on some great information and one of the reasons for me to leave you two and come here was to think about it. Almost as much has happened today as when our sires were killed. That was tragic and sad, and this is quite the opposite."

"Yes, I do have to agree. I mean I ran the total gamut of emotions myself, from crying to complete shock and joy. What else is there to say other than I will leave you to yourself and return to the porch." With that she hugged her brother and left heading back to the porch where Fauul waited quietly.

When she approached the porch Fauul rose and took her hand and asked, "All okay? I know I have thrown a lot at you today. I hope that when I asked for your hand that the answer was not forced and that you felt obligated."

"Believe me, you didn't force anything. But I have to admit you have done a great job of keeping me off balance today. You know what I mean, first announcing you were leaving and would be gone at least a couple of cycles, and then turn around at the end of it all and ask me to be your mate. It is a little much, but I'm a full-grown female now, and I think I can handle it. At least I hope so."

"From what I know of 'you handling it' is the least of your problems. I just wanted to be sure. I'm not the type who will force one into something unless it is required, and this isn't one of those situations. Originally I thought to give us both the time apart to be sure. Yet the time we have had together let me see that our relationship has only grown stronger. Then when I realized when, most likely, the time I would return I knew it would not be fair to you to ask then. It would have been too close to the next major gather and as you know the major gathers are the traditional time of community matings. It overall would not have been right at all. So actually I came to this decision tonight, and really it felt right."

"It feels right to me also. Still it is such a serious and great change for both of us, and as you so aptly pointed out for the ones around us. Not to get off the subject but I can't help but continue to go back to what you said earlier in the evening. It still makes me shudder to think we might have been like that."

"I know, but when you really look around you can see that it would be something that might still happen – anyway enough on that. I'll leave the proof of such events to the Keeper of the Past and his team and do what I can, and right now what I can do is kiss you good night and head out. This has been both a physical and spiritually tiring day, and I am running out of time." Smiling at her he continued, "Running out of time as far as leaving, and running out of time as far as being single and free to do as I please." He then leaned down and kissed her lightly and turned to go.

She reached out and grabbed him and said, "Now is that such a kiss to give the one you promised yourself too?"

Laughing a little he replied, "So that wasn't good enough, was it?"

They then kissed much longer and deeper, and she said, after they broke apart a little breathless. "Wow, that's much better, I think I'll be looking forward to those."

Again smiling he said, "Me too, that had some power in it that's for sure. Anyway, I'll say goodnight again and I'll see you and Lauut in the morn." He then turned and walked to the workers shelter.

At the very moment Lauut had been coming back across the yard and had observed them kissing, and thought. *It's so obvious that they are just right for each other. There is an obvious strength that each has that complement each other. I surely hope that when I find my mate that I can do as well.* Approaching the porch area Lauma did not hear him and jumped when he reached out and touched her shoulder. "Lauut! You need to warn me when you come up that quietly. You startled the heck out of me."

"Sorry sis, I really thought you had heard me approach. He's something special isn't he?"

"Yes, I really feel very special that it is me that he wants. Oh it's both ways I know that, but why me? I mean with his abilities and looks he could probably have any female he wanted. Why me?"

"Probably, if I could answer that one sis, we would be rich and not poor. Who really knows what it is that brings two people together, and then keeps it going? I suspect that the question you asked probably has been asked for probably close to forever. And will probably be asked until we are no more."

"Yeah, I suspect you're right. Anyway I'm exhausted and it has been a very emotional day for me, and after my bath, will go straight to bed. What wasn't finished today will just have to wait until the morrow."

"Okay sis, I think I am going to sit here a little longer. I still have much to think about before I turn in."

"Then brother, I will see you on the morn, goodnight to you." She then turned went back into the house and Lauut was all alone on the porch.

Sighing to himself he, in his mind, went over the day and much of the conversation between himself and Fauul. Yes, in truth, it had been a very busy day. He had to admit that it was busy on all fronts. Mind, spirit, and body all got a great amount of exercise today. He reached for his cup and saw that it was empty. "Darn!" he said to himself, he knew that there was none remaining inside, and he really did not want to make any more. Shrugging, he stayed a few more minutes, and then got up and went inside. Looking down he saw Lauma's dog lying there and said, "You know there's even change coming for you." As if she understood she looked up at him and wagged her tail before putting her head back down on the floor. He smiled and headed to his sleeping space.

He was in that cavern again with the torch almost burned out, and all the different tunnels surrounding him, giving him no hint as to which one was the way out. Once again he could feel the panic rise in him knowing that once the torch extinguished itself that he would be in total and complete blackness. Why was he here and how did he find himself in this situation? Suddenly he realized that he had been here before, and each time that he had been he had never been able to find his way back out. What did this represent? Still looking around he saw no real solution to his dilemma. He felt that one of these many tunnels surrounding him did lead out but once again time was against him finding it. He remembered that when he had gone underground that he had marked his path so he could retrace his steps. Quickly he looked at the entrances for any marks he may have left but found none at this time. Once again he found that he was going to have to pick one at random and see if he would be lucky.

Looking around he found one that looked promising and quickly headed up the passageway. At first it appeared to have narrowed and the roof came down, but then the whole thing opened up and began a slight climb. This time this appeared to be the correct tunnel. It started back down and curved around, and the next thing he realized, to his dismay, it had circled around and dumped right back into the area he had just left. Did he remember to mark it so that he wouldn't repeat his mistake? Before he could check and see it indeed he had marked the tunnel the torch burned out and he was in total darkness. At that moment panic set in and then once again he awoke in a sweat.

It had been a long time since he had had this dream. Yet he was no closer to understanding why he continued to have it. He had really thought that with Fauul here helping and then being able to see things ease a bit that the dream would go away, but obviously that was not what was happening. Already the bits and pieces of the dream were drifting away, and slowly he relaxed and drifted back into sleep.

Lauma, when she had finished her bath, went to her sleeping area and sat by candlelight and wrote in her journal as to what had happened this day. In many ways it seemed surreal. She wondered that sometime in the future, she would look back on what she had wrote and marvel at the words written here, and that this was the time here and now where her life changed.

It all seemed so unreal. It almost seemed as a lifetime of events had transpired in this one day. She had run the complete gamut of emotions and when the day was complete she had promised herself to another. What would this be like to belong to another? It was something she had only witnessed from the outside. Now it was her turn to experience it up close and personal. While sitting there and thinking about this she started drifting into the twilight sleep where one was neither awake nor asleep. Here it seemed that the subconscious ruled and she tended to drift from one thing to another never staying with anything very long.

Suddenly she awoke and realized that she had indeed fallen asleep. "Oh my, not again", she said aloud. She got up and took one last trip to the necessary space and the climbed into bed, blew out the candle, relaxed, smiled a little and turned over finding that comfortable spot and went to sleep.

Fauul after leaving the two of them went straight to the workers shelter. He found, as he continued to work with the sister and brother in the outback that he was finding muscles he never knew he had. Even though he felt that by now most of that should have ended. Cleaning out those water holes had been physically hard. "I'm really going to feel those muscles on the morrow that's for sure", he said quietly. Yes, he could tell that he would be very sore. He had always considered himself to be in pretty good shape, and with what nature had given him he felt great. Still he was finding that slowly this work was toning and sharpening him. At times the work was hot, physically demanding, and very dirty, but he was also finding that he was enjoying it tremendously.

There was something about the outback that just soaked into a person. He found himself starting to listen to what nature was telling anyone who would take the time to listen. It had always been there if one would just stop. But most would not take that kind of time. The township style of life had no time for such trivial things. Plus, with most of what one needed to live readily available, it was not a necessary thing.

He had always noticed that the ones who lived in the outback, even though uncomfortable in a township, seemed to be more confident – not that they purposely demonstrated it. It was just a natural part of their personality. He began to understand why. With the daily challenges that the natural world threw at one, you either overcame, or went running back to the safety of the townships and villages. This outback became a testing ground for one's abilities, and if you were found wanting, there was no place to hide. So you either learned, or you left.

Now he understood the quiet confidence that these people had. He found that when anything was thrown their way that they would, without fanfare, complete the job. It would never occur to them not to try or to even ask for help. He felt that most likely that this life style was tougher, but in the end healthier. He could feel the surrounding countryside becoming a part of him and he was more relaxed and aware. He thought that the mapping project he had completed just a short time ago had taught him a few things about the outback. Now he knew that what he had found there was as a young whelp first entering a learning center. New things were being learned, but it was just the beginning, with much to follow.

While lying there in the bed with the many thoughts going through his head, he was trying to find a comfortable position before drifting off to sleep. He smiled at himself and thought. *I just promised myself to another for the rest of my life. Who would have thought it? Not me for sure.* He thought of Lauma, and that again brought a smile to him. *Wonder what our lives together will truly be like?* Of course he had no answer, and as it had been said time and time again, only time will tell. With those final thoughts he turned over finding a comfortable position. Being totally relaxed he drifted into sleep. Again as always, the morrow would be here soon enough with a new set of problems and challenges.

With Jllon gone work continued. There was an abundance of materials to be cataloged and packed. It would not be much longer before the heat of summer would end this dig. Once the second team arrived to protect and continue to catalog the finds they would move on to the other possible site. Celt couldn't imagine their team being any more successful than they had been here. It had been hot and dirty work for sure. But, in this case, the rewards of finding proof of the *ones before* overrode everything else. Still, they had to continue to be productive here. They had continued to uncover the large trail that lay next to the large shelter where the flyer had been discovered. While this trail was in terrible shape even though covered there were small sections that were still whole. They also had been able to find the boundaries of the same material that seemed to be a part of the flyer complex.

Unfortunately there had been nothing found to identify this ancient township as of yet. Even to have found what they had, considering the approximate age, was a miracle in itself. Now that some of these finds had been re-exposed to the air they were deteriorating. After all, none of these items had been built to last as long as they had. So that was reason enough for these items to start to fail. Unfortunately they did not know how to preserve such things, and it was too bad really. These finds belonged to all the people and not many would ever really know about them or actually see the real things.

Yes, the pictures and descriptions would be in the learning manuals, and the history, as it was discovered, would be presented. Still, it would be an interpretation and not really the true facts or the real objects. And of course, this team would be in those manuals, but they would only be names. Names in themselves would be hollow, as the learners would be required to remember them for some test from the learned . . . what a tragedy in truth. History was always dry in the learning centers. As a leaner he could not wait to be done with it. History was like one of those gourds one found, solid on the outside, but hollow without meat on the inside . . . Something that showed a lot of promise in the beginning, but in the end, disappointing.

Celt knew that the team's job, while Jllon was away, was to continue the work they had started. He had left specific instructions, since seeing the image from the air, to go periodically down the length of the trail the ancients had built to uncover it. If he had not returned by the time this had been accomplished, to start a third dig where it looked promising. Both had thought that maybe, like in the present, that there would be a better chance of locating additional promising sites by finding this trail. In the present many townships and villages were built along major trails. While this team was much smaller than the normal team, even with the volunteers, they had worked well together and had been successful. So he did not know if they would have the necessary time to start a new site by the time Jllon returned.

If Jllon was successful in getting a second, albeit smaller team approved, then they would be packing up and heading for the other area closer to the coast. Still if not approved, he was not sure what would happen. Well, it was not his worry and there was plenty here to keep all of them quite busy. With them now down two more individuals it had been decided that they work only as a single team. The females were moved over to clean and catalog the finds and the males broken down into shifts to haul and sift. Even the camp managers and their assistants were now involved in some of the digging work. While the two camps were still maintained because of the distance of the two sites from each other, the team would work only one area a day and be close to one or the other camp. This left a camp manager team free to assist. They would rotate daily so that all would participate.

The turn was heading into late spring and they would only have a few cycles before summer would arrive. Then it would be too hot to work the digging sites. The plan was to be on the way to the west by then. Leaving his portable shelter Celt headed over to the food prep and eating area and grabbed a cup of hot beverage. Seeing Jahnsyn Lytle and his assistant Mihls Bacr he waved a greeting and then asked, "So how's it all going right now? Are we okay with the supplies or are we in need of making a run over to the merchant?"

"We should be good for at least half a cycle before we need to resupply, but as it comes close to that time some of the things we will be out of. So the meals may become much the same. My recommendation is at the end of the next quarter cycle to send the handlers over and pick up our order and leave the next one."

Celt knew that it would take up to five days for the round trip. So it was a good suggestion. That meant that they would be down an additional three people. Well, there really wasn't much that could be done about it. They had to eat, and maybe some correspondence from home would be there also. It was always nice to receive. "Okay then, that's a good suggestion. Are the rest of the managers going out today or do they have something else going?"

"No, they'll be joining you out there today, and I will be in the working group on the morrow. I must admit that I am sore from the shovel work but maybe I'll lose some of this around my middle from the work. I know my mate back home would appreciate it."

Smiling at the thought, he realized that in many ways the females had a tendency to keep the males in line if only by their looks, glances, and comments now and then. Since most of the regular team had mates it was always fun to listen to the comments being passed around. He was included in this group, and knew that as a male he would try and please his mate whenever he could. After all if momma isn't happy nobody is happy. At least that was the way he had heard it, and he had found that it was pretty close to fact.

Jahnsyn returned to his meal prep and it was putting out a mouthwatering smell. Something about being outside with these smells of cooking food that just seemed to make the food smell and taste better. It wouldn't be long before the team would be eating and then he'd brief them on the present day's assignments after which all would be heading out. He had decided that they would continue to try and expose more of the ancient trail constructed by the ancients.

Here they would run down approximately a hundred body lengths and line up from the past digs and attempt to find it. Once located dig out approximately ten body lengths and then continue the process. They were working this digging generally west away from where the flyer had been discovered, and past where they had uncovered the burned out shelters. Unless they discovered something of significance while uncovering the trail, the distance between the two existing digs guaranteed that they would probably still be uncovering trail by the time Jllon returned.

One of the team entered where Celt was and stated that it appeared the nomads had returned. But, this time it appeared to be a much larger group. Celt acknowledged saying, "Okay, let's call a quick meeting before we go out today and inform everyone. I didn't expect them back for a few cycles yet."

"Okay boss," Danuld said, "do you want to meet here in the eating area or somewhere else?"

"Here in the eating area before we go out would be fine. It's not that a bit of time lost after eating would hurt with what the plans are, but the earlier everyone is aware, not that they aren't, the better."

Danuld left immediately to inform everyone about the meeting. Celt thought. *Why have they returned early, and why so many more of them?* He finished what little he had to do, and went out and joined the rest of the team. That food surely smelled good.

Standing where he could be seen by all he said, "In a short time we all will be eating our morn meal, and you all are aware of what we are doing, so this is something I do not need to pass on. Plus in such a small group you are also aware that the nomads are back. As to why I really have no idea. We are going to be at a disadvantage this time, since neither Doube nor Jllon are here. Since they were the ones that the nomads know and have conversed with, we will have to wait to see what is happening. I, for one, was not expecting them back for a few cycles yet. So be extra careful. Now has anyone here gone over to their area while they were gone?" Looking around at the group it appeared they were all shaking their heads in the negative.

"That's a relief. It has been promised to them that we would not and I am glad that we have honored that. I guess since I am now the one temporarily in charge if they do come over I will be the official representative of this group. I know that half way between where we are and their location was set a neutral area for brief meetings. If any approach you send them to me and we will see if that area is still good for them. For the rest we will just wait and see, and while on that subject I see the camp manager signaling me that the food is ready, so let's eat and get this day going. May it be well with all of you, and thank you."

He turned around and asked one of the cooks, "I do have it right?"

"Yes, of course, come on everyone before it gets cold."

As one the group rose and headed for the food, getting in line. It did appear that in the end, it would be another interesting day.

Celt, while waiting in line for the food, began to wonder if maybe they were the reason for the change in the arrival of the nomads. He knew, most likely, that they being here had made the rounds to all the desert nomads of this branch. And if the wise one of this tribe was an example of the rest then it might be curiosity that brought them here. Well, he could speculate all he wanted; until they came and made contact everything else would be just that — speculation.

Looking around and listening, he saw and heard that the group was much quieter than usual, and there appeared to be a bit of tension in the air. It was understandable, since the nomads could present a threat. The last time they had met all had gone well, but with the additional members of the nomads here now the outcome might be very different.

He remembered, from the report that Jllon had shown him, of how the confrontation between the mappers and the nomads had almost ended in disaster.

It was because of this report, that when they had begun their work here they avoided the nomad claimed area. At first it seemed like a difficult thing to do, as it appeared, at the time of arrival that their area was the only water source around. Fortunately they had found the small stream running out of one of the canyons to the west. And it was here they had set up their main camp, avoiding completely the nomad claimed area.

So by staying north of the nomad-claimed land they felt that they would not impugn the wrath of the nomads. Jllon and Doube had both stressed the point. So what had brought them back early? Well if they were cautious and alert he hoped that would be answered quickly and there would be no issues.

For the next couple of days, as they continued their work on uncovering sections of the ancient trail, the nomads stayed south and did not approach them at all. On the third day the wise one with his whelp approached the dig team. He was obviously looking for either Jllon or Doube, and seemed puzzled that they were absent. Celt, after a short time, felt that he had better approach them and find out what it was they wanted. At the present they were staying just to the south and out of the way. Celt thought that he would head to the neutral area where he would meet officially with the wise one.

The wise one noticing that someone from the dig area was approaching the neutral area headed over to the spot and waited. In a short time Celt arrived, and following the lead of Doube did a small bow acknowledging the wise one. The wise one returned the respect, and asked, "I was looking for either of the two with whom I spoke with before. The one who has been adopted into the nomad society, or the leader, are they not here?"

"Wise one, I must inform you that neither of the two that you are seeking are here at the present. Both left on a quest and will return in a couple of cycles. I have been left as the one who leads while they are gone." He could see the disappointment in his eyes but other than seeing that, there was no other outside indication that it meant anything. Waiting to see what the wise one's response would be, he truthfully was a bit nervous. He was good at doing what he normally did, but left negotiations to others. Well, he was the one in charge right now, so he had no choice. He just hoped that he did nothing wrong here. He said, "It is unusual for your people to be here this time of the turn. Nor I have seen so many of your people gathered in one place."

Smiling the wise one said, "Ah you have not seen our gathers then . . . that of course I knew, as they are in secret places only known to us. The clans you see here today are just a small representation. When we left the last time we were here and when we interacted with others I passed on to the otherwise ones about what was happening here. Many were curious and wondered why such a thing was going on. I passed on the knowledge that your leader gave me, and the fact the Doube who is known to all was here. Many decided that they wanted to both see what was happening here, and to talk with the one you know as Doube. He is known by another name which is secret and known only to the nomads."

"I guess bad timing on our part then. I mean had he known that you would be returning he, they, would have wanted to be here. So with them gone, how is it that we can assist you?"

"It will be a disappointment to the others that Doube is not here and a disappointment to me that your leader . . . Jllon . . . is not here. I will relay that information back to the waiting members. We are aware that you have kept your promise to remain away from our space, and as such there will be no claim made against you and yours. We would like to do as we did before. I will be back with additional of my position in the other clans, and if you have no problem my whelp with others will be in the area to observe. Is the female that assisted last time still here?"

"Yes, and I am sure she will be available. I think that maybe we can start with all the wise ones down at the other site. There have been some discoveries there that may interest you and yours. The only thing I ask is that nothing be touched. We have found the discoveries to be of a very fragile nature, and are actually starting to fall apart since being re-exposed to the natural air. I believe that what we have found may help you with some parts of your missing history, or not – since I do not really know yours. I was told that your verbal history goes back about six thousand turns, and we feel what was found here probably goes back about an additional four thousand – give or take."

"We will appreciate the knowledge. We cannot stay long this time with this many beasts. There is not enough graze for them, so we will remain approximately a quarter to half a cycle then be gone again. To give the grass time to recover we will miss one pass to this area."

"When the two return I am sure they will be sorry that they have missed your visit. I know personally that Jllon really enjoyed the conversations that the two of you had. So when do you want to look over what we have uncovered?"

"I will go back and converse with the rest, and then later today return here and let you know what has been decided."

"Fair enough, thank you for your courtesy and I look to our meeting later today." With that he bowed, and turned and headed back to the dig site. Glancing over his shoulder as he retreated, he saw that the wise one was also returning to nomad camp. But his whelp remained in the area keeping a respectful distance and continued to watch what was going on. Smiling he said to himself, "Ah we have a spy." Then he laughed a little both at his little joke and to shake off the tension from the meeting. Overall he thought he had done quite well. Of course Jllon and Doube had laid much of the groundwork.

When he reached the team where they were working, he informed them of what had transpired so to keep all up to date. He knew this was not a time of mistakes so the whole team had to be completely aware of the situation and of the information that was passed from one group to the other. So far the nomads had been completely courteous, but he knew that one could not just waltz into their domain and expect it to be that way. He was so ever thankful that Doube had been with them. He seemed to have an inside track to the nomads.

It would be mid-zenith before the second meeting would take place on neutral ground so he hoped they could get much accomplished before then. Once the arrangements had been made and the nomads of importance started mingling with them all would have to walk and speak carefully. They were of a completely different culture and had their own ways of handling things. Still he had learned that these roaming people had much useful knowledge, and a great verbal history. It really was too bad that none of it was really known.

Because what he and his team dealt with was history, to have such a rich source just out of reach was frustrating. Each piece that was found and added helped solve the large puzzle of the distant past. At the present that puzzle was missing too many pieces to even make sense. Just like what they had discovered here, the evidence spoke clearly of the *ones before*. Yet, there was precious little to really understand their times, the climate of the world in politics, science, and just how the everyday person lived.

From the time of the *ones before* to the present there were only disjointed pieces to explain why they were who they were at the present. Like Jllon it was easy to see that the *ones before* were well advanced of where they were today. Why the regression? There was too much time with nothing written or surviving to have an accurate record of the past. Even though back in the working shelters of the department what they had was not very well organized and not easily researchable.

So here before him was a people with a verbal history that went back approximately six thousand turns. While he understood that it would be from their point of view, this information could so help in answering many of the questions, and many of the blank spots of this world's history. Maybe in the end, Doube might be the key that opened the world of the nomads to the learned here. All he could do was hope. "So close, yet so completely out of reach," he said quietly to no one. Then shaking his head he thought.

This just isn't getting the work done. Still maybe it is something that I should discuss with Jllon when he returns. It did seem that he and the wise one had hit it off well.

The day continued to pass quickly and before he realized it, it was time to go back out to the neutral area and see what the decisions were. It was obvious, in a way, even before he reached the spot; he saw many of the nomad's whelps excitedly waiting the word that they would be allowed to go explore the area and what these strangers were doing. Smiling, he knew that soon these whelps would be bored, since what they did here was exciting to themselves as adults, but there would be no adventure in it for the whelps. Once their curiosity was satisfied they would drift away head back – leaving only one or two that were drawn to what they were accomplishing.

From the previous visit he knew that a few of them would hang around and even want to participate in what they were doing, and then eventually they too would leave. It would be the elders of these clans, especially the wise ones who would be most interested. What was happening here would add to their verbal history and be spoken around the campfires during those times when the learning was required. *Funny,* he thought, *this team and I will become part of their mythology and will be spoken of during those times of storytelling.* Realizing this just then was quite a shock. It left him thinking as to how they would be described to the rest. *Idle speculation*, he thought. After all, the opportunity to actually hear them would be non-existent. He arrived at the neutral meeting area and bowed to the wise one, awaiting acknowledgement.

The wise one returned the bow stating, "It has been decided that like last time we were here that the whelps can come and see what is happening, but must stay at a specified distance. Is the female with whom they dealt with last time available to keep watch? Before you answer, the otherwise ones will come with me and you can show us what you have been accomplishing here. I feel that since you have honored your pledge to remain away from our sacred and secret area that we will honor this area as yours. If one wants to come and visit either area, they will come to the neutral area, arrangements and a guide can be assigned. With your permission we will start the visiting on the morrow."

"Let's see if I have this right, if I may your name was given me as Soolonge, is that correct?"

"Yes, that is correct."

"As we address you would you prefer to be called the wise one or your common name?"

"Either works fine. Probably when the otherwise ones arrive you may use my name to speak to me otherwise wise one is fine."

"Okay then, Suzzane is available to the whelps since she was the one who they contacted first and seemed most comfortable with. When on the morrow and what time of day did you want to see what has been happening since your last visit?"

"We will be here mid-morn. That will allow us to take care of the normal morn needs of the clans. We, the wise ones, will come first, then afterwards when we return other members of the clan will be allowed to come and see, to satisfy their curiosity. They will be with a wise one who has been here. That way you will know that the ones who approach have been approved by the clans to come and watch."

"That sounds like a fair arrangement. Is there a way that I can send a representative to your camp to observe?"

"No, unfortunately because of our society that is not allowed. Only ones who have been adopted or born into the clans are allowed. I am sorry since you are allowing us access to what you are doing here. Because we are small in comparison to much of the rest of the world it is our protection."

Disappointed, yet the denial was not unexpected, Celt said, "I understand, I was just hoping to be able to exchange knowledge. Maybe it is something as time goes that will happen. I look forward to seeing you and the rest of the wise ones on the morrow. There have been some major discoveries since you were here last. I must ask again that when these discoveries are shown to you that no one touches them. They are very old and very fragile. In fact even with no one touching them they are starting to come apart on their own."

"So understood. I will relay this information back – until the morrow."

Soolonge bowed turned and headed back to the nomad camp.

Shaking his head Celt let out a sigh of relief and then said quietly, "Glad that's over. Now I guess comes the hard part. Since I am the one in charge, it falls to me to be the curator and tour guide." Watching the retreating nomad he turned and headed back to the work area. He would discuss what had transpired at the next meal. While he had the upcoming meeting between the two groups running in the back of his mind, he still faced the work they were doing. He did not understand these ancients at all. This trail made no sense. While, yes it was relatively flat here, why make a trail so perfectly straight? Was there an advantage to it? Very few of the existing trails of the present day were straight. Yes, they had areas where they generally did but never for as long as this appeared to do.

Plus, the first area they had uncovered appeared to have living shelters that were also aligned in a straight line. The trail to them was perpendicular to the main trail, and then the shelters were at right angles to this. The circular pattern they used in the present day just seemed to work so much better than this. Or was it because it had always been that way for as long as he remembered, and it was something that was comfortable and familiar. He suddenly realized that he had a new insight. How did one eliminate thinking beyond what they considered normal and put one's self in the place of these ancients without coloring it with existing prejudges from the present time? Was it even possible? It was something he would really have to think about.

This idea continued to grow, and left him wondering if it was truly possible to be completely devoid of any prejudges when one worked such a site as this. Since all you knew was what your life had brought you, the society that one lived in, and the history as explained. These things became you, making anything different seem strange and wrong. There had to a reason why these ancients had built like they did. Still, with these now known prejudges, could he really see it and understand it? Then he remembered hearing a statement that when one becomes aware of his or her limitations whatever they may be, one can either live within these or find a way to overcome them. After all to solve a problem one must know what questions to ask. If the wrong ones are asked then the solutions will not present themselves. Yet, when one looked at what had been discovered so far, the questions far outweighed the answers, and additional questions were coming much quicker than any solutions or answers.

As Jllon so aptly stated, "We have only found a very small portion of what these ancient people did or who they are. There is not enough here to even know anything about how they lived or how they worked. The discoveries, so far, have shown us that they were far advanced of us. Still, it was not enough to prevent the failure of what they had. This is something that we need to keep in our minds as we continue to discover these people.

"We should also take a lesson from this. The lesson, simply stated, is that even with great advancements it does not take much to destroy it, and leave what may have been a great people on the edge of extinction. From the little we have found it has become obvious that we are their descendants, and they our sires. Which means that we could, and maybe in some areas, equal what they had accomplished, while, obviously from what we've found here, are far behind in others. Who knows, maybe in some areas we have exceeded what they did. Still all is speculation at this point – let us continue our work, attempting to leave out our prejudices that we naturally have, and learn to read the story they have left us to find."

It was obvious why he was the Head Keeper of the Past. He really did see much that was normally missed. Plus his ability to be a learned and to pass on the knowledge was a great asset. Add in his ability to organize just about anything, and all of this seemed to be effortless. At first many had complained when he was chosen for that post. One so young had never filled the position. Yet, he had proven himself over and over again. And finally even the most vocal of the doubters saw he was the right one for the position. And now through his insight and leadership he had led them to the greatest discovery of anyone's lifetime. To have been on one of his teams was always a great honor, but now he had led them to the *ones before*. He wondered if another in this position could have accomplished this feat. In truth he doubted it. Jllon had taken two apparently unrelated facts and found a relationship in them that led to this dig and the discovery. He knew that he probably would have dismissed them as unimportant, surely not important enough to push for this project.

Enough on that, he would be dealing with the nomads soon enough and he needed to get it together for that. Plus he needed to have the team finish with this day's assignments, and follow that with a brief meeting, after the evening meal, to lay out to them what he had talked about with the nomad wise one.

After thinking about it for a while, he realized that most likely there would be more than just the wise ones visiting the work on the morrow. Somehow, probably because it was happening in the desert territory of the nomads, most in the area were now aware of what they were doing. He was now quite happy that Jllon had put that restriction on the nomad's location. He knew that some, figuring that when the nomads had moved on to another location that it would be safe to at least study the area. From a distance, and from the notes of the mapping team, it was obvious that their area had some archeological significance. And yes, while they had plenty to do where they were working, the curiosity of what appeared to be a known area could easily draw them there.

It was now apparent that the nomads had some way of watching their sites and protecting them. Plus it also had become obvious that if necessary, they could gather quite quickly and provide a large force – not a pleasant thought really. It was better to have them on the good side of one than have them as enemies. He suspected that if necessary, all the different nomad clans, the desert, the mountain, the meadows, and who knew how many others, remained in contact and probably would support each other. That, in itself, was a scary thought.

* * *

The next early portion of the day went quickly and before he knew it, it was time for the nomads to approach the neutral ground. He hoped that he had planned well enough. He headed out to the meeting area, noticing that many of the whelps that were free were already approaching, but at the same time keeping a respectful distance to their elders who were also approaching. He turned around and signaled for

Suzzane to come over with him. She seeing him signaling her dropped what she was doing and started heading his way. Again he found himself becoming nervous. There just were too many things that might go wrong here.

She caught with him just about the time he reached the neutral ground, and because of having to almost run to get there with him was a bit breathless. Smiling to himself he thought. *Even with those work clothes she wears it is almost impossible to hide her beauty. Still, this female is self-sufficient, and strong. Guess it has to do with living one's life in the outback. It just seems to naturally develop in one that way.*

There was no more time to think about anything else as the group of nomads reached the meeting place, and he with Suzzane bowed to the nomads. They returned the respect, and were introduced to the additional members who had come along with Soolonge. Celt returned the favor by re-introducing himself and Suzzane. As he had thought, this was a pretty sizable group here, probably numbering close to ten to fifteen members. One of the unusual things he noticed was that one female was there with them.

He asked why, since such a thing was unusual with the leadership of the nomads. Soolonge replied, "She is here to go with your female. She will assist in controlling the whelps, if it is necessary. That way your female will have the full support of us behind her and they will not attempt to do something they are not supposed to do."

"I thank you for that Soolonge, and I am sure that Suzzane will appreciate this courtesy also." Turning and catching her eye he saw relief there. Then turning back round he continued. "It is a wonderful offer for which we accept." Celt then asked, "Shall we head on over to the large shelters that we uncovered there in the distance?"

"Yes that would be fine. There is one more thing I would like to pass on to you."

"Yes, and what may that be?"

"On the morrow there will be a heavy wind coming in and will blow the sands around. You will not be able to work, and must prepare. Otherwise your temporary shelters will be blown down, and much of what you have will be contaminated."

"I thank you for the warning and will definitely pass on to the team what you have said. May I ask how you know this?"

"We, as a people, have always lived here in the desert. As such you learn her signs. It is not a place where one can live against, but must live with. So while many of what is presented is subtle, it is plain to us. I cannot explain it better than that. Let's just say it is the way the air feels and the desert speaking to us."

"While I know I will not live in the desert as you do, I hope to learn from it."

"Always a good plan. Here the lessons are harsh. Either you learn or you die. Rarely is there a second chance. After the wind leaves we will also so as to not destroy our grazing land."

Inwardly he breathed a sigh of relief, *only a short visit this time*. He hoped that what he presented today would be enough. "Again thank you for that information. Without the warning I am sure we would have lost things and would have been sorry that it happened. Again, I know I will not be here long enough to learn what you have, so any assistance like this is most appreciated.

"Okay, just a little information here . . . what we have discovered is a major trail built and then used by the ancients. Along the edges of this trail are mounds and small hills that look promising as places that may have been shelters in the past. I know when you first look at them it is no different than all the others that you see. But, as it is with your understanding of the desert, it is ours to understand that by looking at many factors we conclude that there might be a shelter or shelters existing under them.

"That is how we determine where to do our initial digging. Now that is not to say that we are that fortunate anytime we see what we consider a good site. Many . . . most really do not show anything. That is why overall we do not get the opportunity to do this very often. Anyway, here the two areas we worked both produced results. Where we are going now is the more spectacular of the two, as the other site shows heavy damage from a fire and not much remains."

As he continued to talk they were approaching the large shelters. He brought them along the ancient trail and up to the back of the shelters so they'd appreciate the size and bulk. As he expected he could see they were in awe of what was here. Soolonge, who was the spokesperson for the group commented, "These are large. We have never seen anything of this size, and look at the amount of metal used. The whole shelter is nothing but metal, and yet it has been covered in something to protect it. You can see the difference from where it has come off from heat and where it still is on the metal."

"Yes, exactly, we don't even have the ability, right now, to produce this amount of metal, let alone build a shelter this large." He led them around to the front. At the moment the large door was closed to protect the ancient artifacts they had found. He would lead them through the small side door they had found, and from the decision last night to open the large one for effect. "We are going through this small door here, and, obviously, it will be dark inside, so once we are all inside, I want the last person to hold the door open to let in light and to give us time for our eyes to adjust to the gloom." *They all seem fine with it so far. We'll see how the react shortly to the finds. Glad we were able to determine how to unlock this door.*

He opened the door and headed inside. Soolonge volunteered to be the last and to hold open the door. It took a few moments for the ten or so individuals to enter, and it was dark inside – the only bright area being around the open door. Immediately the nomads noticed that the floor was flat cool and smooth. One of the group commented, "This is not natural. What is it?" The rest of the nomads squatted and felt the floor with their hands. Their eyes not yet having adjusted to the difference in the light waited.

"Again, this is one of the ancient's skills we seemed to have lost. But this is not all this shelter revealed. I am going now to open another door, one that is very large. Please remain where you are, and when I do you will momentarily be blinded by the bright outside light." He quickly headed over to the large door, shifted the pins on both sides, and with a flare pulled up the door which immediately raised revealing the interior, and briefly blinding his audience.

There before them was the flyer and the ground transport vehicle. He could see from both their silence and from the looks on their faces that he had gotten the response he wanted. "These are things the ancients built and used, and, for whatever the reason, abandoned them here before they disappeared. Because of the way things are here it appears that whoever had left these things had planned on returning. But it did not happen, obviously.

Remember, please do not touch them. If you look on the floor you can tell that they are coming apart all on their own. Please walk around them, and then, I have more to show you here before we leave." He gave them as much time as they wanted to look over the two items.

He saw the excitement in their faces as they talked among themselves attempting to come up with some answers for the questions that these objects threw their way. He did not interrupt as he felt that they needed as much time as was necessary before continuing on.

Soolonge approached him and commented, "This is really a great find. There is nothing in our verbal history that talks of these things. It does change views quickly. It makes one think and asks too many questions, and it immediately changes the way one sees all things."

"Yes, you are correct, but as great as these are, it is not enough for us to know much about them. What I have left to show you here is not large as these, but will leave with just as many, if not more, questions as these two objects have."

He led them over to the closest desk that had the images of the family under glass, and again stated that because of the fragile state of everything he was showing them not to touch anything. "If there is any doubt that we are their descendants, then this one image removes all doubt. Other than the strangeness of the clothing they are wearing, they might be any one of us from our time."

From there he led the group into the necessary space. While he knew that this was something they had no use for because of their lifestyle, it was still something they were familiar with. Lighting a torch to illuminate the area, he stated, "This space is their necessary area. I know that's obvious, but what I wanted to show you is the fact that there are no windows and no place to put a torch to have light here. It appears from the globe on the ceiling they had other ways to light the darkness. Plus, look at the quality of the looking glass. Anything here in this space we cannot make today. Even though we have looking glasses it does not come close to this. The rest is beyond us completely." Then leaving the area he doused the flame in a small container of water.

He led them next to the last desk that sat in the back corner where the debris had been cleared. "This is the final thing I can show you here. Then I will lead us out of here and close down the large door. If you look again on the top of the desk you find it covered with glass like the other was. This was damaged from debris falling on it. Still we cannot duplicate this quality, and like the metal it seems to be abundant. Again look through the glass and you see a large image of what appears to be taken from the air by one of these flyers looking back at this area. You can see many more shelters than the ones we have discovered here." Then stepping back he allowed them time to look at all he had just presented to them. He did not want to hurry them, and as long as it remained as it was there didn't appear there would be any problems.

Finally it appeared they were through looking and as one headed back outside into the bright sunlight which momentarily blinded them. He closed and locked the large door, and exited through the smaller one. From here he led them over to the sorting shelter where the smaller artifacts were being cleaned and logged. It was here the drawings were being kept also. These drawing were made at the time of discovery of many of the objects. They depicted the location of these objects. That way as time went on they could hopefully piece together from location what they may have represented.

He handed them many of the small flat disks they had found in the burned site. On one side there appeared to be a bust of a person, then on the other some sort of shelter. They were of many different sizes and had numbers on the bust side. The back sides were not consistent from one to another. While some indeed had shelters others had flyers, and some had what appeared to be some kind of torch. The one consistent thing on them was the writing stating UNITED STATES OF AMERICA.

Looking over the group Celt stated, "We believe that these disks were some form of exchange like the marks we are now using. Again these are of metal and if you look closely it appears the silver looking ones are made of at least two metals somehow sandwiched together and then stamped with the images you see. We have absolutely no idea how this was done. If you notice they all have numbers on them, which consistently consist of four numbers. We think that these numbers represent when these disks were made, but that it only a guess at this time." Collecting the disks and returning them to the containers he left the tent.

"Okay, we will finish at the first site and then you can let me know what you need." Throughout what he had presented to this point, the group had remained respectfully silent. Whenever they spoke it was in quiet tones and to each other. It took a bit of time to finally reach the first site, and like them when they had discovered it, the nomads saw the destruction the fires had caused. The nomads paused, got together, and discussed something in private.

Then Soolonge approached Celt and said, "What you have shown us today has left a deep impression upon us. It is obvious to us, as it is to you, that indeed these *ones before* are our sires. And as you have so stated, it is very obvious that much has been lost. You have left us with much to think about. We would very much be interested in continuing our contact to see what else may be discovered. But for now it is enough. I am to thank you for being honest and allowing us to see all that you have found here. We must now return and prepare for our departure. With the heavy winds coming on the morrow there is much we have to do. Fortunately the signs say it will only last the one-day. With this we bid you farewell and hope we can see each again." With that he bowed backed away and joined the rest of the nomads. They turned and left, heading back to their camp.

"Whew!" he said to himself. "I for one am glad that's over with." Looking around he could see that Suzzane and the one female from the nomad camp had pretty much corralled the nomad whelps and many appeared to be giving up and heading back toward their camp. He knew that shortly they all would return as the work at the nomad's camp involved all. This was just a brief respite for the whelps. And sure enough before he had come close to where Suzzane was the nomad female had signaled the remaining whelps and they were returning back to the nomad camp.

Continuing to approach Suzzane he asked, "Well, how'd it go with them?"

"With the help of Jade it went fine. I could tell that the whelps would not try anything strange with her here."

"Jade, huh . . . that's great; I guess it went well with the group I showed around also. But now we can get back to what we are here to do – soon anyway." They both started walking towards the rest of the working team, and he said. "They did inform me that the winds are going to be blowing heavily on the morrow. I should have remembered to ask from which direction. Oh well, too late now. I was also informed that they would be leaving after the winds."

"I wonder how they know this?" Suzzane asked.

"I asked the same thing, but all I got was something about living here all their lives and just knowing. Something about them being able to feel the change, I really don't understand."

"I think I do . . . at least a little. I believe that you must have grown up as a township whelp, right?"

"Yes, that's true, but how would you know that?"

"It was just a guess on my part, but you see I am one who lives in the outback. Not in anything like this area of course, but when one lives with the natural world you have to learn her ways."

"Now you are sounding like Soolonge."

Laughing she asked, "Am I?"

About that time they reached the rest of the team and Celt called them over. "We are going to need to stop our work for the day and go and prepare the campsites for a strong wind that is supposed to come in on the morrow. I was warned that it will do damage to much of what we have worked including our shelters and artifacts. So we need to all go to the two sites and double tie down everything. I forgot to ask as to direction so I am guessing it may be from the prevailing direction. Still I could be completely in error. With what we have found we cannot afford to lose any of it.

"Let's break up into the two teams we originally had when we first started this dig and go from there. If either needs additional assistance send a runner to the other camp and we will assist. It is getting late into this day and as far as I know our time is limited in fixing this. The good news from all of this is that this particular wind is only supposed to blow one day. The last thing I will say about this is as the winds start to blow everyone will remain in the camps and be prepared to fix anything that may come loose or break. I'm sure that the morrow will be no fun at all.

"Now it is close to the zenith meal, so let's all head into the camps and begin the necessary work, and when the food is ready the camp managers will let us know." With that, he signaled them to head for camp.

Just before sunrise the winds hit, and hit hard. There was a slight warning and then the blowing sand and debris surrounded them. Visibility dropped to almost nothing. It would almost be impossible to see something break or blow away. All they hoped for was the preparation was good enough. Still, with the strength and fury of the winds they really didn't know. Instead of coming out of the prevailing wind direction it was the opposite. Prevailing winds came from the west and southwest. This wind came directly out of the East, but it changed direction often – appearing to be a live demon attempting to find the weakness in their preparations, so that it could destroy. Most of the team had never been in winds this fierce and it humbled one quickly. It was so loud that one had to yell to be heard, and if one were not close to the person speaking the person would hear nothing.

There was fear that the portable shelters would not stand up to the punishment the winds were putting out. At times they were laid flat on their sides, with the poles that were used to support them flexing to almost the breaking point. Every once in a while over the din of the winds they heard something crashing. When they heard it they knew something had been blown over and was probably being scattered across the desert floor. It was only hoped that whatever the winds had found to destroy and spread was not of a critical nature.

It became obvious to Celt and the rest that they would be recovering from the wind for a few days. He had to admit that he was quite happy that it would only be one day. He knew now that their preparations were sadly lacking and he had underestimated the strength and power the winds was presenting. He only hoped that any damage was minimal. Now that the ancient shelters were exposed he had no idea if they would remain standing in winds such as these. One of the two was severely damaged, and in its partial fall had damaged the second. Nothing he could do about it now – still it left him antsy and wanting to get out and check for any damage.

That was completely out of the question. There was too much blowing sand. Even with the portable shelters closed as tightly as they were, the sand was filtering into everything. He was now thankful that the nomads had chosen to warn him. He now knew that if they had not been aware of the approaching winds and had not done any preparation at all, then most likely, everything would have been damaged or destroyed.

Trips outside were brief, and when one of the anchoring pins would pull out then they would rush outside and do a repair as best they could. In many cases they now had to use two pins for each rope. Each trip out for these emergency repairs pounded them, filling their eyes with the blowing sand and as it bounced off of exposed skin would sting. Once they were out a quick inspection was made, followed by a quick return. It turned into a constant battle just to keep the shelters standing.

The winds blew most of the day and as evening approached they started to diminish. The change was subtle and it took a while before they noticed a change in the force of the winds. Still they did not stop all at once but would pick up and blow with the same intensity before subsiding into a dead calm.

Finally it was just that calm and the quiet was overwhelming. After the howling the winds had created to have nothing move and to be completely silent seemed almost deafening. Their ears were still ringing.

Stumbling out of the shelters they saw a world changed and of one that had much of their supplies scattered across the landscape. One of the shelters was half buried in the sand that had piled against it. Another, a supply shelter had partially collapsed and lay under a heavy layer of sand. Everywhere they looked the sands had invaded. Yet in a few areas just the opposite happened. The sand had been removed right down to the hard packed ground laying bare rocks and boulders that had been completely buried.

Assessing the damage was going to take much time, but it'd wait until the morrow. Celt knew that most likely he would not get any word from the smaller campsite until later anyway. He immediately put together a work party, and they began the immediate cleanup around the food prep area. There had been little chance to eat, and he knew with what the team had just experienced and finally being able to emerge to see this destruction, that they had to be somewhat overwhelmed and depressed. One couldn't help it. At least with all of them working on this area they would have a hot meal and a chance to catch their collective breaths. Darkness was rapidly approaching and as long as they had some food and a place to sleep the real work would wait until the morrow.

CHAPTER SEVEN

Lauma, looking at the blowing dust in the bare yard, thought about all that had transpired in the last turn. Other than the other tragic incident in her life more had changed for her than at any other time period. She had gone from being frustrated with her situation to becoming someone's mate in the near future. That in itself was shocking. The winds had returned early which was not a good sign at all. It could mean a very dry spring and summer. That meant the threat of wild fire would be great. She felt, at the moment, she had more than enough excitement in her life and did not need to complicate it with nature's fury.

Fauul would be leaving shortly to return to the township and take care of many things. He had also said that he would spend time with his immediate family there to inform them of the upcoming event. Fauul was sure that his mother would especially like to attend the ceremony even though it was not close to where his family lived. He had told her that he would try talking her out of it but knowing his mother he thought that would be next to impossible – still impossible did happen now and then.

Most likely she would drag his father, sister, and brother down for the ceremony at the major gather – or not, he really couldn't be sure. While his siblings were grown as he, they still lived in the shelter with their sires. It helped all on the upkeep and expenses. Both of his siblings were still attending the higher learning center, and could only work part time. Of course their only excuse for being able to avoid the trip down to the remote village was attending the learning center. That would probably work for them but his father would not be so lucky. While Fauul was sure that his male sire would not mind, attending these functions as a guest, it was more to the females' liking than the males. While the gatherings after the ceremony were great for all, the actual ceremony was most important only to those who were directly involved. He felt it would be better if he could convince his mother that she could meet the new family member later.

At least for her it would be easier, although it would have been wonderful to have her mother here at this important time in her life. She thought that her mother would have been proud of her choice. Again, she found that now, at this present time in her life, she was missing her more. It was during this critical time in a female's life that the wisdom of the past generation was often passed on. There would be no one to ask those important questions. This almost brought her to tears. She had always known that the mother-daughter relationship was a close and special one, and it was one she would never have.

The shelter shook from a gust of wind and she heard something pushed across the yard by the wind and then a crash. Distracted, she got up and peered out to see if anything had been damaged, but could see nothing other than the dust and swirls raised by the wind. Looking at the dust swirls she remembered, as a whelp, laughing and running through them, dreaming that they had the strength to lift her high in the air so she could look down from the sky as a flyer. In her mind's eye she would feel free and turn around and see that her mother would be standing on the porch watching her and smiling.

Yeah, those carefree days of youth, of being a whelp, with what you thought were great responsibilities that, of course, you wanted nothing to do with and preferred the imagination and freedom to play those games. This brought a smile to her face as she recalled those events. It was a sad smile all the same since her sire would never be around. All these thoughts were starting to put her in a melancholy mood. She found herself being both happy and sad at the same time. She also felt herself being very nervous with the unknown future that was beginning to present itself.

She found that she was starting to second guess herself, to question everything, and to wonder if it was right. It was at that moment she remembered her father saying, "You can 'what if' yourself to death and that doesn't change anything. Worry most of the time leads to nothing but problems for the worrier. So once you have honestly weighed everything that you could, then trust in your answer or solution. If things change, then at that time, make the adjustments." He was right, but it was hard not to worry. This was one of those decisions that would have a major influence on her for the rest of her life.

Life in many ways is not fair, she thought. When one is young and without experience one, many times, is required to make decisions that will have a major impact on the rest of one's life, be it positive or negative. Because of that lack of experience and many times no one to discuss it with who has any more experience, the choice you make can be wrong. Yet, at the time of that decision it seems right. Then after turns have passed and one has gained the necessary experience one can then look back and see the error. Where at this time, it is much too late to be able to correct it, or change the path or the direction one really had a desire to go or should have gone in the first place.

She thought that she was in that situation now. She had weighed all and hoped her decision was right, but at the same time having little experience in life, as of yet, hoped she would not be blindsided by something that would have been obvious to someone with much more experience in life. She had looked briefly to her friends from her youth, and while not being able to really talk with them about it, had observed briefly what was happening in their lives.

From the outside they both appeared to be happy with their mates and what life was giving them now. Still outward appearances can be so deceiving. What was presented to the public could be so different from what actually happened behind closed doors. Right now she was happy that she had a half-day to herself. While normally they could take a down day now and then, most of the time they were unable to make it a complete one.

Again hearing the wind gusting and the shelter shaking, it continued to take her back. It seemed that the winds, from her perspective as a whelp, were exhilarating. Again she would see herself running and giggling in the sheer joy of the moment. Such a different picture of herself than the one she now saw in the looking glass. She wondered what she would think about herself from a whelp's point of view looking at her now. Would she approve or just go off running and laughing – really not appreciating the seriousness of the near future, and its implications.

Would she ever reconcile the two of them? Seeing herself in her youth, before the accident, running and loving what life and her imagination allowed, and this grown female about to take a mate. The one who had known so much tragedy, and in many ways, while projecting a strong façade, knew that deep down she had many doubts and weaknesses. Many that she even tried to hide from herself.

On a whim she got up and went outside to the porch, while it was still mid-spring the winds held some heat. Now from here she again traveled back in time. Only this time she became her mother watching the daughter playing and laughing in the winds. Again that sad smile came to her, and then choked up with emotion from the images in her mind she ran back into the shelter to her sleeping area and cried once again. She knew, as she had back then, that nothing would ever be the same. "Oh mother, why can't you be here now? Now, when I really need you, and your ways", she whispered. But, in truth she already knew the answer. Still it did not comfort the hurt she felt in her heart.

While Lauma was by herself in the shelter both Lauut and Fauul were out hiking the property. The winds were warm, and because of them the skies and surrounding landscape was perfectly clear. It was as if they could see from the hilltops forever. The sky had a startling blue tint to it and the hills shown bright green. The whole sight was just beautiful. Fauul, was really beginning to appreciate and understand the outback life now, and was beginning to wonder why he had ever preferred the township style. He was beginning to feel more alive than he ever thought possible. Yes, he had been involved with the mapping project and had been outback for approximately a turn. But for some reason even after that project was completed he never changed his mind and still considered living in that township.

Suddenly Lauut changed direction, and said to Fauul, "Come with me I have something to show you."

Curious, Fauul looked at Lauut and asked, "You have something to show me – now what?"

"You'll just have to wait until we get there. Once we do all will be explained . . . well at least some things will be explained."

They were presently east of the shelter and Lauut headed purposely southwest at a good clip. Shrugging, Fauul started following and eventually caught up with him and then kept pace. Fortunately they had packed both food and water, as they had planned to be out past the zenith meal. It was an opportunity to show Fauul the size of the property and what lay beyond.

After about an hour of hiking, Lauut stopped and pointed to a semi-hidden area and stated, "This is where I set up camp. As you can see unless you know it's here you would just dismiss this as one of the many similar areas that exist in this place."

"So, you camped here, why is that important?"

Smiling at Fauul and seeing no comprehension in his face he said, "Well it seems to me, not long ago, you asked me something, and I replied that it would be later. It's now later."

Puzzled, Fauul couldn't remember what he had asked, and why would this campsite be so important? "Okay, you have my attention . . . continue?"

"Just follow me and all will become clear."

"Really?"

"Yes, really." With that he headed out and within a few minutes they were at the crack in the hillside that led down into the cavern where they had found the fire starters.

Suddenly it dawned on Fauul where they were. Looking at the entrance he almost repeated word for word what Lauma had told him when she first saw the entrance. "This is the entrance? You went down there? You're either braver than I thought you were, or a real fool. That just doesn't look safe at all."

"Laughing Lauut responded, "You sound like my sister. Yet, the second time she went down with me, and while down there we found that fire starter that you ended up with."

Fauul looking around said, "There sure appears to be a lot of small hills here, and look many are bare or have very little vegetation on them at all. So why here?"

"Yeah, it's true. They have always been that way. You can see that they are not easy to climb or to get up either. So we pretty much have left them unexplored." Then smiling he continued, "I guess the only real exploring I have done here has been under one of the largest of them. There is no time today for a trip down there, and besides the first time I went down I learned my lesson very well. I almost did not come out. So before another trip down there I want someone who is on the outside to know that we would be entering the tunnel. And why here? I just happened to be in the area at the time."

"Smart of you, at least now. I guess it is important that we learn from our mistakes, and if we don't we deserve just what we get in the end."

"Now you're sounding like my sire. Of course, he had many such little words of wisdom. It's funny how even though I was still a whelp when he died; I can still recall most of them."

"I understand, and most likely, like most of us when we were whelps, we did not want to hear it at all."

"True, true. Yet once you are grown you find yourself repeating the same things, even after you had told yourself that you would never do it."

They both laughed realizing how true that statement was. Fauul asked, "So how far into this hillside does this go?"

"Distance wise I really do not know. But it goes down deeper and has a few twists and turns. On my first trip I didn't bring enough torches and the last one burned out before I got out. Fortunately I was close to the entrance at the time. Had a scare there, not only because of the torch dying early, but because once I had actually left the tunnel I did not realize it right away. While I was underground a fog had drifted in and it was also a dark night with no moon, so the combination of the fog and night made it as dark as the tunnel had been. I really thought I was a goner. Then I felt a slight breeze and then felt the mist from the fog on my skin. It was then I realized that I was out."

"It would have been easy to panic at that point. I mean thinking you were underground and no light, no way of knowing which way was the correct way. That would have been tough. I'm surprised you didn't panic."

"Believe me, I came close to it. But I kept telling myself that if I did that I might as well lie down and die. I did bang my shin hard and ended up with a bone bruise which left me limping for quite a while. So it was a hard lesson, but one I took to heart quickly."

"So it took some of the daredevil attitude out of you huh?"

"Yes, a whole bunch of it. Much went through my mind as I realized the danger of my situation. Things like leaving Lauma alone, and putting her in a situation where she would have lost another family member. I really realized how irresponsible I was. It was just stupid, and dangerously so."

They left the entrance and retreated back to where he had set up camp and there they ate the food they had brought with them. Lauut continuing said, "I took a lot of misconceptions with me when I entered that tunnel or cave."

"How so?"

"If you remember during your learning time, they had briefly covered the subject of some of our ancestors who had explored caves and such. What they cover does not begin to cover the true reality of caves. Still, because of ignorance, you think what you learn is adequate." Shaking his head he continued, "My knowledge is much greater now, and after my adventure, I give all the accolades to those early explorers. Overall it was tough.

"Some of the misconceptions I had, well, I expected the floor to be flat. It was anything but flat. I felt the roof would be high up and easy to walk under. Wrong again. There were times where I had to crawl. I expected it to be cool. After all, it's underground, and away from the sun's heat. In truth, it was hot and sticky. I did not bring near enough water with me. I could go on, and on, and on. There was just one thing after another that this little adventure taught me."

"Listening to you, I guess you were lucky to get out in one piece. I have a feeling that I may have entered that with the same misconceptions, although I don't know if I would have at all. Guess I'll never really know. So why did you decide to show me now?"

"Don't know really. I think it is because you are becoming a family member and have been more than willing to help us operate the business. I know, by tradition, that when the female mates she and her new mate are supposed to leave and not work the family business. This is one of those unusual cases where if she left the family property would be lost anyway. So to have you so willing to help has been a life saver."

"As you know I had never planned to do any of this. I was quite happy working my way up in the cartographer division. I knew, in a few turns, that I would have a great opportunity to be one of the bosses. That was one of the reasons I took the assignment to help on the final field mapping. Then I met your sister . . . or should I say I was confronted by her and her dog Sadie. After that neither she nor I could stay away from each other. At the time was neither looking for a mate, nor expecting to find someone of interest. I guess plans do change, and in this one it is a major change in direction."

"I guess she blindsided you huh?"

"Guess you could say that. Still I would say it happened to both of us. I really didn't expect it to be this way . . . what can I say? I mean, none of us has a clue what our future will really be. So you plan and do the best you can. Then in a moment everything changes and all those ideas and plans go out the window and either you adjust, or give up. I'm not just talking about the positive changes as between your sister and myself, but those major negative ones also . . . if anyone knows about that it's you two. Whether you know it or not, both of you chose to go with those changes and not to give in."

"I think once again you're giving me a headache here. At the time we didn't look at it that way. After all we were just trying to come to terms with it all, and all we had was each other. I, being the oldest, felt it was my duty to help her as much as I could, and I am sure in her own way she probably mothered me. So we became our own support. I'm not saying it was easy, but we still are here today. Still struggling, still being strong for each other, and even that now is changing again."

Laughing quietly Fauul then said, "Yeah, really, it does seem the only constant thing we have in our lives is change. Now if that isn't a contradiction I don't what is?"

"Agreed. I think we are both finished here. Why don't we head back. Unfortunately there is work to be done before dark, and I would have loved to have a complete day out here showing you around, but responsibility won't let me."

Getting up and laughing Fauul replied, "Funny thing that responsibility, I mean when you are a whelp you so want to be big so you can do as you please. It appeared to be so with our sires. Still, when we were whelps, we could never see what was really happening. Now I think being a whelp again with the small responsibilities one had would be wonderful, don't you?"

"Ah yes. I do have to agree. It was such a romantic view as a whelp. Grow up and do as you please." Shaking his head and smiling, he continued, "Boy were we wrong on that one."

They picked up their trash and headed back in the direction of the main shelter. As they went Lauut continued to point out landmarks and boundaries. He also told Fauul that, if time permitted, and if he wanted to do so, that once he returned from his trip home that he would take him down to the natural cavern at the bottom of the tunnel.

"Oh by the way," Fauul asked, "this wind that we are having here today, it appears to be coming out of the east – generally any way, do you have them often?"

"In truth, more often than I like – but this one is really early this turn. If it follows the normal pattern it will blow in series of threes."

"Series of threes, what do you mean?"

"Oh three days, six days, nine days, but being this early it may only blow for one. In comparison to the how hard they can blow this one is mild."

"Really, this one blows hard enough that, at times, you have to yell to be heard, and the gusts can knock you off balance."

"Believe me this one is mild, but it's not the winds in itself that are dangerous. As summer approaches, leaves and then into fall, and sometimes in the winter, these winds come and go. Then, at times with them blowing we end up with wild fires."

"I guess even paradise has it problems. But why would fires be such a problem? I know that at times from where I come from there are some wild fires but they are handled pretty quickly. Of course in areas where there is no one they just burn themselves out. Still where there's a population everyone pitches together and protects the properties."

"Pretty much the same here – that is if it is a normal wild fire. If haven't seen one being pushed by these winds, then you have never seen a wild fire. Let's put it this way, you've got a rough idea of how much land is on this property now. At least I think you do. You know that if you walked the perimeter of these lands here it would take you about one day, and that would be if you pushed. My ancestors knew, because of the mild winters here, that it would take a good-sized piece of land to support their beast business. Are you still with me here, because you need to see the size in your mind to appreciate what I am going to tell you next."

"I think so, I mean after all I am a cartographer and have to deal with mapping and land all the time."

"True and I knew that but I just need for you to see the size in your mind. Now, if we had one of those wild fires pushed by these winds approach us from the east with a front as long as the length of one side of this property, how long do you think it would take for it to travel across the entire piece?"

"My guess would be, comparing it to the ones I know of, a day or two."

"Normally I would agree with you. There are times when fires do burn that slowly. It makes it easier to protect things when it's like that."

"Burn that slowly? I thought that that was a fast moving fire truthfully."

Laughing a little Lauut continued, "If that was only so. No, until you experience one of these you just don't realize how fast these fires can move. Anyway, it would burn this whole property in only a couple of minutes."

Incredulous Fauul asked, "In a couple of minutes? You're kidding right? I mean this is a pretty good sized chunk of land here. I can see a day or even in an extreme maybe half a day, but a couple of minutes?"

"Scary huh? Imagine how far you can walk in a day, or maybe two keeping a good strong pace. These fires, when at their peak, can burn that in hours. Even the fastest wild beast cannot outrun them, and to make it even tougher, overall these fires have no real established front. Oh there is a main fire, and of course, that main fire has a front, but it throws burning debris ahead of itself, continually starting new fires in front of it. Then they combine with the main fire and on and on."

"That's a pretty ugly picture you're painting there. Are you sure you aren't exaggerating a little here?"

Shaking his head he said, "No, I really wish I was, but until you live through a few of them you really have no idea. There is just nothing that can prepare you for them. At times the smoke completely obliterates the sky, and at night you can see the glow from the approaching fire and that glow covers just about as far as you can see. It is eerie, and the smell of the smoke gets into everything. Then it starts raining ash from the advancing fire. This ash covers everything, and at times it becomes hard to breathe."

"This description sounds like the end of the world to me."

"I can understand that, and it does seem that way at times. But I do have to admit that in its own way it is absolutely beautiful. How can I describe it to you? I guess you will have to see for yourself."

"So, how do you stop something like that anyway?"

"You don't, you just protect what you can, and hope what you did is enough. Then eventually, either the winds die, or the fires slow down, or the fires run out of things to burn. Then, and only then, do they finally stop."

"From the sounds of it there really isn't much you could do to protect anything, so what kind of protection works?"

"Even though you probably didn't think about it, it's one of the reasons the yard area by the shelters are nothing but dirt. We keep it clear down to bare soil out fifty body lengths, and I know you never asked about those barrels we have on the roofs, but we keep water in them to soak the roofs down. And all the windows have enclosures in an attempt to make the shelters as air tight as we can. You see, with these winds at their peak, they can blow burning embers right through any opening you may have missed. So it is important to stay with the shelters while the fire is close so that if anything does get inside or on the roof and might ignite it you can put it out. Finally one must also have a couple of planned escape routes."

"More than one, why?"

"More often than not, as one of these fires approach, one of your planned routes becomes unsafe, as the fire has either jumped it or is approaching it. So, one must even consider a safety place right among your shelters."

"From your description it almost makes me not want to be here at all, let alone live here. That's sure different from my first impression back when we visited here when I was on that project."

Smiling Lauut said, "Most of the time it can be like that. The winters are mild and short, leaving water to be the major problem, but even still there has been enough. There's about thirteen cycles in a turn, give or take, and we have nice weather here somewhere around nine to ten cycles so it's easy to want to be in this area. We rarely see snow at all, even up in those mountains."

"Still those wild fires . . . how often do you get them?"

"Fortunately, not very often at all. Although some turns it's worse than others, and while they do burn every turn many areas aren't touched for up to fifty turns. But then when they do burn, it is with a great intensity and you do not want to be even around then. Enough on that, we are almost back, let's see what Lauma has been up too while we were away."

Looking around Fauul had a new appreciation for his soon to be brother. He seemed to not be bothered by the possibility of these wild fires at all. He, now with new eyes, saw much of what Lauut had explained to him as they were heading back in. He needed to remember to ask about where, here by the shelters, their safe area was located.

They had stopped on a rise that overlooked the shelters and sat under the shade provided by a tree. Shortly they would head back in as the time was almost up and they would have to get back working. Turning to Lauut Fauul asked, "How was it growing up here? I mean I grew up in a township. My father and sire is a merchant and while we are not rich he does well with the business. And yes, as I grew up, I had to learn the business, so in some ways I guess I can help around here on the business end. Still I had time to do things all whelps do, but obviously more limited."

Smiling and staring off into the distance Lauut sighed; he leaned back into the tree and said, "Like you, there were always things to learn, things that had to be done. As a whelp, I always hated the responsibility of it all – would have been out playing all the time if I had my choice. I mean look around you here. So many places to explore, so many challenges to test yourself on, and unlimited areas for your imagination – it was great. That is until that disaster – then it wasn't so great. I was fifteen turns, a youngling at the time and she was twelve. We had some assistance after we were left without sires until I turned sixteen. Here that is considered the time you had to be responsible. The rest you pretty much already know."

They both were silent for a while just enjoying the coolness of the shade and the warm breeze. Then Fauul said, "I can see how it would have been. I think I would have traded my youth to be able to grow up in such an environment. I mean back there, there just aren't many areas to get away that you cannot find yourself in trouble, because the owner just doesn't want noisy whelps running around. Here there aren't any of those problems at all."

"True, but there are others."

"Such as?"

"Such as being too far out, or pretending to be too far out and then coming back and finding out you are in trouble, because you were to be back at the shelters to do something, and you did not show up." Laughing he continued, "I am sure that somewhere in the past we both were in trouble for that one. Avoiding responsibility is the ways of youth, or so it seems."

"True, true, speaking of that word, I do think we should go back in. I believe you said that there were things that we needed to get accomplished before dark. This has been a great day for me. I have learned more and am beginning to appreciate this outback life more."

They both stood up and headed down the hill into the yard area. Then looking around for Lauma Fauul saw that she was not in the yard area at all. Figuring that she was inside the main shelter, he first headed to his to clean up a little. He turned to Lauut and said, "I need to clean up a little. I'll meet you inside shortly."

Lauut acknowledged that, and headed into the main shelter. He was thinking that after the hike something cool to drink would be wonderful. As he entered the shelter he yelled, "Sis? Where are you?

We're back, and something cool to drink would be wonderful."

Lauma hearing her brother enter and call quickly got up, and looking quickly in the looking glass she could see her face and eyes were red. He would know she had been crying. Guilty about her feelings overwhelming her, she quickly headed out to meet him. Lauut seeing his sister approach from her sleeping area did immediately notice and the asked, "Lauma, what's wrong? Why have you been crying? I mean, I thought with what was happening for you that you would be happy?"

Not sure herself why, she said, "Oh Lauut, I . . . ah . . . oh I just don't know. When you two left me here all alone, which is fine, I was enjoying the peace, of course except when that wind would gust . . ."

Just then as she was attempting to explain, Fauul entered the shelter looked over at her, and immediately she saw that he knew that she had been crying, and there seemed to be a deep concern on his face. Fauul looked at both of them questionably with a look that wanted some type of answer. Lauut softly said, "I found her this way when I came in and she was just in the process of trying to explain." Then turning back to his sister he then said, "Please continue."

Now feeling embarrassed, her face flashed crimson. Then catching her breath she asked, "Is this an inquisition?"

The two males looked at each other and Fauul gestured to Lauut to continue, "No sis, and you know it's not. It's just that this was the last thing we expected after returning from our hike."

"Oh I know, and it's the last thing I expected of me. Just log it as a female thing okay? You know that we females are more emotional than you males. Always have been and always will be. That's why we are considered the center of the family . . . the glue that holds it together if you like."

Nodding, Fauul said let's sit, I'll get us something to drink and we can continue to talk." He got the drinking cups and went outside to the hanging gourd where it was kept damp to use the evaporation to keep the liquids inside cool. There, using the dipper, he filled the cups and headed back inside. When he came back in he found the two sitting in the family area and joined them there. He handed both of them their drinks and he sat down. "Okay, if you like, you can continue with your story, or if you prefer we can just drop it."

Lauma seeing the expectation on their faces at first thought let's just drop it, but realized that in truth it wasn't an option. "Okay, I guess I will try to explain, I, as I was saying when you came in Fauul, am not really sure what set it off. I was inside here enjoying the time off from our work and then the winds as they gusted, started reminding me of being a whelp. So I went out on the porch to watch, as the winds picked up the dust and create those whirls. Then, in my mind's eye, I saw myself running in the yard as a whelp, laughing and playing, and just enjoying the freedom of the wind. Then I remembered that mother, at times, would come out and watch. I could see her smiling some secret smile. Then, for some reason, I became her briefly watching me in the yard, at that point all sorts of other regrets started entering my mind, and when it became overwhelming, I started crying. Once the tears started there was nothing I could do until I had cried it out. Not long after that you came in and here we are."

Looking at both of them she still could see the concern, and actually the love both had for her, and while she had hoped not have had to explain herself, she saw now that it was a good thing. Then sighing she said, "That's pretty much it."

"I can understand it. I know for myself, while I never would have the bond that a mother and a daughter have, our father and I had a good relationship. Still I know that males just don't, I don't know how to explain it, but there seems less of an emotional tie between males than there is between females."

"Oh it's much more than that. Still it would be difficult for me to try and explain that to you two anyway. Anyway let's just say I realized a greater loss today, and one that can never be made up for. So the cry was for as much for that as it was for the images I saw in my mind earlier. Remember, there is a great chance, as other similar situations come up, that you may find me crying again. If it's your fault you will know, but if it is something else that I have just realized at that time, then I must come to terms with it, okay with you two? And please don't grill me. When I'm ready I will try and explain why. Do we have a contract on that?"

Again the two males looked at each other, then at her, and silently they both nodded. Fauul said, "Lauma, we really weren't really trying to grill you or even question you. We both, your brother and me, really care for you and to have come back from what I consider a nice day out and find you here this way left us a bit concerned. It, in truth, was one of the last things I expected. It is the only reason we asked."

Drooping her shoulders in resignation she said, "I know . . . I really do! Believe me it was the last thing I wanted to do. The day, once the two of you had left, was quiet, and I was enjoying being by myself, and relaxing. The winds started me on the track of memories, and it kind of just spiraled from there. I know now that I will have to go visit my two life friends in the village. I have much I need to talk with them about, and no before you ask it is not something you can help me with. This is strictly a female thing, okay? I know that as of right now I am promised to you as you are to me, and no I am not thinking of backing out of that. So, if in the next few days, or such that I am a little different or a little distant it has nothing to do with either of you. I have much that I must come to terms with right now and today was when I finally realized it. So I have much to think about.

"It's surprising to me how quickly the time of our mating is approaching, and in its own way that's very scary to me. It is a lifelong commitment and a major change. I'm going from being single, and only having to be responsible to myself and my work, to being part of two, with later, whelps becoming part of us, and knowing that much of this will fall on me as the female. It is a very serious thing we contemplate here, and I think too many enter into this too lightly, not thinking it completely through."

"It still sounds as if you are not sure, and if that is the case, I am not the type to force one into something they do not want. So if that is the truth then we can hold off until you are sure."

"No, that's not it at all. Funny, but from almost the moment we met I had a very strong attraction to you. And if anything it has grown stronger on all levels. I am very sure that you are the one I want to go through life with, and if you were a stone mason I would say you can carve that in stone."

Lauut feeling a bit left out and felt that in some ways he was listening in on a conversation he shouldn't be hearing felt uncomfortable. "Are you two sure you want me here as you discuss this? I feel a little like I should not be here right now."

"Lauut you are as much a part of this as is Fauul here. He will be family soon and you are. In fact you are the only family I have right now, and we both know what is happening here has a big effect on you. So I am comfortable with you being here right now."

"Thanks for the confidence, it just seems that what is being discussed is more between the two of you than me, and I just feel a bit out of place that's all."

Smiling at both of them she said, "Enough on this, let's get something more to drink, and get the work done we have to, for now let's forget this, and just do what we have to."

"Okay by me, okay by you Fauul?"

Shaking his head and smiling, "Of course, you two. I know that really I'm the outsider here, the one learning, so I will just follow your leads. After all what else can I do?"

Jllon had prepared as much as he could and could only wait until he was notified that the council would see him. He decided to make a trip over to the mapping division and see if he could find and talk with Bihl Kaetr, Fauul's boss and friend, and to see if he could find out any more about Fauul, if he was back and if not, when he planned on returning – he really needed to talk with him. In truth, it was critical. While he had Doube with him, who had been with Fauul at the time, it was Fauul that ended up with the object, and he had hoped to use it as an example to show the council. While what he brought would provide a strong case, these objects and drawings were from the present dig – not that this was a problem. This other object that Fauul had was from where he wanted to do the second dig. If he couldn't contact him directly before that meeting, then all he could present was the original drawings made at the time. He hoped it would be enough.

Of course, having a team presently in the field would be a plus, but with the cost of the major projects, it had not been a good time to add another. It had only been because of the strong evidence he had presented to the council earlier that had led to approval. Even then he had to find ways to make it work with less than a full team. Successful they had been, but now he needed to protect that site and move his team on to this other area.

He finally reached the mapping division and headed inside. The first person he ran into was Joellie Trag, the one who had been in charge of the team that Fauul was a member of.

"Isn't it the Head Keeper of the Past," Joellie sneered. "I understand that you want to talk with Fauul. Why? I was the leader of that team. You should come and talk to me. He was only the second in command, and as far as I am concerned, not very good at it anyway. It is because of me that things went as well as they did. It just seems that no one around here is willing to recognize that fact."

"It sounds like you do", Jllon replied sarcastically, "and it appears that you want to make sure everyone else knows also. Okay, did you barter, off one of the locals from the village, an artifact?"

"No, why would I want to. It was a small village just filled with simpletons, no one there would interest me, and I couldn't wait to leave – especially since we were finished anyway. As far as I am concerned he and Doube delayed our return with that trip out to get the pack beasts. It should have taken them much less time. I said as much in my final report."

"It sounds like you don't care for Fauul, and why would that be."

"He was such a pushover with the rest of the team. They walked all over him, and even though the rest of the team praised him for his abilities, I could see the real reason. He was working to turn the crew against me and my leadership."

"Okay, if that's the way it is, if you did not get the object of interest, then I have no reason to continue with this conversation. I need to talk with the one who owns it, and that is not you."

"Oh whatever, he's not here anyway. Took an open leave of absence to go back to that god forsaken little village. I say good riddance to bad trash. He can just stay there. While there he's out of my way, which is just fine with me."

"Well, thank you for your time. I must get on to Fauul's boss. Since last time I met him, it was outside of this shelter, can you direct me to his space?"

"Yeah, it just over there and to the left . . . but remember, I warned you."

"How can I forget?" He left quickly, happy to be away from Joellie. His impression, simply stated, was that this male was really into himself. He had read all the reports and personal logs from the project, and knew that more than once, Joellie had put the team in danger, and his leadership skills turned out to be poor. If Fauul had not been there the team would have probably failed, and most likely there would have been some major injuries if not death. Now that he had met Joellie he found his original assessment to have been well off. This male was much worse. He wondered how Fauul had been able to bring the project to a successful conclusion. His view of Fauul, because of this unplanned meeting with Joellie, had risen considerably. It was obvious that Fauul was very competent – especially dealing with the hostile environment that Joellie had presented to Fauul and the team.

Shortly he was at Bihl Kaetr's space, but he wasn't there. Talking with his assistant he found that he was down working with some of the drawings from the ten teams that had worked the final rough mapping. Again he knew that these were not complete. There still would be many areas that were blank spots on the maps, but now all the major trails and most of the villages would now be located on a map. That is, once all the data was consolidated. That, like in his area, and present project, would take many turns to complete.

He headed in the direction the assistant had pointed him. He found that this department was larger than his own. He knew that his was one of the largest, since they were working the known history, and of course attempting to learn about the unwritten history. With the discovery down south he knew that much of that unwritten history would soon be revealed. He just hoped it would be in his lifetime. Again, he knew they had just scratched the surface, and how deep it would go was anybody's guess. What had been discovered so far had truly wetted his appetite to find more. These few small things they had found gave him just a little more than what the myths had passed on. Eventually after going through many different spaces he caught up with Bihl who had his back to him, "Bihl you are a hard person to find," Jllon said.

"What?" Bihl asked, as he turned around. "Oh, it's you Jllon . . ." He turned back to the members working there and addressed them, "People this is Jllon Jafrey, the Head Keeper of the Past."

"Thank you for introducing me, and let me not interrupt too much here. I know the work you do is of great importance. I only want to take a brief time of your boss here, and then I'll be gone."

"In the meantime . . ." Bihl discussed what he wanted them to accomplish while he was talking with Jllon, once finished, he turned and asked, "What is it I can help you with today?"

"Do you have a place we can go and talk in private? What I have to tell you must be considered confidential and cannot go any farther than the two of us. At least until it is official."

"Yeah, hold on a moment here." He headed around the work area confirming that the crew would be completing his request. Then turning around he signaled Jllon to follow him. They headed back outside and over to a small grove of trees. When they arrived Jllon saw that there were some wood tables and benches here.

"I didn't even know that this existed? Looks like a nice place to be on a hot day."

"Yes it is. Normally many eat their zenith meal here, but that is still a ways away from now. I am pretty sure that no one will bother us, and you can hear the flyers so if someone were to approach then the flyers would be quiet or leave. So I think we are pretty secure here. Now what was it you wanted to discuss?"

Sitting down on one of the benches Jllon said, "I, as you know still need to talk with Fauul. I take it he is not back as of yet."

"That is correct, but that was something that didn't require privacy."

"True, you know I ran into Joellie after entering your shelter. He's really into himself isn't he? I guess that team was lucky to have Fauul as a second."

"That I have to agree. But there isn't much that can be done. He's from an influential family and as such got himself assigned here. He believes he's better at all of this than the rest here. And, as you discovered, is not afraid to let anyone know who's willing to listen, or not, as in your case. Still this doesn't require this type of privacy? So again what's going on?"

"I really do need, now more than ever, to talk with Fauul, so do you first know where he is, and secondly when he is due back here. I am only here for a short time before I must return south and it would be of great benefit if I could talk with him."

"Not really sure where he is, but I do know it is that last village the team spent time in before returning, and that's well south of here also. As far as returning, recently I received correspondence from him that was delivered by runner, saying he would be returning in the near future – sometime after the next minor gather."

"Darn, that's too late. By then I will be back. I have to present something to the council and whatever the outcome, once completed, I have to head back to my field project. If I remember right, you saw that object that he had, and encouraged him to bring it over to our department to look at it."

"Yes, that's true. Once I really looked it over, handled it, and felt the weight I knew it was beyond anything we could do today. So I felt really strongly that it had to be an artifact from the distant past. I knew that by going over to your department that it would either be confirmed as such, or identified as a fake. It was soon after that meeting with you that he asked for an indefinite leave of absence and headed south."

"It was real as far as we can determine. I myself never saw the object, and one of the reasons I needed to see Fauul is to see the real thing. That object and the personal notes from the team is what prompted me in seeing a relationship, and a strong chance of either proving, or disproving, the existence of the *ones before*."

"Ah yes, the infamous *ones before* . . . the same myths that were used by our sires to keep us in line as whelps. So is this why we are here right now? Did you prove that they were really only myths, or did you prove they were real?"

"Oh they are real alright, and not only that but I can now prove that we are their descendants. It was a combination of that object and notes allowed me to put a team in the field and to make the discoveries that we have. But the location must be kept a secret, let alone the proof of their existence." Leaning closer to Bihl he continued. "You see if word got out of our find, then the site we are working would be looted, and any useful information would be lost forever. Then there would be fakes everywhere claiming that what they had was from the *ones before*. It, most likely, will cause a frenzy anyway when it is finally announced. But where we are working is only one of the two major sites we want to dig. The second is only known to Fauul, and yes while Doube was with him, and knows where the property is, I believe that Fauul has a better idea. And yes I do have Doube working with me right now. What a great individual he is. How'd he ever end up on one of those last groups going out anyway? With his skill he should have been on one of the first."

"You are so right about that, and he was to go out with the first group. But he had some issues to deal with at home and was delayed. So as you say in your business, the rest is history."

"Yeah, and that's a great statement. I'll have to remember it. Anyway Doube has been a great help to me, and I know sometime in the near future we will lose him back to the property, and what a great loss that will be."

"I do have to agree. So if I understand what you have told me . . . you have positive proof of the *ones before*? Wow, it was something that had always been the back of my mind, but nothing has ever been found . . . anything. How'd you get so lucky?"

"Well, I'd like to say luck had nothing to do with it. It was hard work, research, and much thinking. I needed to find something in common, and I knew that just the object would not be enough to be able to get approval for a field dig. It was within that combination that I found that there was enough circumstantial proof to get the project approved. I knew it would be difficult with the outlay that had just been made because of your work. So I had to work on compromises and show the council where I could save them marks over the normal operating expenses. It was difficult, but in the end very successful. I also knew that this was the only chance our department and I would have. Permission is rarely granted."

"I will definitely inform Fauul when he returns that you want to see him. I still have no idea what his plans are. I really could use him here, but I suspect he has found someone down there with whom he will mate with. Still that is only rumor. He has not really said, but it is a very strong supposition on my part. He had definite plans before the fieldwork, and all of a sudden afterwards, everything changed. I really suspect that some female has won his heart, and that is something that would not be easy. I know you have never met him, but nature granted him many good things, and he has always been attractive to the females. Yet, even so, none had ever seriously interested him here. He knew that many pursued him simply because of his position and a promise of a greater rise in the future. Don't get me wrong, he went out with many but absolutely none of it was serious."

"I wonder how close he is to where we are, down there. It would be funny if the two of us were within a day or two of each other, and like me chasing you down today just continued to miss each other."

"Okay then, until I hear otherwise, this conversation never took place, other than the discussion about Fauul. I do have to get back to work, and I am sure you still have much to do before you return. By the way, it has been a pleasure, and to be a part of the generation who now knows that some of our myths are in truth fact just adds to our meeting."

"You are so right, and while I know history will mark this time and I and my team will be listed as the discoverers, it is not totally accurate. If the work done by your cartographers had not happened then our discovery would never have happened. So overall it's that 'cause and effect' that has brought about the success."

The two got up Jllon preparing to head back to his department, turning he saw that Bihl was doing the same. Overall, he was disappointed that Fauul once again was unavailable, but felt confident that Bihl would keep the information given him confidential. He would have to remember this spot. It was quiet, peaceful, and in the summer heat, shaded with a breeze. Overall a nice place to spend time during breaks in the work.

Now he had only to meet with the council and then with either an approval or without, head back to the primary dig site. He knew if approval was not given that somehow he would have to split up his small team further, making the other site a little more difficult to work. When he got back to his work space his assistant informed him that on the morrow, first thing in the morn, he was on the schedule to see Alvina Scorcher, the assistant to council, which presently consisted of Jerry Karten, Kris Foruner, Floh Fisk, and Rowbard Garseya. Jerry and Rowbard were the two males on the council and Kris and Floh were females. Here it was felt that a balance of both sexes was important. So it was always filled this way. While this was not the complete council it was the one who ruled over the day to day generalities. Only at the two major gathers was the full council in session to handle all of the major requests and requirements.

Again, as in the townships and villages, the positions were filled and held for up to two years, one year as a minor only attending during the major gathers, and one year on the major council. No position was elected, but a requirement of service. He himself had served as the one in charge of the township he presently resided, but as of yet to have served on the council. With the research he was presently involved in, it was unlikely he would serve on the major council, which, in truth, was fine with him.

The next morn he reported promptly at the opening of the council. The discussion with Alvina was just a formality. Since he was known to the council and had, in the recent past, been before them, they were eager, in their anticipation, to see him.

Probably more for updates, as to the investments made, than the request he had come to present. Sitting on a bench he waited while the assistant went in to see if they were ready to see him. She came back and stated, "Jllon, they are ready to see you, so please go right in."

"Thank you." Picking up his many items and drawings he headed down the hallway and into the council area. From past experience he knew that when this shelter had been built that the chamber where the council met had been designed with the idea of showing the power of the council. The area where the council sat was semi-circular in design and was set above the area where one presented information to them. When you entered you were required to walk down a short series of steps which put one more in the position of a whelp to his or her sires than being on equal footing.

"It is wonderful to see you again, 'Keeper of the Past'. What is it that brings you back so soon?" Jerry asked, "And I mean that in the spirit of what you had relayed to us before you left on this present project."

"First let me state that what I reveal here today is something of great importance, but at the same time cannot leave this chamber. As I reveal what I have, and explain its significance it is important to understand that an early release of this would compromise all that has been accomplished so far. Do I have the promise that this will not leave this chamber after I leave?" He knew that the assistant would be recording what was said, and if the council accepted the silence requested, the record would be unavailable to the public.

The council put their heads together and talked softly among themselves, and then Jerry asked, "Is it that important? Part of why we are who we are is the availability of most, from this or any council. If we start creating secrets where would it stop, and would we, in the end, really put ourselves above all other citizens?"

"That in itself is a good question. I am not asking for a permanent ban on public revelation, but until more is found and understood, revealing what has been found would destroy much."

"I assume that the materials you have brought with you will shed some light on the importance of this ban."

"Yes, but I must ask your indulgence. I cannot display or explain what I have here unless I have your cooperation on the matter of revelation."

Again the council members talked among themselves, with Jerry asking, "Is what you have that important, *so important* that we must consider a change?"

"Again let me say that I am not asking for a change really. I am only asking for a delay in the dissemination of this information until we have protected what has been discovered. If it was released prematurely then all that we have found and learned will be compromised and destroyed. This loss would be too great a burden for us and our society as it is now."

Taking in the words that Jllon had just spoken, Jerry appeared to be thoughtful, and the rest appeared to be just as deep in thought. "Okay, before we have a decision on this we will need to discuss it among ourselves. You cannot give us a hint at all at this point to help make a decision?"

"No, unfortunately I cannot. Anything I say will immediately reveal all."

"Okay, come back after the zenith meal, and we will have an answer for you. Is this all you have for us now?"

"Yes and no. But the rest cannot be asked until the first is accepted. I thank you for your time and I will return at the requested time. Until then I take my leave."

"And thank you for being so forthright. This you ask is quite serious, so we really have to discuss it. We do not want to set a bad precedent that will be looked back upon as a way to make this council become a force for controlling the people to our will."

Jllon bowed to the council and took his leave. Once out of the shelter he breathed a sigh. He really never liked these encounters but this time there was little choice. What they had found was just too important. He headed back to his workspace and placed the objects and drawings in a safe place and headed out. He had much time to kill before he returned to the council chambers.

Jerry looking over to the assistant Alvina asked, "Do we have any more people this morn that has an appointment to see us?"

"Yes, but only one other, and it appears to be a minor matter. I, because of who it was, had scheduled much time. At the present all after zenith is open."

"Is this one available now? We would like to discuss what has been requested by the "Keeper of the Past", as this is a very serious matter."

"I will go and check and then report back", Alvina replied. She got up and headed back to the area where citizens could come in and set up appointments to see the council.

While she was checking Floh said, "This thing he asks really bothers me. Can we begin to hold secrets from everyone, and if we do where does it stop?"

"I don't know," Rowbard responded, "and with no information as to why, it's hard to agree."

"Okay, he seemed very serious and very worried about whatever it is. Is he the type who just wants to keep things secret or is he one who makes information available? What is Jllon's character really like? This will help to know." Kris paused before continuing, "I think you could see he was torn between wanting to reveal what was important, but at the same time seemed to know that even one word or hint would give it all away."

About this time the assistant re-entered the space and announced that the other appointment would be with them shortly.

Jllon was at a loss. He knew the importance of the find, and yet understood the questions that were thrown his way. It would be so easy for a ruling council to begin to hide things from the ruled. So far as he knew it had been avoided. And here he was requesting just that. Still it was a legitimate request. The complete and successful outcome of the endeavor could change all their futures. The discovery had already done that. But to what level would be determined by how much undisturbed work and research they'd complete. He did not envy the council in their decision. Plus if they refused, then his trip back here was wasted.

So, would this discovery end up affecting them in a minor way, or would it be major? He really had no answer, but he knew that the council's decision could determine it. If the information he had was released too early then all would be lost, and to him, it would be a major tragedy. Shaking his head, he thought. *They have to go along with what I am proposing. It's just too important . . . just too important.* By seeing where they had once been and where they were presently, he knew that there was much to be learned from these ancients.

Sitting in his workspace he racked his brain for some solution. What could he tell them to make them understand the importance of this find without giving away what had been discovered? Was there a way to talk about the find in such a way that nothing of importance would be revealed? There had to be a way. Everything he had brought to show the council would reveal the truth about the dig and if he couldn't get their cooperation, he would not be able to present any of it. Plus he knew that to continue to have the council on his side was of great importance. Without their support the funds necessary to continue the work would be lost leading to the closing down of the project.

He knew that in the past some had faked their results so that they could continue their work, and had, in the end, tainted everything they touched. Even, if after it was all finished, and the final results were accurate, it left disbelief because of those falsehoods. And because of what they had done earlier they ended up compromising their careers and their work. He wouldn't, and couldn't. It went completely against who he was as a person.

While he was involved with these thoughts his assistant entered and said that Doube had returned, and did you need him? At first he thought no, shortly, one way or the other, they would have to return to the dig site, and then he realized that Doube might be able to provide a partial solution to his dilemma. "Is Doube close by?"

"Not at the moment, he said that he would be heading over to that eating area that you both liked, and if you wanted to talk with him he would be there."

Thanking her, he got up and said he would be going over to see Doube, and would return later. Quickly, heading out the door, he made his way to the eatery where they both had last met before Doube had returned home. It had been brief, and neither had entered to eat. But when they had gone their separate ways, they had agreed that this would be a good meeting place. Both had enjoyed the food that was served here. He now was thankful that they had made these arrangements beforehand. This made locating each other much easier, and while he had not expected Doube back yet, he thought how fortuitous this early return was.

Entering the eatery, he had to stop a moment to let his eyes adjust to the gloom that permeated the room. He had always thought, not seriously of course, that the reason such places were always so dark was to prevent the patrons from knowing what they were really eating. Finally his eyes adjusted and he noticed off in one corner someone signaling him. Looking closer he recognized Doube. Then waving at the staff he pointed in Doube's direction and headed over to join him. He said, "I really didn't expect you for a while yet, but I'm glad you are here."

"Things wrapped up pretty quickly on the property and I enjoyed the visit very much. But something kept nagging me that it was time to leave and that I was needed somewhere else. Eventually it almost became overwhelming so I gave in to it and here I am. So was I right?"

"I believe so. I have to go back before the council after the zenith meal. I was there this morn and had asked for their silence with what I want to reveal to them. They then posed some interesting questions, and said they needed to discuss my proposal before giving me an answer, thusly the delay."

"So what's the problem the council has?"

He quickly filled him in on what had transpired earlier in the day and brought Doube up to speed as far as to why nothing could be revealed unless he received their guarantee of silence. Of course being in a public place as they were, he did not say why. Doube agreed, after the meal, to come with him back to Jllon's workspace and they would discuss strategy if the council had decided to balk at his request.

Back in the workspace Jllon said, "Now what I thought may be a good approach is for you to present your theory of a worldwide disaster and the reasons that you have come to that conclusion. I will support you with what we have found on the dig so far, but come far short of actually mentioning what we have discovered. Of course none of this will be necessary if they agree to remain silent."

They continued right up to the time of the meeting to plan their strategy, and hoped that it would not be needed. Still, with the importance of the find, it was better to have a backup plan. They headed over to the meeting and again met with the assistant. She told them that the council was not quite ready to see them yet, and please be seated. Once again, like earlier in the day, he sat on the wood benches and waited for his opportunity before the council.

It seemed like forever, making him nervous as the two of them waited. They continued to pass small talk back and forth just to pass the time, nothing of consequence being spoken, and probably nothing of the conversation being remembered. Finally Alvina said that the council was ready for them and led the way to the meeting space.

Once again, as in the morn, Jerry commented first. "You have left us in a difficult situation here. You ask for our silence, which we do try to avoid. In an open society like this almost all is public knowledge. I am sure, as is always the case; there are small secrets that are kept. Things like what makes one product better than another and such secrets as those are understandable. Yet, when the council starts to do the same, holding themselves above the common people, then that council, at that point, has failed in its duty to the people. Then too much becomes secret and this is followed by the lies to cover those secrets, and eventually that government becomes the enemy of the people, since it now feels that it is above them and will rule as a sire over a whelp – feeling that they, the council, the government, know better than the common person."

"I do understand your, and I am sure, the council's point of view. I do have to agree completely with your statement. Still sometimes there has to be a delay in information, both for the protection of the information, and to prevent deceit to enter."

"So you want us to use deceit to prevent deceit?" Kris asked.

"Shaking his head in the negative, "No, not at all. All I am asking for is a delay in what I want to pass on to you until we have gained all we can from what we are presently doing. Once this is complete then it can be shouted from the rooftops by all of you. In fact I would join you."

"I see you have brought another with you to this meeting. Can you introduce him to us?" Rowbard asked.

"I am sorry; this is Doube Mickles, the scout of both our project, and one of the scouts on the mapping projects that preceded ours."

"Ah, the Doube Mickles. Your name is not unknown to us," Jerry said. "Word has it that you are one of the best if not the best of your profession."

Bowing to the council, Doube replied, "Thank you, but I only do what I can, and I feel there are others who are just as good as I."

"Yes, that would be your response. It seems to be the nature of ones that are good in what they do. They normally do not brag and usually downplay their abilities and skills. It is usually the incompetent that must continually brag. You and your type let your actions speak for you."

"Thank you for the compliment. I will accept it in the manner given."

"So Doube why are you here with Jllon?"

"I am here because, while I know that what he asks is against our ways, and once such a thing starts the question arises as to when will it end, still I find what he has to present is unique, and must be provided all the protection one can give."

"So you agree with his request," Jerry stated.

"Yes, and I understand his reluctance on revealing anything until he has the requested promise. What he has is that important."

"If I may interject something here," Floh said. "From what has been said so far I can assume that something has been found. We have checked the archives before your return and have found that claims have been made in the past about such finds that you are not willing to discuss, only later to have been proven as fraud. Is there any guarantee that what you are presenting or should I say want to present is not the same?"

"First let me say I can neither confirm, nor deny the team has found anything, until once again, I have the requested guarantee. Second, I am quite aware of the fraud that has been perpetuated in the past. Many times by a respected member who then lost everything once the fraud was discovered. I have no desire or plan to repeat such a thing. I also want the council to hear from Doube on a theory he has developed. You may be unaware that Doube is a trained geologist as well as a first class scout. His knowledge in both areas has given him insights into things others probably would have overlooked."

The council then looked expectantly at Doube and Jerry asked, "First what is this theory and how does it apply here?"

Doube, looking over the council said, "First let me say that I am still waiting answers from the other continents of this world to confirm what I have found here, and once confirmed what I have found will then be proven as fact. So until I have those answers it is only a theory.

"That said, being a scout has allowed me to see much of this continent. At first I didn't think much about it. On one of my early scouting I found this dark soil line. I put it away in the back of my mind and generally forgot about it. Yet as time went by and I worked more and more of this continent I found that the dark line existed everywhere, although some places it was much wider than others. I found the evidence mostly in the riverbanks and ravines, and then along earth shake lines. It was everywhere. That got me to thinking as to what may have caused it. In many ways it reminded me of volcanic soils. Then it hit me that this was proof of a worldwide disaster sometime in the past. In geologic time it wasn't that long ago that it happened, and I was guessing somewhere around ten to hundred thousand turns ago.

This, as it turns out, puts it in the time frame of the myths of the *ones before*. Since the past, as the Keeper of the Past keeps it, is different from what I look at, I did not see the correlation until both myself and Jllon here started discussing it. All of a sudden, for both of us, it made sense . . ."

Interrupting Jerry asked, "What makes sense?"

Jllon then replied, "What we came to realize is that if indeed, the *ones before* were real that they would have been affected by this worldwide disaster. In fact it might have been a large enough event that it could have brought that civilization to the edge of extinction. Anything they would have had that we could find to confirm their existence would probably have either been destroyed, used up, or buried deep. By bringing these two disciplines together we were more able to understand what may have happened and why there had been nothing to either confirm them as real or to completely dismiss them as fiction."

"This indeed is new knowledge. Is this why you need our silence? Theories alone do not require protection and from what you have told us others are searching in other places to confirm this."

"True", Jllon responded, "but you need to see that with this new knowledge it gives us a better understanding of where and what to look for. It provides a way to confirm whether what we find actually belongs to the proper time period. In the few digs I have been involved with, we were always guessing if what we found belonged to us, or maybe those elusive myths of the *ones before*. Now, with something that exists everywhere in a known geologic time, it gives us something to make an educated judgement. That in itself has never existed before."

Jllon found himself once again becoming excited and he saw that it was flowing into the council as they began to see the implications that this new knowledge presented. He saw that the council was beginning to see what this might actually mean. Jerry asked, "This isn't something that could be faked is it? We really do not want to deal with any falsities here."

Shaking his head, Jllon continued, "No it is very easy to confirm. So with the use of this new knowledge we have been working a very promising site. Here again I must stop until I have your promise of secrecy. One of the reasons I have come before you is I need an additional small team to come down where we are. Only you the council can approve such a thing. Right now that is as far as I can go until I have your word. If I neither have your word nor get the additional team then my trip back here has been a waste of time. So again I ask, do I have your promise?"

Again the council put their heads together and for a short period of time a heated but quiet discussion ran between the members. Finally one of the members turned to the two of them and said, "We need a little more time to discuss this and the new information that was just presented. Please go back out to the waiting area so we can discuss this. Once we have decided we will call you back. I promise you will not be out there a long time."

Bowing both of them left the area back to the waiting space, with Jllon hoping that what was just presented was enough to get the council's approval. He knew he was asking much, but it was so critical. Either they as a whole won, or if revealed to all without that guarantee, lost.

"Well, how do you think it went?" Doube asked.

"I'm hoping that what you presented is enough. I know that overall we are asking for something that is rarely if ever granted. But, this just happens to be one of those very rare times where it just has to be. I could see the excitement in the council members so maybe it's enough . . . I just don't know really."

They sat out in the waiting area for much longer than they thought they would. As time continued to pass Jllon was becoming nervous. He did not know what to think, and it would have been easy to assume that it was going badly. Both sat in silence more interested in seeing Alvina come back in and let them back into the council area, than talking. Still she continued not to show. Jllon was just about ready to get up and head outside for some fresh air when Alvina approached them and said the council was ready to see them again.

With the amount of time that they had been waiting, he really had no idea which way the council had decided. So with some trepidation he re-entered the council space. Jerry, who appeared to be the speaker for the council on this day said, "We have come to a decision of your request. First let me say before I give you an answer that even with the new information that was given to us the decision was a tough one. As said earlier, this can lead us into a dangerous direction. The final vote taken was three to one. We have agreed to keep silent on what you will present. I hope that we the council have not erred on this decision."

With relief Jllon said, "I thank you for your honesty, and I myself would not have normally requested such a thing. With that said I now can tell you that we have found proof of the *ones before*, that they do exist, and we are their descendants. What I will present to the council today will be that proof, and the reason silence is requested is that we have barely begun our discoveries. It is important that we learn all we can before any official announcement is made. If this information were released early then the area where we are presently working would be compromised – looted and then many fakes would be presented, all claiming to be from the *ones before*. Once that happened then all knowledge that may have been gained would be lost forever."

"You mean that you truly have found proof of the *ones before*?" Jerry asked incredulously.

Jllon started passing around the drawings and artifacts he had brought with him. While the council was initially studying the items Jllon turned to Doube and said, "I thank you for your assistance here. I think without it I would not have gained this promise for the council. If you would prefer to leave now, I have no problem with it. I can explain everything here, and had more or less planned it that way anyway."

"No, no this is fine. I want to see the reaction of these council members to what you present. It will give me a pretty good idea of what to expect from the rest out there if word did leak out."

Turning back around and watching the council members they saw the excitement building as they examined the items that Jllon had presented them. Kris asked, "Are you really sure about this? I mean it has always been something we have all wondered about. Were they real or were they just fiction?"

"Oh they are real, and if they were not we ourselves would not be here to ask," Jllon replied. He continued. "If you look at the drawings of the family you will notice, other than the strange clothes they are wearing, that they could be any one of us. These ancients had a way of catching an image of anything that gives the appearance of being real. While some of our artists can paint close to realism, these, from the ancients, are as close to an exact copy as one can make. We cannot come close to even explaining how it was accomplished."

As the after zenith continued to pass with it heading into early evening and the council with their excitement, continued to ask questions, with the two of them attempting to answer to the best of their ability. Finally, it appeared that most of the questions they could answer was answered, Jerry asked, "If I remember correctly the main reason for you to come before us was for an additional team, can I ask why it is required?"

"I do know that with all that has transpired in the last turn that it is a difficult request. But, this is only one of two promising sites, and I need to take the team I left with over to the second site. This new team, which does not need to be large, will protect this first site. Since it lies in the desert and soon it will be too warm to work, it will be a good time to move to the other site. Still, we cannot afford to abandon this first site without protection."

"So, as I understand it, you want guards, is this correct?"

"Yes and no. Part of the new team must be someone who can protect, but I also need part of the team to be learned. I want no time wasted in what we have uncovered. It needs to be studied and cataloged. After all, with something of this importance, and even with the promise of silence, I cannot guarantee how long it will remain unknown. I will leave it up to the council to make the choices as far as the protection goes. I have a list of prospective learned whom would be good choices for the rest of the team. I do not expect this team to be larger than ten members, and less is fine. Because of the remoteness of the site there will be a good chance that it will remain hidden from the public.

"Once the team is formed then you can send a runner to a remote merchant whose location I will give you. With the letter you can include the details and when we can expect arrival into the port that is closest. Doube, at that point, will meet them and bring them to the site. Once they arrive, we will move on to the second promising site. Now, of course, before I leave the council I will need all the items back that I have shown you. We have barely learned anything about our ancestors, and have very little overall. So, even these few objects are important to our research."

He went up to the members and collected and accounted for all that he had passed out to them. Once he had everything he said, "I know what I have asked without revealing much to you made you decisions difficult. Still, I had no choice and now you can understand why I could not say anything until I had your promises. I couldn't even hint, as it would have given it away. What little I have presented here gives us the proof but doesn't tell us much about them. I hope, before these digs are complete, that we know much more and we can start taking advantage of some of the technology they apparently had. Still the lesson in all of this is, simply stated, their advanced technology didn't save them from this world wide disaster, and if happened to them it could repeat itself, and this time wipe out all of us forever."

Thanking the council for their time, both Jllon and Doube bowed and left the area. In the background they heard the council talking excitedly about what they had just been revealed and explained. Once outside they saw that it was dark, and both found they were hungry and a bit exhausted. The session with the council had been nerve racking and actually had left them drained, as if they had been digging all day. "I don't know about you, but I'm ready for that eatery and then off to bed. I am finding myself tired. Doube if you will join me for a meal, then on the morrow we will collect any correspondence followed by booking a return voyage so that we can return. I truthfully cannot wait to return. Does this work for you?"

"You know me; I am not a township type of individual – too many people around, so yes that works find."

"I'm sure the details will work themselves out. But I suspect, in the near future you will be heading back to the coast to get that new team. I really do not know how long it will take for the council to put it together. I left a correspondence with the assistant as to our needs. We will just have to wait until a runner informs us."

"Well, I am glad that this part is over. I did enjoy returning home. All of my family is in great shape, and my sister has all the males who might be interested running scared." With that statement Doube laughed, "She has no patience for stupidity or ignorance, takes after our father on that one."

Once they had arrived back at Jllon's apartment they spent a quiet evening discussing many different things, and Doube finally said that he really had just arrived in the township, and was tired. He headed off to the guest space in Jllon's apartment. Jllon wanted to remain up a bit longer, as he still had much to think about. One of the most important remaining, in his mind, was still contacting Fauul, and he hoped that somehow that could be arranged. He suddenly realized that he was starting to drift off, got up, stretched and yawned, smiling as a stray thought of his mate crossed his mind, he headed off to sleep. The morrow would be very busy as everything would be wrapped up here, and the two of them would head back to the dig site in the desert.

A half of a cycle later, they left the water-craft at the northern township, picked up the supplies they would require, and headed inland to the southeast. As before, when they came to this port, they kept a low profile, appearing to be any of the many who travel with nothing special about them. Unknown to them they could have found Fauul here while they were there also. He was in the process of taking the water-craft up north to talk with both his family and his friend and boss. He, of course, was hoping to find the Head Keeper of the Past to find out what he wanted with him. But as fate would have it, with the crowds and chaos, they never crossed paths.

Finally, the two of them were on the hills just outside of the main camp looking down. From the distance that they were observing it appeared that there had been some changes. Not knowing what might have caused them, they headed down towards the desert floor. It had appeared, as they went through the abandoned village, that winds or something had ended up doing some major damage. So, it could be that these same winds had made the changes they were observing at the site.

The two of them walked into the camp unnoticed, as the team was out working the sites. It was strangely quiet with the winds flapping the material that the portable shelters were constructed. A slight rattle as a bit of sand would be blown against something solid. It almost seemed like a ghost camp. Then one of the camp managers came around a corner and jumped. "Where'd you two come from?" He asked. "You scared the living daylights out of me. I mean I wasn't expecting anyone in for a little while, and the last thing I expected was the two of you."

Smiling, Jllon replied, "Sorry about that. It was just as much of a surprise to us that this camp appeared to be as empty as it is."

"Yeah, I can understand that. There's been much happening since you left."

"Really? How so?"

"I probably should let Celt tell you since he's in charge, but I'll quickly cover just a bit for you." He mentioned the return of the nomads, and the warning of the winds, and then the damage. "For a detailed report you can ask Celt. I think under the circumstances he ended being under, he handled it well. Of course that's just my opinion."

"I guess there was much that happened. Thanks for the update, and yes I will talk with Celt later, but right now can you direct me to where my mate is working, I would like to see her again before we get serious again."

"You and her? Or do you mean serious as far as the work here?"

Smiling he replied, "Now, I'll let you figure that one out . . . however you want to take it." Then listening to the answer from the camp manager Jllon replied, "So if I understand it, she is over at the other camp, working in the sorting shelter. Okay, see you both later, and until the morrow Celt is still in charge. Doube go relax for the rest of the day, and on the morrow we will get into the next portion. At this night's meal I will fill in the team on what transpired while we were gone, and they can bring us up to speed." He left and headed out towards the second camp eager to make contact with his mate. It had been a long time since he had seen her and he was really missing her right now.

"You know he probably won't mention it tonight, but we really nearly failed on getting that second team. I guess it really doesn't matter . . . I think I'll just go check out my shelter and put everything in order." With that Doube left and headed over to the temporary shelter he was staying in.

Jllon walked quietly deeply in thought, thinking about all that had transpired up to this point. It, truthfully, was incredible. He knew that it had been hard work that ended up producing these results. But, he knew that others had tried, and had come up empty, as he had in the past. Looking around he noticed that it was extremely clear and it seemed he could see forever. The breeze was soft enough that he heard his footsteps crunching in the sand. While the desert would eventually be too hot to work in, right now it was almost perfect. It would be easy to relax and then fall for one of the many snares this land would present if one wasn't diligent.

Finally, he saw the sorting shelter ahead of him, and he made sure that he approached it from the back side wanting to surprise his mate. No one knew exactly when they were to return so there would be no expectation. The first person he saw was Suzzane who looked up and was about to speak when he motioned her to silence. Nodding that she understood, she smiled seeing his intent. This she had to watch. So walking back a short distance she watched as Jllon approached from the blind side threw open the partially closed flap and entered the shelter.

She could see that Nouma was concentrating on something that had been dug up and wasn't watching the individual who had just entered, assuming that it was Suzzane being that she had just saw her coming her way.

Jllon standing there and smiling said, "Now is this any way to treat your mate."

"Catching her breath she yelled, "Jllon! You're back! You could have at least warned me. I mean I must look a mess, is this any way to greet me? Darn you!" She then got up and the came together and hugged tightly, she then saying, "Oh how I have missed you."

"Do I ever understand that statement! I too have missed you greatly. While Doube was okay, he is not you, and I couldn't discuss things with him to the level as I can with you, and of course he isn't you in so many other ways."

"Well, I'm glad to hear that!" she said rather severely. Then not being able to keep a straight face started laughing.

"I'm not taking back command of this team until the morrow, so why not take the rest of this day off, and we can go explore."

"How do you mean that sir?"

"Anyway you want to take it."

Now feeling like she was intruding Suzzane decided to withdraw tactfully, and leave the two of them alone for a short time. She knew they would be leaving shortly, and she'd take over what Nouma had been doing. It was great to have Jllon back. Probably later he would bring the team up to date, but right now the two needed time to themselves.

It didn't take long for the word to get around that Jllon was back. But at this moment no one could locate him. Doube has told them Jllon had gone over to see his mate and would probably be back later. After all, it had been a couple of cycles since they had seen each other. So the team continued through the after-zenith and headed in for the evening meal at which time they figured the two of them would show up. Sure enough one of the team caught sight of the two of them walking arm in arm coming into the camp. Jayson pointed and said, "Hey look, there they are!"

The rest turned around and tried to locate them in the dusk and finally saw two figures approaching out of the gloom. Eventually they reached the firelight and entered the camp. Jllon, once again, had found the quiet of the desert creeping back into his soul, and to be with his mate again he felt quite fulfilled and happy. Something about being in the outback did that to him every time. Looking at Nouma he saw the happiness in her face also. Turning towards the team he said, "It has been an interesting journey that Doube and I have taken, and from what Nouma tells me it has been no less for all of you. Anyway, after we have all eaten and had an opportunity to relax a bit, I will let you know what transpired while I was in the township and what the council finally decided. But . . . oh yes I almost forgot."

He left his mate's side and headed into the shelter where he rummaged through the stuff he had returned with and moments later came back. "It took a moment there to locate this." Holding it up for all to see, they understood that he had correspondence from home. This raised the excitement level up another notch. To get letters from home was always special, and it was something that did not happen often because of their remoteness from any other village or township. Jllon passed out what he had, and a silence grew over the team as they eagerly read the personal messages sent their way.

As they completed the reading they began excitedly to share and discuss what they had just received from home. While Jllon felt fortunate to have his loved one with him, he understood quite well what was going on with each one of his team as they related to each other what they had received from home. For the moment Jllon was forgotten, as he expected. Besides he really would not take over the leadership until the morrow anyway, and this was so much more important.

The two of them grabbed some of the food and sat down and began to eat, listening to the conversations and just enjoying the moment. Celt himself was glad that Jllon was back, and while he had not yet had a chance to talk with him, he knew that soon they would have a meeting in which both would exchange detailed information. So with the rest he read his letter and enjoyed the somewhat festive evening.

Fauul had prepared as well as he could and with the end of a minor gather had joined a group of traveling merchants that were heading up the coast. The trip would only take a few days, and then he'd book passage on one of the water-craft heading up the coast. From there it would take a bit of time to reach the township. Once back he'd first go see his family, something he hadn't done in a long, long time. Then he would set up a meeting with his boss and friend, and hopefully from there go see the Head Keeper of the Past – at least that was his plan. Still he knew from experience that what one planned wasn't necessarily how things worked out in the end.

The trip to the port had proceeded without incident and he thanked and said good bye to the traveling merchants, and went to book his passage. He was thankful that he still had much of his funds that he had earned from the mapping project available. While paying for the passage, he realized that he had been lucky once again, since it could take up to a cycle for passage to become available, yet today one would be leaving in his direction in the after-zenith. Unknown to him while he was finalizing his place, outside and heading south, Jllon and Doube passed his location. Both, at that moment were deep in thought, and didn't even glance in his direction. Had they, Doube would have recognized him immediately. But as life and the fates seem to play with ones' lives, this was not the time of meeting, and both being ignorant of each other, continued on their chosen paths and headed off in opposite directions.

He made a quick stop at one of the local merchants at the port to bring home some small gifts for his family and to have enough supplies to make the last part of the journey, which could take up to a cycle to complete. It, of course, had more to do with how the weather was than the actual distance. One in a hurry, or began each day before sunrise, and continued on well into darkness, could cover it in less than half a cycle. Again the trip aboard the water-craft was uneventful, but he couldn't help but reminisce about the last time he made the trip in the current direction.

Thinking back it was before he had decided to return and see if Lauma had felt as he did. He was on the final leg of the mapping project, and his future was heading in a different direction than what it was now. There was no prospect of a mate, and the idea of taking a little time off was something that sat in the back of his mind. Smiling he thought. *My how things do change . . . they really have changed!* Leaning on the rails and watching the craft cut through the waters his mind would just drift from subject to subject with nothing staying long enough to even remember. The waves were almost hypnotizing and the sounds of the flyers, which seemed to follow them, seemed to mesmerize him, making the passage of time seem to fly.

Before he knew it they were swinging into the port where he would disembark. Patiently he waited for much of the passengers to leave before he headed down to dry land. The trip had left him in an introspective mood and he had no desire, at the moment, to talk with anyone. He felt that doing so would break this mood and he was, in a way, enjoying this inner view. Still he knew that once on dry land and on the trail to the township he would have to leave the mood behind and become alert to the normal dangers of the trail.

Again, he hoped to tie in with a group heading in his direction. While bandits in this area were rare, it didn't mean that they were not around. So, the larger the group one could be a part of, the greater the chance of avoidance. The movement and energy of the port snapped him out of his reflective mood, and again he began to feel the energy that flowed around him. It had been one of the things he had always enjoyed about the township life. He began to smile thinking that now he would be comfortable in either environment, at least he thought so.

As it had been when he had left the village luck was with him and he found a large group that was also heading to the same township. He joined them, finding out that they would be moving out the next morn. They had said that one more or less was not a problem. And one who had trail experience such as he was always an asset. One of the first things he noticed was a number of young females that were staring at him. *Trouble*, he thought. He could tell that they would most likely be pestering him.

Maybe he could stop that if he casually informed them he would be mated at the next major gather. He hoped that would be enough to discourage them. He really didn't need that kind of trouble, since he was the newest member of this group. Such a thing might lead to dangerous misunderstandings. He almost thought of declining the invitation and finding another group heading in his direction, but realized that there really wasn't one that would be leaving for another quarter of a cycle. Time was something he didn't have much of. So he would have to survive this group in one piece and continue from there. He informed the leader of the group of his concerns, and what he suspected, leaving it in his hands to handle. At first the leader of the group denied that such was the case. Then he glanced around and looked at these young females and how they were staring at Fauul and realized that Fauul had not lied. Fauul would just attempt to help and hopefully stay out of those females' way.

"I suggest that you make it clear to them, as I will that I am to be mated when I return south, and I am no looking for any companionship. I will also state this to them, but sometimes as you well know, once a female gets an idea in their head it is difficult to make them change."

"Yeah, that's true. My mate decided that I was the one for her a long time ago, and I really wasn't so keen on the idea. No offense, I mean I did find her someone to be interested in. It's just, at the time; I wasn't interested in that way. Still we have had a wonderful relationship through these many turns. Okay, you have stated your intentions clear enough. So hopefully between the other males here, me, and you we can convince them to leave you alone."

While this group did move up the trail rapidly, and they covered the distance in the half cycle it had been an uncomfortable trip for Fauul. Even with the warnings from the sires to these young females, they still attempted to draw out Fauul's favors in their direction. It would have almost been comical, if there hadn't been such seriousness to their ploys. Still he thought that probably sometime in the future he would look back on this and laugh. But for now he was happy to leave in the good graces of the group and with his whole skin. While he was used to females being interested in him, he had not had that much attention from so many in . . . well, he really couldn't remember.

Looking around the township he knew he was back on familiar ground. It felt right and comfortable. No one here knew he was back, and even though his boss would be expecting him, no time had been set. He went back to his apartment that he had kept, because when he originally left he did not know if the journey would be a short one. Remembering back he knew that his decision to leave had been a quick one, and he had left quickly. Smiling at himself, he remembered what his state of mind was back then. He had become quite unsettled, and finally had realized that he had probably been captured by some female, but enough on that. He needed to get cleaned up, go get some food, followed by checking up on his accounts to see where he really stood. While it would be a busy after-zenith, at the same time, he'd work through it at a leisurely pace. On the morrow he'd go see his boss, and if what he proposed be accepted, from there he'd possibly move on and go see the Head Keeper of the Past.

Once all the business was taken care of he'd go visit his family. His father was a local merchant, and all the family participated in keeping it a going concern. Of course, once one became of age, one could choose his or her life direction. He had chosen to become a cartographer, and had found he was very good at it. Still much of what he was as a person could be seen as a result of the way he was raised and the responsibilities that were placed on him early in his life. While, at the time he hated them, he now saw how they had given him advantages over others that never were placed under similar responsibilities.

Thinking of his family, his mother first came to mind. She was a loving person, but one who pushed all who were around her to greater heights. While the family was not rich, they were well off. The many turns of hard work by the two sires, and as the whelps became old enough to help; they would join in the business, resulting in it being very successful. His father was a respected member of this large community, and had served his turn on the main council, as possibly he would one day. His other siblings, a younger brother and sister, who both were young adults now, were both in the secondary learning centers, as he had many turns ago. He knew from the time of the turn that they should be there or maybe they would be assisting their father. And if assisting back at home they shortly would be returning to the learning centers.

This was something his father had always pushed, "Ignorance is the fault of the individual", was always one of his favorite sayings. As a result, both of the sires always pushed learning. "If you don't know, then go find out", was something both would say, not that they didn't help. But their way was to assist and direct one in the proper direction, and make one find the answer to the asked question. At times it was frustrating, but now he saw the advantage to such an upbringing.

Smiling, again to himself, he could almost picture his mother's reaction when he announced that he would be mating soon. Knowing her, it would be a wonderful surprise, but at the same time she would think he was only joking with her. Since she was well aware of the females being attracted to him and the attention he always received from them. So her view was one of patience. After all, when one has his choice of so many, it is very easy to delay.

The rest of the day went rapidly, and he headed back to his apartment for the night, ready to face the morrow. Still, he had to admit that it was great to be back on familiar ground. After all he had spent most of his life here. Now his plans were such that when he finished here, he probably would only see this place very rarely. His new life direction was a long way to the south.

The next morn broke bright and clear, with a promise of mild weather. It appeared to be a great day to be out and about. Heading out to an eatery he had a hardy morn meal, and noticing he still had a brief time before his boss would arrive, headed over to the grove of trees outside of the working shelter. He had to admit, like so many others he worked with, he found this area to be peaceful and relaxing. Sitting on one of the many benches he let his mind drift a bit, and wondered how Lauma was faring without him there.

He could see when he had left that she did not want him to go. It was written in every part of her body. Still, she understood that there was nothing either of them could do about it. This was a trip that was necessary. Yet on the parting neither said much. They just hugged and kissed lightly, knowing that if either tried to talk that one or the other might break down. So with a wave he took his leave, joined the traveling merchants, turned around one last time seeing her there looking a bit forlorn, and then she was out of sight. It really had been hard to leave.

Suddenly he realized that he was hearing many voices and more time had passed because of his reminiscing, and people were already at the shelter beginning the day's work. He got up and headed into the shelter, a place where he had spent many a workday himself. While it was all familiar, at the same time it felt a little strange. He couldn't put his finger on it as to why. Looking around carefully he saw nothing had changed. Still something just didn't seem or feel right. Finally it dawned on him that it was he who had changed, and while this had been his workplace for many turns, it was now only a place to visit. He was a visitor – what a concept. Smiling at this thought, he headed on down to Bihl's workspace.

When he came to it he saw that Bihl and his assistant were deep in conversation. Not wanting to interrupt he waited quietly until they had finished their conversation. The assistant then turned around and exclaimed, "Fauul! What the blankly blank are you doing here?"

"About time," Bihl replied, "You know while you have been gone, you have become very popular around here. It seems this person or that person needs to see you about something . . . always coming in to bother me." Then Bihl smiled and continued, "Glad to see you back. So was that trip down south you took successful" You never did mention why, but I know you said it was personal, so it was not my place to pry."

"As to your question about success, yes the trip down south was quite successful, and later when you have time I have much to discuss with you. From the look of that conversation, when I came in, you have much going on right now. And, not that you don't know it, but I am still on that extended personal leave, so my time is much freer than yours. So please let me know when you can give me some major time. I have a few things to run by you, and some ideas that need to be addressed. I have also heard that the Head

Keeper of the Past wants to talk with me. So, maybe if you cannot talk with me until later today I can go there and find out what he wants."

You're right, but I think I can give you the time you need this after-zenith. In fact why not come by at the zenith meal, and we can start then. Unfortunately once again you both have missed each other. The Head Keeper of the Past was here looking for you, but has left, heading back down south on a field project they are working."

"South? Down where I just came from?"

"Not sure really, since you never really identified where you went . . . but maybe. Of course there is much that is south of here so it might be anywhere. Anyway back to the original subject, where do you want to meet? And since you're still on personal leave, I'm making you pay for the zenith meal – after all that's only fair."

Laughing a little Fauul said, "Well, you do know our favorite. I'll meet you there. Say, can I walk the work areas for a little while? I'd like to see some of the new maps that have come out of the projects."

"Don't know why not. After all, you do work here, don't you?"

Fauul laughed saying, "Not right now, I'm just visiting."

With that they both laughed, and Bihl said, "Go ahead I'm sure there are many who would enjoy seeing you again. But I must warn you Joellie is quite unhappy about the attention you have gotten. I would recommend avoiding him if at all possible. He seems to be bitter about it. He even jumped all over the Head Keeper of the Past when he came looking for you."

"Warning well taken – I will attempt to put a wide path around him if I see him." Fauul left the workspace to wander the areas and see what had transpired since he had been gone. He had had enough of Joellie when he worked with him on their section of the field-mapping project, and he really didn't need to run into him now.

As he walked the areas he did run into members of the past field team. Still he was lucky and was able to stay out of Joellie's way. He spent some time talking with the many people he knew and saw some of the maps as they were being completed. He was especially interested in some of the areas the other teams had worked. As the morn continued he came to the conclusion that this continent was huge. He saw that even though most of the major trails and much of the side trails were now represented, there were still blanks. These unknown areas would be filled in as time went, and wouldn't require the massive cost and workforce that this final push had cost.

As he had expected, where he was now living down south there was a large unknown area. This worked well into his plans. So now that he had confirmed his suspicions, and had reacquainted himself he bid his friends and team members a good bye. He related to them that he was still on personal leave, and would be in the area for a few days or so, and would be available if they were interested in making contact. As he left, he realized that there was still some time left before he met Bihl.

On a whim he decided to head up to his father's business shelter and see what may have changed there. He knew he had only a little time before the zenith meal, and the meeting with Bihl, so this would be a quick visit. Later after he was able to either get approval for his ideas, or not, he would come back to his sire's shelter and spend the evening with them. He knew that it would be an interesting evening, and probably the conversations would carry on late into the night. He found himself in front where he paused for a moment. He entered inside and immediately the memories began to flow. He heard his father talking with someone in the back and he thought he caught the voice of his sister Kayleh helping a customer, which was a surprise, as he had expected that she might be in the learning center. He heard a sound that sounded as if someone was chopping wood for the fireplace and cooking unit. He guessed that that would be his brother, concluding if his sister was not at the learning center most likely his brother would not be either. So he went back out of the front entrance and walked out behind, and yes he saw him there splitting the wood down to a manageable size. His back was to him and so he walked up quietly to his brother. But not too quietly as he did have a tool that would do much harm if one wasn't careful. "Hey Chaze, how's it going?"

"What . . . what . . .?" Turning around Chaze said with surprise in his voice, "Oh it's you Fauul. What the heck are you doing here? From the last word we had received you were down south on some personal business that you didn't even let the family know about."

Coming together and grasping each other's arms in a personal greeting Fauul smiling said, "Yeah, I know. But I wasn't sure myself if the trip was going to turn out the way I had hoped. So there was really nothing I could say. At least until I knew."

"Okay then, why are you back here now?"

"I'm not trying to be secretive here, but I will reveal that tonight when I'm finished with the meeting with my boss. What he tells me will have an influence on what happens with me."

"Missing mother's cooking is that it?"

"Now we both know that our sister is a better cook than she is. Truth be known, we both are probably better at it than she. But don't say that to her, and if you do I will deny it and say you're just trying to start a fight for old times' sake."

Marks realized that for some reason the sounds of work had ceased in the back and came out curiously to investigate. Seeing his oldest son he yelled, "Fauul! What are you doing here?"

Chaze turning toward their sire laughed and said, "I asked him the same question."

Looking at his sire Fauul replied, "And as I told my brother, I cannot say much at this time, but will reveal what I can tonight. I have a meeting with my boss in a short time, and what comes out of that meeting will let me know how I am to proceed."

A slight look of disappointment flashed across Marks, but he didn't say anything. He asked, "So you are coming over tonight, right? . . . And if so, at about what time? I'm sure your mother would like to know, and actually so would I, I guess."

"Questions, questions. Hey Chaze doesn't this sound like the grilling we used to get if they thought we had been up to no good."

"Yeah!" Chaze replied. Then they both laughed at the puzzled look on their sire's face.

"Actually I am planning to be here around the evening meal so I can share that time with the family. Then we can sit around and I will attempt to bring you all up to date as to where I have been and what is happening. After that all of you can do the same for me. After all you four are still here together, and I am the one who has been gone."

"Chaze, can you go over and inform your mother that we will have a guest tonight for the evening meal. And yes you can tell her who it is so she doesn't get too uptight."

"Will do," Chaze said, as he headed over to the living shelter that was close by the sutler's shelter.

A brief uneasy silence hung in the air as the two males – father and son faced each other. "I only wanted to come over for a brief period of time to inform you and the family that I would be over tonight. I really have much to discuss with all of you, but until I find out how this meeting is going to end with Bihl I just cannot say anymore. Anyway, I've got to go . . . this place does bring back many good memories I do have to say that."

"Probably true, but now you're looking at it from a different perspective than when you were a whelp trying to find ways to sneak out and not do your work assignments. Don't get me wrong. When I was a whelp I was the same way. It's just the way of things. When you are a whelp you cannot understand why you can't just be carefree and do what you want. Then you always want to be grown up, since you think you can do anything you want, and no one can tell you otherwise."

Smiling, Fauul replied, "So true. The view of being an adult from a whelp's point of view is romantic and so far from the truth. Once one truly becomes an adult then he or she is completely responsible for their actions. To me it's a sign of one who has left the whelp period behind. You find many that never seem to grow up. They are always blaming others or the circumstances for their problems instead of looking into the looking glass to see where the real cause is."

"You are so right. Working here in my own shop I see it all the time. So I guess I will see you tonight then. Fathe, your mother I know will be very happy to see you."

"I'm sure, but I do have to go for now." They grasped arms and Fauul departed heading for the eatery to meet Bihl. This brief meeting with his family flooded his mind with many good memories, which brought a smile to his face. Even though it had been a short meeting it had been wonderful to see his family again. Later there would be time to catch up on everything.

He arrived at the eatery only to find that Bihl had preceded him and was waiting for him. As he entered and his eyes adjusted to the dimness he saw someone waving at him and realized that it was his boss. He went over to join him and Bihl stated, "I've went ahead and at least ordered us something to drink. I have come with you often enough here to know what you like, the server said that once you showed up that she would be here immediately to get our food orders."

"As always Bihl, well prepared and well organized. Anyway thanks, I know that with your schedule that even, at times, getting this brief break can be difficult."

"True, but when one of my best takes off, and then comes back wanting to present something to me I'm willing to take the time to find out what it is and to be in a place where we will have time to discuss whatever it is uninterrupted. And speaking of interruptions . . ." Both of them saw the server approaching their table, with both ordering before continuing.

"I thank you for your confidence and praise."

"Your welcome, but I don't just give that type of compliment out unless it is deserved. Do you think that I am unaware of who actually kept the field team you were second on from becoming a disaster? If Joellie had had complete control, there is a great possibility that the team would have been lost, and none the wiser as to what happened to them."

"Joellie definitely wasn't easy to work for, and he did put us in a few dangerous situations, still I only did what I had to."

"You can be humble about it if you want, but the rest of the team vouched for you and your skills. There wasn't one of them who would have refused to go out on some other field project with you. It basically was unanimous. They would have wanted you as their leader. I say, when as a group, that is their feelings, it pretty high praise."

"Again what can I say? That Joellie was a bad leader? I really do not need to comment. He does enough for all the rest of us. I know that he does not like me, and less so now that the team considers me as the one who kept it going and safe. Still Joellie is my superior here, and I try to stay out of his way."

"True, and how he ever got where he is, is beyond me – probably something to do with his influential sires. Anyway we didn't come here to discuss Joellie."

"True. Look, I don't know quite how to say this, but the reason I went on that personal leave was in fact very personal. When I left I had no idea how it would come out and as such I could not say anything other than what I did."

"Okay, so if I'm understanding things now, you can now let me know quite a bit more than then, right?"

"Right. The reason I left had to do with a female . . ."

"A female? You? That's one area you never had a problem with. They always seemed to be attracted to you."

"Yeah, and that can be a problem . . ."

"A problem? Most of the rest of the males that I know would love to have that kind of problem."

"Ha ha, very funny. No, I can understand that, but it still can be a real problem. You begin to wonder if it is just you and the position you hold and that they may be looking for someone who holds a higher status than they do, or are they truly sincere? Its fun when you are not looking to get serious, and just to go out and enjoy a female's company. But when you finally want to get serious, how can you make an honest attempt when you don't know the real motives?"

"Okay, I can see how that could be a problem. I mean you are very attractive to the females physically. And it is known that you are on your way up within the area where you work, again being very attractive to the females. So how can you be sure that they are truly attracted to who you really are and not to what they perceive? Is that about right?"

"Close enough. I know that you are mated, and you and your mate seem perfect for each other. I've visited you and her a number of times and thought how wonderful to have such a relationship."

"Oh, it isn't perfect, I guarantee you that. Still, it works well for both of us, and truthfully I don't think I could find another that would work as well. I have learned that there are so many levels to make a relationship work. While we have been together for many turns I am still learning. I know you have heard that it involves is a lot of compromise. And I have to say that's true. Still there is much learning, and that learning continues as long as the two of you are together.

"One of the most important things is talking. Talking and listening . . . it's both. If this would ever stop I feel that it would be the beginning of the end. There are enough problems outside of your relationship to make life hard. If you quit communicating, then it begins to break down, and from there the problems within the relationship are far worse and destructive, than the ones outside. We both have seen those kinds, and have wondered why they were still together."

"Yes that is quite true. So when the two of you met, did you know that she was the one for you?"

"Funny you should ask, but yes. Still I had a harder time convincing her. Why all the questions on relationships anyway? Am I detecting a trend here? Have you found that someone special to you?"

Laughing Fauul said, "I thought you had figured that out by now. Yes, and in our view it is mutual. She was attracted to me, and I to her. No, not like the females here who appear to be status jumping, but a deep honest attraction."

"Well, are congratulations appropriate? So how did this happen, especially to you."

"As I have said, it was totally by accident. I wasn't looking and neither was she. In fact we had a major confrontation when she thought we might be part of a bandit gang that had been working the area. If it hadn't been a dangerous situation, it would have almost been funny. I mean here I am one of the taller and better built males, and with me was one of the best scouts we have, Doube. She, being a slight female, and her dog, standing off the two of us, having the upper hand and winning the situation. We were definitely on the defensive, and she had a strong control of the situation."

"Yeah, that would have something to see that's for sure."

The server, trying to get their attention said, "If you will allow me, I mean I don't want to interrupt this conversation but I have your food."

Apologizing, they let her place the food on the table, and thanked her.

"If I remember right Fauul, she was one of the ones who had an interest in you."

"Your memory hasn't failed. But she and I could never get along. Our personalities clashed, and had we pursued it would have been war. You know one fight after another, and that would be no fun at all." Fauul laughed at the thought of it. "So how long do you have before you have to return to the work shelter?"

"I have as much time today as I need. I told the staff that I would be with you working out whatever you wanted to present, and that was a priority right now."

"Well, thank you, and I still hold our friendship in high regard . . . although I would never use that to force anything. You know this food is really excellent!"

"That's why it has been a favorite. Now let's get back to what we were discussing."

"Anyway, Doube and I found out later that one of the reasons for the strong front she had put on was due to the fact that the property was operated by her and her brother. At the time we had arrived he was out working the beasts and she was alone there at the main shelter. Not knowing if we were honest or part of that group of bandits, she took the offensive.

"You must understand that it is rare in these small villages to conduct a major business transaction away from the gathers. I mean contact can be made, but usually the actual business is conducted there. So when we showed up presenting a possible business transaction, immediately she was suspicious. I probably would have been myself. Anyway to make a long story short . . ."

"Ahhh, I think you're a little late on that on Fauul," Bihl said while smiling.

"Sorry, but I felt you needed to know the circumstances. Anyway, when all the misunderstandings were brought to light, everything went well from then on. The only problem was she. She is a rare beauty. In that I mean that normally you wouldn't look twice at her, at least until she smiles. Once that happens it completely transforms her. Anyway we, Lauma and I could not keep the strong attraction we had for each other from showing. Both of us tried to just ignore it but it just kept getting stronger."

"Yeah, I can understand that. I had a very strong attraction for my mate also. So continue if you would."

"Anyway we finally had to admit that we were interested in each other and spent much of the last day together. When I left I thought that that would be the end of it and I would move on. But as you know it wasn't happening, and that's when I requested the personal leave to return there. Still, even at that point there was no way to be sure that she hadn't forgotten about me and moved on. So I planned on going back, contacting her brother and see what was going on. After all, she could have been mated by then and been with whelp, if you know what I mean.

"So in the end after all that, it turned out she was just as serious about me as I as her. So we spent much time together to find out if it was what we wanted. Along the way I declared to pursue, and then asked her to be my mate. And that's part of what I want to discuss with you."

"So you want my advice, is that it?"

"No, but it is important to know this before I continue."

"So, there is much more. I have a feeling that once the word gets out that you are to be mated, that there is a whole lot of females that are going to be unhappy."

"Probably, but knowing them, they'll just move on to the next interest."

"So, I guess congratulations needs to be offered here."

Smiling and thinking about her, Fauul said, "Thank you and I know that the romantic view of this says all will be well, but life and reality says different."

"At least it sounds like you're going into this with an open mind. So different than some I have seen."

"Yes, I am, and I had better as this female is strong willed and strong minded. One you walk beside, knowing she is your equal. Yes, I do think I know what I am getting myself into. Still, what can one really know when you enter into such a thing?"

"That's a very true statement, so anyway, continue."

"Here's the problem that I face. I mean I could force her to live here in the township with me – this allowing me to be close to where I work. But it would leave her terribly unhappy, and would most likely cause her brother to lose the family property. A property their family has had for many generations. Plus she has been raised as an outback type of person, and the township style of life would drive her crazy. It's something that I am now just beginning to understand. So I will not do that to her."

"I am beginning to see the dilemma you have put yourself in. Do you bring your new mate to live here, and chance losing her, and alienating her only family, or do you come up with some alternative? Does that cover it?"

"Not bad, and you're right about him being her only family. They lost their sires in a freak accident when they were still whelps. The four of them were the last of their heritage. Anyway, as I learned their business, which is beasts by the way – they work both field and pack beasts – I grew to appreciate the outback. I began to understand why these outback people seem to be so confident and strong. The world they live changes all the time and most of the time without warning. You either learn to deal with it or you leave. Thusly the ones who remain become strong and confident in their abilities."

"So what has that led you to, and what do you want to propose?"

"I know it has taken me a little time and much explaining to get here, but I felt you needed to know why I came to this decision, and with the background now known it allows you to understand."

"Makes sense. I guess it always better to explain one's self then just to throw out something."

"I guess it helps the other to better understand why. So, and I confirmed this at the work shelter, I began to realize that where I'm located, there down south, is largely unknown and completely unmapped, other than the trails that we, as a team, mapped. So what I am offering is one of two things here. First, if you approve, I can open up another mapping shelter there in the area so that I can map the areas down there. It would be a place some of the new workers could be sent for experience, and this would allow me to continue what I love to do. Plus it would provide additional mapping into these unknown areas at no additional cost since I would work out of the property where I presently live. But if this is unworkable I will have to quit and change my path and become a beast-master with them. I would prefer to stay with mapping, but if that turns out not be workable then so be it."

"Hmmm, let me think about this for a little while. It is a great proposal overall, but I think to get approval I am going to have to go higher up. The idea of no increased cost to the division, and to have one as you in charge will be pluses. I do like the idea. I mean, while yes we were able to get much of the areas generally mapped, especially along most of the existing trails, we still have too many blank areas. That area being one of the largest areas marked unknown and is where you said you are.

"Tell you what, let me run this past the department heads and see if I can get approval. I believe what you are offering will work. Contact me again at the end of this quarter cycle and I should know more. In truth, I will hate to lose you from my staff, but what you offer is of a greater benefit."

They continued to talk for a while longer. Both began to notice that the shadows were getting longer and that they had better break this up and continue with what they had planned. Both grabbed arms in the greeting of the day, and headed in opposite direction – Bihl back to the mapping shelter, and Fauul heading over to his family's mercantile shelter.

At least Fauul had presented his solution to the situation he now found himself in. He had hoped that Bihl could have given him a definite answer, but had to admit that what he was told made absolute sense. So he wouldn't be able to express everything he wanted to his family as of yet. Still he had to admit that he felt good about how well their discussion had gone. The time was passing very fast, and he knew that soon he would have to be returning.

He wondered how Lauma was faring with him gone. Even though the trip here had been a busy one, he was finding that he was missing her tremendously. He now began to understand that statement, "Absence makes the heart grow fonder". Now, again, he started to appreciate what some of his mated friends' statements about how he would not understand until it had happened to him. There was a comfort beginning to develop between the two of them. Each beginning to know the little things the other did unconsciously. These little things that made each unique in their own way, and yes he found himself looking for her without even thinking about it. Then laughing at himself when he realized he was doing just that, and knowing there was no way that she was here.

He arrived back at the mercantile, and assisted his father in closing it down for the day. They talked a little, both from the memories they had and their own point of view. It was different when one talked with their sires when one was grown. Still that aura of authority that being a sire required still was there – even if it was not as obvious. With the closing of the shelter they headed out the back door, and there met Chaze who had come over to help finish if it was necessary. Seeing they had completed the job he fell in with them and they headed over to the living shelter and the rest of the family. Fauul realized that this was probably one of the first times in a couple of turns that the whole family had been together. He also knew that as time continued these gatherings would be less and less. It was a sad thought truthfully. You spend your early life with your sires and siblings, living both the good and the bad, and then suddenly everyone goes their own way and what you had is gone forever.

While on this train of thought he went back in his mind thinking about when he was growing up. He, like most other whelps, dreamed what it would be like to be grown up. Then came that day when he realized that he had. He had been out with a couple of his whelp friends at the local swimming hole enjoying the respite from the heat of summer. When a small whelp came up and stated that "You grownups need to stay in your own part of the pond and to stay away from our part." It was the first time that statement had been pointed directly at him. He remembered using it when he was younger. Now those younger whelps had considered him an adult while he still did not.

They entered the living shelter by the back door and had washed up before entering. From the smell coming from the food prep area his sister Kayleh must be helping. There came no smells of something burning, which had been common with their mother. It seemed she would be distracted by something, forgetting she was cooking. It would enviably be burned, and of course, they would still be required to eat whatever it was.

"Marks, is that you?" Fathe asked.

"Yes, Fathe, and yes before you ask both Chaze and Fauul are here with me. Is there anything we can do to help?"

"No. No just go into the family space and relax a little. We'll join you there shortly. It will be a little while before we eat so we can catch up while it's cooking."

"Okay, sounds great. Chaze you want to get us something to drink. I think some of the hard stuff would be nice before the meal."

"Fine with me – wine or distilled?"

"Fauul since you haven't been here for a while what would you like?"

"Wine is fine with me . . . maybe after dinner some of the distilled to help settle the meal."

"I heard that!" Fathe said, "Are you already complaining about the food?"

"No, mother, I have found that a nice sipping drink after a meal helps to settle a meal that's all."

While Fauul was defending himself, he heard both his brother and father laughing quietly. Then Marks said, "You used to complain about her food all the time. And if you remember she has outstanding hearing. So what did you expect?"

In a short time the rest of the family joined the males in the family space and relaxed while the food was cooking. They all talked much about growing up and what it was like from the view of their parents. Many a humorous moment was passed on from their view of things. And now that the three of them were adults themselves they could join in the humor even though it was at their own expense. Finally Marks said, "Yes, whelps do many funny things. The one thing most whelps forget is that their sires were whelps once themselves. And anything they would try probably had already been tried by their sires, and probably with just about the same results."

"Yes, I have to agree with that statement. As a whelp one only sees their sires as adults, the ones in charge. It is really hard to see them as whelps themselves. So that view of the sires never really seriously enters one mind – at least in my case – how about you Chaze?"

"I have to agree. Sires were always adult and bigger – you sis?"

"Well I guess it makes it unanimous. Still I thought some of the stunts you two used to pull were stupid anyway."

"Yeah, and we would just say it was because you were female," Chaze answered.

She turned to both of them and stuck her tongue out at them, and made a face. This got them all laughing. "Yes, in many ways you tried to mother us, but since I was the oldest I thought I knew better," Fauul stated. "Still what a joke that was. I knew better, right! I'm sure if that conversation had been overheard by our sires here they both got a good laugh out that one."

With the meal ready they all went to the table and enjoyed a good meal. Fathe asked, "Fauul you have been gone quite a while, what brings you home now?"

"As I was telling dad earlier, I have some announcements to make, and hoped to be able to give you all the information tonight. But I cannot since the meeting I had this afternoon with my boss concluded without a definite answer. But before I head back down at the end of this quarter cycle I will know and let all of you know." He went into what had been going on in his life the past couple of turns. Covering the mapping field project, the meeting of Lauut and Lauma, becoming friends with Doube, and saving to the last, his upcoming mating with Lauma. He wanted to save that to the last knowing the impact it would have, and to be able to answer any questions that he knew would be asked. He took a deep breath and stated he was to be mated.

Looking around he could see the shocked looks on the faces of his family. He said, "Come on now. It's not that bad. I mean most of us eventually find a mate. Why should it be different with me?"

Finally his mother, after the shocked silence said, "Let's just say that with the way the females were attracted to you, and boy were they attracted to you, that you would just enjoy what was there, and not settle on any one special female. After all, why settle for one, when you can have any you want. If I remember it right, I think you even said that once when you were still a growing whelp."

"Yeah, I probably did. But deep down, I was looking. I knew that what you and dad had was good – even I could see that. And yes, while having it easy with the females is nice; it became obvious, over time, that many only wanted to be with me so they could brag to their friends. So like anything else in life, it got old after a while."

"Well, if a single female could catch our brother here, I guess I better watch out." Chaze said, trying to keep things light.

So far neither Marks or Kayleh had said anything and he was waiting wondering what they were thinking. Still he knew that much of the conversation around the shelter was from his mother. He always thought that dad had grown tired of talk by the time he came home each night, since he had to do that all day in the mercantile.

"So Kayleh do you have anything you would like to ask or add?" Fauul asked.

Shaking her head she said, "No, not at this time. I am really in shock. It would be the last thing I expected from you. I mean you could have had any female you wanted, at just about any time. I was never happy about that. I mean, after all I am a female. And it appeared to me that at times you were cruel to them, and that just made me mad."

"Well, Fauul are you sure? This will probably be the biggest decision in your life", Marks said, "and one of the toughest steps to make."

"Oh, I am quite sure. I've done a lot of thinking and second-guessing of myself. I've continually questioned my motives, and even this trip back here in a way is a test to see if it is real. So far the only thing I can say is yes it is quite real. I have no intention of backing out of my promise to her."

"Okay then, when do we get to meet this female? Her name is . . .?" His mother asked.

"Unfortunately because of the danger of the trip here, and the fact that there was no other female to go with her, she is still in the village where we met. And yes I did mention her name, its Lauma Ktrove."

"You mean I don't get to meet the female that has stolen my oldest son's heart? Is that fair to your mother? Well, that settles it. I am returning with you when you go back."

First there was a stunned silence as everyone in the space absorbed the comment that Fathe had made. Then Marks responded and said, "Now Fathe, I really don't think that's such a great idea. Fauul said the area was remote and because of the dangers of the trail that traveling with a female is unsafe."

"Well how else am I going to meet this up and coming new family member if I do not go and see her? Plus if I understand it she has no mother to help her prepare for the mating, and it would only be right if I helped."

"She doesn't even know you and you want to take over her mating? Do you think that's such a good idea? I'm sure she has friends that will be more than willing to help her. Isn't that right Fauul?"

"Yes dad that's right. She has two female friends that she has known all her life and I am sure they will assist her in any way she needs. Plus, if necessary, she can talk with her friends' mothers and get advice from them if she needs any."

"See Fathe, it's all covered. Besides it's their mating and I am sure afterwards you will have a chance to meet your new daughter. So while I understand your desire to assist here it appears that it has been well covered. Besides, if she is outback's female, I guarantee that she is pretty self-sufficient."

"Yes mother, we are planning to come here afterwards and spend time up here. Also when I return back there this time, I will not have as much safety on the trails as we will when we come back. Remember it's after a major gather so we will have many people on the trail with us."

"He does have your safety in mind Fathe. I know from talking with him earlier he said that he tied in with a group of traveling merchants when he returned, and that on the return trip he would have no such luxury, and would have to find a group heading in his direction at the port."

Still somewhat unconvinced Fathe continued, "Are you really sure? You're not just trying to prevent me from going are you?"

Both Fauul and Marks shook their heads. Thinking to himself. *Yeah just as I thought.* Instead Fauul said, "Not in the least. It is a surprise that you want to go there. But because of the remoteness of the region there are active bandit clans working the areas. Since the distances between villages are great it makes it easier for them to survive and do their worst. And I promise that when we do come up here, after the mating ceremony, we will visit often so you two can get to really know each other."

Somewhat mollified she reluctantly gave in saying, "Okay, but I still would feel better if I could help."

"I have an idea mom. How about you work on planning a get-together for the family and friends where we all can be involved and she can meet everyone that you would like her too. Does that work?"

"I guess it will have to . . . yeah I can do that, and I think it would be fun for all. I'll, of course, have your brother and sister help, and Marks when you can. Of course you will have to let me know by runner when you plan on being back here."

Glad that he was able to deter his mother Fauul said, "Of course I will. Just know that the runner will not be able to give you much of a lead-time on this. So I'm sure, knowing you that most of the work will be done before it is even close to that time."

* * *

She found that she kept looking for him in the morns when he would come from the workers shelter, and still knowing that he was gone she just couldn't help herself. *How has it come to this?* Now without Fauul around she felt empty and really wanting to see him. It bothered her that she was this way. After all she had been self-sufficient and strong and was able to do for herself. But now it seemed that none of that mattered. *He's not here.*

Still, there was the work that needed to be done, and again since he was gone it was back to the two of them. It was strange that without really appearing to do so Fauul had taken over and helped in so many different areas that now all of a sudden it seemed there was just too much work. Guiltily she knew that the burden would be increasing on her brother since she would be spending more time in the village working with her friends as they prepared for her up-and-coming mating ceremony.

After contacting the town leadership she had learned that there would be two others, making hers the third. She, thinking about the ceremony, knew that there were three points where one could back out and leave. It was something that had been developed over time. She realized that some of it probably came about from the history that Fauul had revealed to them. This gave either member a way out. In the present society arranged or forced matings were frowned upon.

These ceremonies were based on three aspects of a lifelong relationship – mind, spirit, and the physical. While there was a way to end a mating, the most prominent was the inability to produce offspring. At this point in their history the population was very small, and there was a need for more people. Yes, there were other ways to break up but being unable to reproduce was the main factor.

Going over in her mind the ceremony she felt she had no problem with the first two aspects. She was sure that she was not alone in being nervous about the third. This, of course, was the physical. This meant that they had to come together intimately. That meant they actually had to perform the act, it was a requirement. Yet even here there was a way out. The public sleeping areas would be converted for the newly mated. Spaces for privacy would be created with a small space included. When they entered the main space the door to this smaller space would be open. It had a way to be locked from the inside so that if someone still wanted to back out, they could go into this space lock the door and not be forced into anything.

Of course since all would know about this portion of the mating ceremony there would be much joking and kidding of the newly mated. Still none was mean spirited, and all was in fun. Of course part of the game was to see how many times they could make the new couple blush from embarrassment, as sly comments would be made, or suggestions given.

Still she was extremely nervous about this. She bred beasts and was well aware of the process. Yet this had always been something that did not involve her directly, and now in the near future it would. It was downright scary. Yet, the female beasts seemed not to be bothered about it at all, and at times seemed to enjoy it. Well, she had better put it out of her mind for now. There still was much to do anyway. She would be leaving in the next couple of days to visit her friends Sooma and Traylu. They both were eager to assist her in the preparations.

"You seem lost in thought sis," Lauut said.

"What? Oh, yes . . . I guess I am. I miss Fauul, and I know that I am leaving here for a couple of days shortly, and I feel guilty about that. I mean it will leave you responsible for everything and there's really more work here for two of us than what we can do. His help has been great, but of course, he had to leave, and now I am abandoning you too."

"I'll get by. And as you said it will only be a couple of days. I know I will be behind on many of the things but what is coming up for you is very important, and I think you have chosen very well. Besides, as if you didn't know, I really like Fauul. Plus when you leave to visit his township, he has stated he would assist in the costs of hiring someone to assist me while the two of you are gone. I really feel that finally things are changing for both of us. I really do mean that."

She turned around from the window and sighed, "I have to agree. Still right now I do miss him. I guess it is another proof that we really do love each other." Thinking about it, much had changed and seemed to continue to change. In fact since Fauul had entered her life there had never been so much change. It seemed that he influenced every part of her. She wondered if it was the same for him. "Better get to this day's work. One thing for sure it will not wait on us."

Laughing at her comment Lauut said, "You are so right. Tell you what, let's work this one together. It will make each project go faster even though at the end the day's work will be just as long. It will give us a chance to just be sister and brother again. Who knows maybe we will just talk about some of the stunts we used to pull on each other, and of course the trouble we would get into."

"Smiling at her brother she said, "Works for me. Let's do it!"

They headed out to begin the work that always seemed to be there and also never seemed to be finished. Such is the life in the outback.

CHAPTER TEN

With the meal completed and everyone relaxing and re-reading the letters that Jllon provided, Jllon got up and said, "This will be a quick and brief summary of what transpired back in the township. Let's just say that for a while there I was unsure of the outcome. Doube had taken a little time away after we arrived, and I did much of the preparation work for presentation to the council. Still, because of what we have discovered here, I had to get their cooperation of keeping this information under wraps.

"It first appeared that it wouldn't happen so I would not be able to present what we had found, leaving us to further reduce our team's size. Doube returned and between the two of us we were able to convince the council of the importance of this find without actually stating what we had found. Once that part of the presentation was accepted we passed around both the artifacts and drawings, and showed them the confirmation of the *ones before*. Once they realized the importance of the discovery it was simple to get them to put together a small team that will come down later to protect and continue to catalog our find.

"So in the near future all of us here will be packing up and heading west over, or around the mountains and heading out to another promising site. It is from this second site that the object was found. Unfortunately I have yet to have seen it. Still, I have it on good authority that there were no way we, in our time, made or created it. So there is a good chance that this second site could be as rich as this one has turned out to be. Still . . . . still it may have been just a fluke and this site here might be the best it gets.

"I will be discussing with Celt in the morn all that transpired here while we were gone. I want to thank you for being calm under the stress you had when the nomads showed up unexpectedly. While I only have a bare outline right now, that will change on the morrow. As you know I am not officially taking back the leadership until then so if anything comes up tonight talk with Celt. Tonight Nouma and I have much to talk about and catch up on, and would prefer not to be disturbed."

That brought a laugh from the team as he hoped it would. He looked over at his mate and saw that she had blushed and that had brought a deeper laughter.

One thing about it he was glad to be back with his mate and the team. He wished there were a way he could help the rest, but knew the letters would have to do for now. Maybe once they setup on the second site . . . well he really wouldn't know until he was there. *Just where is Fauul?* He really needed to talk with him, and see that object.

Talking with Doube he knew that most likely Fauul would be around the village where they were heading anyway. So the chances were good that he would finally meet him. Still for some reason they kept missing each other. There had to be a reason for that happening. Oh well, there was nothing he could do about it. Time to enjoy the evening, and the company of his partner in life, then back to the daily problems, the work, and the desert on the morrow.

The morn came too quickly and it was time to be back and working the site. After the morn meal he met with Celt who brought Jllon up to date with all that had happened while he had been away. Jllon asked, "So how much damage did the winds do anyway? I really haven't been back long enough to notice any difference."

"Surprisingly little. And it was all because of the warning we were given by the nomads. So while they were here they made me quite nervous – I mean you and Doube handled them last time, and I figured I wouldn't have any worries. Then out of nowhere they were here – downright scary if you ask me. When I first saw them I did a double take. There were more nomads at their location than I have ever seen in my entire life. I thought, oh no, now what did we do? But later I learned the word had gotten around to the other camps and they were curious as to what we were doing."

"I can see you are all alive and well, so I guess you did well on answering whatever concerns and questions they had."

"That's easy for you to say. Still I have to admit they were well mannered, and Soolonge acted as their spokesman. I gave them a tour of what we had found and didn't keep anything from them. After all, if they had so wanted, they could have looked anyway. There really would have been nothing I could have done to prevent it. I am so glad that you two had laid the groundwork. Because of that I feel they had respect for what we were doing here, and because you had shown them similar respect they had come this second time showing the same respect back.

"Anyway, because of their warning about the winds, we tried to make sure everything was tied down as best that it could be. All the operations were closed down, and we closed down, as well as we could, the flyer site. Still with the winds blowing as hard as they were, and the damage from the past on the main shelter much sand blew into it. And, as strong as the winds were, I was afraid that the winds would level the shelter. Fortunately they did not. Mostly the damage was from our temporary shelters blowing down, and some objects in the camp being blown around. Plus, like that flyer shelter, sand got into everything.

"Interesting thing though, in some of the areas where we had been working on the artificial trail built by the *ones before* the winds ended up covering some parts, but also uncovered other parts. I really have something to show you in that regard. Somewhere between the two sites we have been working, along the artificial trail, something was uncovered that I think you will find very interesting. After we finish here I'll take you there and you can judge for yourself. Until then I don't want to say any more."

"All I have to say is, when I left I figured it would be an easy time. Just a continuation of the work we were doing and a better understanding of these ancients. Instead it seems you had one adventure after another. So you have something you want to show me? Okay sounds good, but I know we probably have much more to cover here before we go out. What do you have the team doing today anyway?"

"Believe it or not, we are still recovering some items from that wind storm. So I have a couple of members out searching. The rest are still inspecting and looking for damage. I learned something from the nomads, and it was about these winds. They happen often in the late summer, and at times are stronger than the one that struck us. If that's so we will need to find a way to protect these sites. We were lucky as this one only blew for one day. They said that in the really strong ones it could blow up to nine days.

"The other problem about these winds is their direction. Generally out of the east but it varies enough during the blow that you can never be confident on the direction. While the steady winds are bad enough it will gust, at least it seems to be, at least twice as hard. Just like it had a mind of its own and it was attempting to destroy what we have built. I've really never been in such winds before."

"That bad. Hmmm, that does add another dimension to what we've found. I figured by being here in the desert, and with little humidity that there would be few problems in preserving what we found. As usual, I have been proven wrong. At least I can say that I am thankful that it happened now. I really would have hated to been out working our other location and then have to abandon it to come back and try and salvage our work here. It is something we are going to have to seriously consider."

They discussed many things over the next couple of hours, ironing out ideas as to the preservation of the discoveries. It was now mid-morn and the westerly breezes had picked up. It was a beautiful day. There was a hint of the heat that is normal in the desert, but the westerly winds coming off the ocean far to the west helped keep it temperate. Jllon wanted to inspect the sites to see for himself what the winds had done, and then between the two sites view this new discovery. He felt that by the zenith meal he would be caught up and have an understanding of all that transpired while he had been away.

Celt led him down the artificial trail that the ancients had constructed, in the direction of the two dig sites. Jllon saw that in a couple of the areas where they had uncovered this trail the winds had subsequently covered it again. He was beginning to understand how destructive these winds were. Thinking about what he had seen so far he began to wonder how they were going to be able to protect the large shelter that they had uncovered at the second site. Not knowing how stable the shelter was or even how it was built he was very worried. They couldn't afford to lose such an important find.

As they passed the first dig site he watched as part of the team worked on uncovering some of the finds that the winds had reburied. He learned the winds had also destroyed one of the portable shelters they had been using as supply storage. As they continued down the trail he noticed up ahead of them that the rest of the team seemed to be working another part of the trail. Although it looked a little different from what they had found so far there was no hint as to its importance. At this point Celt commented, "I guess I would like to curse these winds for undoing much of the work we have completed. Still at the same time I have to thank it also."

"What do you mean by that? From what I have seen so far it has undid much of what we have accomplished."

"True, but if you remember, as we walked between the two sites we had to skirt this hill where you see the team working. Well the wind uncovered some of the trail on the east side. It wasn't straight like the rest we have uncovered so far. It turned out to be curved. As we followed it around it continued to curve. We believe now that it goes in a full circle. Interesting thing is that there are additional trails that come off of this circle, almost like spokes in a wheel. Although not that many. You know, kind of like ours presently do around our villages and townships."

As they skirted the hill Jllon could see exactly what Celt was talking about. "Interesting . . . it makes me wonder what is under this hill."

"My thoughts exactly. So after the cleanup is completed I thought we would put the full team here and see what we find. This seems to be out of character to what we have found so far. I mean everything seems to point to angles."

"Right, hard lines, nothing soft – and really nothing to the way we build now. Still maybe they weren't all about lines and angles. As you know, we really know very little about them as of yet. This further complicates things. Who were these people anyway? I know they were our ancestors", Jllon said, "still other than what I see about their similar looks we have nothing in common."

"At least not yet. I mean, just as you have said, we have so little knowledge of them yet. The few pieces we have only identify them, but do not define them."

They stayed at this new site for a short period of time looking over the new discovery before continuing towards the second site. Jllon wondered what this third site would produce. Still it might end up with nothing more than a trail that went in a circle. He saw in the distance that the large shelter was still standing, and that was a great relief. When they finally arrived at the shelter, Jllon walked around it to inspect it and see if he could detect any new damage. The first thing he noticed was the partially collapsed shelter appeared to have been further damaged by the winds. This posed a threat to the other since this one leaned into it. "We've got to find a way to strengthen that one." Jllon said, pointing at the damaged shelter.

"Oh, I agree, but wood is not very available here, and I don't know what to do, any ideas?"

"Truthfully, no. It just has to be done or we will lose everything here." Continuing his inspection an idea was beginning to form in his mind but again he did not know if it would work. "Looking at this, I wonder if we could dismantle this damaged one, and then use what we salvage out of it to reinforce this other one?"

"I didn't think about that – probably why you're in charge and not me. It's something to think about that's for sure. I guess my next question would be, is it safe to do so, and should we?"

"Yeah I know what you mean. It would mean that we would be destroying part of what we have uncovered, and changing what the ancients did. Still if we are to preserve any of it, we may just have to do it."

"I'm glad I am not the one who has to make that decision."

"It's really one I don't want to make either, but it may become necessary, and if we don't come up with a solution soon, these winds may provide one we don't want."

They spent the rest of the morn inspecting and studying the two shelters and trying to come up with the best solution to the problem presented. But as the zenith meal approached and they began their hike back to camp, they had come up with no solid answers. "I think we need to discuss this with the team tonight after the evening meal and see if they may have some ideas. I would prefer not to destroy anything we have found, but at this moment cannot see any way around that possibility. Anyway, I want the artists to go over there on the morrow and do detailed drawings and paintings of the shelters so if the unthinkable happens we will have accurate information and images of them."

"A good idea there Jllon. Do you want the teams to continue as I have assigned them?"

"For now. Until there are some answers I'm not changing anything. I'll be up there studying the site to see if any ready answers come to me, and I will leave you in charge to continue as you have been. That way we can continue the important work, and hope the winds hold off." Thinking about the site Jllon realized that things were getting very complicated. The engineering the ancients used to build these shelters was beyond their understanding at the present. If it finally came down to having to dismantle that one shelter could they? Or should they just chance it and hope they would remain standing . . . just too many questions again with no ready answers.

The next cycle proceeded without incident. At the end of this period most of this circular trail had been uncovered – including the area inside this circular trail. From what evidence they were able to recover there appeared to have been three small shelters plus many of the same strange trees they had found earlier in the canyon. But here, as in the first site, everything had been destroyed. They were coming to the conclusion that anything they excavated towards the mountains to the west was destroyed either by earth shakes and or fire. It seemed that only something as far out as the flyer shelter avoided this type of destruction.

Still, even these two showed damage. One had almost been destroyed and had partially collapsed into the second. This had, obviously, damaged the second. Yet if that had not happened then most likely the shelters would not be standing today. It was the type of collapse that led to a stronger support over all for the remaining in-tact shelter allowing it to remain standing. The only other area that seemed to have taken less damage was located where the nomads had claimed as theirs.

Looking at the notes from the cartographers, they had mentioned ruins around a water source. From talking with Soolonge Jllon found that the area had always been used by the nomads and had always been in their oral history. So Jllon figured these shelters probably belonged to the same township. Still, because of the sacredness of the area, he knew they would not be able to study the site close up. It would only be from a distance, and from a distance much would and would be missed.

He knew, from the notes of the cartographers that were involved with the incident that they had almost come to harm. If Doube had not been with them there would have been a good chance they all would have perished right then. Doube, by being an adopted member of the mountain branch of the nomads, was able to smooth the incident over and correct the wrongs made by his team members. Since Doube was now the scout for their project they were able to avoid the same mistake. For that he was thankful, and the conversation he had with the wise one from the nomads had only been successful because of Doube.

On the morrow the pack beasts would be returning from the merchant on the other side of the mountains. He was hoping to hear from the council, and then know approximately when the new team would arrive. He knew that there was much to be found here, but the summer heat was not far off. Once it arrived, then there would be no digging. It simply would be protection of the sites and cataloging of what had been found.

He still marveled that these ancients had successfully lived in the desert. Yes, he knew that the nomads did also, but there was a vast difference between the two groups. One of the reasons for the nomads' success lay in the fact they moved, never staying in one place long enough for it to fail – while these ancients were sedentary. Even though they had a much faster and better way to get around, evidence pointed to a permanent settlement. And this evidence pointed to a township-sized settlement. Not a small village or temporary stop over.

What was it that drew the ancients to this spot? He could see that through three seasons it would be a nice place to be. Temperate, with much sunshine and comfortable temperatures, still the summer heat would make it almost unbearable. And that would be enough to keep him away from living here.

On another subject he and the team had come up with no solution for the winds. Before they made the move to the other proposed site an answer of some kind would have to be found. Then that night as the team was discussing things over the evening meal, one suggested that since it had been covered by sand and dirt the winds had not done any additional damage, which was true. Adding to it that the location was the desert, which was naturally dry; this had prevented any water damage. All this was known, so he was asked what his point was. The one making the point responded by asking, "What if we were to bury the east side of the partially collapsed shelter with sand, and then the winds simply would blow up the sandy hill and over the tops."

It was such a simple solution, and none of them had even considered it. One thing about it, there was plenty of sand and dirt. It probably was the best way they would have to save the shelters. But it would be a little more difficult than just covering the east side of the shelter. Celt had stated that the winds had been variable, east, southeast, northeast. So that meant they would have to build their protection covering all three of those directions. It would require the whole team, and probably all the time they had left before they moved. Still he knew it had to be done if they wanted to come back to still-standing shelters. It did seem the best solution.

After the meal he pulled in the rest of the team leaders and discussed the idea with them. No one came up with a better solution so it was accepted as the only solution they had for now. He asked how long it would take the team to finish what they had been working on so he could get an idea as to when the team could shift to the building of the sand barrier. Celt, who was the second in charge said, "The area around that circle could be roughed out in about seven days. Won't get much research done on it but at least we can see what it represents."

"Good, make sure you have the artists do a detailed work up of the area so we can add it to our archives. So Nouma how's the research end going? Can we work on closing it down soon?"

"As you really know there's enough stuff here to keep us researching for turns, but I think we can wrap up much of what we are doing in about three or four days."

"Bayleh, is there a way in the next few days that you and your group can pull down the smaller camp and move everything back to main camp? We need to be working towards a single camp for the new team."

"Once the beast handlers return from the outpost, which I believe should be on the morrow, we can start on it. There's plenty in the second camp, so I haven't a guess as to how long it will take. I will go there on the morrow and look it over and give you an estimate. Does that work for you?"

"No problem. Before I break this up, there is one last thing I need to say here, or maybe two. First it has been great to work with this team, with all of you. We have made the most important discovery of any generation. Secondly, we have to get it in our minds to look at our work with the idea that in a short time we will be leaving these sites. So as you work you need to start looking at them with the idea of preservation. It would be tragic to have found what we have only to have all the evidence destroyed. By the way, we haven't named this site. Anyone have an idea of what we should call it other than the desert dig?"

"We did find that sign which stated Desert Sands, if you remember," Flar stated.

"Does that work for all of you? I guess it would be an appropriate name – considering we found all of this under the desert sands."

So it was decided that temporarily they would call the site Desert Sands. Jllon knew that this was not the name of this township, but until they found something that identified the township this name would have to do. "Okay then, keep me informed, especially if there is a change in the times for completion. We need to move as quickly as possible to preserving what we have discovered. We have already seen deterioration in both the flyer and the ground transport. Thanks for all the input and pass on to the rest of the team what we have discussed. Find out if there are any other ideas out there that we can use. I have always found that we work better when everyone contributes, good night and see you all on the morrow. We will meet again after the evening meal on the morrow after the arrival of the pack beasts."

The meeting broke up and everyone left to their own temporary shelters. The time ahead of them had much work in it and that time appeared to be short. Jllon walked over to Nouma and took her hand and they walked out into the desert. It was going to be a full moon tonight. They saw the first hints of it rising over the distant hills to the east. When there was a full moon over the desert it took on a different life. As the down canyon winds started to develop there would be a subtle breeze. The sands would catch an eerie glow and the desert plants would be indistinct and at times appear to be someone or something standing there watching. It was a different kind of beauty that one could not describe, but had to be in to appreciate. The quiet of the night soaked into them as they leisurely hiked around the camp. "You know I really never did like the desert," Jllon said.

"Me either, if truth be told, still . . ."

Smiling, catching her unspoken thought Jllon said, "Yeah, funny how that works. As we have worked here that stark ugliness has vanished, and now I can see and appreciate the beauty that is really here. Still one cannot be too careful. It can lull you into being careless and here you cannot be."

"Still, I just love it here with the full moon. I feel that I could sit out here and just quietly enjoy it all night." Smiling and sighing a little she continued, "Of course it is much nicer when I am with you here. It allows one to share . . . to share how I am feeling, and to feel the warmth when you are close like this. It makes me feel like we are the only ones here. Even though just over there is our camp and it's full of people."

"I guess we are lucky to have chosen the same field of work. For so many their mates work a different area and they only see each other when they can."

Smiling she said, "For some that is all they want or need. And probably in some cases can stand."

Both then were silent for a while. They got up from where they had been sitting and continued to hike and enjoy each other's company. He, with his arm around her waist, and she the same. Jllon saying, "I feel fortunate that we have this closeness. We just seem to connect on so many levels and not that I haven't told you but that trip back to the township without you was pure torture for me. I feel naked without you."

"Laughing a little she then teasingly said, "I do like you that way."

Puzzled a little, he asked, "What way?"

Laughing again she then replied, "Naked, of course."

That got both of them laughing, and he turned around and hugged and kissed her deeply. "You know, I really, really love you. Shall we take advantage of probably our last night of being together? You know after this as we work towards leaving here we will see very little of each other."

"You have to ask? Of course you do. You're always that way."

Laughing again they headed hand and hand back to his shelter.

While they all knew that there was turns of work ahead of them here at this site, the mood was one of anticipation as they shifted their direction to packing up and preparing the change in location. It was in the after-zenith that the pack beasts and handlers arrived back from the trip over the mountains to the outpost located there. When they were first spotted, heading down the trail out of the west, the word passed through the team like a wild fire. As always there was an anticipation of correspondence from their families. And while they knew they probably would not actually have this in hand until the evening meal, it lifted the spirits.

The work they were performing now consisted of trying to conserve what they had found. To build a large enough mound of dirt and sand, to block the winds to the east of the large surviving shelter, was hard back breaking work. Still having had a taste of how severe the winds were there were no complaints. It had been decided that most of the fragile items they had found would be moved into the flyer shelter giving the items the most protection they could. So like the honey makers, the whole of the camp was extremely busy.

It seemed that there was always something that had to be completed, and the list of items continued to grow instead of shrink. And this list didn't include anything personal. Before they might even think about packing their own items the entire growing list had to be finished. They were hoping that they'd be in the village for the major gather but knew that as time continued they would probably miss it. Still, if this site were any indicator of the time involved, they would be there close to that remote village for the next major gather in the fall.

The camp staff helped the handlers unload the pack beasts and pass on the correspondence to Jllon. He took time out of his schedule to sort through the letters so that they could be distributed with the evening meal. As expected, there was one from the council, and once the immediate needs were taken care of he would take a break and find out when the additional team would be arriving.

One of the first things he noticed was the date. It had been sitting at the outpost for a cycle so whatever was stated inside was old news now. It couldn't be helped, but still reading it would have to wait. He needed to get back out and see how the mound was progressing and assist in moving the fragile items. *Funny how things get messier before they are put away*, he thought. Looking around he could not help but think, *"Organized Chaos", that's for sure*. Still he had been on enough of these projects to know that what he was seeing was the norm.

Celt approached him and the asked, "Was there correspondence in with the supplies?"

"Yes, and as usual I will pass it out tonight with the meal. How's the mound coming? And by the way, one of the letters was from the council – haven't had time to look it over other than when they sent it, so will have no answer until tonight."

"It's hard work, actually harder than when we uncovered it", he paused briefly, "partly because we are running on a much tighter schedule. I'm rotating the crew and we are working it until dark. I've basically assigned the females to provide water to the diggers, and to assist in moving the fragile items into the flyer shelter. They are rotating those duties also. Two will bring items and one will provide the water. All the camp managers and assistants are involved in breaking down the second camp and moving it back to the main camp, then packing what is not needed."

"Good, it sounds like it's in full swing. I'm coming down where the diggers are to assist them. If you will work with the camp managers and start looking at what we want to pack over the mountains with us . . . I am not sure as of yet what our accommodations will be. Still, with a working property close by and a village a short distance away, I hope to be able to get the crew into a more permanent shelter situation than what we have here. Yet I know we will need a few of the temporary shelters on the next work site even if it is just a place to get out of the sun."

"So how do you want me to set it up?"

"My thought simply is to make a judgement call, and have them put the items we probably would want to take in a separate location. You know, one that we can either add to or remove from, but enough out of the way that we don't trip on the stuff. I'm going to be talking with Doube later and find out what he remembers about the area we will be going into, and then I'll let you know what I find out from him. Anyway, that's enough for now, I need to get out there and help. See you tonight at the evening meal, and good luck on your end."

"Okay, I'll go ahead, and yes I'll see you tonight. I suspect it will be a quiet evening, both because of the letters, and the fact that all will be exhausted from the work." They headed off to their separate tasks – Jllon to assist the diggers and Celt to overseeing the camp managers, and preparing for the next move.

Jllon, as he headed off to the area where they were building up the soils, stopped briefly at the first site where they had uncovered the destroyed shelters. He was beginning to develop a theory of what happened in the area closest to the Desert Mountains to the west. It seemed that anything south and east of this area showed no sign of burning, yet everything close in had been destroyed by fire. Even the new site on the artificial trail showed the same signs of scorching.

Remembering the notes from the cartographers, Doube had mentioned that the area appeared to have had volcanic activity in the past. And while there was no known volcanic flow found, it would not have been necessary to super heat the air in this area, to then consume anything that was burnable. Since they had yet to uncover the entire township they would not be able to establish boundaries to this burning. Again it would be turns before this site was completely explored and studied.

He continued on to the one standing shelter they had uncovered – he was hoping they would find others. Still other than the ruins where the nomads claimed as theirs, there had been none. Again, he knew that they had barely scratched the surface, and there was still a possibility of finding other standing shelters. Coming in sight of the work he saw Suzzane as the one who was presently on water duty, and she was talking with Flar, who was overseeing this work for this day. Both had their backs to him as he approached so they did not see him come up to them. They both jumped when he asked, "So how's it going?"

Suzzane turning said, "You scared me there. I almost spilled the water. And you know how far back it is to get more. And if I had, I should make you go back and get it."

"Sorry about that, I didn't think you two were that deeply involved with your conversation. Anything I should know about?"

"No, not really," Flar responded. "We were just considering the many mounds out here and wondering if there could be as many new discoveries as there were in these sand hills. After all the first two you chose both produced. So we were wondering whether it was your skill, or just luck, and that we could choose any of these out there and find something."

Smiling a little Jllon said, "Partly both, experience and luck. Still I believe luck is spelled W O R K. I have found that studying the way things get buried over time that you start to develop a feel for what may or may not produce something. It's not 100% accurate, but I have found that I can usually identify a promising site. Like many of these out here just don't look right. I think most are natural and if we dug there, in the end, they would produce nothing, other than another pile of sand."

"Really? I didn't and still don't see any difference in the hills where we uncovered the finds at the two sites and these that we can see. The difference must be real subtle", Suzzane stated, and looking around she said, "Oh look one of the others is signaling me. Think I better get back to getting this water around to the other members of the team here." She picked up the water bucket and headed off.

Flar asked, once Suzzane left, "I noticed that you waited until the packers returned before you joined us. Did you happen to see if there was correspondence?"

"Yeah I did, and yes everyone will have a letter or two to read tonight, including me. I have received the correspondence from the council and should know when the new team will be arriving at the port."

"You didn't take time to read it now?"

"No, we need to complete this work here, and the time between now and dark is not going to change anything in that correspondence."

True, so are you here to take over from me?"

"Not really. I'm here to join the work force and get this job done. One more body to move the dirt will help speed things along. And as the camps are reorganized then the camp managers will be joining us here, since this is so critical. It would be a shame, after all this time, that this shelter, which was buried for such a long time that in the end, we lose it to the same forces that originally, buried it."

"Yeah, it has me worried. I was really surprised by the strength and variability of that wind. Before you start let me show you what we are doing and see if you may have some suggestions that would improve our work."

"Okay, lead on, please."

Flar led him around the work area explaining what they had in mind and how they felt it would protect the shelter. Since Jllon was not here during the winds he only nodded and agreed. It did appear they would be providing the best protection with the resources they had available. Once the tour was complete he grabbed a tool and joined in the moving of dirt and sand to the ever-growing hill they were creating.

Before he realized it dusk was approaching and it was time to head back to the main camp. By the time they reached the camp it would be approaching dark. He noticed, as he had expected, that he hurt a bit and knew he would be sore on the morrow. Since he had been away from the project for a while he had gotten soft. So now he would pay the price for that softness. Still as tired as he felt he did not think he would have any trouble sleeping.

They placed all their tools inside the shelter and as a group headed back in. Everyone was anticipating a good meal and receiving mail. Followed by quiet time as everyone would be absorbed in reading and rereading their letters from home and attempting to see what may be unsaid, or implied within them. Jllon, knowing the time the correspondence from the council had sat at the outpost located to the west, hoped that the council was just sending an update, and not the new team. They were not quite prepared to receive them yet. And he did not want them to be waiting at the port. He wanted Doube to be there to meet them so that they could come directly here – less chance of any information leaking that way.

The first part of the correspondence was just that an update to what had transpired and a statement that the team they would be sending would be smaller than originally asked for. Again because of the burden of cost they had no choice. Jllon knew that this work they were presently involved in was not cheap. To support a team in the field for as long as they were going to be working could, in the end, be just as expensive as sending the ten mapping teams out. He knew it was a burden on their society, but he thought that it would be worth the cost. Looking at what they had discovered so far, should help them advance technologically, and learn much about their unknown past. What he had seen so far pushed him on to find and to learn more.

Somewhere he hoped a depository for knowledge survived the suspected worldwide disaster. To find such a thing would change everything – not that these finds did not influence views and thoughts because they did. He saw it in the way the council reacted when the items and drawings were finally presented to them. It makes one eager to find the keys to those advancements that the ancients enjoyed and they themselves lacked. And it brought forth curiosity, leaving one wanting to know more, with so many additional questions that had no answers at this time.

Going back to the correspondence he found that indeed the new team was on their way, and consisted of five individuals. Three who would assist in the security and two were scholars, and even though the three were security, they also had a background in learning. So any member could do any part that was necessary. And especially here it would be necessary. The desert conditions, during the summer, were harsh; so much of what this team did would be curtailed by the heat.

One of the plans for this team was to remain here until relieved again when part of the present team would return in the fall or winter months to continue the work. At that point they would come over the mountains and join the other portion of the team that would hopefully be working a new successful site. If this new site turned out to be as productive as this one then they would have enough work for a couple of generations of the keepers of the past.

Getting up he went to find Doube. From what he could glean from the information he knew that soon the new team would be at the northern port. So Doube would need to head out on the morrow to be there in time to meet them. Looking around the camp he noticed that most of the team members were still deep into their personal messages from home and not really saying much to each other. He understood it completely. He was sure part of the silence had to do with fatigue. Still not seeing Doube, he continued his search – asking one or another member if they had seen Doube. The answers were generally negative.

Knowing Doube for what and who he was, he suspected that he was outside of camp looking over either some rock or just the lay of the land. Doube liked to look at the same piece of land all times of the day and night. He said that it gave him a different perspective each time he looked – making it easier for him to recognize different aspects of the land. So once he knew that Doube wasn't in camp he went outside of camp and started and general search. With the full moon it made it easier to see and search.

Eventually after circling the camp a couple of times he saw him out sitting on a rock. He approached from the front so that he wouldn't surprise him. Actually he laughed at himself for that thought. *Surprise him, right!* If anyone would be surprised it would be him not Doube. One just didn't sneak up on this scout. He was too good at what he did. And, as he expected, as he approached Doube said, "Been listening to you walk around out there. Didn't know for sure what you were doing so I waited to see if you were looking for me or just enjoying the full moon."

"Can't help but enjoy the full moon. It changes the desert, makes it softer, almost dream like in its appearance, but I really was looking for you."

"Okay, now that you have found me what has come up?" Doube asked smiling.

"As you know, I received the correspondence from the council and unfortunately it has sat quite a while before I received it. The new team is on their way and . . ."

"And you need me to go meet them. Do I have it right?" Doube interrupted.

"Yes, that's right. We need to have them immediately on the trail from the port so there will be no chance of a slip up."

"Fast trip there or can I do it a little slower? In other words do I have time to do some side exploring or must I get right there?"

"From the gist of the council's letter I would say speed is of the essence. In fact there is a chance this new team may arrive ahead of you. Coming back, if you want to show them a little of the land I have no problem with that. It may help them if they know what they will be facing and I cannot think of anyone better to explain it to them, can you?"

Smiling Doube said, "No, I guess not. So when do you need me to leave?"

"In the morn just after the meal would be soon enough. If you beat them there here are some marks to cover your time. Who knows, you might find something there you need. On the way back bring them through the abandoned village, and then up and over so they will be able to have an overview of the entire work area."

Okay with me. Will you need me to let you know when I leave?"

"No, not at all, when you are ready just go. Here is the contact letter and the names of the new team members, plus the location where you are all to meet so as to avoid any misunderstandings or problems."

Okay then, I guess I will see you again when I return. I'm going to remain out here for a while longer. I just love the quiet here. Let's me think and contemplate things."

"Okay, I'm heading back in. I'm tired from the work performed today, and probably will most likely turn in. Good luck, and as always be careful . . . not that you are never so, and with that I'll just say g'night." Jllon turned and headed back into the camp. Once back in the camp he looked around and saw that most had already turned in for the night. Other than the two who had the watch, the camp was quiet. He knew that he had duty around dawn, everyone except the females were required to be involved. The females had other assignments that were required of them. That way most of the work was shared equally. He briefly talked with the two and then headed off to his sleeping area.

Doube remained outside of camp for a little longer. Then sighing he got up and came back into the camp. He saw the camp manager who had been on duty that day and was still working. He approached him and said, "Jahnsyn, I'll be heading back out to the port on the morrow – early if I have my choice. I'll need travel food put together for the next seven days and can you inform whoever is working this position on the morrow that I would appreciate an early meal so I can be on the trail just after sunrise."

"Okay with me. If you come back just before I leave my shift tonight I'll have the travel fare ready for you. So the boss got word the replacement team was on its way huh?"

"Yeah, looks like it. Guess that'll put more pressure on you all here to get these final projects finished."

"So how long do you think you may be gone?"

"Don't know really. But just going there and returning can be half a cycle. So if the team is there when I get there, then it should be a quick turnaround. I wouldn't worry about arriving at our other location before the major gather though. It's just not going to happen. We will probably miss it by at least a half of cycle – which probably will in truth be a good thing."

"How so? I do so enjoy the major gathers, and to be at one that is new to us is a wonderful experience."

"True, they can be exciting, but I suspect we would find no room in which to stay. We are only taking enough shelters with us to provide a covered work area around the next dig. So if there is no space at the hostels then we would be without a place to sleep. Not that sleeping under the stars isn't nice now and then."

"Ahhh yes, I see what you mean. Anyway if I miss you tonight, the supplies will be stacked over there and you can pick them up. I guess then I'll say my good bye to you now since you will be gone before I am back working on the morrow. Have a safe trip."

"Thanks and thank you for putting this together on such a short notice. I think Jllon was surprised to have learned that the new team was already on its way." Doube turned and left to put together his necessary items for the trip. He would be on his own at least in one direction and would have to be careful and avoid any detection by anyone, especially the probable bandit groups that might be in the area.

The next morn, as promised, the meal was waiting for him. The activity for the rest of the team's meal was just beginning and it would be after sunrise before any of the team would be up and looking to eat. He hoped to be through the abandoned village by that time and well on his way. He wanted to put as much distance behind him the first day. Heading for the table he thanked Jahy Delb, one of the assistants, and ate quickly. He picked up his pack and immediately headed out. Before coming to the table he left a quick note attached to Jllon's temporary shelter so that Jllon would know that he was on the way to the port.

It was great to be out on the trail again. While he enjoyed working for the many different teams that he had been with, he felt most free when he was out by himself. Even though this would not be a sight-seeing tour it did not matter. He now only had himself to depend on and if trouble came he would be able to, most likely, avoid it. Since one individual was much more difficult to locate than a group.

He knew that he would stop early have a quick meal, then move on and cover additional ground. That way if one of his temporary camps were marked or had been discovered, by the time anyone would approach, he would be a long gone and away from there. At night he would be keeping a dry camp. No fire, no food, and a place that would be hidden and unexpected. Once back in the outback he became one with it. It was as if he was one of the many beasts who lived in this world. It had been one of the main reasons for his success over the turns.

Still he understood that even the wild beasts eventually made mistakes, so he continually checked himself. He avoided patterns and if he felt he had unconsciously created one would then immediately change. He knew that even by not creating a pattern was in itself a pattern. Still he hoped that by doing what he did, in the end, he would be less of a target.

Too much trouble when there were always easier targets out there for the bandits. Like that group of traveling merchants they had found. He wondered if they had ever been identified. He had to admit that he probably would never know.

CHAPTER ELEVEN

Fauul knew his time was short. He would have to be heading back south after he learned of the decision. He found that he should be able to book passage on the water-craft for the next morn after getting the answer. Until then he walked the township and visited his old places. He ran into old friends and helped at the mercantile. And of course, continued to talk with his family, and had to continue to discourage his mother from wanting to take the trip with him back down to the village. She had always been a strong willed person and one who usually got her way. Still he knew that the trip would not be good for one of her status to take, let alone a female. She really had no idea of the hardships and dangers. She only saw that her oldest was becoming mated and felt it was important to be involved.

For that he could not blame her. Since the ceremony would not be performed here locally it just was not possible. So she would just have to settle for meeting the newest member of the family when they returned here after the ceremony and spent a half cycle here. He thought about that meeting and sort of laughed to himself. "That meeting should be an interesting one." He said to himself. "After all what we will have here are to strong willed females. Maybe I should just stand back and watch the sparks fly." He then laughed to himself as he pictured it in his mind.

Yes strong and self-sufficient Lauma meets Fathe, the mother of her mate. He thought that maybe he should warn Lauma. But that could come later when they were on their way back to here. He knew that until that time Lauma would have plenty on her mind and did not need anything else to make her nervous. Thinking of her brought a genuine smile to his face. He had to admit that he really missed her, and honestly could not wait to get back. At least it wouldn't be much longer.

He made contact with his boss on the requested day, and found out the higher ups had approved the plan. Mostly because there would be no direct cost involved and since the department was paying him a salary anyway, there would be no change or increase there. He would be solely responsible for what happened down there, and they would expect results to be regularly sent by runners. Thanking Bihl for his effort he headed out and put together what he needed for the return trip, went back to the family to bid a farewell, and finally headed back to his apartment to close it down. On the morrow he would be heading back to his mate to be, and he couldn't wait.

Lauut and Lauma headed into the village, he on some pretext to see the beast master, and she, to meet with her friends as they helped her put together her mating ceremony. Lauma knew that in truth Lauut was only coming along to make sure her trip into the village was a safe one. While the trail that went into the village from the area of their property was not a main one, it was traveled enough that usually she could find someone to travel with. While rarely did anything happen, it was still better to travel in groups.

As usual, this trip was uneventful, and they parted company at the edge of the village. He, heading over to Aurto Satrneze the beast master, and she going to the mercantile where she would tie in with her lifelong friends Sooma and Traylu. Thinking about them she realized that at one time she had come close to losing them. After the accident that had left her and her brother without family she had completely isolated herself from the past, which of course, had included her close friends. It was only after meeting Fauul that she finally made contact with them again, and found the closeness they all once had.

Now, because of that accident, she had no mother in which to guide her on this journey. So she was falling back on her friends for help and advice. If she had never renewed these friendships she would have been at a loss as to what to do, and how it all was to work. Still she was practical enough to know that somehow she probably would have figured it all out, but any assistance was more than welcome. Both of her friends were mated so they had gone through the ceremony and would pass on what they had learned.

Stopping briefly before entering she took a deep breath. She had so many questions, and she was sure her friends would have answers and advice for her. Finally steeling up the nerve she went into the establishment and true to their word her friends were there waiting for her. She saw the excitement on their faces. Sooma said, "There's the mate to be. The last one we ever thought who would become mated." With that all three laughed.

"Now what do you mean about that statement?" Lauma asked.

"Come on now", Traylu said, "there had been many a male who has attempted to attract you but you would have nothing to do with any of them. So we thought there was a good chance that you would just be without a companion, a life mate."

Smiling she couldn't help but see their point of view. It was true that none of the males in the surrounding area held any interest or attraction to her, but she didn't think that others had noticed. After all it was her problem not someone else's.

Then Sooma continued, "Yeah, now look at you. You've captured the best that we've seen. Not that I have a problem with my mate. Still the one you have chosen is surely easy on the eyes."

A little embarrassed with the easy way her friends were describing her mate to be she actually blushed, and felt somewhat shy. Feeling the heat in her face all she could do was to keep smiling. Yes, Fauul was quite a person, and how come it was she that he wanted, was a complete mystery to her. Still she wasn't complaining, as she wanted him too. Looking at her friends she saw that they were smiling back at her.

"I think we've touched a nerve here, don't you Traylu?"

Both walked up to her and put their arms around her and led her to the back and then out the back door. From there they went into Sooma's shelter which was directly across from the business. Once inside they went into the food preparation area, and sat around the table that was close. "Okay," Sooma asked, "now before we start here, do you have any questions you would like to ask?"

Still a little embarrassed she said, "Of course there's much I want to ask . . ." Not knowing where to begin she was at a loss for words. Something that never had been a problem in the past seemed to happen more often since she had met Fauul. The silence hung in the air and she felt herself reddening again. *Darn why am I doing this?* She thought. *After all they are my friends.* She noticed that the two of them just sat there expectantly and waited for her to get her composure.

"I understand completely", Sooma said. "What you are going into is such a big deal and nothing will be the same afterwards. Many of the things that were always private will be no longer, and even the way you look at things change. So it is so easy to be completely off balance right now. It is also the time where we start second guessing ourselves, and wonder if what we are doing is right? Believe me he is doing the same thing. While males are much simpler than we females they still go through much of the same doubts and questions as they approach becoming mates."

With a questioning look on her face Lauma asked, "How can you know that? I mean what you are saying is so right, but how can you know that about the males?"

"We mated didn't we? Besides, if you have a good relationship communicating is important. And not just communicating but being honest in those talks. It's more than just saying your piece, but you have to listen to his also. I have found that while I get what I want more than he does, we still have to compromise on so much. And if you are not willing to listen as much as you talk then it won't be long until you have nothing but an empty shell of what might have been great. So now that I've preached a little, Franc revealed that to me and it's the same with Traylu. After all, we get together often, and complain about our mates, but believe me we really would not want another – take too long to break another in." With the final statement she started laughing, which helped break the tension that Lauma had been feeling.

"Funny that you should say that about communicating, Fauul said much the same thing. Is it that important really? I mean, I'm sure there are days were neither of you say much."

"That's quite true, but your body talks, even if you don't. So even if you don't realize it, you are always talking with each other whether it verbal or physical."

"Speaking of physical, that part of the ceremony scares me completely."

"Oh we understand, but we'll talk on that later. There is so much we need to work on before we deal with that little detail, and no, we are not putting you off, even though you may think so. We just want to get everything else done first, and then when we have most of it finished then we will have a frank talk about the third part of the ceremony."

"Well, if you say so," she replied in a meek voice.

"Come on now. This should be a time of celebration not of meekness. After all you are to be mated. It is a great time in your life. You know something that even as whelps you dream of. So now you are the last of our special group to join us", Sooma said, "and we are honored to help with this important event." She got up and said, "Come follow us, we have something to show you."

Lauma, getting up from the chair, wondering what now, followed them into the sleeping area, and saw a mating outfit. It was absolutely beautiful. Yet she knew it was something well beyond anything she could afford. It must have come from one of her friends. "That's not for me is it?" She asked.

"Of course it is", Traylu stated.

"I can't afford anything like that . . . I thought I would just have something simple that I made . . . nothing like this . . . I mean this is so far beyond . . . oh I just don't know."

"Don't worry about it dear friend – and no this is not either Traylu's or mine. Your mate to be left marks here to cover what we felt was appropriate for you, and he said that he would leave it completely in our hands. So we knew that this one was the one for you."

"You mean that Fauul stopped here and has talked with you and made these arrangements and didn't say anything at all to me?"

"Yes, he said he was on his way back to his township and wanted to make sure that you had what you needed. He knows that you and your brother are having a tough time, and he thought that he would at least help you here. I must say the male you have chosen is quite considerate, and thinks over everything. I'm almost envious of you. Still you two seem to be right for each other. I cannot deny that at all."

Choked up with emotion, Lauma could only stare. Here was something so beautiful, something that was well beyond her wildest dreams, and yes, while it was only an outfit, probably to be worn only once it was still . . .

Traylu interrupting her thoughts said, "Well female go try it on so we can make the necessary adjustments. You know your day is fast approaching and we must make sure you are prepared."

Giggling, and filled with an overwhelming joy, she with the help of her friends, undressed and put on this mating outfit. Then she noticed lying on the bed was another outfit. This one was small and made of something thin and light. It was almost transparent, but at the same time wasn't. "What's this? Does it go under the mating outfit?"

Smiling a knowing smile, the two female friends looked at each other, and then Traylu said, "No, no that's your outfit for the third part of the ceremony."

"That! Why it wouldn't cover anything! You expect me to wear that?"

"Yes, and believe it or not it covers everything of importance and it enhances who you are physically. It leaves the male intrigued and very interested", Sooma said.

"Yeah I bet. I can't see me in this thing, I mean . . . oh boy, must I?"

"Yeah, I know we are all private with our bodies. But that will be changing now. Yes, you will still be private but not nearly on the level you are used to. Now, or soon you will be sharing who you are with another who will be doing the same. It is a whole new experience – at once embarrassing, and still at the same time wonderful. You know, as females, we are painfully aware of our bodies' faults and try to hide them", Traylu said. "Then all of a sudden you are revealing them in ways you never imagined,"

"And you will try this on also. So we can see what we need to do to it so it can better do its job," Sooma continued.

Still looking at that almost nothing outfit she just couldn't see herself dressed in it. She really did have her doubts. Then looking up at her friends, she asked, "Did you both wear something like this for the third part of the ceremony?"

Both enthusiastically nodded their heads in the positive. Then Sooma said, "Yeah we both had the same reaction that you did. You wouldn't catch us dead in something like that let alone alive. But all I can say is that once you have it on, it seems to bring a change. It makes you feel, how can I say this, it makes you feel very different than you ever have.

And you find it is something that you will want to wear again."

"Really? I mean that thing just doesn't provide one any innocence at all."

"I can see how you could make that conclusion, but you haven't tried it on yet to see how this works. Anyway we'll look at that a little later. Now come over to the reflection glass and then we will make adjustments."

Lauma walked over to the reflection glass realizing that it was full length. Something like that must have cost a fortune. Looking into the glass she saw a stranger. It just couldn't be her. Suddenly she saw some of her mother there in that image and it surprised her. The outfit was beautiful and what she saw there was a beautiful young female. Her friends worked a bit on her hair piling it high on top revealing a beautiful neck that was highlighted by the outfit. Her friends continued to fuss and adjust and make the necessary modifications to the outfit. Then Sooma stepped out saying that it was getting late and she had to prepare food for the evening meal, and Traylu, realizing the same thing, quickly left to do the same in her shelter. Sooma, yelling from the food prep area told her to go ahead and get back into her normal outfit, and that she would be staying in the guest space tonight. Traylu would be returning and they would continue with what they had started.

Once changed back into her normal clothes Lauma came out to assist her friend but instead Sooma told her to move everything to the guest space, and once that was accomplished then she could help with the meal. So she picked up the mating outfit carefully. She had never owned anything so beautiful in her life, and to find that her future mate had been responsible almost left her breathless. Smiling to herself and shaking her head she thought, *Fauul sure thinks of everything, and even is willing to surprise me.* He sure kept this away from her, and left her with no hint of what had awaited her.

After carefully placing this outfit in the guest space she went back and collected that other outfit. This one she definitely was unsure of. To wear something like this was beyond her. After all she hadn't revealed this much of her body to a male since she was three turns old and she would share a bath with her brother. It wasn't long after that these shared baths ended. She seemed to remember that somewhere between three and four turns old that she went from running around without clothes to where she was embarrassed if her mother entered her sleeping area and she didn't have a top on.

Now, and just like that, it was supposed to change. Still, she knew that it was something that happened to most, and she thought that her feelings probably weren't much different than other females out there. Although, she had to admit, handling this small outfit that it had a wonderful almost sensual feel to it. It seemed almost to beg for her to put it on – seemed like it would feel really nice against the skin. Well, it would have to wait; there was work to do before as she and her friends continued the preparation.

She then left the guest space and assisted her friend in preparing the evening meal. Before Sooma's mate arrived Lauma had some questions she hoped to get some answers for. "So, now that you have been mated for the last three turns how is it living with a male? I mean I live with my brother, but that's not quite the same thing."

Sooma looking over at Lauma said, "Hmmm, let me see. Well it's definitely different. We see things differently. I don't know if it's because of our differences or because our backgrounds are different."

"I don't quite understand what you mean."

"Well, males are just out there. I mean most of the time you generally know what and where they are. I mean that generally they are easy to read and know their moods and thoughts, and sometimes I expect things and it doesn't happen. So at those times I don't know whether to blame him or myself. They are not as good at reading us as we are reading them. They just don't seem to be able to communicate as well as we do among other females. I am sure that when they are around other males they have little problem with that, but it seems harder for them when they deal with us."

"So does that mean you don't talk a lot, or that there are many misunderstandings?"

"I think, in the beginning, when you first start living together, and because your sires raised you differently, that there is a great chance for misunderstandings. Still, I think that both of you are trying hard in these first stressful times to learn, and I mean really learn about each other. I think that during the time of pursuit and such, you think that you really know the person, but you find that you have really only scratched the surface. Each of you, during the time of pursuit, is on your best behavior, and is really drawn stronger to the other. At this time, you are not living with the other, and because of this, you do not see them when they are sick or tired or unhappy, or even angry.

"So you go from someone who appears to be just wonderful all the time to the reality that it's just not possible for anyone to be that way all at all. Then you learn that on that physical side that makes us so nervous in part three of the ceremony is much stronger in the males. I believe in many ways that if they had their choice that we would be involved that way every day."

"Really, every day?! I mean, I understand that it's a part of life. Without it there would be no new generation to continue on. Still it can't be that big of a driving force in them . . . I mean; well I thought that something like that would only happen, oh maybe, a couple times a cycle."

"I can understand your reluctance at this time and can actually feel for you. But I think that you will find it much different and at times enjoyable. One of the surprises for me was how different it felt every time we have been involved physically. You would think that it would be the same every time, but it's not. We'll leave it there for now. Later, when Traylu comes back on the morrow, we'll both relay our first night to you. In many ways it is just down right funny."

"Okay, if you say so."

"Oh don't let it worry you. By the time the third part of the ceremony begins the two of you will be so exhausted from the day's activities that most likely neither one of you will be able keep your eyes open. To finally get away from the joy, and frivolity, and chaos, that is happening around you, to finally get somewhere where it is quiet, and finally are able to relax and actually talk without having to yell. And to finally be away from the crowds, who are having fun at your expense, even though it not meant to be mean hearted. It is almost a joy to finally be alone there.

While one is not allowed inside one of those spaces before the ceremony, you really never know what is put in there. It's surprising how much thought goes into the setup. I cannot tell you much more than that. Since it is important for you to see it as it is and not to have one tell you. Again enough it's time to put the food on the table and eat then we will retire to the gathering space have a quiet evening, and afterwards you can go to bed and we will continue on the morrow, okay?"

"Okay, so the mercantile will be closing soon?"

"No, but Franc has someone cover while he comes in to eat. He will remain here a little while and go back and finish the work there and finally comes back to the shelter for the evening. It is tough to keep a shop open in such a small village, but we manage. Of course, as you know, I help there as much as I can."

"Part of the sharing, huh?"

"Yes, in all things, and I mean in all things."

It surprised Lauma, but the rest of the evening went rather quickly. She found that she did like Sooma's choice of a mate. Franc, overall, was friendly and outgoing and seemed to treat her friend Soma with much consideration. Of course, she didn't know if this was just because she was here or that this was how he was normally. Still, she thought as she made her final trip to the necessary space before heading off the bed, that she really had learned much. She wondered if her other friend Traylu would generally agree with what Sooma had passed on to her. Of course she knew of the two friends Traylu had always been the shy one. Yet, it did not seem to be that way anymore.

This put her mind on a different track. She then wondered if Traylu's mate had anything to do with the increased confidence that she seemed to be projecting at this time. She would have to remember to ask. She had to admit that right now that she was tired. The day had been full of excitement, surprises, and emotionally she felt somewhat drained and physically tired. Even though it would be a strange bed, and a strange shelter with its own unique sounds, she thought that there would be no problem with falling to sleep.

She returned to the guest area put on her nightclothes and climbed into bed. Her last thoughts as she drifted off to sleep were about Fauul. "Fauul where are you?" She said sleepily, and quietly in almost a whisper she said, "Even though you can't hear me, Fauul I love you."

To her surprise the morning sun awoke her. She hadn't even realized that she had fallen asleep. "My, I really must have been tired", she whispered. Listening, she could hear activity in the outer spaces and realized that she was in her friend's shelter and that the two were talking softly to avoid waking her. Stretching she got up and put on her robe and came out to go to the necessary space. Seeing them at the table she said, "Good morn."

They both turned and smiled with Sooma saying, "Good morn to you too."

"Franc nodding his head said, "Yes, and how'd you sleep? I know how it is to be trying to sleep in a strange place."

"I guess like a rock. I remember lying down in the bed, thinking about Fauul, and then the sun hitting me in the eyes."

"Fauul?" Franc asked.

Sooma turning back to him said, "Oh sorry, my fault there, Fauul is her mate to be. He had to go north to tie up some business and should be on his way back by now."

"Ah I see. Well, got to be back at the mercantile shortly, and I know that soon Traylu will be here, you three enjoy the day. I know from experience, my own of course, how much planning goes into these things. Even though it is a group ceremony, and it would seem that it isn't necessary, I now know better."

"Sorry, but I really have to make that trip to the necessary space. Nature you know, and yes I'm finding out much the same thing – see you." She said as she smiled and headed off to take care of the nature call.

"You know your friend seems to really nice", Franc commented. "It is such a shame that she lost her sires. Still it doesn't seem to have affected her in a bad way."

"It did break us up for many turns", Sooma replied. "I am sure that there will always be scars that we will never see. It really cannot be any other way.

Losing one sire would have been bad enough but to lose your foundation like that has to be devastating."

"True, true, anyway, I have to leave." Getting up from the table France said, "Lauma don't let these two friends run everything. Make sure you have input in the end."

"Oh, I don't think that will be a problem Franc. If anything that loss has made her stronger and she never did have a problem speaking her mind."

"Thanks Franc, I'll keep it in mind. Hope your day is a good one." Lauma said from the necessary space. She heard chairs being pushed back and the door opening and closing, followed by the sound of dishes being cleared. She finally came out to find that Sooma had placed the morn meal for her on the table. She rarely had been waited on this way and again felt a little embarrassed by the attention. She noticed that her friend sat back down and was drinking the hot beverage.

"Well, don't let it get cold sister. Come on over and eat. We have much to talk about and to plan. Your time as a single female is just about over, and we have planned a small get together among the other females to celebrate your up and coming mating."

Again surprised, she asked, "Get together, really? Is this something that is a normal part of leaving single life?"

"Yes, and I suspect it will be the same for Fauul. But since he isn't in familiar territory it may not happen. Still I wouldn't be surprised if your brother has planned such a thing for him. I suspect, knowing your brother, that he will just spring it on him after he returns. So you may have to do without Fauul for at least a day." Seeing the frown on Lauma's face, Sooma laughed. "Now I know he has been away for a while, but one more day isn't going to change things. Besides, after the ceremony, you will probably see way too much of him anyway."

"What do you mean by that? Was I that obvious?"

Well, to your first question. You will be living with him, and he with you, and no, I wasn't necessarily speaking of him without clothes . . . and to your second one, yes you were that obvious."

Looking down all she could say was, "Oh . . ."

Laughing again at Lauma's reaction, Sooma continued. "Today we will be going down to the eatery and meet many of the village females; this will be around the zenith meal time. We will spend a couple of hours there and then come back here and finish up. We have to finish that outfit before we go out to your celebration, and then come back and deal with any of finalities that may arise. I do wish we had another day, but we have to deal with what we have and make it work."

"Boy you sure have this planned out. I really had no idea. I mean I appreciate the get-together, but I really never had much contact with the females here. You know, the property kept me much too busy to even find time to be social, other than at the gathers. And even there I was desperate to sell the needlework and sewing products so between that and the beasts we could continue to survive."

"And don't we know it. You have been on all of our thoughts. We just didn't know what we could do to assist. So anything that was done was done quietly. Then you found your mate, and now allow the village females, who have respected you, to celebrate with you. It is only right. We have to keep the sisterhood alive. We are our only real support. Yes, the males do much, but they really can never understand us as other females understand us. We are your support. Don't expect everything to go perfectly after you're mated. There will be problems you just don't expect and we are here for you to look for answers or just support.

"It's not that the males in your life don't care or don't love you, because they do. But there is enough difference between us to create problems, and situations that neither sex expects. So while discussing it with your mate is critical, and very important, sometimes it takes someone who has already lived it, to allow you to see it in a different way, and from a different point of view. This, many times, can open your eyes to a solution. Oh by the way, you will also be receiving small gifts today. It is also part of this new direction. So please accept them in the spirit given. Mostly they are given with the idea of a new shelter being set up. You know things that you probably always use but never think about, but if you did not have them you would be lost."

It was overwhelming; all this was new to her. She had never even realized that the community had respected her and was just waiting until they could assist. Who would have ever thought it? Then to be allowed into this network of females, again something she really never knew existed. With everything that was leading up to now, and the property taking all of her time, there had been no time for anything else. She rarely had the opportunity to stay in the village let alone talk with anyone other than on business. Emotionally she was full and almost overflowing. Never in her life had she had so much attention placed directly on her. Was she even worth it? Well, personally she didn't think so. Suddenly she realized that Sooma was still speaking and turned to listen.

"I can see that this seems to have overwhelmed you a bit. Am I right about that? Ah I can see it in your eyes; you don't think your worthy of any of this. Well female, buddy, get used to it because you are."

Choked up and unable to reply all Lauma could do was mod her head. She felt that if she tried to speak that she would break down and cry again. This was such a new concept, a new direction, one she never knew existed. She just didn't know what to say, what to think, how to act or react. She was totally confused by what was being revealed to her right now.

Again Sooma seeing the emotions running across Lauma's face got up and came around to her and hugged her. "I can tell this is something else that was completely unexpected. Did you think we would let you enter this new world without help?"

About this time there was a knock at the door and Sooma said, "Ah that must be Traylu. Now just sit here and soak in everything I've said, finish your meal, and then over some hot beverage we will continue, all three of us." She moved over to the door and opened it and Traylu entered. Both of them talking among themselves and then Traylu seeing Lauma at the table said, "Good morn, and how goes it for you right now?"

Sooma turned to Traylu and said, "Oh she isn't speaking right now."

"Not speaking right now? Did you make her mad or something?"

Smiling Sooma said, "No, I just overwhelmed her with some of the facts of sisterhood and she's just too choked up to speak, isn't that right Lauma?"

Again all Lauma could do was nod in the affirmative. She knew it would be a few minutes before she would get enough control on her emotions to be able to say anything.

"See I told you. Anyway just get a cup and come sit. We can just talk for a while before we go finish the outfit. I am sure once she can speak again that she has some rather personal questions she would like answered. Especially about that third part of the ceremony that always scares us to death."

Traylu, thinking about that portion of the ceremony, started laughing and turned to Sooma saying, "Yeah that sure was the way it was for me. I know I have talked with other females and it was the same for them. I wonder why it is so? I mean if you look at the beasts of the field or in the wild or even our dogs, you cannot but admit that you have seen them mating. It's always been a part of life on all levels. So you knew that your time would come where you would find yourself involved in the same way. Still it was a very nervous time."

"Oh I have to agree there. Anyway, let's just sit here and enjoy each other's company for a little while until she is ready to question us. Does that work for you Lauma?"

Again while her emotions were coming under control she still felt as if she would still cry if she said anything so once again she just nodded. She watched her two friends grab a cup of hot beverage and come over to the table and sit with her.

Sooma said, "Traylu why don't you fill her in. I know we aren't going to get into the nasty details of the actual physical thing here, but at least we will both explain how we felt and things like that."

Thinking a minute, Traylu went into her description of the third part of the ceremony. "Okay, first before I go there I want to talk a little about after the second part where you are attached to your new mate with that two body length tether. While it is done all in fun there is a serious side to it. Part of what it is all about is cooperation. If, when you are tied together like that, you don't work together then you run into all sorts of problems. So consciously you have to work together the rest of the day, or you end up falling, because one went one way and the other a different way. Then comes the first really embarrassing moment when nature calls. I mean, as a female, you do not like to make noises such as burping and such. Plus when we have a nature call to pass wind is natural, but again because we are who we are we try to keep such things private. It's just the way we are . . ."

Listening to what was being said, again it was something new. She saw, while it provided problems for the newly mated, it provided fun for the village. Still the serious side of it demonstrated, to the newly mated, that they would have to cooperate. Traylu continued, "Anyway, there is no way to avoid nature calls. You can try, but in the end you would just wet yourself and that would be something none of us want. So now your new mate has to literally hang outside the door of the necessary space. He cannot get far enough away to where he would be unable to hear what is happening inside. So you sit there trying your best not to pass wind or take a leak slowly so it makes no sound. Yet as the late zenith continues to pass you find that you have to go there many times, and eventually you just give up and do what you would anyway. I'm sure that my face was red a couple of times coming out of there.

"Anyway the tether cannot come off the two of you until you enter your space that night. By then we both were exhausted. Between the emotions, and anticipation, the involvement in the ceremony, the celebration afterwards, and all of the attempts to work together because of the tether, and then all the off color remarks, you're numb. There just seemed to be little time to rest, and then suddenly here I was. Alone with Gohn, and we needed to fulfill the final portion of the mating ceremony.

"For a period of time neither of us moved. It was just nice to sit there say nothing and just relax. But once we caught our breath we starting looking around this small room and seeing what was there. Now I am not telling, as again that is part of the discoveries that you are to make. No there isn't anything there that you wouldn't find somewhere else. Let's just say that because of the traditions and time of this ceremony that they have supplied it with most everything one would need, including believe it or not a portable pot that is used for the necessary space. First time I've ever seen one."

Lauma now completely involved with the story being told her said, "Okay I'm with you so far . . . continue please."

"Anyway, we decided that before we fell asleep that we should just do it. Anyway I went and changed into that outfit, you know like yours and he in something almost as revealing. Then if you had been able to hear you probably would have laughed. I mean we are supposed to be superior to the beasts, and yet something they seem to do so naturally was almost a joke. We had no instructions, not that we needed them, but there is a great distance between thinking you know, and then knowing.

"Again let's just say, the first time there, is, other than the fear and nervousness, forgettable. Then you find out some other unpleasant things, but you get through it fine. Later in your relationship, this mating becomes much better, as you learn about each other's bodies. That final act there just about finishes your depleted reserves of energy and sleep just sounds wonderful. But, again, you find that for many turns, probably since you were a whelp, you have slept alone, and now someone is there with you. So while you are very tired, that first night is very uncomfortable. It becomes another area of cooperation that one just does not think about. Then when the morn comes, both of you are still very tired. It was as if you really never slept, and it is at that point that you notice some other side effects. But you will need to find out those on your own. I am sure it is different for everyone. And that's just about it."

In her mind's eye Lauma had followed Traylu's journey through the end of the ceremony and could picture most of what had transpired. It gave her confidence. After all, Traylu who had been the shy and quiet one of the threesome could come through as she had, then Lauma felt that she probably could also. The story definitely helped on relieving some of her fears. Turning towards Sooma she waited to see what she would tell her.

Sooma then related her story. "I was much the same." She said that she had been the first of the three of them to become mated, so had no inside information. So when it had been Traylu's turn to mate she helped as they were doing for her now. It was a good thing for her nerves to hear how it went for her friends.

"Enough on this! We'll not talk any more of this unless you have other questions. We need to get to finishing that outfit. Then, when we come back from the get-together, you can try on that other outfit that seems to have you scared. Oh by the way, you will need to bring both to the gathering. The other females are always interested in the mating outfits. You'll even put on the one that you will wear in part one and part two of the ceremony. The other will just be passed around. Not many of these mated females have handled silk. A few yes, but not many."

"You mean they'll see this little outfit? Are you sure?"

"Of course, it's not like they don't know what will be happening in there. Plus many had something similar themselves. But, as always, things change over time. They like to see how things change. Don't worry about it. No one is going to say anything to embarrass you. In fact you will probably hear other stories as some of them reminisce about their mating ceremony. Here let me show you mine. Like the main outfit, I have kept it – probably more for memories than anything else." Sooma went into the master sleeping space, was gone for a short period of time, and then came out with both outfits. The main outfit was beautiful, but not quite to the quality of the one that Fauul had paid for, and the other was actually smaller than the one she had. Sooma being bigger than Lauma left Lauma wondering what it covered. "That's small!" She blurted out, suddenly embarrassed and flushed red again.

Smiling at her Sooma said, "Yeah isn't it. But you know something, I love it. Yes I was very nervous about wearing this thing but I just loved it, what can I say?"

They spent the rest of the morn finishing the outfit. Lauma kept glancing over at the other outfit. Trying to imagine what she would look like wearing it, but just couldn't come up with an image. Well, later she would be trying it on – then she'd know. Finally it was time to head out to the local eatery, and she was reminded to bring both outfits with her. The day was flying. Before she would know it the day would be done. She'd possibly spend one more night, and with the next morn her brother would meet her and they'd return. Her outfits would remain with Sooma until that day.

They ended spending almost three hours at the get-together. While again feeling nervous at being the one honored here, and really nervous about parading around in her mating outfit for the first two parts of the ceremony, she found, in the end, that she actually had fun and enjoyed it tremendously. There was much advice given and many stories told. And yes, the females who had come, just about a dozen of them, passed on many small and useful gifts. And they all loved the small outfit, many loving the feel of silk. Then before she realized it, the time was over, and she was heading back to Sooma's shelter. The gathering had filled her with energy and an overwhelming joy. She had never had time to visit and enjoy the company of so many. She had a warm feeling all over. She felt as if she had just entered a wonderful new world, and it had been one she had never known to exist.

"Wow, thank you, thank you so much! I really did not know what to expect, and they all were so wonderful. They sure had a lot of advice that's for sure, and many of their stories were really funny . . . and to think I was just thinking, when I came over yesterday, that it would only be the three of us. You really have opened my eyes."

Again smiling Sooma said, "Unfortunately, for you, because of your tragedy, there was little chance for you to find this. Life had become very difficult for you and your brother, and all consuming. Plus we knew that there was no male here locally that even held an interest to you. I mean it's not like they didn't try. But they just couldn't live up to what you needed. So when we learned of this Fauul and that you had finally found your life mate we rejoiced. Thinking that maybe finally the hardships would be lessening and maybe actually end, and finally that you would be able to join us instead of just trying to survive in a bad situation. I'm not saying your brother is a bad situation, but what you two were forced into was."

"Yes, when we saw your reaction to Fauul after he came back – you know, back at the gather, when he and your brother approached your booth. It was there at that moment we had hope that finally you had found your mate", Traylu stated. "It really was written all over your face."

"Was it that obvious? It was such a shock. I mean I finally had put him out of my mind. I figured that he was never going to come back and be a part of my life and it was time to move on, and then there he was." Her two friends smiled a knowing smile.

They entered the shelter where they sat at the table for a short period of time while they went back over the get-together and the different females that had attended. Lauma knew that she would treasure these two days for a lifetime. She just couldn't remember the last time she felt so happy and so full of confidence and joy. Even that little outfit didn't seem to scare her now. "You know what", she said, "I think I will try that thing on now."

"Oh good. Then you can come out here and let us see okay?"

Lauma nodded as she headed into the guest space.

Sooma said to Traylu quietly, "It will take a little time. I'm sure she'll be tentative at first, probably look at herself in the full-length looking glass, and then carefully come out. I'm sure it was the same for you when you first got into yours. I know it was for me. After all, it's such a different way for us to look at ourselves. Think about it, with these we become the temptresses, the ones that are out to seduce our males. And we are taught, all our lives, not to be that way. It is something that is difficult to overcome. Besides, we females don't like to show off our bare skin anyway, or at least not in that way."

"Yeah, isn't that true. We always seem to want to hide what we think is our bad parts from our mates, as if they care. It's just our lack of confidence in our bodies that makes us do that. I know that Gohn has told me many, many times that he became my mate for what and who I am, flaws and all, and he could care less about them. I know it's true but I find myself still doing it. I'm sure it frustrates him, but he doesn't say anything."

She heard her friends talking out in the eating area but couldn't understand anything they were saying. Right now she stood by the bed looking down at that outfit still not sure about it. It was a two piece outfit – the bottom piece to cover her privates, and the top that draped over her shoulders and came down to just below her buttocks. "Well what can it hurt?" She asked quietly. She undressed completely and put on the bottoms. She had never felt anything like them. They were soft, they were warm, and some of the most comfortable unmentionables she had ever worn. They had a silkiness that she had never felt before. She followed this by slipping on the top and saw that indeed it covered just past her butt, and the material again was soft and warm and very comfortable.

Standing in front of the looking glass she saw a different picture of herself again. One of the first things she noticed about the outfit was how it hid everything important to her, but at the same time suggested it was there. She suddenly smiled in self-conscious way. It was almost freeing. She suddenly found herself imagining Fauul's reaction to this and was pleased with what she saw. *I'll definitely have to be careful in something like this. I just can't sit down or turn quickly . . . might show too much.*

She now had enough nerve to come out of the space and show her two friends. She came out of the doorway somewhat tentatively, stood there and asked, "What do you think?"

They both clapped their hands and Sooma said, "Now that looks like it was made just for you. It's perfect!"

"I agree, I think your Fauul is in for a real surprise, and I know it will be one he will love."

Smiling at her friends she did a little curtsy, and paraded a little, feeling really sexy. Then the door opened and in walked Franc. Seeing him she gave a little scream, panicked, and ran back into the guest space – this was the last thing she expected.

Franc asked, "What the heck was that? Who screamed, did I miss something."

Both Sooma and Traylu were laughing too hard to be able to answer. While Franc's appearance was completely unexpected, Lauma's reaction was classic.

Finally catching her breath, she said, "No Franc not really. Lauma was just showing us one of her mating outfits and you were the last one she expected. It was just a natural reaction on her part."

"Oh." He said, then yelling a little he said, "Sorry about that Lauma. I really didn't see anything at all."

Thankful for that she quickly undressed from the outfit and got back into her regular clothes and came back out. "I guess I need to apologize to you to Franc. It's just you surprised me and it was the last thing I was expecting."

"Apology accepted. I know normally I'm not home at this time, but wanted to let Sooma know that I would be working a little later tonight and to delay the evening meal. I had one of the outlying properties come in with a large order that I have to fill before I finish."

"So how late will you be?"

"Don't know really. Only have about half the order put together right now. I have to finish it tonight as they will pick it up in the morn when I first open."

"Okay, I'll come over every once in the while and see how you are progressing. Then I'll know when to have the meal ready. I have Lauma here to help so it won't take very long."

"Okay then, I'm heading back, and once again Lauma, sorry about the intrusion."

"Oh it's okay, after all this is your shelter not mine. I am only a guest here."

"True but a close friend of my mate, and as such . . . always welcome here."

"Thank you and I guess I will see you at the evening meal. On the morrow I will be leaving. Still have much to catch up on back at the property."

"Looking forward to meeting the male who captured your heart – must be someone special."

"Oh he is, very special, and I really love him", Lauma exclaimed.

Franc returned to the mercantile and once again, this time, all three of them laughed, which helped, melt the tension and shock that had built up in Lauma. She said, "That was a surprise. Here I was parading this thing like a temptress, and your mate shows up – scared that feeling right out of me."

"Yeah I must admit it looked like you were having fun there for a moment, and then you should have seen the look on your face when Franc walked in. That's exactly why we couldn't stop laughing."

The final evening went by rapidly and before she knew it she was back in bed and preparing for her return trip. The last thing the two reminded her of was that on their mating day they, she and Fauul, would not be allowed to see each other until the actual ceremony began. It was a tradition that went back to the dawn of time. No one knew why this was observed; still it seemed appropriate and had remained. Again, before drifting off to sleep, she wondered how Fauul was making out. Had he been successful in his plans, or were there to be changes? Of course this was all idle speculation . . . because until he returned she would have no answers to any of these questions.

As she looked back over this day, much had happened, and she found that in some ways, she had already changed. Although she thought that part of her would always be that little whelp female looking in awe at the many things that happened in the adult world. She knew that soon she would be making passage into another part of that world, and while a little tentative about it; she really was looking forward to it. This was her last waking thought, since before she knew it the morn had broken once again.

The last two days had been exhausting, but she wouldn't have traded them for anything. She found out many things about her life friends, and also about the other females in the village. She had met many of them and had become a member of the sisterhood. This, an unofficial support system that the females had and the only requirement for entry was being female. No, it was not some official group that one signed up for or paid dues into, but just females supporting females.

Finally, she found that she could be brave enough to wear the outfit needed for the third part of the ceremony. When she had first laid eyes on it she had thought. *No way.* But with the encouragement of her friends she had tried it on and found that it was freeing. So many other thoughts about the two days entered her mind, and she wondered, if indeed, it had been just two days. But they were gone now and it was back to reality and the daily work to keep the property operating.

Still her day was approaching rapidly and once again, all would change and change forever. Once this step was taken there would be no turning back. Even who she was would be different. That young innocent female would be no more, and she would have become another knowing one, with the promise of being a mother in the future.

CHAPTER TWELVE

On the day Fauul left it was the morn and he had gotten the earlier of two water-craft trips heading down to the port where he would disembark. Overall it had been a successful trip, one that he was thankful that would be ending soon. He found that as he expected, he seriously missed Lauma and could not wait to see her again. Again, he was thankful that his family was able to convince his mother to remain there. That turned out to be the most difficult part of his trip. Then, to his surprise, a number of his old friends from both his work area and the ones he had grown up with, kidnapped him and threw him a leaving the world of the singles party. It had been at one of the local drinking holes, and they had an evening of frivolity and drinking. He endured the many rude remarks about leaving his friends behind and the suggested comments about his upcoming mating. All in all, it was done in fun, and nothing was to be taken as mean hearted. He personally could remember planning a couple of these for some of his friends who had crossed the line. *Yes,* he thought, *these will be good memories for the future.*

Back in that remote village, wanting to help the local merchants, Fauul had left marks to cover the mating outfits for Lauma and himself. He would be picking up his when he returned. He knew by tradition that he would not see the ones for her until the ceremony. So he hoped that her friends had chosen well. He also knew that at the beginning of the major gather that all who were to be mated on the last day would have to report to the elder to get their directions as to where to meet on the last day and how they were to approach the ceremony. That would be the only practice they would get.

Funny . . . He thought, *now, at this very moment in time, this seems to be the thing that occupies my mind more than anything else.* Still he knew why, but also realized that probably it was not a good thing at this point. It could lead one to be careless, and there still were too many trails to travel, and he needed to be alert. Again he hoped to tie in with a group heading south providing less of a target for the bandits.

The trip down took a few days by water-craft so there was much time to think about everything that was happening in his life. Still, most of the time he just stayed on the deck staring out at the waves the water-craft made. Eventually pulling into port close towards late morn on that second day, and happy to have this portion completed, he left the water-craft and stood for a short time getting his land legs back.

Doube had made good time, and from the correspondence that Jllon had given him, he knew that the new team would arrive on the second water-craft. He had just seen the first arrive, and he had confirmed it with the dock master that it was the first. This meant he would have a few hours before their arrival. It would give him time to catch his breath and relax a little.

Idly leaning against a shelter and watching the people disembark, he took a double take. He thought he recognized someone coming off of that one. *No*, he thought, *can't be just probably someone who looks like someone I know*. He kept an eye on the individual who had stopped and appeared to be getting used to being on land again. The more he looked at him the more he was sure he knew the person. So walking over in his direction he wanted to make sure his eyes were not deceiving him.

Still, as normally happens, a crowd came between him and the individual of interest, and when it cleared that individual was no longer there. "Isn't that the way of it", Doube said to himself. He turned to go back to the shelter where he was standing and ran straight into the individual of interest. "Fauul! It is you! Wasn't sure, and this was the last place I thought I would find you."

"Yeah, Doube it's me. When you started walking towards me I could tell it was you just from the way you walk. So I headed in your direction only to be blocked by that same crowd, I worked my way around and came in from the back. I could tell that you had lost sight of me and when you turned around we kind of sort of met."

"What the heck are you doing here anyway? I figured you would still be down south there with that brother and sister. I kind of guessed you were sweet on her."

"I know it was that obvious to everyone but us. So what have you been up to lately? I mean I really didn't think you would be here in this area either."

"I'm working for Jllon right now. Here to meet a team that he needs. Then take them back with me to where he is."

"Jllon? Don't recognize the name – someone important?"

"Yeah you could say that. He's the Head Keeper of the Past."

"Him? He wanted to talk with me, but we keep missing each other. I thought I would have run into him back in the township but he wasn't there. So I just gave up, figuring he would have to find me."

"I could take you to him now if you would like. After all that's where I am heading on the morrow."

"Thanks, but no thanks for now. Just don't have the time. The major gather is just about here and I have to be back there for it. You see that female I was sweet on when we were there is to become my mate. So if he wants to see me it will have to be after we get back."

"So you two are becoming mates, I guess congratulations are in order then . . . ah, back from where?"

"Thanks, and after the ceremony we will be heading back to the township for half a cycle. You know, a chance for us to be with each other, and a chance for her to meet my family."

"Ah, makes sense. So I know in the near future he will still want to talk with you. Soon he and his team, myself included, will be at that village anyway. Hopefully you will be back by then and you can talk with him at that time."

"Works for me, anyway got to find a group that's heading in my direction. Prefer not to go down the trail alone."

Understandable, I think I saw a group forming back at the mercantile. Guess I'll see you around, and once again, congrats on your up and coming mating."

"Thanks, and I look forward to seeing you down there. Love to catch up on what has been happening since we parted ways."

Yeah, me too."

Fauul left and headed for the mercantile and Doube went back and leaned against the shelter waiting for the arrival of the new team. Fauul saw, as he approached the mercantile, what Doube had been speaking of. There appeared to be a group forming there. He knew it was a common place for this to happen here at this port. When the person who owned the mercantile had looked for a location he had picked this one. Not far from the docks, and not far from the major trails leading out of the port, with plenty of room to grow. It was almost a perfect place to setup. Over time he added an eatery and a drinking hole, and from the looks of it probably a place for one to spend the night other than the hostel, which wasn't very close.

When he contacted the first group he was disappointed, as they would be heading east inland, and then generally north. So he continued to look and found a small group heading in his direction. They were a lead group heading down ahead of the up-and-coming major gather and were to scout it out to see if the ones they represented wanted to put it on their circuit of places they visited.

As Fauul knew, the location of the village was remote and there was little to attract major interests at this time, so he held out little hope that once the area was surveyed by this group that the village would become a regular stop. Once he made contact he found that he was welcomed with them, and as fate would have it they were leaving shortly so he would not have to spend the night at the hostel.

A few days later he bid farewell to the group and headed over to the mercantile in the village. He had a few questions he wanted to ask Sooma, and then pick up the supplies that he had ordered before he left. Secretly he had put together a list of major needs for the property, and he would need to set up with them supplies for the mapping section he would be adding to the village. At this time his plan was to use the property as a base of operations. The property had the shelters for this, and since it had been built to house a much larger operation there would be plenty of available space.

Again he knew that bringing this to the village would help its economy since there were not many things close to it to help. He hoped that as he worked the mapping that other things would begin to show up that would provide an increase of marks to help them out – only time would tell. Other than being in this village, mapping the major trails into it, and then hiking the property, he knew very little as of yet. He had been told that there were a few other settlements further south, but these were extremely small, making the village he was in look like a township.

He entered the establishment and said, "Hi Franc, is your mate around? I just want to see how it went with Lauma when she came in and spent those two days here."

"So you must be Fauul. My guess is that it went well. From my point of view she was almost glowing when she left here to head back to the property, but if you wait a minute I'll get Sooma and she can fill you in on what she will allow you to know."

"Great, I know that she will only tell me in general terms because of tradition, but even that will be more than I know now. Anyway after you get her go ahead and fill that order I left here with Sooma before I went up to the township. Then I have another order to leave with you that will become a continual one."

"Really? Something for the property, or something else?"

"Something else, but first let me talk with your mate, and then after she has gone back to what she is doing I'll cover this new list with you."

"Okay . . . be right back." Franc left and was gone maybe five minutes when he returned with is his mate. Pointing out Fauul, he directed her to him.

"Fauul! It's wonderful to see you again. I know that Lauma will be mad when she learns that I get to see you before she does. So what is it that I can help you with, as if I didn't know."

Briefly at a loss for words Fauul finally asked, "Ah, so how'd it go? Now I know you cannot tell me much . . . tradition and such, still it's such a big and important day that is coming, well you know what I mean."

Smiling at his apparent fumbling of words she said, "Oh it went well. In fact, very well. We really wished we had another day, but such things are out of our hands really. You really did surprise her. I knew that you had told me that she would know nothing about it, but I had figured she would have guessed. So how are you doing anyway?"

"As you can guess, I want to get back there and see her again. Everything to the north went very well and my old friends threw me a leaving single get-together. They had their fun and I guess so did I. I figured that Lauut would think about doing the same thing for me down here, but I know that it is something he or they cannot afford. So hopefully he does nothing."

"You know those outfits that I chose, since you are not allowed to see them until the ceremony, were not cheap. How are you holding up financially? Not that it's any of my business, but these costs do mount up."

"Believe me I'm fine on that end. While not rich by any means, I ended up with quite a bit of marks from the mapping project I was on. It was at least a turn long, and all my earnings just accumulated over that time, since all the costs incurred during the project were paid for."

"Glad to hear that. I'd hate to have a friend like her end up not being able to do much because you both ended up hurting financially. It can be devastating on a relationship. Not that she has seen much financially during her lifetime. She has worked hard for what she and her brother have, but they have come close, a number of times, to failure."

"So, I guess what I'm asking, is do you want her back for another day or two? You suggested it, and with me returning I can cover. As you know the time is rapidly approaching, and I want her to feel as comfortable as she can."

"No, not really necessary. You know on the morn of that day, you two will see each other for the last time until the ceremony. It will be then that the one who performs the actual ceremony will walk all of you, and remember there are two other couples involved, through exactly what you are to do. Then you will not be allowed to see her and she you. The males will keep you isolated and the females will keep her the same. Then, of course, when it is time you will approach and see her for the first time in the ceremony outfit. I do believe, like her, you will really be surprised for what it has done for her."

"You know it really doesn't matter, she is who I am interested in anyway, not the clothes she wears . . . wait that didn't come out right!"

Laughing she said, "Oh you males! Sure it's exactly what you meant."

"Now that's not true . . . well partially true, but still I simply meant that it is she, and whatever she would be wearing would not change anything."

"We will see about that. Just remember that the next morn and then come back and tell me the same thing. I'm curious to know."

"Yeah, I bet. Still if there is to be an answer about that I'll let Lauma tell you. She will probably know anyway."

"Oh I have no doubt about that. After all the three of us, Lauma, myself and Traylu have been lifelong friends and we keep very little from each other."

"Oh joy, that's comforting to know."

Laughing again, she continued, "Now don't take that in a negative way. Not everything is said or told even among us."

"I'm glad to hear that. Anyway thanks for the update, and I'll be sure to pass on to her that you are thinking of her. Now I have to discuss some additional business with your mate Franc, and I'll let you get back to whatever you were doing."

"Believe it or not, I was working a little on your mating ceremony. After all I am involved a little. Lauut asked my help since both of their sires are not present for the ceremony. Anyway see you later . . . I'm sure that I will, and good luck." With that she turned and left leaving him standing there thinking over what she had just told him, and he thought what a great friend Lauma has. And he had to admit to himself that while at first he thought she was a little pushy, that once he got to know her better he really liked her.

Turning back to Franc he said, "Okay now here's the other list." He went into an explanation of what was to transpire and how often he would need it re-supplied and where and who to bill. Plus he gave hints as to where he could order the necessary materials since it was something Franc would not normally carry. "I'll be back shortly for the first list, the one for the property. I'm going over to see Aurto and see if he will rent me pack beast so I can get this order over to the property. Then with Lauut's help get it returned quickly."

"Okay Fauul, this should take about an hour to put together. Should just be enough time for you to get the beast, get something to eat, and still be out of here in time to get back to the property . . . and thanks, not just for me, but for them. We've always been pulling for them, but could only cheer them on, since we are not a rich community. They've always have had it tough, and to actually see a possible change in the right direction makes the whole village feel good. Plus what you are adding here will be of great help."

A little embarrassed by the praise Fauul said, "It's nothing really. Both of them are great people. They haven't allowed the difficult times to destroy them, and of course your village supporting them helped. Anyway thanks, I'll see you then in about an hour."

He turned and left. Deciding to eat first, followed by heading over to the yards. It had been a long time since he and Doube had spent a brief time there, sitting on Aurto's porch and drinking ale – a lifetime ago really.

It was close to dark when he arrived back at the property. Overall it had been a long time consuming trip, from here to the township and back again. Still he felt good about it. Much had been accomplished and he had come back in time for the up and coming ceremony. He knew that in truth, while it had been in the back of his mind, that with all he was involved with, there really had been little time to really think about it. As he entered the yard he heard the dogs start to bark and knew that shortly the two of them would be out to investigate why the dogs were barking.

Sure enough no sooner had he thought it and they both were standing on the porch. He heard Lauma yell, "Fauul!! You're back!" She came running across the yard to fall into his arms. "I have missed you so much. And yes while the time has passed quickly, at the same time, it just seemed to drag. I can't explain it but now you're back!"

He could see a great smile on her face and he thought he had caught a sign of tears also. "Are you crying?" he asked.

"Oh, Fauul don't worry about it. I am just very happy to see you and what you see is joy not sadness.

Something you'll just have to get used to when you start being around females. Unlike you males we show our emotion. What are we standing here for? Let's go back inside I want to hear about your trip and if everything was successful. And of course I just want to be with you anyway."

"Whoa a minute here . . . I have to finish, and with the help of you two, unload the supplies I am bringing back. I really don't think this pack beast would appreciate having the supplies strapped to his back all night."

"Supplies . . . pack beast? Oh yeah, sorry, I only saw you." Turning she saw that her brother was standing there grinning. "Now what's that all about?" She asked.

"You never greeted me that way, and I'm your brother," he said with mock sadness. Turning to Fauul he said, "So what did you bring us? That looks like a pretty good load on this beast. Did you pack it or did you get some help?"

"Now what's that supposed to mean?" Fauul asked, "Of course I packed it. I might not be as good as you are but I can at least do that. So are you two just going to stand around talking or are you going to help unload this and then help me put this beast in with the rest?"

"Oh, sorry," they responded together.

With the three of them working together it wasn't long before they had the supplies unloaded and put away and the beast placed inside the pens. "It has been a long day, and with the travel and such I have to admit that I'm tired." Fauul said

"Now if you think you are just going to sneak away and not fill us in on what has been happening then you are dreaming – even if it is just a short version tonight, with the details coming on the morrow that would be fine." Lauut responded. "Besides Lauma has been nervous for the last couple of days wondering what you were doing and when you would be arriving. After all it isn't that long until the major gather. Isn't that right sis?"

Trying to look exasperated, she said, "Lauut now come on, you really didn't need to tell him that, I mean really." Then turning to Fauul she said, "Yes, I have been worrying a little . . ."

Lauut interrupted and said, "A little she says . . ."

Stamping her foot she turned again to her brother and said, "Would quit interrupting me, I am trying to explain myself here."

Smiling at her he said, "Go ahead, this should be interesting."

Listening to the two of them bicker back and forth he couldn't help but smile. He could tell that Lauut was having fun teasing his sister, while she was trying to have nothing to do with it. "Okay you two, you can joke and tease all you want, but I would like something to drink, and would like to sit down for a little while before I retire."

"Oh, sorry – just couldn't help it. She left herself open and I couldn't resist. I mean you haven't had to live with her while you have been gone. I can at least tell you, from my own time here with her, that if you were to back out now, she probably would kill you – if not with some weapon, then with the glare that you would be getting from her."

"Has it really been that bad with me gone?"

"You really have no idea. But I'm sure if you ask her she will deny all of it . . . to be honest she has been lost in thinking about you, and I could really see how much she missed you. So I guess I have to say that it has finally happened. I thought so before, but now I know for sure. She has found her mate."

Humbled a little by her brother's statement she said, "I guess I cannot deny it. You have been with me every day even though you were not here. I would, every morn, look for you coming across the yard and then realize that you were not coming. Still, each day I would continue it, just like I could will you here. Anyway we are dominating the conversation here. Tell us what happened. And while you are doing that I'll get us a snack and something to drink."

For the next hour Fauul talked about his time away including the get-together his friends had thrown for him, and the success in getting the department to open a branch down here with him in charge, Plus his brief conversation with Sooma. When he had mentioned he had talked with Sooma he saw Lauma blush a little, and since Sooma had only told him things in general terms he didn't quite know why she had blushed. Anyway, he continued his story up to arriving here. Taking a deep breath he said, "I don't know what I said to make you blush, but let me say that when I talked with your friend she really only said that your two days went well, and that she had wished there had been more time. I said if you needed it, the additional time, with me back I could cover. She said, not necessary, and then filled me in on the day of the ceremony, and that was all."

"So she didn't tell you about anything that happened during those two days?" She asked.

"No, she said that was between the three of you. You know yourself, Sooma, and Traylu. And with your friend there, I knew that was all I would get – which is fine really. I just wanted to make sure that all had been well and everything that needed to be done for you were completed. She assured me that everything was fine and ready."

Smiling she said, "Well, I am glad of that. Sometime after we are mates I'll fill you in on those two days. All I can say right now is they just flew by."

"Well, I am glad to be back, and I for one, am ready to go get some sleep. So I will head on out, and leave you two and see you in the morn." With that he got up went over to Lauma gave her a hug, kissed her deeply and then said, "You know I have missed this."

She replied somewhat breathlessly, "Yeah, me too."

He turned and left to go to workers shelter as he was very tired, happy to see Lauma again, and was quite happy the journey was complete.

CHAPTER THIRTEEN

Doube watched Fauul as he headed for the mercantile area and thought. *You never know when that special someone will show up. When we went there it was only to try and get some additional pack beasts, and it ends up for him that he finds his mate.* Smiling while shaking his head he turned back around and watched for the next arrival. He knew that the additional team was to be on this one.

After a short period of time he talked with the dock master and found that it probably would be just after the zenith before the other water-craft arrived. He decided that he would go get something to eat instead of just standing and people watch. It would be the last chance for such a meal until they arrived at the village. If he remembered correctly they called it Rancho. No one really had any idea what it meant but when the sign was discovered there had been other words on it but this one was the only readable one. So the village thinking it probably was the name of their village originally, had adopted the name.

Whoever owned the mercantile by the docks had been smart and had continued to expand. So for any disembarking they could find just about anything they needed. It included an eatery and that's where Doube headed. He had a quiet meal in the corner and just people watched as the time progressed. He saw a young couple with their whelp, who could barely walk, talking about their domestic life, and their hopes. It always seemed to be this way. He knew he could go to almost any place and find close to the same conversation going on.

We seem to think that we are so unique, he thought, *but after a while you find someone else has already done what you have done – and those thoughts and dreams appear to repeat also.* And here he was seeing it repeated again. He wondered if there was someone out there studying this phenomenon, but, he had to admit, it was just idle speculation. Before he knew it the time had come to head back to the docks and see if the water-craft had come in. And as luck would have it, the water-craft was just pulling up to the dock as he approached. Again he leaned against the shelter. From here he had an excellent view of all that left the craft.

This time there were many more passengers and it took much longer for everyone to leave, and come ashore. A couple of times he thought he had his group identified, but these broke up and became too small to be them. Wondering now, whether they had actually made the trip he started heading for the dock to try and catch the captain to see it this team had actually boarded. But as he approached a final group left the craft, and he knew immediately that this had to be the group. Approaching the one who he thought might be the leader he asked, "Are you George Diamond?"

"No, I'm Han Smit, George is over there. And you are?"

"Sorry, I'm Doube Mickles, the one who will be taking you and the team out to the site where you will be working."

Turning and then yelling over the noise Han said, "Hey George here's our guide!"

"What? Can't hear you, one moment I'll be right there." Coming over to join them George continued, "Sorry it's just too noisy, I could only understand my name. What was it that you needed?"

"George this is Doube Mickles, he said he is the one who will take us to our work site."

"Yes, that was the one we were to find, and here it is that he has found us." Then turning to Doube he said, "Anyway I'm George Diamond. We have to wait for a short time while our supplies are unloaded."

"I hope it's not much more than you can carry," Doube replied. "I've no pack beasts here with me and to get one here would be much too expensive."

"No, no it's just what we can carry. We were under the impression that there would be pack beasts at the site and that regular supply trips were being made. So we were to pack accordingly."

"That information is correct. So how long before you and your team will be ready to travel? I want to get down the trail as soon as we can. I'm assuming that you have eaten on the trip down, and that you have enough food in your packs for about seven days."

"That is what we were told to have when we got here."

"Good, I have learned when you deal with too many different people who are in charge, that sometimes the requirements get changed, and what is really needed, ends up not showing up at all. Anyway, I was prepared either way. While it would have been expensive to purchase what we would need here, I have checked it out to make sure it was available. I think we are blocking progress here, let's go over there out of the way. It will be less chaotic and I think a less noisy so we won't have to shout over anything to be heard."

"Sounds like a great idea to me." Turning around George signaled to his team to follow him. He said to Han, "Why don't you hang here and watch for our stuff, and when it's unloaded signal us and we'll come and get it."

"Okay boss, shouldn't be much longer."

They headed over by the shelter where Doube had been watching. George asked, "So where is this site we are going to, and why all the secrecy?"

"All I can tell you right now is that it's in the outback – kind of really isolated. As we get close I can fill you in on the rest. Oh yeah, here's the letter of introduction to show that I am the one you are to meet, and you are to have the same for me. So show me yours and then we will have the formalities out of the way."

Digging into one of his pockets George found and handed his letter of introduction to Doube who passed his to George. Doube said, "Yup looks about right to me. Oh look, it looks like Han is signaling to you. Your stuff must have been unloaded, shall we?" They headed back collected the items and immediately left the port area. Doube wanted to put some distance from the port before evening and push the new team while they were fresh. He had a destination in mind that would be safe, but with a start later than he liked, it might be dark by the time they reached it.

Six days later and ahead of schedule they entered the abandoned village, and stopped briefly so that the new team could see it. Doube stated, "This was one of the places we visited both as a learning exercise for the learners on the team and to understand what had caused it to fail."

"And what was the conclusion on the reason it failed?" George asked

"The water source dried up. But it was a slow process. If you study this area a little you can see that this village was abandoned slowly."

"So how far are we from our destination, and can you now reveal why the secrecy?"

"I can, but I'll give you a choice here. We are not far from the main camp now, and will be there before dark. Jllon, you know the Head Keeper of the Past, is down there and he can give you a complete explanation or I can give you a brief one here as we take this break."

They talked among themselves for a couple of minutes then George said, "Tell you what, how 'bout just giving us an idea, and then Jllon can give us the details. Is that fair?"

"Sure, and I think you probably deserve it, since you will be here quite a while anyway. I'm sure, why so far out here and what, would be so important anyway. Simply stated, we have found evidence of the *ones before.*"

"The *ones before*", George exclaimed. "You're kidding right? I mean they're just a myth, not real . . . just something to scare the whelps."

"No, they were quite real, and what we have found here will change everything and challenge your beliefs. It has to be kept a secret because there is much work still to do and we have barely found out anything about them yet. If word got out, then people would come down here in droves and destroy anything left that needs to be found and understood. Believe me, when you see what has been found so far, you'll understand."

"Who'd ever thought it; the *ones before* . . . you're not joking are you?"

"No, quite serious really. Anyway, with the location of this place marked in your mind let's continue on to the main camp."

"Fine with us, and with that information, you really have my curiosity up, and it has kind of re-energized me."

"Kind of thought it might, okay let's go."

It was approaching dusk when the new team finally arrived at the camp. Before descending into the desert, they had stopped briefly at the high point to see the panorama of the surrounding area and to see that it was desert. From there the camp was clearly visible as was the two dig sites and the large shelter at the second, off in the distance. George had commented that he had never seen anything that large that was man made before. He was informed not only was it the largest that any of them had ever seen, but that it was constructed entirely of metal. Again, he thought that Doube was joking with him, but was informed that he could on the morrow go check it out for himself to confirm it.

Jahnsyn Lytle, who was the camp manager on duty, when they arrived stating that he had seen them approaching and had made sure there would be enough food for the increased numbers. As the new team entered the camp, a group that was at least twice to three times their size, were all sitting and eating a meal. Jllon stood up and said, "We'll deal with the introductions later. Grab a plate and come eat. Once everyone is comfortable we'll talk."

"Don't have to tell us twice." George responded, he turned to his team and said, "Just don't stand there do as he says. Grab a plate and some grub and let's eat. There seems to be a table there that would do fine for us," pointing out an empty one that was behind the people who were eating.

Once everyone finished the evening meal Jllon got up and addressed everyone. First looking at the new members he said, "We welcome you here. What you are unaware of is the fact that we have been here for close to half a turn or there about. As Doube told you before you entered the camp, the reason for the secrecy is what was discovered here. On the morrow you will get a tour of what was found and its importance. Then you will join the rest of us as we work on preservation of what we have uncovered. With you, as the new team here, we should be able to wrap this up much quicker." He made the introductions of the existing team for the new members, and had George, who was in charge of this second team, introduce his.

From here Jllon briefly pointed out the areas that would be important for them tonight, and stated that they had placed a new temporary shelter for them located just outside of the light. "I'm sorry, but until we leave it will be a little tight for space, but other shelters will then be available and make things a little easier. We will have much to cover and to understand before the site is turned over to you, and little time in which to do it. It had been hoped, originally that we would be able to move to our next objective around the time of the major gather, but as it turns out, that is not to be. Probably a more realistic time would be a half cycle to a full cycle after." He wished them well and be free to talk with anyone here and please understand the importance of the secrecy of the site and the why, and asked if their journey had been okay, followed by saying that was all he had. George got up briefly and stated that when the information was finally revealed it was a shock. Their sires had scared them all, when they were whelps, about the *ones before*. This brought a laugh out of the group as they all could relate. Once they had grown up they considered these *ones before* just something that never had existed and was just one of the tools their sires had used to keep them in line. Now before them was proof that they were more than legend, more than myth. It was a shock, and of course there was a little bit of denial.

As expected the two groups stayed apart for the first evening. Since neither knew members of the other personally, it left a feeling of nervous tension hanging over the teams, as it was unnaturally quiet. Eventually they all retired. Jllon knew that as they worked together that most of the nervousness would disappear.

The next morn broke bright and clear, as it usually does in the desert, and after the morn meal Jllon took the new team immediately out to bring them up to date on what had been happening and what they were doing. He wanted them to understand the importance of what they would be doing here. Then he would have Doube take George and Han over the mountain with a pack beast and introduce them to the outpost on the other side where they were getting their supplies and messages from home. With the time they had spent here it was hard for Jllon to even admit that it was winding down for him and the team. He wanted this initial survey by the new team to be completed by the zenith meal so that they could join the work on the preservation tasks.

Like Celt before him, when Celt had to give a tour to the nomads, Jllon did the same for the new team. By the time they had finished they were ready to believe that truly the *ones before* were real and the proof lain before them. As they toured the finds Jllon also passed on to them what they would be doing and since it was the desert the summer would be hot. He especially warned them of the winds and the damage they'd do to their campsite let alone to the finds.

This explained the growing sand hill to the east of the shelter. It was asked if similar protection would be provided to the site closest to the camp and the answer was no. Since everything there had been destroyed by fire, and nothing was left standing, the only importance here was to insure that the areas they had sifted remained marked. So, if at a future time, they decided to continue the work they would know what had already been worked.

"So, as I understand it . . ." George said, "We are here to continue to catalog and to protect the sites."

"Yes, that's just about it. You will not be doing any more digging unless it's to repair the hill, but that doesn't mean you cannot mark other potential areas for future digs. Still if word does get out about what we found here then truthfully it won't matter. People will descend on this place in such great amounts that all will be lost anyway. So let's hope that doesn't happen."

"Agreed. I for one would not want to face the crowds of eager people wanting to get their own piece of these ancients. And think of the chaos it would cause . . . just the amount of fake stuff that would start showing up would be unbelievable."

"Now you see the problem quite clearly. Normally such things are open for all to view, but we just can't . . . not yet anyway."

It was soon after that Doube took George and Han over the mountains to see the merchant located at the outpost and to establish the names that would be receiving correspondence there. Doube also informed the owner that the rest would be transferring theirs to the village that was located west. Handing him a bunch of letters from the team, he stated, "The ones who will be moving to the new location, are informing the family members of their up and coming move, so you shouldn't be getting much more for them. If you do, we will leave the marks necessary for you to send them on to the village. If I remember right, since it has been a while since I was there, its name is Rancho. Anyway we will confirm that for sure since we will pass by your location on the way there."

With the business completed they headed back to the camp in the desert. George asked, "How much does he know?"

"Nothing at all. As far as he knows, we are just working the mountains and the edge of the desert; he was told that we are researching that abandoned village as a major learned project. That is one of the reasons for you to have gone through it when you first arrived. If he had asked about it and you hadn't known anything about it, it just wouldn't make sense."

"Yeah, I understand now. I couldn't figure out why that was such an important stop. I mean there are a number of those all over the place – why this one?"

"So now you know why, and I would suggest that now and then you and part of your team go into it just so that you are familiar enough that if a question is thrown your way you can answer it honestly."

"Makes complete sense – helps cover what was really found and leaves no curiosity. I like it. Jllon sure seems to think of everything."

"You don't become the Head Keeper of the Past if you are stupid. And the one thing I can say since I have worked with him he's anything other than stupid."

"And he seems to care about who is working for and with him", George commented. "It shows in everything he does. When I first met him there I thought this one is much too young to be in such an important position. But, once I began to see how he works and anticipates and cares about things I realized that he's wise way beyond his turns."

"Yes I would say that is a good assessment of who he is. I have worked with some bad leaders . . . a Joellie Trag comes immediately to mind. He always thought that it was his to take and do. That leadership was owed him and his style showed in every fiber of him. In fact I came to appreciate the second in charge on that one. In the end we became friends. All I have to say is that if Fauul had not been with that team there would have been some tragic outcomes, and even possibly death.

"The one thing I have noticed over time is that there are natural leaders and ones who say they are. Usually the ones who can lead, but of course there are exceptions even here, just naturally step up and do the job without any fuss or even trying to bring attention to themselves. They usually will see a job and see solutions to getting it done and then just do it. Jllon is one of those as is Fauul. I wouldn't be surprised to see the two of them becoming friends. They are similar in so many ways."

"Fauul? Who is this Fauul you are speaking of — part of the team that I haven't met as of yet?"

Laughing a little, Doube said, "No, you haven't met him, but he plays a big part of this discovery. Anyway, when your team takes over the desert site, we will be heading to a village where we will see Fauul who will be involved heavily with the next phase of the work. So no you don't know him and probably will not meet him. It was just that I saw much of the same with these two males . . . he's getting mated shortly, did I mention that?"

Laughing out loud George said, "Ah ha! Some female has trapped him in her snare. So he will join the ranks of those who have mates then. So when is this loss to being single happening anyway?"

"I actually had talked with him at the same port where I met you and your team. He was on the earlier water-craft. He related to me that it would probably be close to right now. I suspect that the major spring gather is happening there right now, and if so, on the last evening is the ceremony."

"Shaking his head, George said, "I see we have lost another one . . . gone to the other side. As for me I will remain single as long as I can. I can enjoy the company of a female now and then, and leave when I feel like it. No strings attached for either of us . . . eliminates the complications that way. Actually everyone on our crew is single, makes it easier that way. Isn't that right Han?"

Han who had not participated in the conversation but was listening, replied, "Right. Of course I'm sure that you saw that most of our team is young. Just out of the higher learning, and with nothing going on, and the idea of a little adventure appealed to them."

"Oh they may get more than they bargained for, especially if they decide to violate the nomad's sacred space there. So I must reinforce right here and now, stay away from that area. We have established a relationship with them by being open and honest. With your team it must be the same. Jllon, Celt, and myself, will cover it in detail . . . not only with the two of you but with the whole team. Curiosity, which drives us forward, must have a control, and this is one area where it is not allowed to rule."

"That serious huh?"

"More than you know. Violation, besides destroying what we have established, would mean death. They are that serious about these areas and will protect them at any cost."

"That's serious! I've never dealt with the nomads so I really have no idea about them at all. They would really use deadly force?"

"Yes and think nothing of it. It would be instant and brutal with no mercy. I believe that they may have extended their protection to the site you are to protect and continue to catalog. Obviously it is modified to allow us to do what we are doing. And that came about because we honored and respected their right to the place that they had established as theirs. Then when they arrived and saw that it was so they came and spoke with us. We openly showed and explained what it was we were doing. We did this as equals and with respect. They were very interested in what we had found, and later, many of the additional clans came to see what had been found here."

Thinking about what had just been said George said, "I bet all of you were pretty nervous, right?"

"Careful is probably a better word. I have some insight into the nomads and their lives, and I was able to advise Jllon on how to approach them in a way that would not leave any misunderstandings. So you can see that with communications being established we cannot jeopardize what we have begun."

"I think I understand. Is there more on this subject?"

"Yes, but we are not going into it now, as you will need to talk with both Celt and Jllon. They were the leaders at the time and it will be them that must pass on how to deal with the nomads when they arrive back there, and I will guarantee that they will be back."

"Okay then, you've left me with much to think about that's for sure."

Doube, on the return trip, took them the alternate way, stating that sometimes it would be a good idea to approach from this direction, since the abandoned village could be reached from either direction. While the mountain route from the desert was a shorter route, the one he was showing them was the easier one.

Once again they went through the abandoned village, and George with Han could then connect another portion of the trails on the maps that existed in their minds. George said, "You know, as we were coming around the hill back there things started looking a little familiar. I thought – no, it can't be – and then we made the turn towards this village and it all fell into place. I had no idea."

Smiling Doube said, "Funny how that works. I know with the map I have in my mind that when a piece is put into it, the map seems to shrink, and many times opens a whole section for me. I suggest that you and your team do a little bit of exploring to really familiarize yourself with the area, including that burned village located there in the mountains. People are slowly returning so you should probably establish a presence there also. But continue to use the outpost. With the mountain village go there only enough so that you are not strangers but not so often that they become curious and try and see what you may be up to."

"I didn't see any when we came that way, where is it?"

If you remember, even though it is showing green now, that old burn area is close to it. It is located further up in the mountains there. While not hidden, it still is not easy to see."

"You think we will have that kind of time on our hands do you?"

"Probably more than you think. Since most of your job will be protection of the site, and repairs to the sand hill when the winds leave, plus a little of cataloging, and even with all that it still will leave much time for you to explore."

"Okay, so where should I explore? I mean I know that we are supposed to see if we can find and mark some additional promising areas there, but other than the abandoned village where?"

"I'll show you some areas to search and to learn when we are back and if there is time. Others I am sure you will find on your own."

"Just a thought," George said, "I've always wondered why when you enter places like this that it just appears to be silent. Like someone or something is just waiting . . . waiting for what I don't know . . . but it has always made me uneasy."

"Really", Doube replied, "and I understand. I mean, you expect at any time, to see someone come out of one of those shelters and for life to continue. But it's just not going to happen. In a few turns there probably won't even be a sign that there was even a village here. And the only place it will exist will be in the minds of the ones who once lived here."

They left the abandoned village and headed back to camp arriving at the zenith meal. George saying, "Good timing I say. Always like a hot meal."

The next few days was going over in detail what the new team would be required to accomplish. The members were taken within viewing distance of the nomad claim and shown the extent of what they claimed. It was again reinforced to stay away. While there Jllon, Celt, and Doube went over in detail the protocol on communicating with the nomads when they returned. It was critical for the continued good relations between the two groups.

Doube went into the explanation of the "close to disaster" that had almost transpired between the nomads and the mapping team – explaining that his intervention was probably the only thing that kept the members, who had violated the area, alive. It was hoped that with continued contact, that eventually this site and others would be open for scientific advancements and learning. But until that day, one had to proceed with a great amount of caution.

The work also continued on the building of the sand hill. There was no proof that, in the end, it would save the shelter, but with no other solution available it was the best they could do. Again it was explained to the new members that maintaining this was critical. They couldn't afford to lose such an important discovery, or what they were now storing inside of the same shelter.

With the work behind them they finished packing up for the journey over the mountains and down the valleys into the village. One pack beast would be left with the new team and the others would be used to take what the rest needed. Doube had relayed to Jllon the message from Fauul about what was happening with him. There was a good chance that by the time they reached the village that he and his mate would have returned, but that still was an unknown. Again they would only know once they arrived. Then bidding farewell to the new team they headed out.

CHAPTER FOURTEEN

It was almost impossible to believe. She found herself almost scared to death. Up until this moment she could have backed out and remained as she was. Second thoughts, about what she was about to do, kept entering her mind, and the doubts were building. Was it the right thing to do? Should she have taken more time? Is he the right one for me? On and on, the questions continued to enter her mind unbidden. She had to admit she was a nervous wreck. In a short time they, the three couples, were to meet for the one walk through they would be doing. Then, for the rest of the day, until the ceremony in the early evening, they would remain separated and not allowed to see each other.

The quarter of a cycle at the major gather was a blur. She honestly couldn't say whether, she with her business, and her brother handling the beast sales with

Aurto, was successful or not. She had been much too distracted. Still, as the time neared she was finding it harder and harder to concentrate. So the day before the ceremony she gave up and closed the booth down. She couldn't concentrate, period. She went to find her two friends and find solace with them. She needed to find out if what she was feeling now, as the time approached, had been the same with them.

When the major gather had begun, she originally thought she would not open the booth at all. But realized that by having it open, and doing at least some business, that it would keep her mind off the mating ceremony and she would be able to worry less. But it really hadn't worked, as many of the community members would come by to talk and congratulate her on her becoming a mate. So, for her, there was no escape. Every once in a while, either Traylu or Sooma, would come by just to encourage her. They were great friends, and she really appreciated what they were trying to do.

Walking into the mercantile past the crowds that were at the tables they had placed outside, she looked for Sooma, and did not immediately see her. Franc, who was quite busy, noticed that she was looking for something and excused himself went over to her and asked, "Are you in need of something, Lauma?"

"I was really on looking for Sooma, but I can see that you are very busy so I'll come back later."

Another customer signaled him wanting something, he turning towards them said, "One moment please . . . I'll be right there." Then turning back to Lauma he said, "Yes quite busy, but she went over to the shelter briefly. You might be able to catch her there. If you do can you ask her to come back as even with the help I have, I really need her help."

Smiling at Franc, she said, "Of course. That's if I see her. Looking at things, she may have gone somewhere else to assist. She's that kind."

"She is, isn't she?" Franc responded, "Sorry but I do have to help them . . . see you around Lauma. And I'll definitely be there at the ceremony." He left to help his next customer.

Lauma thought. *Thanks really thanks a lot. I know that he meant well but I am so wound up that another reminder of what is about to take place is something I just did not need.* She headed out the back door and over to the shelter. As she came near she could hear voices coming from the shelter and knew that someone was there. She knocked on the door and in a few moments Sooma opened the door and said, "Lauma! It's great to see you. I've only got a couple of minutes here, and I am sure part of what you are doing is relaying a message from Franc saying he needs me, right?" Then motioning her in she saw a couple of the females from the village who was visiting with Sooma. She remembered them from the get-together they had in her honor."

Lauma seeing how busy Sooma was said, "Sorry, I'll come back later. It's obvious that you are quite busy, and yes Franc did ask me to relay that message. He and the others there are quite overwhelmed right now."

"Oh you're no bother. I was just dealing with some orders that these two wanted. It was easier here than in that chaos in the mercantile. Anyway, you are welcome to stay if you like, but once I finish with them I will have to go and help. Remember, that once you have done your walk through on the morrow, you will be required to return here. Now don't worry your little head about it, because there will be plenty of females coming and going during the day to keep you involved, and then most of the after-zenith will be in you getting ready."

"That's okay, I'll let Franc know what you are doing, and then I'll just walk the gather. It's something I usually don't get to do anyway. You know, usually tied to my booth. Anyway, thank you for the offer. I promise I'll stop back by this evening before retiring at the hostel."

"No you don't. Tonight you will be retiring here in the guest space. You need as good night's sleep that one can get. Still I know that it will be a rough one anyway. After all the biggest change of your life is happening on the morrow, and who can sleep when that's happening?"

"Thank you so much. The hostel can be so noisy making it hard to sleep anyway, so I'll definitely take you up on the offer. Then I guess I will see you later." She turned and headed back into the mercantile to let Franc know what was happening with Sooma. Once she had informed Franc, she headed back out into the chaos that was the spring gather. Making contact here and there with different members of the community and thanking them for congratulating her on finding a mate and hoping that she wasn't too nervous.

Even with the nerves, she found that to her surprise, the after-zenith went far too quickly. With dusk approaching she went to find her brother and to remind him that he would need to be with her in the morn as the family representative. But search as she may, he did not seem to be anywhere. She asked down at the yards expecting him to be there and was informed that he had not been there most of the afternoon, and neither had Fauul.

Then remembering that the village females had thrown her a surprise get-together she suspected that the village males were doing the same for Fauul. What worried her was the timing. Knowing that, most likely, much ale was being passed around, she suspected that when they left wherever it was that they had located themselves they would be pretty incoherent. She finally gave up, knowing that it was getting late, and no one seemed to know anything. She figured it was a conspiracy against her, but again had no proof. Yet there just seemed to be too many who knew nothing Oh well, she would have to trust her brother, and Fauul. But it left her frustrated and a little angry. She really had wanted to talk with both of them. Now all she could hope was that they would show up in the morn like they had promised. Turning around she headed over to the mercantile to see how it was going there. She knew that soon it would be closed down for the evening just before the nightly entertainment began.

Walking into the mercantile she saw that Sooma was watching her. Sooma smiling, said, "I can see that something hasn't gone right. Let me guess . . . you tried to find either your brother or your mate to be and neither could be found, right?"

With a quizzical look on her face Lauma asked, "How'd you know that?"

"It seems to be a tradition with the males that they kidnap the one who is about to join the ranks of the mated. I suspect that the other two were grabbed also. So the three of you, you and the other two females, will be without them around tonight. I'm sure, in the end, they were willing victims. So don't let it bother you. It happened to me and Traylu also."

"Yeah but . . ."

Again smiling Sooma continued, "I know, you wanted to make sure that they would be where they were supposed to be in the morn. I guess it's that mothering instinct that believes that they must be reminded all the time. Still Franc showed up the next morn as he was supposed to – even though he looked a little pale. All I can say is it must have been quite some send off."

"So you are telling me not to worry, and all will be okay?"

"Well, as okay as it can be. Fortunately the morn meeting is straightforward and simple. I do believe if it was other than that he probably wouldn't have remembered a thing."

"That bad, huh?"

Then laughing Sooma said, "Yes, that bad. I think it's the goal of the kidnappers to really get them drunk, and usually they seem to be pretty successful. Plus, I am sure; it would not be a place a female would want to be. I'm sure that the remarks that are going around would make one of the worst of our kind to turn red from embarrassment. Of course, I really don't know, as nothing is ever said to us about what goes on there. Still it's not that hard to figure out."

"So you are saying that I just need to forget it, and continue on tonight as if nothing has happened, and just leave it at that."

"Yes, and don't worry . . . which I know is something we are good at anyway. Knowing what I do about your Fauul he'll be there as he should be. So why not just go back to the evening celebration, get something to eat, enjoy the celebration, and then come to the shelter when it gets a little overwhelming, and the noise too much. At that time we can quietly talk about whatever you want."

Still not sure she hesitantly said, "Okay . . . if you say so . . . I mean . . . how do you go and enjoy yourself when I'm so nervous, I'm afraid I'll just break down and cry. I mean I just cannot keep from second guessing myself as to whether this is right or not."

"You'll do that even after. It's just natural, but at least try to forget about it for now and go have some fun. I guarantee that Fauul is, so why shouldn't you?"

While standing by the yards Fauul had been talking with Lauut and just passing the time. It was early after-zenith and he figured that he would soon go over and see how Lauma was doing. But before he could excuse himself he was grabbed by at least six of the local males and hauled off to a private location only known to them. He fought them a little and then realized that they were laughing and having a good time so he knew that they meant him no physical harm.

Looking ahead of him he saw the other two males who would be joining him in the mating ceremony and realized that the village males were sending them off from the brotherhood of males to join their females. He remembered that he had done a similar thing to a couple of his friends, and now it was his turn as well as these other two. Smiling at the crew he said, "Alright, alright I'll quit fighting you. I should have realized what this was all about, but had forgotten that I had done the same for a couple of my friends."

He was introduced to many of the village males he had seen but never met, and then the drinking and comments began to flow. Time passed quickly and he could tell that he was really beginning to feel the ale. Also from the position of the stars and the darkness he knew that it had to be approaching the middle of the night. He really needed to make a break soon; otherwise he would be in no shape for the meeting in the morn.

The next morn dawned with a light fog. Still there was a promise of a warm spring day in the air. He thought that the fog was very appropriate. If it had been sunny he would still have felt as if he was in a fog. He had to admit that last night was fun, but he knew now he would pay the price. He was also sure that even though this seemed to be a tradition, that along with it came the other tradition of the females, who would be joining the males in the mating ceremony, and would be most unhappy with the shape that their males would be in. Now he would find himself being the one who would be taking the wrath of his mate to be. Even if it were just in the looks she would throw his way. In truth, the way he felt, right now, he could care less. He knew again that in a few hours that he would feel better and eventually be back to his usual self. So it was time to go to the morn meal get something hot, and a good couple of cups of that hot beverage, and he thought once consumed that he just might be close to normal.

Even though he had no idea where Lauma was, he suspected that she probably had spent the night with her friends, and slept in Sooma and Franc's shelter – which meant that she would be eating with them. So the earliest he expected to see her was just before the one walk-through they would do. While he knew that he had promised himself to Lauma as her mate he suspected that the true reality of the enormity of it would not hit him until they were going through that practice.

Thinking back, once he really knew the truth within himself, he had no doubts. There always had been something, a spark . . . a draw, between them. As he had contemplated this back in his apartment, before he knew if she had really had the same feelings for him, he had come to the decision to find out. And now here he was. Once they had started really seeing each other and living the daily life in close proximity with each other there was absolutely no doubt. All he saw of his future included her, and that was enough for him.

While on the other side he suspected that she was probably having second thoughts. How could it not be that way? She had lost her sires when she was young, and she and her brother had to survive on their own leaving them self-sufficient. Now she was about to let someone else in her life that would make her dependent. He thought that that idea, in itself, had to be scary. Let alone knowing that she would be having whelps by this male. So for a female the prospects for a mate were much more serious, not that he didn't take it seriously, but he knew that emotionally, the female was the center of the family. So finding the right mate was critical, if her life was to be livable. He had seen relationships where it wasn't, and the female looked worn and beaten down, not that it didn't affect the male, but it seemed most obvious with the females.

Looking up he realized it was time. While he had eaten the meal he really had barely tasted it. He found that he had been drifting, in his mind, in many directions including the contemplation he had just gone through. He really had not been aware of the time at all. Getting up, he immediately sat back down and said quietly, "Slowly there. I seem to be a bit off balance this morn." Then laughing at himself as he said to no one in particular, "Not a surprise really."

He noticed the fog was breaking up. *Wish it would in my brain,* he thought. There just seemed to be no energy and with the warmth of the sun it would be easy to fall asleep right here. Still he knew that wasn't possible he had somewhere he needed to be. He would nap later in the day before the real ceremony. Fortunately, for him, the distance wasn't far, so once again he got up and headed over the meeting area where they would have the practice.

Finally arriving, he first noticed that he was the last to get there, and even Lauut had arrived ahead of him. The next thing he saw was the other two males that would be involved with the ceremony looked as bad as he probably did. Smiling while he observed the females, he saw, by their body language that they were most unhappy about the appearance of their males.

Then he realized that there were sires here. He remembered that before even the practice would begin that the sires would have to affirm that nothing was coerced, and indeed they, the females, were doing this of their own free will. Listening, he realized that the person who would be performing the actual ceremony was talking.

". . . as I was saying, the history of why it is necessary for permission to be given has nothing to do with the fact that your daughter must have your permission to mate. It has to do with a distant fact of history where females were nothing more than property and breeding stock. It is a dark time of our past, but one we cannot deny. We cannot change it, so from that period came the rules that we now abide by. The ones that show up both in our ceremony and the way one pursues a mate. So sires before I continue, is this relationship being entered into by the free will of your daughters? Looking over at Lauut he said, "And, of course to you Lauut, your sister, since you are the family representative here."

They all agreed, and then the speaker continued. "While I know that you who are mated and are presenting your daughters here have heard this before, the ones who are here to join us have not. It does not hurt to hear it again and to be reminded. Now as you know you will be asked to do the same tonight during the ceremony. Your daughters, in their mating outfits, will approach from the east, and as they approach, you will be over here. Then you will join them and walk up on the platform.

"At the same time the males will be approaching from the west, and will stand over here on the platform. I will again ask you sires if this is entered into as free will. You will answer as you have here and leave and join the village. Spaces will be reserved for you in front so that you may have the best views. So if you understand it we will see you tonight about thirty minutes before so that you can be ready to join your daughters as they leave your family and join their own."

The sires and Lauut, understanding their role, left the stage, but only went down and sat to listen to what would be said to the participants. "Now that we are finished with the sires we now come to the guests of honor here. While we have gotten the approval of the sires here, I now ask you females who are to be leaving your families, are you truly entering into this relationship of your own free will?"

Looking around the speaker saw that two of the three were blushing and seemed shy. But all three remained silent and just nodded their heads.

"A loss for words, huh? I suspect it will be one of the few times that you will be", he said as he smiled. "Okay, we have much to cover and then your friends will take you away. As you know this will be the last time you see each other until the ceremony tonight. I will be walking you through every part other than the third – which you will have to figure out on your own." And with that comment, it brought a bunch of nervous laughter from the females, leaving the males smiling. Yes it would be interesting that was for sure.

"Just one thing about the third part, and it's this, every portion of the ceremony is built to allow either party to stop the process. At any time you can say that you are not party to this and for you it will end there. In the mating space where you will consummate your relationship there is a space within a space that allows you to reject even this. In that smaller space there is only a handle on the inside. Yet initially there is one on both sides. This prevents someone who is dominating the situation and forcing some into something they don't want a way out. If you decide this is not right for you then you can remove the outside handle, and you can enter this room and be safe. Then in the morn the contract between you and the other will be incomplete and as such be null and void. So if any of you have been forced into this, when the two are alone, you still can break the relationship right there and then.

"Only one thing left to discuss before we actually walk it and that is after you leave the stage and go to your mating feast before part three later that night. As you know, these relationships you are entering, requires cooperation on almost every level. So while it has a serious side to it, take this portion in fun. I guarantee the village will. You will, during part two, receive the leather bands that you will be wearing on your left wrists. Between the two bands will be tied a leather strip approximately two body lengths in size. This means that you two will be tied together until you retire. There can be no removal of this strip until you enter your space.

"So what this simply means is that you must cooperate in all things. So while it will be frustrating at times, since you have done things on your own, now you must work together. It is symbolic of your up and coming life together. This also means females that the male is stuck outside the necessary space and can hear all that can go on in there. It will be the same for the males, although, from experience, I would say that such a thing is more embarrassing to the females.

"The last part I will talk about is the next morn. Once the two of you have confirmed the completion of the final part of the ceremony then you will be allowed to remove the leather bands. And then you will be given your copper ones that have the first name of your significant other on the outer side and the last name on the inner side. It is up to the two of you to decide later if only one last name is to be used, or both, or the last names to remain as they are. Any questions before we start actually walking through?" Looking around it seemed that nobody had any. "Okay then, let's get started. Now . . ."

Before they knew it the rehearsal was complete, and they were led away to be kept separate until that evening ceremony. Looking over at Lauma he realized that any chance to talk with her was gone. She seeing him had questions in her eyes, and all he could do was shrug, and mouth that he would attempt to answer her questions during the mating feast. But he really suspected that the earliest any of the couples would have to talk with each other would be when they finally retired to the third part of the ceremony. It would only be then that the chaos of the day and evening would be over, and they would finally have time to themselves.

Still he knew that for both of them, this was going to be a difficult time. Since neither had been involved to this point, he figured that it would dominate both their thoughts. Even though there was nervousness there, he really couldn't wait until they were finally alone, as mates. Both of them, starting out in a new direction, and with a new commitment – he followed the other two males away from the platform. While he knew that there was a chance for the evening to end without them becoming mates he was confident that both were ready.

Lauma leaving, had questions she wanted to ask Fauul, but she was being led away, and knew that she would not have a chance to get them answered. She saw that Fauul had recognized her questioning look, but only shrugged. She could see that he was in the same fix as she. He had wanted to talk but now it was not allowed. They were being separated until the evening when by the law of the land they were to become one . . . a new family and a new direction. She would have to wait for any answers and knew that from now until the end of the ceremony things would become crazy.

Her friends, Sooma and Traylu, came and led her away, back to the shelter. From now until the ceremony she would not be able to leave as it was for Fauul and the other two. "Well, you are one step closer to joining us," Traylu said.

"What?" Lauma asked, she had been thinking and had not heard her friend.

"Ah you must be a million body lengths away. All I said was that you were not too far from joining us."

Smiling a little nervously she said, "Yes I was . . . we didn't get a chance to talk this morn and I had something to ask him."

"Don't worry about it," Sooma replied. "Later when you look back you probably won't remember what you wanted to ask anyway. I know I was questioning myself all the way to the ceremony. And yes before you ask, I was a little ticked at Franc. But it was just a little thing anyway, not something to get bothered about at all."

Timidly she said, "If you say so. Oh I am just a nervous wreck, and there is much of the day ahead of me with nothing to do but think."

"Oh, you'll be busier than you think, and while, at times, the day will drag a little, before you really want it to, it will be time, and then you will find yourself walking down the trail out of the east heading for the platform. And you will see the one you love approaching from the west and then because of what it means to both, you will only have eyes for each other. In fact in his eyes you will positively glow. But not only will his eyes see this in you. All the females in this ceremony just seem to become beautiful and glowing as if the love each of you feels cannot remain contained within you. But you won't see it", Sooma said, "as he will be the one that has all your attention."

"Yeah, that and you not wanting to embarrass yourself by tripping over something as you walk to the platform," Traylu added. "It happens . . . after all we are not used to wearing these outfits and we can end up being a little clumsy."

Fauul knew that Lauut had borrowed space with the beast master. So in his family's shelter he would be spending the remaining time. Being that Aurto did much business like Franc the shelter of his had guest spaces to accommodate prospective buyers. It was here he would stay until it was time to head out for the ceremony.

Lauut said, "It's sure easy for one to become nervous. I mean I'm nervous and all I have to do his confirm that Lauma is entering into this of her own free will. While the two of you are facing him and then the village . . . right now I am quite happy it's not me. How are you doing by the way?"

"Oh, pretty good, I guess. I suspect as the time gets closer I'll keep thinking of things that might go wrong, or that your sister will have decided that it was a mistake, and back out. The mind just keeps coming up with different things that say we will not be mated. I guess, as you say, it's just nerves. Anyway after what you and the village males did for me and the other two last night, I am a little beat and suspect that I will just nod out here for a little while, if that's okay with you?"

"Of course, why wouldn't it be?" Then smiling, he the continued, "Kind of surprised you didn't we?"

"Yes, I have to admit that it wasn't something I was expecting. Really, at the moment, I was thinking of going over and talking with Lauma and see how she was holding up. Yet, something happened that prevented that . . . yes, please thank them for me. It was a nice send off." Fauul took off his boots and lay on the bed and said, "If I'm out too long here wake me. I was just a little late to the rehearsal this morn, so I better not be late to the important one tonight."

"No problem Fauul." Lauut turned and left. He had some final thinking to do himself. Since Fauul had arrived they, he and his sister, had been changing. Tonight he would be giving his sister to this male to start a new family. It, in truth, was still a shock in so many ways. After the accident it had just been the two of them for so long to have it now change so drastically was something hard to imagine. He stayed by the door for a short period of time and then heard the regular breathing of one asleep. He went out to the yard and pens to talk with Aurto and see if the spring gather had been good. With the mating of his sister happening at this gather he had not really paid much attention to business. While he had beasts here, he really did not know for sure if there had even been a request for any. Seeing him leaning against one of the rails Lauut approached him and asked, "So Aurto, how's it going so far?"

"Lauut! How's it going? Okay I guess. I've had better gathers, but, of course, much worse also. So how are your friend and your sister?"

"As far as Fauul goes he must be made of ice. At the moment he doesn't appear to be nervous at all. But he is probably good at hiding it. After all, because of his work, he has been in pressure situations before."

Laughing Aurto said, "Yeah, but nothing like this. I know myself when I made that walk I was almost shaking."

"You? Nah, you're joking right?"

"I swear it's true. Ah the memories, it seems so long ago now. But enough on me, you didn't mention anything about Lauma."

"Sorry, I really only saw her for a short time today, and my guess is she is scared to death. It seems funny for me to say that. She has always been cool and rock solid, and as you know not afraid of anything. So to see her like this is so different."

"Think of it this way, if she wasn't then probably this would not be right for her. It means she has thought about it a lot, and has considered the outcome, and in the end probably means she does love this Fauul. I, from what I have seen of him, she has picked very well."

"Well, thank you for that. I must admit, I have been impressed by him myself. Not afraid to tackle any job . . ." Then laughing out loud he continued, ". . . including my sister."

"Yeah I know what you mean. At times she can be a real firebrand. Like all females she can put you in your place with just a look."

"Know what you mean there. She has done that to me a few times. Sometimes the way she would do it would remind me of our mother. It does seem that some personal ways of doing things are passed down even if the sires are not there to influence one."

"Okay, so how are you doing? I mean, directly or indirectly you are involved here. The closeness that the two of you have enjoyed is now sort of gone, and she is be putting more of it towards her new mate to be."

"True, we've discussed that quite a bit. It is part of those changes I just mentioned. It has left me with mixed feelings. I mean we all know that this day comes for most of us, and she, with no one here of interest, appeared to not have that chance . . . and then here we are facing that very thing. I don't know, he has helped us in so many ways, I guess only time will tell in the end."

"True, the future belongs to no one as it isn't here yet. I guess we just have to take care of this day and make it right. Anyway I've got a couple of people coming shortly so I guess I'll see you a little later when you come back."

"Yes you will, and thanks again for the use of the space. I think he's sleeping now. As usual the sending away get-together was wild and crazy. I guess I will just walk the gather. I know that things are starting to wind down, and on the morrow everything will be closed down and after the clean-up back to normal." *Well as close to normal*, he thought to himself. He turned and left with no specific destination in mind.

Again not really paying attention, he was thinking about all that had happened to them this last turn, and it seemed to have been more than any other – other than the turn where they lost their sires. Without realizing it he found himself in front of the mercantile where one of Lauma's friends worked and lived behind. He thought that maybe he would go in and see how his sister was doing but did not know if it would be allowed. Standing in front of the mercantile, deciding whether to go in or not, he saw Franc coming out to one of the tables with a customer, and waited until they had finished. He approached Franc and asked, "Do you think it would be okay if I talked with my sister, or is that off limits?"

"Good question and one that I don't have an answer for you. But right now they are back in the shelter, so why not go and knock on the door. Sooma will probably answer it and she will let you know I am sure."

"Yeah I bet she will. Okay sounds like a great idea, thanks and Franc I hope it has been a good gather for you."

"It has, and you?"

"In truth, I don't know. Been kind of involved heavily with this mating ceremony and it has taken most of my time. I suspect that it was okay, but I can't really say."

"Understood, I know when mine came around things were just as chaotic and not much got done either."

"Anyway thanks, I'll go see your mate and get my answer." Again leaving he went around the back of the shelter and headed over to the place where Lauma was presently spending her time. He went up to the door and knocked. He heard voices, mostly female, but couldn't understand anything they were saying. Finally one became louder, and then the door opened.

"Sooma, its Lauut. Can I let him in?"

"One moment please. Lauma your brother is at the door would you like to see him?"

Not knowing how she answered he had to wait for some type of confirmation. He then heard Sooma say okay. Sooma came to the door and said, "Yeah, but you will have to stay here in the entrance. She'll be right out, you'll need to give her a little time she wasn't expecting anyone so she's not decent."

Feeling out of place he waited for quite a while and then he saw his sister come out of one of the spaces. He saw that they had been working on her hair, and while the work had not been completed it had changed the way she looked.

Arriving at the entrance she asked, "What are you doing here?"

"I know that I probably shouldn't be here but I had to find out how you are doing. I mean you seemed to be really nervous at the walk-through this morn, and I wasn't able to talk with you then."

"Thank you for that, and yes I was and I still am. Did you see that this morn Fauul was late? It's not like him. I was worried he wouldn't show at all."

"Yes, I know, but he was just barely and I can honestly tell you that he is looking forward to this, and yes I think he is somewhat nervous also. I mean it's only natural. This is such a serious step in one's life. So can I leave here knowing that you are okay? I know that right now you are in good hands with your friends. I really wish that our sires were here to see this. They would be so happy for you, and I know for a fact they would love Fauul."

"Yes, it would really have been wonderful if they were here, and it was one of the things I cried out while the two of you were working. I was looking for some advice that only a female could give and mom came to mind. Then I knew that I would never be able to get that advice, and I was washed with a deep sadness knowing that we, she and I, would never share these important moments together."

"Okay then, I'll leave you alone until the ceremony where I will see you the last time as just a sister . . . you know that I love you much and have nothing but good thoughts about what you are about to do."

There was a silence for a short period of time, as she was touched by what she knew, but to have him reveal it in such a way was wonderful. "I always knew it, but to hear now at this time, I must say thank you, and I'm really proud that you are the one to confirm for our family. Anyway I am finding that there is much that still needs to be done so I have to go back. I guess the next time I see you will be as I walk up to the platform brother." She led him back to the door, since he was standing just inside of the entrance, gave him a big hug, and closed the door. Quietly, as the door closed, she said, "And brother, I do love you too, again, see you tonight."

He was glad that he was at least able to have a few moments with her and that she appeared to be okay. Well there was just too much on his mind right now. So he decided to go back to the yards and sit on the porch and daydream a little, and probably reminisce about their lives up to this time. It wouldn't be too much longer before Fauul would need to be wakened and he himself prepare for the ceremony.

Dusk was settling over the area and there was anticipation of what was to come. It was always a joy when there were members of the village who were to be mated. All shared in their joy of discovery of the new lives they would be starting after this night. The ones who had been mates for many turns would look back, in their memory, to the time when they had been up on the same platform saying their vows to each other.

The mating feast afterwards with the music and dancing and of course the joking and teasing that went with it filled them with pleasant memories. While this signaled a new beginning for these who would be mated, it also signaled an end to the major gather, and the return to their normal lives. The seating area was filling rapidly and soon the sires would be standing on the east side of the platform awaiting their daughters as they approached.

Fauul, still trying to wake up, was glad that he was the third in the group of three. When Lauut had awakened him he had been deep and it took a little time for him to realize that someone was attempting to wake him. It really seemed that he had just gotten to sleep, but when he finally opened his eyes he saw that the sun was setting and he needed to get ready. He got up with the taste of metal in his mouth and headed out to the trough to splash some water on his face, figuring that the cold water there would snap him out of it. He had stripped off his shirt to splash the water on himself and got some admiring comments from a couple of young females who happened to be passing at that moment.

Smiling at them, he turned around and headed back inside, slightly shaking his head. He figured that by now he would have been used to that reaction, but he never really understood it. He suspected that it probably was the same with some of the females who received a similar reaction from the young males. Realizing, as he entered the shelter, that he would not have as much time as he had hoped, he immediately started to get ready. He knew that now that it was here he would have no time to think of anything but being properly dressed, to listen for the cues, and when it was time, approach the platform. From here until the morrow, time would fly. And until they were alone and possibly have a moment or two to be able to catch their breath and have things slow down, it all would be a blur. He had always wondered what it would be like to be on this end of it, and tonight he would find out.

Lauma saw dusk approaching and knew that shortly she would take her place in the line and start her walk to the platform. She had taken a critical last look at herself in the full-length looking glass and was pleased with what she saw. She had never owned an outfit like this in her life, and after the adjustments that her friends had made, it fit perfectly. When looking at herself she could barely see the same female that had been working on the property. The working of her hair had again changed her appearance and the light use of some makeup that the village females used highlighted her face in a way that again was very pleasing. While still nervous, she couldn't help but marvel at this female standing there. She would have never believed that she could look like this. Yet, here she was, and it was her that she was looking at. Turning around at the sound of a voice she realized that Sooma had just commented to one of the females who were present.

Turning to her Sooma said, "Oh Lauma, almost time for you to join the other two. As you know I'm going to be with your brother as the representative of the family so that he doesn't feel too out of place. So I have to leave. I'll see you shortly as you approach the platform. Oh, by the way, not that you can't figure it out for yourself, but you'll be knocking your male off his feet when he sees you. I suspect that he is going to be shocked at the transformation here."

"Yes, I do look nice don't I?" Lauma asked, in a quiet voice.

"Well if you want my opinion, I would say that what you just asked is an understatement of the facts. You've always had a wonderful and beautiful smile, but now you are radiant, just radiant. Anyway got to go . . . will see you soon." Sooma quickly turned and left to go join Lauma's sibling at the platform.

Stepping out the door she heard the music being played by the small band of the village – just members who play different instruments who get together for these occasions to provide the music. As had been explained in the morn, two specific pieces of music would play signaling a warning to be ready. She was hearing the first of those two now. Suddenly her nerves really kicked in. She was almost shaking, but thought that most likely once she started walking to the platform that some of it would probably leave.

She walked over the east entrance to the village and saw that the other two were already there. Since she and Fauul was the last to sign in for the ceremony she would be the last to walk. This would give her a chance to see how the other two did it and give her a little respite before it would be her turn. She wondered how Fauul was doing, but figured since he was a male that he probably wasn't even nervous about it at all. Well, they could talk about that later. She heard the pause between the music being played knowing now that the ceremony was just about to begin.

Listening she heard the elder, who would perform the ceremony, start by making the opening comments. He said, "We are here tonight as part of what life is about. When we come into this world we don't know that we are incomplete, half of the whole. To be whole takes one female and one male, the opposites. So in symbolism during the ceremony the females will approach from the east and the males from the west – this, to show the separateness of each of us. As they come closer together this represents the growing closeness and understanding that there is a need for the opposite in their lives, and then when they join me here on the platform it is an acknowledgment of the promised union as one."

The music started again and the procession began. She watched the first female start her walk and across the way in the distance her counterpart doing the same. Torches had lighted the entrances to the village as well as the paths they were walking so that all was brightly lit and easy to see. Both the participants and village would have a wonderful view of the proceedings. Initially there was a silence from the people as the two groups started approaching the platform, but then the village started clapping their hands in encouragement. She watched as the first female came up to her sires, and at the same time the male on the other side waiting until she and her sires then stepped on the platform at which time he joined them.

The second one was now about half way so she knew it was time for her to start her walk. Once she was out in the open she had the first chance to see Fauul. Wow! Was all she could say. The outfit he had chosen worked well for him. She, looking at some of the young females, saw the surprise in their eyes as he approached, and at the same time something else she didn't quite understand. For a moment he stopped, which puzzled her, but then he continued and before she knew it she was with her brother and friend Sooma. They stepped up on the platform and all waited for the music to stop.

Fauul, approaching the stage, looked across to see Lauma, and he stopped and stared. This definitely wasn't the same female he had been with. Never had she looked more beautiful. When Sooma had told him that the outfit was right for Lauma, he had no idea how right it was. Realizing he had stopped he started walking again and approached the platform a step behind her. When she stepped up on the platform he did the same. He was smiling and found that he couldn't stop if he wanted to.

The elder began by saying to the couples softly, "Turn around to the village please," which they did as one, following his directions.

"Sires I ask the question that I asked earlier today are your daughters entering into this relationship freely?"

The sires, Lauut, and Sooma all nodded.

"Now that we have confirmation that all is as it should be, sires you may go sit in your place of honor."

When the sires left the couples turned back around and faced the elder. Smiling he said, "I have many things to say, and then there will be a point to where you will repeat your vows to each other. Do you all understand?"

Once again the couples nodded their heads confirming their understanding.

"What you enter into tonight should in no way be taken lightly. Your promises made here are for a lifetime, and if one does not see it that way you should not be here.

"A relationship is three parts. These are mental, spiritual, and physical. All have to come into play as the two of become one. Mental, as you first were attracted to each other, and the discussions you have made over time. The compromises, the disagreements, the understandings you have found, the truths you have learned about each other. While, as you go on in your life, these beginnings are just what they are in comparison of what is ahead of you.

"Spiritual, this is the building love that you feel for each other. While you feel, at this time that it cannot get any stronger, you will learn that it will. You are a conduit for the love the Creator has for His creations. Your emotions, good or bad, can be considered to be from that side of you.

"And the third and final is physical. From the physical comes the next generation. If shown properly, is a strong part of the others. Each complement each other, and in different times of your lives together you will find that each one of these three attributes changes in importance.

"There are many things out there beyond your relationship that can destroy the beginning foundation you have been creating between the two of you. Most dangerous of these are pride, anger, and jealousy. Most important to the continued health are communication, compassion, compromise, and wisdom to know what is important at the moment.

"The two of you must show a united front, have much humor, forgiveness, and forgetfulness, and in all things cooperation. As you, in the eyes of all, are one. Males, I am speaking to you as each of you has an important place in your relationship. Soon, if it is so willed, there will be whelps added to your new families, and each of you will go from being the most important to being part of the new. You must, at all times, keep these principles in mind – understanding, protection, provisions, learning, guidance, cooperation, and discipline lies upon your back.

"Females while the list is smaller for you, it still is a tougher one. You have your eyes and spirits on forever. It is through you that the next generation will appear. So family, sharing, nurturing, and the peace keeper are what you face. Do all of you understand what has been said here?"

All of them answered yes.

"Now as you know we will be dealing with the first two parts of the three here. As the vows are repeated you will place the leather bracelets on each other's wrists, and then I will attach the strap between the two, this being again symbolic of the cooperation necessary for your relationship to survive. Then you will join the village in the celebration of your newness. Once this second part then is over, you will retire to the spaces that have been provided for your use to consummate your relationship. It has already been explained to you what is there. Only there can the strap be removed, and then in the morn you will be trading your leather bracelets for the copper ones.

Males repeat after me . . . By placing this bracelet on your left wrist I am claiming you as my mate . . . I am promising to be there for the best and worst of times, and to support you in your needs . . . knowing that as time passes many changes will happen that are unforeseen and unexpected . . . and that you and I will remain one until our passing from this world."

At each pause the males repeated the wording as presented, and then the elder turned to the females and asked them to repeat the same phrase to their mates – Finishing with the males and females placing the leather wrist bands on the left wrists of their mates.

Once completed, he walked between each of the couples and tied the strap between them, and turned to the village saying, "They have completed the first two parts of the ceremony of mating and are considered such. These couples, understanding the mental and spiritual sides, and have accepted their responsibilities. In the morn, with the confirmation of the third part, they will receive the copper bracelets confirming to all they are to be lifelong mates. May I present our newly mated!"

With that statement a cheer went up from the village, the music began again and then the elder said, "Go join your loved ones and enjoy this celebration." He smiled saying, "Since it is in your honor that we do this."

All three couples hugged each other, and kissed their new mates and headed off the platform to the cheers of the crowd.

The evening celebration was a blur of people congratulating, the food and drink, and the difficulties of navigating the areas tied together. Fauul thought that overall it would have been easy with just a little thought, but found instead that it was anything but. What seemed the logical easy way to go was not necessarily how Lauma thought it would be. They ended up a number of times almost falling or pulling the other off balance. Then there were the individuals who would walk between them purposely and become entangled in the strap.

Of course, as expected, there were comments about the third part of the ceremony. Most were subtle, as with most of these ceremonies, whelps were present. Ah yes, the adult world where many statements had a double meaning. Fauul, in a spare moment, as there had been few so far, whispering in her ear said, "You are absolutely beautiful tonight.

When you approached the platform you stopped me in my tracks. For a moment there I thought, who is this person . . . and they were right you absolutely glowed. When I had asked your friend about the outfit they had gotten for you all she would say was it was right for you, and all I can say is that right doesn't come close."

"Thank you my new mate." She whispered back as another couple from the village came up to congratulate them.

As time went on she felt nature building but thought she would wait, but it appeared that the celebration would run late into the night and as such was the case there would be no way she could hold it that long. Finally surrendering to the need she told Fauul that she had to use the necessary space. He said that it would probably be a good idea if he did to. Like her he was hoping to be able to wait until the celebration was complete before attempting the use of the necessary space.

Both headed off still attached to each other. She wondered why this was so important. After all, nature's call was something all had to deal with, so why make them stay tied together? All she could figure out was it had to do with something about sharing everything including embarrassing moments. And while this was done in fun, but required, there was a serious side to it. She was seeing that this simple strap enforced cooperation. And if you did not cooperate then you would fall flat on your face – a simple lesson right out of being newly mated.

They reached the necessary space, and barely able to hold it she entered the female side. He then leaned against the shelter. There really wasn't anything else he could do. Limited by the strap he was not even able to pull far enough away to feel comfortable himself. She, when she sat down to relieve herself, thought maybe I can just let it go slowly, but her bladder was so full that it ached, and she said to herself, "The heck with it." and let it go. From the outside it sounded a little like a flood of liquid, but he tried to ignore it.

Shaking his head a little he really didn't see the importance of this, but he was sure that there was a reason. After all, everyone had this need, why embarrass anyone? The door opened and she then came out with her face a little red and she said, "Glad that's over, now it's your turn." So, once again, they went to the male necessary space, and the roles were reversed, she on the outside and he on the inside. She heard what sounded like a stream hitting something solid and then the sound tapered off and a short time later he emerged. Looking at her, he shrugged, and they both headed back to the celebration.

The celebration ran late into the night. The ones with whelps had bowed out earlier. Leaving the older couples and the singles still enjoying the company of the three newly mated. Eventually even this group started drifting away, and finally the three new couples were able to gracefully say goodnight and head for their prepared spaces.

As Lauma and Fauul walked to the third space reserved for them they felt exhaustion in every step. After the nervousness of the day, the ceremony, and the celebration they found that their energy reserves almost completely gone. It was almost an effort to even think let alone walk. Finally they entered the space and found that there were a number of small surprises. But they should have realized that this tradition in the mating ceremony had been going on as far back as anyone could remember. So there had been plenty of time to know what would be nice to have.

Looking around the first thing of course was the bed. Yet that was not the only furniture in the room. There were a couple of chairs and a small table. On the table food and drink was visible. On the door of the smaller space were these words. IF THIS IS A FORCED UNION THEN HERE IS THE SPACE FOR YOUR PROTECTION. IF NOT THEN PLACE THE PORTABLE POT FOR YOUR NECESSARY NEEDS IN HERE FOR YOUR PRIVACY.

"Now they think about our privacy. What about out there?" she asked

Laughing at her comment he said, "I think it's probably because if things progress as they are supposed to then privacy is no longer an issue."

Making a face at him she said, "Yeah right. Bet you can't wait."

"Now, don't think that I didn't know that a few times when we were kissing pretty heavily, back during the pursuit, that it did not appear that you were unwilling."

"True, but it wasn't going to happen, so it was fine to test the waters so to speak." Looking around she said, "Let's see what else they have provided." The area within the room was bathed is soft candlelight which left shadows in many areas. They found additional candles that would brighten the space if they felt like it. Also they found a basin with water, plus an additional supply, if it was needed. Both drying and washing cloths with a cleaner were found. Then they discovered that their everyday clothes had been placed there along with a place for their celebration outfits.

She knew that the outfit for part three had been placed in the small room and soon she would be changing into that. Although right now, she felt very shy around Fauul. *What if he didn't like what he saw?* After all, she had what she considered a number of flaws. At this moment, she hadn't figured out a way to hide them. Would they turn him off and make him not like her?

They both sat down in the chairs and were silent. Fauul said, "It feels good just to sit, and to finally have it silent. If I'm not careful it would be easy to fall asleep." Looking over at Lauma he could see her smiling, he continued, "Now you know we must complete this part of the ceremony so it will be a while before either of us sleeps."

"I guess that's so. So I'll get changed and you can do the same." She got up and went into the smaller space, leaving the handle on the outside went inside, which had a small candle burning, closed the door and undressed, and put on the small outfit. While she was doing this he in turn undressed in the larger room. While he had no special outfit for this night he stripped to his under shorts, and went back and sat down.

Time passed and Lauma had yet to put in an appearance, so he asked, "Is there something wrong? Can I help in some way?"

"No, no problem . . . I'll be out shortly." Knowing that she would have to come out sooner or later, she worked up the courage and slowly opened the door. She felt so exposed. While she had partly gotten over the fear of the outfit when she had worn it in front of her friends, she found that the fears had returned.

Fauul remained sitting and saw the door crack open and continue to open slowly. Then she slowly emerged from the room so that he could see her. Standing quickly because he saw the doubt and fear in her eyes he said, "Lauma! Wow, is all I can say. If you are worried about me not wanting you this way you are so wrong. Come here and let's hug, and yes that outfit makes you even more desirable to me."

"Are you sure? You're not just saying that are you?"

"Are you kidding? Just look and you can tell that's not the case at all."

Looking close at him she realized that he was not lying at all. It was there for her to see, something that a male could never hide. This gave her confidence to come out and to go to him where they hugged.

"Okay, I know we will have a life time for this part of our lives, but tonight we probably should just get this completed, try to get some sleep, and truly start our new lives together on the morrow. And I'm not trying to downplay this at all. I wish there were a way to make this memorable. But most people I have asked said that this first time was very forgettable, and only with time did things work better. Plus you work with the beasts including their breeding. So I do think you know where we are going with this."

"True, but now it's me this time and not them. After all it will be me who had to take something inside of me instead of them. It makes all the difference in the world. But, I'm tired, so you lead and we'll go from there," She said softly even though the nervousness still showed in her voice.

He led her to the bed and he sat down, saying, "Okay, my love. You sit here between my legs with your back to me. I want to massage you a little and get you relaxed and enjoying my touch."

She did as he asked and he started working her shoulders and back. Slowly working down and being slow and deliberate. "Fauul, that feels wonderful."

He continued to work her over, every once in a while, he would touch her in private areas, with a very light, gentle touch, which was beginning to have an effect on her. Slowly but surely she felt her body responding to his touches, and was feeling the passion rise within her. Finally she was beginning to understand what those female beasts might have experienced. And suddenly she no longer cared.

The next morn, after cleaning up, and eating a light meal, wearing their normal clothes, they packed their personal items and opened the door heading outside. She wondered, if indeed it had, after what they had done last night, left any lasting impression or if she had somehow changed in such a way that it would be noticeable. The only thing she noticed at this moment was a small bit of soreness down there. She attributed that to never having anything in there. It did make her walk a little gingerly, but other than that all seemed to be normal.

Waiting out front sitting at one of the tables was the elder who had performed the ceremony, and smiling, he said, "I see that all went well with you two last night. But I am required to ask, did you consummate your relationship as required?"

How is it that he knew immediately? Maybe there's a subtle change. If it were that obvious to him would it be the same with others? "How did you know?" she asked.

"Oh, it's the way you two are when you come out. You see the physical ties you even closer together than anything you have done up to this time. Anyone who has been around mated couples can tell. While the act is up close and personal, and messy, it brings another type of closeness that one can see. Anyway, I ask again, did you consummate your relationship?"

Both looked at each other and then at him and answered yes.

"Okay then, can you give me your leather bracelets, and here are your copper ones to replace them. May your lives together by happy and may there be many whelps."

Trading the leather for the copper they eagerly placed the new bands on their wrists, thanked him and headed off to find her brother. They would spend just a short time with him. He had their bags that they would take with them for their time away. They would join some of the groups heading up the coast so that they could catch the water-craft and head to his apartment in the township where he grew up. There she would be meeting Fauul's family, and they would have much time alone and together with his family.

CHAPTER FIFTEEN

Jllon, taking one last look of their first discoveries, finally turned to the team and said, "I guess we have done all we can here, so let's head over to the new area. I really wish that we had been able to arrive at our destination in time for the major gather. It would have been a nice break before we start again. Still there is nothing we can do about it. There's a possibility that we will be within one quarter of the next minor one, and we can use it as a small break."

The sun was just rising touching the edge of the desert, and with first light they had decided to head around the mountains by the alternate trail to make the travel as easy as possible. They left one pack beast and took the remainder with them. The needs of the smaller crew would not be as great as theirs so one would be all they would have need of.

They climbed out of the desert floor and took a brief halt so that they all could look over the panorama that was before them to the east. Someday they would be able to uncover other secrets that lay deep in the desert, but for now that was for some time in the distant future. Watching the sun continue to rise over the desert they finally turned, with the coolness of the morn upon them, and continued into the abandoned village, down to the main canyon trail and generally west to meet the trail to the south that would take them to the outpost.

They pulled into the village in the late after zenith, with Jllon with Doube making arrangements for the use of the hostel. On the trip down he and Doube had decided that the best course of action was for Doube to head out to the property and see if Fauul was back as of yet. And if so, to have Fauul come into the village where they could discuss their hoped for course of action with him. But first they would take a day off from doing anything and just relax. After all, it would be their first time back in civilization in a very long time – even though it was a small and remote village.

It seemed strange, at first, to actually hear others talking and seeing strangers walking around. The only such things, from where they had come from, were the many small creatures and crawlers that seemed to exist everywhere in the desert. So to find one among people again would take getting used to. Once the team was settled in at the hostel, with the females having their own shelter, Doube led the males over to the yards and introduced them to Aurto, and asked to purchase some of his excellent ale that he brewed somewhere close by. Smiling at the crowd Aurto went to fetch the requested ale and the team seeing that there were not quite enough places to sit on the covered porch sat on the boardwalk – some leaning against the rails that supported the cover and others against the wall between the chairs. Like Fauul and Doube, who had visited this area so long ago, they started noticing the cool breezes that seemed to be blowing out of the southwest cooling the lingering heat of the day making it quite pleasant to just sit here and relax. Again, like the two before, they found it easy to let the day, the breeze and the quiet soak into them, with only idle conversation passing between them, and many silences, as they just enjoyed the moment.

Aurto arrived with the ales and a promise of more if they so desired, and that brought a cheer as there had been nothing like this available to them for a very long time. Even though they knew this was just a short respite, it almost felt like a real vacation. Aurto asked Doube, "So what brings you back, and with a different crew?"

"This time I am with some learned, and their fieldwork team. Jllon is the leader, and like last time

I'm working and scouting for him. Of course last time I was with the mapping team. He's the 'Head Keeper of the Past', and is planning on a learning dig around here somewhere. So they will be here, well not here in the village, but here in the area for quite a while I suspect. So I'm sure that there will be an increase of business for the village."

"Ah, we can always use the additional business. This keeper of the past is he a good one to work for or is he like so many of the ones in charge . . . you know like that ah . . . who was it last time you were here?"

"Do you mean Joellie the one who was in charge the last time I was here?"

"Yeah, I think so. Is this one like that one?"

Laughing Doube said, "The difference is like night and day. You will find that you will like this one quite a bit. His mate is even with him on this project."

"His mate? Really, she must be not much to look at if she likes that kind of work. I know that the weather can ruin a female, and if she does much of this, the sun would have done its damage."

Smiling at his ignorance, Doube said, "Well, I think you are going to be very surprised. In fact there she is now. I suspect she is coming to find out where I am, and again I suspect that Jllon would like to see me. And before you ask, no, she does not do his errands for him, but they work very well together."

Turning around to where Doube had pointed Aurto saw a female approaching and to his surprise she was one of the most beautiful females he had ever seen. Turning back to Doube with a questioning look he asked, "Her? You don't mean her do you?"

Laughing again Doube said, "Yes, I do mean her. And she doesn't see it either. She just doesn't understand why males act like they do around her. But understand this she and her mate are very close and work very well together, so even though a few get ideas about her it won't happen."

"Then all I can say is that he is a very lucky male to have such as her. I have known other females that do not come close to matching this one and are really into themselves with the exclusion of everyone else."

"Yeah haven't we all, and that can go for both sexes."

Nouma, seeing the team over by the yards came over and found Doube and smiling said, "There you are Doube. Jllon said he would like to see you, but no hurry. He said he just had a few questions that came to mind once we got here."

"Thanks Nouma, when you see him, tell him that once I finish my ale here that I'll bring him one, and then we can talk. Oh, by the way this individual is Aurto, the local beast master."

"Aurto? Glad to make your acquaintance. As you've heard, I'm Nouma and Doube that sounds great. Hey you know what; it's kind of nice to be back in civilization again. I almost have forgotten what it's like to be honest." She turned and left heading back towards the hostels.

"So why is she on this project? I mean someone like her should be anywhere but here."

"True, but she is unique as this is her other love. And she is in charge of the other females who are working this project."

"There are other females who are doing this?"

"Yes, but they are learners from the higher learning, and by doing this are getting a couple of turns of free learning out of it for their work."

Shaking his head Aurto said, "I would not have expected this. While many of the females here help their mates in the hard work, mostly they try to keep closer to the shelters. Since time and the sun can take away from them their youth and they fear the loss of their looks. It can be harsh, but there is very little any can do about it."

"True, and it in itself, is a tragedy. Time is the ultimate conqueror. It takes it all from us and allows us no respite."

"Now you're a philosopher, and all this time I thought you were a simple scout."

Laughing at the comment Doube said, "Okay, guess if you can get me a couple more of your ales I'll go see what the boss wants." After receiving and paying for the ales he headed back to the hostel to see what Jllon had in mind. Suddenly he realized that this was what he and Fauul had done the last time they both were here. It almost seemed a lifetime ago. Much had happened since that inauspicious beginning. Who would have thought that their trip out to the property would have been the beginning of a journey that would lead to the discovery of those elusive *ones before*?

Arriving, he saw Jllon sitting and talking with Nouma. He waited until he thought he could interrupt and approached the two of them and offered the ale he had brought for Jllon to him and then apologized to her for not bringing her one. Then turning to Jllon he asked, "So what was it that you want to see me about?"

"I've just come back from the mercantile, and ran into some friends of Fauul and Lauma, and they have stated that they have returned from their mating break and are back on the property with Lauut. So what I would like you to do is simply return to the property, since you have been there, and talk with them. See if I can have a meeting with them. I know that because of their situation that I will have to go to them, which is fine with me. I want the team to break for at least a quarter of a cycle before we start again. But at the same time I would like to have this set up beforehand."

"Okay, I can leave right now, as there still is enough time left today to be able to reach the property before dark. If I wait much longer it will not be so.

Unless it doesn't matter if I start out in the morn instead of now."

"It's your call. Once we start the work again I suspect it will be a long while before we can break like this again."

"The rest of the males of the team are over at the yards with Aurto enjoying a few ales. He makes some of the best in the region. You'll see that once you drink yours, anyway, I think I will just grab something to eat here and head out. Who knows how long it will take to get things arranged?"

"That's quite true. I know that especially in the outback here, that many still live by the right of the 'benefit of the majority' law – which states that if you have something of benefit for the majority, then for the period of the good of the people, you can lose the use of your property until such time as it is deemed over. While I know it can still be invoked, I have never liked it. So I must be able to convince them that it is not my plan to use that law at all."

"Yeah, I know what you say is true. While it was always supposed to been used for good, I know personally that many times it was used for personal gain by someone in power at the time. Anyway, guess I will see you in a couple if not sooner." At that he left and headed over to the eatery to get some food before heading out.

It definitely was approaching dark when he reached the gate. It had turned out to be a little further than he had remembered. *Funny how that works*, he thought. Anyway he was here now, and now came the fun of trying to enter without the dogs coming after him. He hoped that they remembered him.

Inside the shelter the three of them were talking after a long tiring day of work. Even with the one working with Lauut, while they were gone, the work had continued to pile up and things kept getting further and further behind. So presently they had been working from dawn to dusk with little break to get caught up. Suddenly they heard the dogs barking. But unlike their barks when chasing something it was different. "I think someone is approaching," Lauut said. "Although I would almost say that they know whoever it might be."

"Approaching at this time of day?" Lauma asked

The two males got up and went into the yard to see if they could see anything. But when they arrived they saw the dogs heading towards the gate, but because of the coming darkness could not see anything. Listening carefully they thought they heard a voice over the din created by the dogs. To Fauul the voice sounded familiar, but who it was did not come immediately to mind. Turning to Lauut he said, "You stay here, I'll walk down there. For some reason I know the voice and the dogs seem too also. Anyway this way if it turns out bad you will have a warning and can act accordingly."

He walked down towards the gate, being careful. As he approached he could barely make out someone standing on the other side away from the dogs and again there was something in his stance that was familiar. Then it came to him it had to be Doube. He said, "Doube! What the heck are you doing here anyway?"

"I don't know . . . keeping myself on this side to keep the dogs off of me I think."

Laughing, he turned around and yelled up to Lauut and said, "It's okay it's Doube. As soon as I can get these dogs away from the gate we will be back up."

Listening he heard Lauut reply giving an acknowledgement. Lauut returned to the shelter to let Lauma know so she would not worry. Fauul was finally able to get the dogs away from the gate and let Doube in. "I haven't seen you since I ran into you at the port."

Coming through the gate carefully and giving the dogs a chance to sniff him he said, "That's very true, and I really didn't expect you there either. So now that you have a mate how's everything going with you?"

"Oh very well. In truth I couldn't be happier. We have been good for each other. You know I was one who figured it would be many turns before I became serious – having too much fun being single, so why would I want to spoil it? Yet here I am and quite happy about it. So what's up anyway?"

"Let's get up in the shelter so that I can speak to all of you, and then hopefully you can give me shelter for this night before I return."

"You know better than that. They provided for us the last time we both were here, and that hasn't changed."

They entered the shelter and headed into the meeting and sitting area where Lauut and Lauma were standing and awaiting his arrival. With both smiling at Doube, Lauut said, "It has been a long time and many changes since we last saw you."

"Can we get you something to drink or eat?" Lauma asked

"Actually yes, both would be nice. I ate before I left but that was quite a while ago."

"Okay then, let's all go to the eating area where he can eat, and we'll get some hot beverage and join him there. Does that work?"

Both Fauul and Lauut nodded and moved to the table where they all could talk. While Lauma, whose turn it was to work the meal that night, grabbed a plate of food for Doube. Fauul grabbed a bunch of cups and Lauut the beverage and they all sat down at the table. Initially, as Doube ate, there was just simple small talk as they reacquainted themselves with each other. Then Doube said, "As it was the last time I was out here, I'm here at the request of the one I'm working for."

"So I suppose that it's still the 'Head Keeper of the Past'?" Fauul asked.

"Yes it is."

Both Lauut and Lauma looked at each other questionably and then back at Fauul, "Keeper of the Past?" They asked. After a brief pause and looking at Fauul before continuing they asked, "Isn't he some kind of learned? One who deals with dusty old records and such? What would he want with us?"

Replying to the question Fauul said, "Don't ask me. I've been here with you. I just knew that was whom Doube was working for. The rest will have to come from him."

Smiling at the exchange from the three, Doube said. "First off he is much more than just a learned, and yes I suspect that he does deal with dusty old records and such, but he also deals with finding out about our past. And that requires work outside the shelters. It requires much time away from home and getting quite dirty. It probably is harder work than what you do here believe it or not."

"How would you know that?" Lauma asked, curious now.

"I have been with him since the beginning of fall, and he, unlike someone we know Fauul, is a great leader. Once you two meet I think there will be an instant friendship. You two are more alike than any two I have met. Plus Lauma, I think you will love his mate."

"His mate? She is with him and works these projects with him?"

"Oh yes, she is just as passionate as he is, and they are just a wonderful couple. Anyway, this is going off the subject. I need to get permission from you for a meeting. And because he is aware of your circumstances, he will want to come here to talk with you. He has much to tell you and ask of you. From my time with him I would say listen carefully. What he tells you he believes in, so if he says it you can trust his word."

"Coming from you Doube, that's high praise," Fauul said.

"Yeah, probably so, but he deserves every bit of it. Anyway that's why I am here. So can I let him know that you will meet with him?"

Not seeing any reason why not to meet they agreed. They set the meeting up for three days from the present to give Doube time to return back to the village, to take a break, and time to come back with Jllon.

They spent the rest of the evening just catching up. Then Doube found, that unlike before, when he and Fauul went out to the work shelter to sleep, it was Lauut and he. Asking Lauut why he had changed with Fauul he said, "I figured since he and my sister are now mates that they deserve the main shelter, and I would just live out here for now. It's a change yes, but I think that they deserve their privacy, and if I had stayed there even though my sleeping space isn't very close to the master space it might have been a little uncomfortable. After all they really haven't been mates for very long yet, and there are adjustments both have to make. I just don't need to be there right now to complicate things."

"That's really nice of you to do that. After all Fauul is the outsider here, and the two of you have fought to keep your property running, so I thought that maybe they would move here."

Smiling at Doube he said, "Now why would I do that to my little sister? She is very special to me, and I think she deserves the best, and honestly I don't think she could have done much better than finding Fauul. So it is just a small sacrifice on my part. Believe me they both objected when I suggested it. But right now I think it is for the best."

"I can understand your feelings for your sister. I feel the same for mine. Only she is the oldest so I am her little brother, even though I am bigger than she is. Yes sacrifice for family is not unusual. Eventually I will have to give up scouting to go back and work my family's property when my sires are no longer able. When that finally happens, it will be a tough day for me."

"So how large is your family anyway?"

"We are a little unusual. With my sires there are only four of us. Normally, as you know, families can be pretty large. I really suspect yours would have been larger if your sires hadn't been killed."

"Probably, most likely, and very true. But who can say? I find that there are all sizes of families here and I suspect that there is no usual size. It probably comes down to what the sires are comfortable with."

Doube laughed, "Or ends up with. After all I'm sure many of the whelps are not planned."

The next morn after the morn meal Doube headed back to the village and the three of them continued their daily work. Now with less assistance from Fauul, it was a little more difficult, but he had to work on his regular assignment as a cartographer. For some of the work he required an assistant, so had hired a local youngling. He and his assistant would work four days a quarter cycle on the mapping, and Fauul would assist three days with Lauut and Lauma.

With this schedule, time was flying, and before any of them realized it the three days were up and late in the day they saw Doube and a stranger approaching their gate once more. Seeing them Lauut commented, "That sure was a fast three days. What happened?"

Looking at the two males standing there Lauma said, "Well, quit standing there and one of you go let them in. After all, we said we would talk with them when they returned, and having them approaching now and no one to greet them is just not nice."

"Okay, okay, I'll go meet them at the gate. Why don't you two finish up and while you do that I will show this Jllon around – hopefully giving you enough time to finish. Then we all can retire to the main shelter and get a meal put together. Once we've eaten and feel comfortable we can retire to the family space and see what he wants to ask. Does that sound like a plan?" Fauul asked.

The other two agreed and headed out to finish the work while Fauul headed for the gate to meet the two approaching people. He got there just ahead of them and leaned on the gate waiting to see what they would say. Doube was facing Jllon and making some type of comment that he couldn't hear. But Jllon nodded and looked back at him. Finally close enough to be heard Doube said, "Jllon this is Fauul, the elusive one, and Fauul this is Jllon the other elusive one. I've told him that you were trying to find him just as much as you were he. But neither of you were able to make the connections."

Opening the gate and stepping outside he grabbed his arms in the greeting of the day and then said, "That is very true. I even made a trip back to the township figuring I would be able to find you there only to find you were not. No one knew why you wanted to see me. I had learned that you had left again on some project before I had arrived. While it did not necessarily bother me it still left me wondering why someone of your importance wanted to see me. Oh by the way, watch out for the dogs. I am sure they will want to meet you. But I think that the other two are keeping them in the yard presently."

"I've wanted to meet you since I first saw those sketches of the object. But for whatever reasons it was not to be . . . dogs you say?"

"That seems like a life time ago. Why is that object so important anyway? And, by the way, Lauut discovered what they were, and yes dogs."

"Who's Lauut, and what did he find out?"

"You know what, instead of standing here and just talking, let me show you around. Then I can introduce you to both my mate and her brother. He can tell you personally, what he has learned." He led them back through the gate, followed by closing the gate, making sure to latch it, and led them up into the yard between the main shelter and the works shelter. Here they ran into Lauma who was heading into the main shelter. Once again, since they rotated cooking chores, it happened to be her turn again.

"Lauma, I'd like you to meet Jllon, and of course Doube you already know."

"Good day to you sirs." She responded, saying, "We'll get better acquainted a little later but if we are going to have anything to eat I need to get there and get started." She excused herself and headed into the main shelter.

"So is she your mate?" Jllon asked

Smiling he said, "Yes, and as Doube probably has told you we are just mated. He was with me when we met, and maybe even relayed the story of that meeting."

"Not a whole lot of it really, but enough to know that she had the two of you cornered."

"That's an understatement, but what can I say other than we were right for each other. It became evident almost from the beginning. It just took me a while to realize that it was so." Shaking his head he laughed as he remembered that time.

He led Jllon and Doube around the area showing off the pens and beast shelter where they ran into Lauut. Again Fauul introduced Lauut to Jllon, and found out that it would be a little while before he was finished. He showed them the area in the workers shelter that he had set up as an office and finally left them on the porch to enjoy some quiet time while he went inside to assist Lauma with the meal preparation.

Jllon, once sitting on the porch, commented, "This place looks like it has been in operation for a very long time. Wonder how far back it goes?"

"I really don't know for sure, but I do know it has been with them for many generations, and as you can see, at one time was a much larger operation. Now, it's just the three of them."

"Fauul seems like a great person, and I can see why the females would be attracted to him. It looks like he could have had any he wanted, why her? I mean she seems like a nice person herself, but is really not a beautiful female – not that something like that is important, but it does seem like an unlikely match." He laughed, "Not that Nouma and I would be considered a great match if someone saw us together."

"I can understand that view, but you have never seen her smile. Just wait, then it will change your view of her forever. On top of that she is very sharp and quite strong willed, and is one who is not afraid to make her point of view known. You will know instantly where you stand with her."

"Really? I would never have guessed she seems quite pleasant."

"True, very true, but don't lie or cross her, if you do she can be anything but pleasant."

While the two them prepared the evening meal they heard the two talking on the porch, but it was too soft to be able to understand anything they were saying. Fauul, looking at Lauma, smiled and said, "You know what, you're beautiful even now."

"Blushing again, and thinking to herself he sure can do that to me. "Would you stop that." Then playfully she said, "I know what you want but you can't have it right now so there."

"Can I help it that I love every part of you, and that you bring that want out in me? Anyway that's not what I meant, even thought I would never refuse. I really meant it."

"You know what; I don't think I would find any male refusing such an offer from a female. It seems to be the way all of you are built."

They continued teasing each other while they were alone, and as they finished the preparation Lauut entered followed by Doube and Jllon. Studying Jllon, Lauma thought he didn't appear to be anything out of the ordinary. In fact he seemed to be a little young to have such an important position. Yes, he was older than she, but still she had expected someone around the age of, well maybe her sires, if they were still alive. "So, Jllon, how long have you been the 'Head Keeper of the Past'? I mean I was surprised to see someone like you."

Smiling at her he replied, "I've been in the position for a few turns. And your reaction is quite normal. No one expects someone who appears to be young in charge of such an important position. And before you ask if this was a bought position, because of someone in my life that had high importance, the answer is no."

"Well that's a relief. Fauul was telling me about someone he worked under who had gotten his position that way and was a real pain."

"Could that have been Joellie Trag?" Looking around he saw that that name got a reaction.

"So how is it that you know of him anyway?" Fauul asked

"Let's just say that I had a run in with him, and his reputation precedes him, and from what I have personally seen is no exaggeration. Plus, I had access to all the personal and field notes from your mapping project."

"Food's ready so let's eat then we can retire into the family space and continue."

With Fauul helping and Lauut placing the dinnerware on the table they all sat down and had a good meal. Using the time to get acquainted, and become a little more comfortable with each other. "Does anyone want anything else to eat?" Lauma asked. "I'm getting up, so if you do I'll get it now."

No was the general answer, so she said, "Well then, it appears we are finished. So let's retire to the other space and relax a little. Lauut, how about getting that hot beverage out there so that we can have it available and Fauul you can help me clear this mess."

Smiling at her Lauut said, "Look at that. She becomes a mate and then just starts to boss everyone around. You'd swear she was our sires."

Putting her hands on her hips she said, "Now that's just not so. I'm just delegating. After all this has to be done and since it was my turn to cook, I think, as the cook, I can tell you where to go."

Laughing Fauul interjected, "Yeah and you're great at telling us where to go", which brought a chuckle from everyone. Doube looking at the interaction between them saw that there was fun included in all the seriousness they faced. It was an important insight. He knew that it existed with his sires, and it showed that to survive it was a requirement. Finding a comfortable chair he sat down in the family space with Jllon joining him there close by. Shortly the mess was cleaned up and the rest joined them with Fauul saying, "It sure is nice to finally be able to sit and relax. It has overall been a very busy day."

The other two agreeing whole heartedly with the statement finally sat down with a sigh. Fauul and Lauma took the double seat while Lauut took the other chair. "Okay now, is everyone comfortable?" Lauut asked. "If so, what was it that you wanted to talk with us about Jllon?"

"First off can I see those, what did you call them? Fauul said you learned what they are as I remember, is that right?" Jllon asked

Lauut getting up went over to another area in the shelter, picked up a basket and brought it over to Jllon and handed it to him. "Is this what you wanted to see?"

Taking the basket he looked inside and there were two of the objects, since Lauut carried the third. The very items that had started his quest in determining if the *ones before* had existed or were the myth he had always thought they were. Of course, the discoveries in the desert had confirmed they had existed. Still, there at the desert sites, nothing like these had been found. Again, it was not surprising, since most of the area had shown massive damage from fire. "Finally I see the actual items that started the search for the *ones before*," he said.

Surprised by his statement, Lauut asked, "The *ones before*? You mean the actual *ones before*? I thought that there was a possibility that they could have been, but there was no proof. What made you decide that they could be from them?"

Smiling he said, "Remember who I am and what I have access to. You know such things as all the existing records, drawings, and sketches. So I have seen what had been presented in the past as coming from the *ones before*. All of the things that had been presented, and in the end, had been shown to be false, and made by the individuals who had presented them.

"The interesting thing is that if you laid out the sketches of these fakes from the oldest to the newest, and yes we still have a few of the fakes, you would see that these fakes have become more crude and larger as we get closer to our time. What this tells me is that sometime in our past we could do certain things better than we can now. We have lost skills and methodologies over time and haven't recovered them. It also says that there was a possibility that we were much more advanced sometime in our distant past."

They were all listening carefully to him, as what he was presenting was something they had not thought of at all. "So, if I understand it, you are saying that we may have been able to do much more then than we can now, right?" Lauut asked.

"More or less. But then you found these objects, and Fauul got one from you and brought it back with him. He showed it to his boss who suggested that he bring it over to my department. The one who saw it immediately knew it was special. He was sent to look at it as his specialty had been uncovering the fakes in our generation."

Then looking a Fauul he said, "You were initially happy to show it but, when he requested that you leave it with him, refused. He convinced you to stay long enough so that it could be sketched, but for some reason you were in a hurry and a little impatient. But he successfully got the sketches and then you and the object basically disappeared.

"Once I saw the sketches I wanted to see the real thing. While the sketches did it justice, to be able to see and feel the real thing would have given it substance. So, finally I'm now able to handle part of what started our search. And I must say I can only agree with the first assessment made by that assistant so long ago."

"So if I am understanding what you are saying, you now believe that the *ones before* might be real and not myth."

"That is correct. But for the moment that is as far as I can go . . . by the way Lauut, how did you discover their purpose? Looking at them it just isn't obvious at all."

"The same way I found them, accidentally. I was absently handling one of them after I had cleaned it up. I was opening and closing it in one hand and then dropped it. I quickly reached for it, as I did not want it to hit the ground, and missed it but struck that wheel. When that happened it threw out sparks which ignited what turned out to be a wick. Once it did that it was obvious what they were."

"Before I go any further, and I have talked with Doube on this before, I need a promise from the three of you that what we talk about from here on is kept here. If I cannot get your promise then what I would be asking after this would not make much sense."

"So can you reveal anything at all? So that we know that we are not promising something that would do harm to anyone?"

"Unfortunately, like when I was before the council, there is little I can say. I will say that there should be no harm that comes out of your promise, and maybe in the end, some good for everyone. But, I cannot even guarantee that. Even for me, with the knowledge I have, I have no way of knowing the outcome."

Fauul looking over at Doube asked him, "Doube, what's your role in this? Is what he is asking something we should consider?"

"I'm under the same promise that he is asking you. All I can say is that you trust him. He has only been fair and honest, and I do know his reasons and I understand them and actually agree in this case with them."

"We've been together over a project and I consider you a close friend and would trust your judgement. So if you feel it is something worthwhile and not something that is harmful I guess I would agree to the promise. But I cannot speak for the other two here. Even though I am now part of their family, they are the ones who have been here from the beginning. So I will go with whatever their decision on the issue is. I feel it is only right."

Jllon turning to Lauut and Lauma asked, "You've heard what Fauul said, so I am asking, will you promise to keep what we are discussing here a secret until such time as it can be revealed?"

Lauut looking over at Fauul said, "Gee thanks. You leave it in our laps. Okay Lauma what is your opinion on this?" Turning towards Jllon he asked, "Is there any more information that you can give us to help here?" Jllon shook his head no. "Okay, why don't you two stay here, and Fauul, Lauma and I will go outside to discuss this. Is that okay?"

"No problem. I know I'm asking much with little to help you with your decision, but I haven't been able to figure out how to present this without giving anything away."

The three of them got up went outside into the yard to discuss what had been asked of them. Once outside Lauut asked, "Do you trust Doube that much?"

"Simply put, yes. You know his reputation. And as long as I was with him he has only proven it. Heck, he even saved my life back in the desert. So anyway you want to put it, yes I trust him. He even said that he trusted Jllon also. That's high praise coming from him."

"I guess if it is something that must be kept quiet it must be something really big. But what could the Head Keeper of the Past want with us here. I mean, come on, we are just a small property in a very small remote village close to the coast. I mean big deal right?"

During the conversation Lauma kept quiet listening to what was being said, she finally asked, "Just what's going on? We've been going through quite a bit of change here lately. What is it that he wants to present? I mean someone with his status did not need to come to us. He could have requested that we meet him somewhere, and if you think about it, we probably would have been obligated to meet him."

"You're right", mused Lauut. "So do we trust him or don't we?"

The other two kept silent to allow him time to think. "You know sis, what you said is true. He could have made us come to him. Instead he came to us. Plus Fauul you say that you trust Doube and it appears that he agrees with Jllon on this promise. I guess it must really be something important."

Again both of them kept silent. While Fauul probably was better equipped to make a decision, he again felt that it was not his place being the newest member here. He would go along with any decision that Lauut would make. He said, "Lauut, I cannot make this easier for you. I can only give you the input that I have. Since this is you and your family's property, and has been for many generations, it falls on your shoulders for a decision, and I will live by whatever one you make."

"Thanks for the confidence here. Why is it that such things are never easy? It always seems that you have to make decisions when you have only part of the facts. And because of that you can never know if what you have decided was correct in the first place . . . okay, okay then. From what I have seen, and from what the two of you have presented, I'm going to trust him and tell him yes. Do you two agree with that?"

His sister nodded and Fauul said, "I told you that I would abide by any decision you wanted to make on this, but I, truthfully think, it was the correct one."

"Okay then, let's go back and tell him."

As they entered the door Lauut saw that they had been calmly, but expectantly awaiting their decision. "Okay Jllon, you have our promise. Whatever you tell us will remain here with us."

"You know in truth I hate to have to do this. We, as a society, are pretty open and very few secrets exist. I know that there always will be, but I never figured that I would be one of them hiding the biggest secret of them all." He paused before continuing, seeing that he had their complete attention. "Anyway, we have been digging in the desert and have proof that *the ones before* are real. Not only that but we are their descendants."

Silence permeated the room as the three of them soaked in what had just been revealed to them. "Are you quite sure about that finding?" Lauut asked. "I mean it's just myth right? Something sires use to keep the whelps in line right?"

Jllon saw that the same reaction seemed to be with the others in the room also. Shaking his head he continued, "No they are quite real. And indirectly you are the one responsible for their discovery, Lauut."

"How can that be? I've been here all my life and I haven't been close to anything that even resembled the *ones before*."

"Let me explain here, and then I think you will see how all of you fit into this. First of all, before Fauul and Doube came here to purchase pack beasts, they were working a mapping project, which took them through the desert. In their personal notes were hints of something out of the ordinary. But even they did not realize the significance of what they saw. Now if it had ended there then nothing probably would have come out of their findings. Are you with me so far?" Fauul, Lauut, and Lauma nodded agreeing.

"Then, because of the need of additional pack beasts, and they arriving between gathers, the boss decided to send Fauul and Doube here to purchase the pack beasts. I know that this part of the story is very familiar to you. Anyway from that contact came the, what do you call them . . . oh yes, fire starters. Anyway, to keep this from getting too long, the one that Fauul had was shown to my department. We knew that it was special almost from the moment we saw it. As far as I know we have been unable to make anything that comes even close to them.

"Again, these ah, fire starters, would again by themselves, probably not have started the investigation. But when the two facts were put together and both were in a kind of close proximity with each other it was enough to get permission to pursue a dig. We started with the desert for a number of reasons, the most important being the notes from the cartographers. Isolation of course was another."

"Why isolation?" Fauul asked. "I would have thought that working close to a populated area would be easier."

"Easier yes, but in a populated area or even close to one there is a greater chance that anything that would be found would be contaminated by the very population living there. Making it difficult to determine if the finds were genuine or just something forgotten that had belonged to the ones living there."

"So what makes you so sure that what you found in the desert belongs to the *ones before*? Fauul asked again.

Doube said, "Believe me Fauul, if you saw what was found you would have no doubt at all. We have no way presently to do anything we found there. Truthfully, it was really humbling to see what we have lost over time."

"He is quite correct. It appears that an intense fire had destroyed most of the area, but further out, what we found, was life changing – which now brings us to you and your property."

"Wait, are you telling me that you suspect that there may be something here that may be of the one*s before*?" Lauut asked, quite shocked by the possibility.

"If I have the information right, you did discover the fire starters here, right?"

Looking around at his sister and Fauul he wasn't sure how to answer, but then shrugged and said, "Yes,

I did find them here. But now you are scaring me. Since there is a law of the land that says if something of value is on one's property that will serve the greater good of all then one must give that property up for the duration of time that it applies."

"Yes, I'm quite familiar with that law, and have never liked it. It made it too easy for someone who happened to be in power at the time to declare it and then take something they coveted from someone else. No, I will not be invoking or using it, so you can relax. I have complete control over what happens with the digs and what is found.

"You see . . . what we found will change everything, and I mean everything. But before any of it can be revealed to all, we have to discover all we can so that nothing is lost or destroyed. Imagine if word got out what would happen. Our sites would be descended upon by the mobs looking for artifacts from the *ones before* and everything, in the end, would be destroyed and useless. And then one of our greatest treasures, the knowledge that we would learn from our ancient ancestors will be forever lost."

"That's fine for you to say. But there are others over you that could invoke that law, making the promises you make worthless."

"That is true. But they do not know the location of the desert site let alone this one. If nothing is discovered then nothing will happen. But if there is a discovery then the site will be protected until such time that most of the value can be obtained. I only would want anyone who invoked that law to tie it directly to the findings and not everything your family owns. I think we can safely make that work. We can make a contract that so states that the only area that the law would apply would be exclusively the dig site and anything found related to such sites."

"This is all so unbelievable. I mean just finding out that the *ones before* were real and they were our sires . . . what happened?" Lauma asked.

"Doube, do you want to answer her on that one?"

"Simply put, there appears, in the geologic record, of a worldwide event that brought destruction to almost everything approximately ten thousand turns in the past. It seems that it was severe enough to almost destroy us."

"And it is probably the reason that nothing really has been found. From what Doube related to me this disaster was severe enough to almost wipe us off the face of this planet. So any shelters would probably been destroyed, and if the intensity of the fires we saw in the desert was the norm at this time, then what would have survived initially would have been consumed by fire. Only by sheer chance would some things survive, and probably in the most unlikely of areas, like the desert."

Picturing, in their minds, what had been presented they all shuddered at the thought of having been there when it happened. What would one have done to survive such a disaster? And if it had been worldwide, as was suggested, there would have nowhere to run or to hide.

Lauut signaling to the other two said, "We've got to go back outside and discuss this. I'll give you my answer shortly." He led the other two outside into the yard again and began pacing. Immediately he realized that just by having the information given to them that everything had changed. It became clear of the importance of this and the protection. Turning to the other two he asked, "What do you think?"

"First of all . . . to have been there . . . to see it happening, not to know if you and your family will even be alive in the next few minutes, or to see them destroyed right in front of you – how horrible!" She exclaimed.

Fauul, looking at Lauma, saw that what had been revealed to her about that awful event sometime in the ancient past had really upset her. "From the sounds of it I agree it was awful. But I guess the only good we can see from it is not everyone died. If they had, we wouldn't be here to be able to see in our minds what it may have been like."

"I guess you're right, but . . . oh I don't know. I can just see mothers trying to save their whelps, and mates trying to find each other all without success. Then the pain of not knowing, and then just trying to stay alive – it's almost too much."

"Hey you two we are getting off the subject here. I need your input as to whether to give him permission or not. This is so critical that I don't want to make it myself. Wow, the *ones before* are real. That's so hard to believe."

"Yeah, see you are doing it too." Lauma said.

"Yes, I guess I am. But, to think that maybe there is proof right here on this property and never even realizing it. Then all the generations of Ktroves who have occupied this land, and none ever had been the wiser of what may lay beneath our feet. You know I almost want to give him permission to just to find out if it's true."

"From knowing Doube, and he agrees with Jllon, just from that I would agree to it. But then again I am new here so it should be only the two of you making that final decision."

"Here I thought making the first decision was hard – you know agreeing to keep quiet. Now we are putting our property and lively-hood on the line."

Lauma said quietly, "I trust him. You know it's kind of like when Fauul and I were attracted to each other, he is honest, I can sense that in him. And yes, the more I'm around him the more I like him. You can tell he cares and that he thinks quite a bit to make sure that his decisions are as right as they can be."

"So if I am interpreting what you are saying sis, you think we should agree."

"I'm not saying one way or the other here. I am just telling you what I feel and think about Jllon. You're the oldest here and I know it's not always the easiest position to be in, but it still is your decision, not mine."

"Okay, both of you have stated your feelings I guess that is two to one for accepting the offer. I must admit the idea intrigues me. So for all of us I will accept his offer with the inclusion of the contract to protect us. Is that agreeable?"

"Works for me", Fauul said

". . . and me", Lauma stated.

Heading back into the shelter Lauut looked over at Jllon and said, "Okay we can agree, as long as we have the written guarantee that only the area where you will be working will be affected."

"Good. Now come back and sit down. Now that you are with me on this I can offer you more."

"More?"

"Let's say that we would prefer not having to live in our portable shelters again. It would be nice to have a little better place to stay while we work. I have noticed that you have a workers shelter that has plenty of empty space. Included, from what Doube tells me, is a place that mated workers could live. So along with everything else I would like to rent that space. This would help with the support of your property and family here."

Looking at the other two, Lauut asked, "Would you have a problem with me moving back into the main shelter while they are here? I know I insisted on moving out to give the two of you your privacy, but if we accept this, then I feel it would only be right to give them the whole shelter."

Smiling at her brother Lauma said, "Now Lauut we told you at the beginning that it wasn't necessary that you move over there, but you insisted, as you say. So why would we object to having you come back in? After all, you will just have to get used to the two of us teasing each other and other such things. But you always teased me anyway, so that shouldn't be much different."

Smiling he continued, "Yeah I guess that's true. But I'm sure it's a little different than when I teased you." Turning back to Jllon he said, "Okay, I can't turn down some additional income when it has been so hard to come by."

Fauul smiled. "I guess I'll have to move my operation also. No issue really."

"Again, good. But I'm, of course, not finished throwing things your way. First, let me say that what we are using for our cover story here is learning. I have in my team learners who are here of course learning but also earning additional time for higher learning. It was a cost saving method. With all that has been spent on the mapping, there was little to fund this project. So if ever asked, you will tell all who want to know, that you had received correspondence from me a while ago, asking permission to use your property as a place for this learning, and of course, you agreed since it would help with your finances.

Now for the . . . ah . . . probably the most difficult part from you, and that is you must reveal where you found these wonderful artifacts. Without a location we cannot do what we are here to do."

"Yeah I thought I would have to do that. But if what you say is true then of course I will do that. But initially I will show you and Fauul. Lauma has already been there, and by the way, no I am not leaving out Doube. So on the morrow all four of us can go. By the way tight places don't bother any of you?"

"No, why?" They asked.

Smiling he said, "Because where we must go is underground."

When he revealed the location, for a moment there was just silence. Then Jllon said, "Underground, huh. So what made you want to go searching underground anyway?"

"Let's just say I was curious, and leave it at that. When we get there on the morrow I'll explain a little. Is that fair enough?"

"I had hoped to head back on the morrow, but I think we can delay. I don't think another day or two in the village will bother the team, and I left it open with Celt on when we would return. So sure on the morrow will be fine."

"Good, but we cannot leave first thing. We've got to put together some items and then of course, we have the morn work that has to be completed before we can go. So we will pack some food since we probably will leave mid-morn and not be back before early evening. By the way, we have a tradition here, that once everything is finished in the evening we retire for a short time out on the porch, so if you will excuse us that is where we are heading. Of course you are welcome to join us if you would like."

The rest of the evening passed pleasantly enough and with Lauut leading the visitors he showed them the area where they would sleep. Fauul and Lauma headed back into the main shelter, finished the cleanup and retired themselves.

Once again he found himself in that cavern surrounded by numerous tunnels that had no markings to allow him to know which way was out. Again, the torch he was carrying was warning him that his time was almost up. He had no other torch for backup. It was now or never. But this time instead of letting the fear and panic overcome him as it had in the past he stopped. He knew that there had to be a solution here. But what was it?

For the first time that he could remember, he looked up and there before him was the answer. It was not here in these tunnels. They were just dead ends. What he was now discovering was that he needed to look beyond the obvious to find the solution. By looking up he saw another tunnel, but by looking closely he saw a very dim light emanating from it. Now he just needed to find a way to it and then he would be out.

Once again he awoke realizing that it was the recurring dream. But this time he found the answer. Now he realized that his mind had been attempting to solve the problems for themselves and the property. The solution had been there all the time but by continuing to think in the normal way the answer had always eluded him. Now with what had been presented to him this night, a new and different solution had presented itself, and it was completely different from any direction he would have thought of. Seeing that, he felt there would be a good chance that this would be the last time he would have the dream. Finding that it was still night he turned back over and went back to sleep, satisfied, in his mind, that the up and coming changes would be for the good.

Before he knew it morn was dawning and it was time to take care of the beasts. In the air he smelled the hot beverage. That meant that his sister and brother-by-mate were already up and had started the meal. It was Fauul's day to fix the food so he knew that he and his sister would be feeding the beasts in the pens. Sighing, he got up and went to the necessary space, took care of the nature call, got dressed and headed out to meet her. He suspected that she would already be at the pens and headed in that direction.

The air was crisp when he left the shelter. Looking about he could see the skies graying towards dawn. Sure enough he saw that she had put up the railings so that the one area could be cleaned, and the beasts were waiting in anticipation of the food they were about to get. "Good morn sis, and how'd you sleep?"

Turning around pushing a wisp of hair out of her eyes she smiled and said, "Very well, and you?"

"Oh I guess okay. I had that dream again."

"Dream? Oh the one about being stuck in a cave?"

Reaching for the pitchfork he grabbed the vegetation and threw a load over the rails into the pen. She had finished the cleanup and had pulled the rails out and let the beasts back into the main pen area. The beasts eagerly attacked the food as it came into the pens. "Yes, the very same. But this time I found, well I think I found a way out."

"Really? What was so different this time?"

"I really think it was what was presented to us yesterday that provided the answer. I think I was trying to figure a way out of our problems and it manifested itself in that dream."

Leaning on the rake that she was using to clear the manure she asked, "So what was the answer?"

"Look up!"

She had a quizzical look on her face asked, "Look up? I don't understand."

"All I can say is when we normally look at something it usually just ahead or around us and not up. So up was outside the normal thinking. I think it was saying don't continue to think in your normal way but look outside of that and there you'll find your answers."

"Okay if you say so. But I will take your word for now and think on it. By the way you heading back into that crack have me a little nervous. So please be careful."

"Oh believe me I learned my lesson the first time I went there. Plus you know we are going and also know when we should be back. And that was something I didn't do the first time and again almost killed me."

Finished they headed back to the main shelter for the morn meal, "I wonder what he has prepared today? You know he isn't the best of cooks, but it's passable."

"True, and now I know where he gets it. When we were there in the township where he grew up I went to meet the family and of course had to stay for a meal. Fauul warned me that his mother wasn't the best of cooks and he surely was right. Strong opinionated female she is, but I think we got along okay. His siblings are great, and even his father. You can really see where his strength comes from, but cooking will never be one of them."

That brought a chuckle out of Lauut, "I guess we can't be good at everything."

At this point they saw that Doube and Jllon were leaving the workers shelter and joined them on the porch. Jllon commenting that he could smell the hot beverage and was looking forward to the meal. This immediately brought laughter from Lauut and Lauma.

"Did I say something funny?" Jllon asked.

With a twinkle in her eyes Lauma said, "You may change your mind. Fauul tries but isn't the best at this. At least it's edible."

After the meal the three of them left Jllon and Doube and went out to finish the morn work. Once they had completed the work they would meet the two of them on the porch. Then all of them would finish putting together what was necessary for the trip. Lauma would put together a food pack while they worked the rest.

Turning towards Doube Jllon said, "You know that food wasn't that bad. Not the best by any means but edible."

"Yeah, I've had worse, but truthfully I can't remember when. So what's your plan here anyway?"

"First of all, I don't know even what we are facing yet. It was a surprise to find that these objects were underground. But don't ask me why it surprised me. I mean so much of what would have survived probably is buried. We did uncover those artifacts in the desert. But from his description we are going quite deep, and I think that was the surprise.

"Anyway, after we figure out what we are going to do and how we will approach this I want to show them the drawings and sketches we have from the desert so that they will completely understand what it is that we are dealing with. I mean, as far as we know, anyway."

"Sounds good, but what if the area is quite a ways from here making the shelter usage a problem?"

"We'll cross that stream when we come to it. Should know much more shortly anyway. Wonder if there's any more hot beverage. He, at least, can make a decent cup of that even if the rest isn't up to our standards."

"Don't know, but give me your cup and I'll go look. Let's see you want a little honey in yours right?"

"Right, I like it just a little sweet."

Doube took the cups headed back into the shelter. Jllon heard him work around the food prep area and heard something pouring and knew that there was at least a little left. Sure enough in a couple of minutes Doube appeared with both cups full. He handed one to Jllon and they both sat down to enjoy the drinks. "You know what," Jllon said, "This is really a beautiful location. It has been situated where you get the breezes, and the views from here are wonderful."

"Yes, I noticed that the last time I was here. And when you look at the way things were originally laid out you can see that it was also built with protection in mind. Since this has been around for many generations of this family I suspect that things, at one point, were not as peaceful as they are now."

"Yeah now the only things we have to deal with are roving bands of bandits – and, of course, with care, the nomads. But if you deal with them honestly they can be a friendly bunch . . . well sort of anyway."

"The nomads are their own society and a much closed one. As you know, I'm one of the few outsiders that they have let in. Still even with the access I have there is much that I'm not allowed to know or see."

"Look it appears they are finished."

Looking down towards the pens Doube watched the three of them approaching the main shelter. As they came into voice range Lauut asked, "Did you kill the remaining hot beverage? I sure need another cup myself."

Doube replied, "No, but there's not much left, maybe a cup or two anyway. You know it's this stuff that keeps us going."

"Yeah," replied Lauma, "in so many ways it keeps you going. You know especially to the necessary space. It just seems to go through you quicker than you can drink it. And I'm heading there now. See you shortly."

This brought a chuckle from everyone. They couldn't help but agree. The stuff was good but it did seem to pass through one quickly. Jllon turning to Lauut asked, "So what's next? After all right now this is your show and we are just here to assist."

Lauut explained what they would need and they all went over to the supply shelter to put together the necessary equipment. It took at least an hour to prepare as Lauut had stated, he had learned from his first encounter and anytime he went back it was to be prepared for anything. By the time they returned to the main shelter with the packs they found Lauma sitting on the porch drinking a cup and she said, "While you all were busy out there I made a fresh pot so before you go you can have one for the trail."

Thinking that was a great idea they all grabbed their cups refilled them and came out and joined her there. Lauut telling her what he figured would be the approximate time for their return, and if they didn't by that time, to give it additional reasonable time to cover something they hadn't expected. Still he felt that with the number of people going that they were safer than when she and he had taken the journey.

Finally they all put on the packs and with Lauut leading headed out. As they went along Lauut pointed out landmarks and interesting facts, or showed them where they had done some type of work to the countryside. Eventually they came up to the area where Lauut had set up his camp and he said, "We are close here. I used this area, because once you set up here, unless you are aware there is a camp here, well it is completely hidden, and would be just passed over. We're probably fifty body lengths from the entrance right now."

Looking around the area appeared to be somewhat desolate. Even the vegetation was almost now existent. Looking ahead to the hillside Jllon noticed that it was quite steep and again very little grew on it. In fact from the steepness it appeared to be close to impassible. Again, there was little to draw one to it, so there normally would be no reason, or even interest to want to climb it. Then looking closer a little excitement entered Jllon who the pointed and said, "Doube look!"

"What?"

"Look over there. Doesn't that look like the soil you identified for me and that we used as our line of during and after the *ones before*?"

Looking at the hill they saw where some of the soil had slipped, probably because of the earth shake, and a darker soil was now visible. "You know you probably are right." Doube replied.

"What's got you two so excited?" Lauut asked.

"Doube has a theory that is close to being proven, and we have seen this soil everywhere we have gone. It's here also. Although my guess is that here it appears to be much thicker. Let's just say it's a good sign."

"Are you talking about that dark soil up there on the hillside? If so there are areas around here that are just thick with it."

Doube and Jllon walked over to the hillside and looked up at it. The sides seemed unstable and decided not to attempt the climb to study it closer. The other two joined them and Lauut said, "Come on, we need to get going or we will not have time to complete this. I think you will find that when we come back out that you will be very tired. I don't know quite why, but the times Lauma and I have been here we could barely keep awake once we got out."

He led them around until the crack was visible and the reaction was the same. "You went in there? Doesn't look real safe", Jllon stated.

"Yeah, I know. You don't have to remind me. Lauma put me in my place the first time she saw it. Anyway, we'll just use one torch for now. Once we reach the cavern at the bottom then we can light a couple to give us better light. Remember that once there, in the cavern, be very careful. We've found a number of places that have hidden drops that goes down who knows how far. Fauul, you're the biggest of us, so I think a couple of areas will be a little tight for you. So we will slow down at those points and wait for you to get through. Okay . . . ready?"

Nodding their heads, Lauut lit the torch with one of the fire starters with Jllon commenting, "Handy those things, much easier to light then using flints."

"Yes, I agree, anyway let's go."

Lauut entered first and Fauul last. They kept close together, and like Lauut, when he first entered, had expected it to be cool, but instead felt heat. It was not overpowering just a surprise. "It's cooled a little since I was here last. So I guess with this opening the heat is escaping and whatever its source it can't replenish it, which is a good thing. I was soaked from sweat the first trip."

Still, it was obvious that they too would be soaked even if it was cooler. Lauut showed them the markings he had made on the first trip and explained how he had put them together so that if they were separated they could use the same markings to return to the surface. Jllon commented that at least in this way Lauut had planned well even if other areas he was not as prepared. In a couple of the areas, as Lauut had explained, it was tight – especially for Doube and Fauul both being bigger than the other two. But eventually after what seemed like a very long time they reached the wall where it seemed to just become a dead end.

"As you can see, when I first reached this place I was disappointed. Having just come through all of what we just did, and here it ends . . . how frustrating. I mean I did a quick look around and it just seemed like this was as far as I was going. But . . . if you look you can see that there is something wrong with the perspective over there. It just doesn't look right. Do you see it?"

The other three looked closely but at first could discern no difference. It did appear to just be a part of the wall. Then in the flickering light of the torches there appeared to be an illusion and suddenly they saw what he was talking about. Doube said, "I've had much experience in finding such things but it took a while even for me to find it. How did you do it so quickly?"

"You know what, I really don't know. I was ready to give up and just go back but something caught my eye. Something just didn't look right to me so I went and investigated and . . . follow me now," which they did, "and here is what I found."

As they came around the switchback they entered into the open cavern. For a moment the three of the just stood there surprised. Even though it had been explained to them before they had taken the journey, it still was unexpected. Lauut explained the marks he had here to be able to find their way back out. Saying that once they got deep into the cavern that all the walls would appear to be similar and if the marks were not there it probably would take way too much time to find the entrance or exit.

To demonstrate what he was explaining he had them go a little ways into the cavern then turned them around a couple of times and said, "Okay, now if you look at the walls you will see that they appear to be just the same. Even though they are not, they still are similar enough to make it hard to find where you came in. Plus landmarks are not very clear either."

Again they had to agree. "Even if you were not prepared as well as should have been, it's obvious to me that you at least thought out the part of being able to find your way back out. And of course by having little or no experience in the underground it's no surprise to me that you were not as prepared as you should have been", Jllon commented. "After all not ever doing anything like this how could you know what you really would need?"

"Now let me show you a couple of areas that we need to lock into our minds. These are places that one could fall into and probably never be recovered from. Lauma and I were going to come back down and rope them off, but with work being as it has been, and of course her distractions, we never found the time to get back here."

"Meaning me, right?" Fauul asked

"Yeah, you were a pretty big distraction for both of us – obviously more for her," Lauut said, while smiling. "But I will not want to ever get that time back. I feel that it has been right for both of you."

He led them over to the areas he was speaking of and over to the small tank that still held water. "This water here is drinkable, but barely. It's heavily mineralized, but in an emergency it will do. Now it was here that I was testing this water to see if it was drinkable when I caught a flash of metal over there. Time was against me, but I still had a couple of minutes before the results of the water test were complete. So I went over to this debris pile." He led them over to it and said, "Well, this is it. This is where I found the first one, and then when Lauma came with me on the second trip, we found the other three." Pointing up he said, "See up there, there appears to be a hole. But I don't have anything tall enough to get up there, and besides this was just something we didn't have time to pursue. My guess is the same earth shake that opened the way into this cavern also caused the collapse of the roof and created the pile that we are standing next to."

"I would say that you probably have it about right," Doube said. "Looking at this pile my guess is that it's much newer than any of the surrounding debris. That's a long ways up to the roof, but it does make me curious as to what is up there."

"Interesting," was all the Jllon said, "Very interesting." Turning to the rest after looking up he said, "I know coming down here we made a number of turns but my guess is that we are somewhere under that steep barren hill. I think we will have to try and figure out how far and go from here . . . hmmm, there is much to think about that's for sure. Okay, let's head back out and then head back. I want to show you some of the drawings and sketches and get your opinion Fauul, since you have dealt with such things in your area."

"Okay by me. So what's your plan?"

"Don't know yet, but I think we will start some work down here and find a way up through that hole. At the same time we need to figure out how to judge where we are in relationship to the surface. Yes, there's much thinking here before we seriously start anything."

"Okay, if I understand it, you are ready to head back out. So follow me and we'll go." Lauut headed back to the hidden opening and head back to the surface.

Eventually they emerged from the tunnel and found that even though it was warm out, the breeze chilled them. Their clothes were soaked with their sweat, and when they looked at each other found themselves covered in dirt. They went back to the area where Lauut had camped and picked up their change of clothes that they had left there. They changed clothing, sitting down for a short period of time. Like on the other round trips made in the underground, they found that there were very tired.

After a brief rest they headed back to the shelters – both for a good hot meal, and of course, a bath. Jllon was feeling the excitement rise in him again. While the desert had presented quite a challenge it would be nothing in comparison of this one. What was inside of that hole in the roof of that cave? Would he end up disappointed and find nothing. Or would there be a whole treasure trove of items? Of course all was speculation until such time as they explored that hole – if they could. After all, there would be no easy way up to, let alone into that hole – so close, yet so far.

The sun was setting when they finally arrived back at the shelters, tired, dirty, and hungry. Fauul and Lauut went out and finished the work before coming in. They had relieved Lauma and had her fix a quick meal while they finished up. The other two went into the workers shelter and took a bath before returning to the main shelter.

"So how'd it go?" Lauma asked.

"You know I would have to agree with your first assessment of the entrance," Jllon said. "But once down there it has left me very curious as to what might be inside of that hole. Still even for us it will be a challenge as to how to enter it. Overall, I think that the trip there was very worthwhile."

"Yeah, I know what you mean. I called him either crazy or a fool for entering that thing the way he did."

"He did admit that he was stupid for doing that, but looking over what he did when he entered it the first time, he wasn't as stupid as it first appears. It was obvious he had thought out much of it. Of course having never done anything like this, it's no surprise that he wasn't as prepared as he should have been."

About this time both Fauul and Lauut entered the main shelter, she looking up said, "Okay you two, I can use some help here, but not before you clean up. Look at that mess you're tracking in here. At least you could have dusted off before coming in."

Both ducking their heads said, "Sorry, just wanted to get in here as quick as we could. You know to help, but you're right should have at least brushed off the worst of it before coming in." They hurried off to the necessary space to clean up and afterwards, come out and join her in getting the meal ready.

Yelling at them so they would hear, she said, "Fauul you know this was supposed to be your time, but I guess its better that I'm fixing this. Don't want them thinking you are trying to poison them."

"Now wait a minute here. I may not be as good as you are but I don't think I'm that bad. Am I Lauut?"

"Hey, don't bring me into this. I'm just the brother-by-mate, and I know better than to get in the middle of anything dealing with my sister."

"Lauut, I'm not that bad, am I?" Lauma asked.

"Let's just say that you know your mind and stick to it. So one better not try to change it or there might be some trouble. And before I dig my own grave here, I'm shutting up."

Listening to the exchange of the three of them, both Doube and Jllon started laughing. Jllon turning to Doube said softly, "I guess we know who's in charge here and it ain't the two males."

"What a surprise. You weren't here when we first encountered her. If you had you would understand as to why it's probably is that way."

Shortly Fauul made his appearance and said, "Is this better? Yeah I know come over here and help."

Passing Jllon on the way Jllon whispered, "So tell me has becoming mated to her been worthwhile?"

Again surprised by the question he paused and then said with a smile, "Of course. And with her here in hearing range did you expect me to say anything else? No really, I am not sorry at all." He continued over to the food prep area and helped her finish.

Lauut then made his appearance and assisted with the final settings. Once he had finished he assisted bring the food to the table. They all sat down and ate the meal. "So what's your opinion Jllon?" Lauma asked.

"Opinion of what?" he asked.

"Oh of that cavern and what we found . . . did you look for anything else by the way?"

"No actually we didn't. This was kind of a let's see what we are facing type of visit, and for me to get a better picture in my mind. I can't help but be intrigued by what I saw down there. The torches didn't throw enough light on the roof to tell much about it – your opinion Doube?"

"I believe, from the little I was able to see, that this originally was a steam vent from some past volcanic action. From what I can determine it had to happen a very long time ago. The heat and humidity says that somewhere down there, there still is some active hot springs. But they might be lower in the complex. The areas that you showed us Lauut, appears to go quite deep."

"So that accounts for that heat. I must admit when I first entered the tunnel it was the last thing I was expecting. I mean, well look, it was underground, and we put some of our food that we grow in cellars that we have dug out the hillside and they remain cool no matter how hot it gets outside."

"True, the ground can do a great job of keeping the temperature constant and cool, but at the same time if it's hot it will do the same thing."

"I guess that's true," Lauut said. "Have you ever walked an area that had been recently burned? I mean, here fires can be a problem, and if you walk the ground after one has passed the dirt is so hot that it is almost impossible to stand on. So I guess it works both ways. I just never thought about it."

Fauul looking at Doube said, "Yes, I seem to remember when we were heading for the village that we passed through a burned out area. But I really didn't think it was something that happened much. Even where I come from we have them now and then."

"Yeah, I do remember it also – up in the mountains. We passed through it a few times since, and while you can tell that there had been one there because of the damage to the trees, it's hard to tell when it happened."

Jllon listening asked, "Fires are a problem, how so?"

"Even paradise has its problems. We have had many people that pass through describe this area as paradise. After all, we have a very mild climate, nice breezes off the ocean, short winters, you know things like that. Of course that poses other problems that one wouldn't normally think about, coming from a wetter area.

"Things like less water, and wild fires. Lightning starts many, but people cause a few. When one comes from a wetter area it is easy to be careless. Then every turn we go through a period of time where we get hot dry winds blowing off the desert. I think I remember you saying that you faced one of those in the desert. Anyway, if a fire starts during those winds, and until the wind stops the fire burns. If it is close, all one can do is protect what you have, and hope that it passes you by.

"We all help each other during those times, and since you will be spending the summer here I suspect you will at least see the smoke from one. May it be no more than that, but if it is, then be prepared for the sight of your life. If you have never seen one of these, be prepared to be in awe of the fury of nature."

"I'm sure it can't be that bad", Jllon said. "I mean I've been around a few wild fires up from where I live, but while they were spectacular, I could hardly call them awe inspiring."

"Let's just say that the ones up north would be just a campfire in comparison to these down here. The fastest beast that lives here cannot outrun them. And if you are downwind of them the smoke can almost turn day into night. So before you comment any further wait and watch. Only then will you truly understand."

"Wise advice, I guess. I haven't lived my life here, so to be smart I should allow the ones that have the right to put me in my place."

"No, it's not that. I've found that you seem to be one who is willing to listen and then apply what he has heard. It's just that until you see one . . . well until you really do see one, anything that you are told, just won't seem right or logical."

"We've kind of got off the subject a little here. So again Jllon what's your opinion?" Lauma asked again.

"Sorry, it's easy to go off in different directions. Now that we have confirmed that the *ones before* are real and are in truth our ancestors, I would say that by accident you both probably have found another location of these ancients. And it seems, more times than not, that it is by accident things are discovered."

"We thought that maybe these fire starters might be made by these ancients, but were only guessing. After all, someone else could have made them just a little while into our past." Lauma said. "So we were just fantasizing that they were from those ancients."

"Well, from where I sit, and you must remember the past is what I deal with, we have had no capability to create anything like these as far back as our written records go. You must remember that there are always ones wanting the notoriety that will create something followed by claiming it had to be from the *ones before*. So, over time, we became responsible for identifying real from fake. And so far, including what we found in our records, of course until now, there never was anything presented that was from the ancients."

"Wow, nothing?" Lauma asked.

Shaking his head Jllon continued, "No, nothing at all. We even have a member of our staff whose job it is to prove that whatever is presented is real or a fake. And I must admit that he is very good at it. When Fauul presented your fire starter he immediately was excited. Never had anything like this ever been presented. And what made even more believable was the fact that Fauul wasn't trying to pass it off as something from the ancients. As you know, shortly after showing the object, he disappeared to come down here to pursue you. So his interest was not of the *ones before*, but of the heart."

"Yeah, then as time continued I received word that you wanted to see me", Fauul stated. "But, for whatever the reasons, we just continued to miss each other."

"That's true. It seemed like we were avoiding each other. But now we have met, and I have met the rest. Soon you all will get a chance to meet the rest of the team including my mate. Lauma, I feel that the two of you will get along well. Let's say it is just a feeling I have. Anyway, after we finish here I want to show the three of you many of the drawings and sketches. I know we briefly covered them, but this time I want to go into detail. That way you will have more knowledge about this and there might be something about them may jog your memory about something around here, who knows?"

After finishing the cleanup, they all headed into the gathering space and Jllon left to go get the items he had wanted to go over in detail. "So Doube," Fauul asked, "now that you have worked with him for this time period, does the opinion that you gave me back at the port still hold true?"

"Nothing has changed. Like you, he is considerate of his people, and always seems to anticipate what may happen. And if it is something beyond that, say like when the nomads came to actually visit our worksite there, he finds quick and at times unusual solutions." Smiling, he said, "And wait until you meet his mate. Sometimes you wonder what brings about a match and here is one. I mean other than his obvious abilities, there is very little to attract a female.

"You know unlike you that have the looks that make females want to be with you, he doesn't. You can see that. Yet these two are together and are very much a couple. Like you to the females, she is to the males, she is just absolutely beautiful. Although from her attitude you would think that she doesn't see it."

This left Lauma curious and now eager to meet this female. But if Doube's description was accurate, she knew she would have to control her jealousy. Yes, she knew that she had only been recently mated, but knew how a pretty face would turn the heads of any male, and she knew that Fauul wouldn't be any different. Still this female seemed to be ignorant of what she had, strange.

Doube continued, "Now you should have seen him before the council. While he asked for my help I just added information when he asked me for it. I was there as an expert and to give my opinion. Like when he was asking you for your promise to remain silent about the discoveries, he was doing the same with the council. It was a tough sell being that he could not reveal anything until he received their promise of silence. Even there you saw that he was respected. Again, so unusual for one whom is our age . . . in other words, young or younger than any in such a high position."

About this time Jllon returned from the workers shelter with the items that he wanted to present. "Okay, now before I start with this stuff I, as a learned, have learned much on this project and have been quite humbled by our ancient ancestors. I feel that if one stops learning then it's time to quit life. Doube here has contributed much to the success of what we have found. And before you ask, no he didn't locate our finds, but instead gave us something to work with that allowed us to date what we found consistently.

I have learned this time out, that by using other disciplines that you can be more accurate in your assessments and conclusions. I think that probably, it is why our ancient ancestors were advanced as they were. Somewhere in the distant past we got away from that and started guarding our knowledge. While I know why it happened, it now has become clear as to why it is better to share our knowledge. Once Doube pointed out something that he had observed from his discipline it opened my eyes to many new possibilities. Anyway, before I show you these, I want him to give that information to you. Will you do that Doube?"

Doube said, "Okay, but I don't want to bore you all here. So I'll just be brief." He went into a short explanation of his theory and what he was waiting on from his colleagues across the oceans.

"I know you had mentioned a little on this," Fauul said, "but you really think that it was worldwide?"

"Yes, it has been consistent no matter where I have been. And before you ask, it is not always the same depth down but the line is always there. Some places it is very wide and others just a small thin line. Something really large that affected the whole planet happened, and I am guessing that it was around ten thousand plus turns ago."

"Once he told me this I suddenly realized that it was an important fact for me. You see we have been able to find objects above that dark line, but never in or below it. So we have a history related directly to us from above that line and mystery at and below. Now here in more detail is what we have uncovered, and yes these were covered in and below that dark soil."

As they were looking at the many drawing and sketches Fauul asked, "I notice that these items that you have here are drawn well, but how do you identify where these things exactly lay?"

"Can't you see? They lay just as you see them here."

"No, you don't understand what I'm asking. Of course you would know exactly where this was found. You were there and so was the artist. But now as I am looking at this and not being there I have really no idea. Isn't it important to know where an object is recovered and how deep it lay in the soil?"

"Yes, it, over time and study, can reveal much – but I still do not quite understand what your point is?"

"I guess I'm trying to bring in another discipline to your work. If, as a cartographer, I did the work as you have here, then the ending result would be worthless.

And from my eye this is close to that." Seeing the reaction from Jllon, he continued. "Now don't take me wrong here. What you and your team have found is priceless and the most important find any generation can lay claim to. But if another group, at a later time, decided to study your work that is represented here, could they find the exact location where it was originally discovered? And once there could they go to the exact point or spot where the object was uncovered? Say, I decided ten turns after your work, to try and duplicate it, could I even begin to find the exact work area? And not only that but the exact distance and relationship of the two sites, so that I might be able to draw additional conclusions?"

Thinking a minute before answering Jllon said, "Probably not. I guess when one is intimately involved; something like this it doesn't come to mind. I mean, of course, I can go exactly to the spot, but could anybody who was never there? Why would that be important? Because, as I know from our own discoveries, there may be a time when a new interpretation needs to be considered . . . and many times that exact location and placement is needed to confirm or test it."

"Right. It's generally the same. When we map an area we know it from traveling the area. But, if I passed on the data as you have here, then for anyone who hadn't traveled it, the map would be useless unless they happened to line up whatever landmarks that would still exist on that map."

"So if I understand it now, you are saying that while this information presented by these drawings and sketches are good, because it has no reference other than other objects within the work area that one would not even know where it came from or its significance with the overall site."

Nodding Fauul said, "Exactly. Fortunately all is not lost even for this work. Why, simply because the team that made the discoveries is here, and the drawings and such are accurate. You just need to tie it all in with maps and then add a grid system to your drawings. At that point anyone could go back to exactly where these were found."

Smiling when he understood what Fauul was saying he said, "See what I mean? Here again another discipline that has nothing to do with my field and yet by adding it to what I do, we gain accuracy and repeatability. Plus it allows anyone in any time period to come back and confirm our initial findings. So now you are going to have to explain how all this works and how to tie it into what we are doing."

"No problem really. I obviously cannot teach you everything involved with mapping. But I am presently mapping the areas down here, and with the help of your team I think we can get the area where you are planning to work mapped quickly and properly. Then with a map in your hand you can sketch in the site and include the areas you plan to dig. I'll show you how to set up a simple grid so that anything that is found can be placed exactly."

"This is great. And what you have been telling me makes perfect sense. Just as what Doube presented did. Okay let's finish looking over these, and then we will head back to the village and bring out the team. I want you to show us all how to do what you have suggested. I have learned that if everyone knows each other's jobs then anyone can fill in any position at any time. This of course, includes mine."

They spent the rest of the evening looking over and discussing the different drawing and sketches. As expected the sketch of the flyer brought the most comments and surprise. They finally all retired out to the porch and had a final cup of hot beverage before retiring for the night. It turned out to be another beautiful evening.

Lauma said, as the two of them were preparing for bed, "I think you have something I want."

Turning to her and smiling he asked, "Now what would that be?"

Again smiling at him and she teasingly said, "If you haven't figured that out then you're not the male I think you are."

"Oh, it's that way is it?" He laughed and continued, "And it seems to me just a short period ago you were afraid of what you are asking for now."

"Yeah, and that was then and this is now. I've found that it can be very nice, and . . ." Again teasingly she turned away from him before continuing, ". . . besides sometimes you get it right," which brought an immediate laugh from both of them.

"Oh, you mean that sometimes I get it wrong? So, oh mighty experienced one how would you know", as he tried, without too much success, to look serious.

Then looking deeply in his eyes she took his hands and led him to the bed and said, "I only have what we have had, but I must admit that it has turned out to be something I want to have with you for a very long time. It is the closest I can get to you, and afterwards when we talk a little, and touch before going to sleep is overall just wonderful."

"In truth you will not get me to argue. I think you have done a wonderful job of summing it up so shall we. After all it does sound like a new adventure is about to begin for all of us." He kissed her deeply and they hugged and climbed into the bed.

She was up before he was the next day – nature call. *My I think I must have had too much of that beverage last night. Nature is demanding that I get rid of liquid or pay the price.* Looking over at Fauul sleeping she knew that even though she was a little early the day would be in full swing before she knew it. She thought that when they became mates that she had loved this male, but was finding out that it was just the beginning. Even now she was finding that she was becoming more in love with him the longer she lived with him. It left her wondering how deeply one could love another. Well, she had a lifetime to find out.

Once having taken care of the nature call she thought that she had time for a quick bath, and while she was taking her bath Fauul entered, yawned and asked, "Why didn't you wake me, I could at least have washed your back while you are in there."

Sticking out her tongue at him she said, "Now every once in a while I would like to have a little privacy."

"Oh really!" He grabbed one of the drying cloths and threw at her. "Here catch!" She screamed a little by being caught off guard, and he began to laugh. "Yes if there was a way I would like to have captured that moment. You should have seen your face when I tossed that at you. Look I'm going out to get that hot beverage started, and then head out and start the morn work with the beasts. I think it's your brother's turn to fix the meals . . . and enjoy your bath. Oh by the way, thank you for last night." He left the necessary space leaving her by herself once again.

She thought, *how nice . . . I mean thanks really isn't necessary, but still it shows the respect he has for me.* Again she was beginning to understand the bond that must have existed between her sires. She felt that as time went on and her relationship grew that in the end she would understand many things about them that could only be learned when one was in a similar strong relationship.

She came out of the necessary space feeling clean and refreshed and found a cup waiting for her with a single flower next to it. Smiling, she again thought. *Wow always some small surprise.* Taking the cup she went out to the porch and sat down for a few minutes just relaxing. This, she knew, would be very short lived. The day was just about to start and if it was a normal one it would be very busy.

Listening, she heard Fauul down by the pens working with the beasts who were bawling their impatience at not getting their expected meal. Then looking over to the workers shelter she saw the three coming out. Sighing she thought, just not enough time here to relax, but with becoming an adult comes responsibility, and you just can't shrug it off.

The three of them crossing the yard towards her greeted her with a good morn, and seeing that she had some hot beverage entered into the main shelter to get some of their own. She knew that her brother would be starting the morn meal, and she would, once she finished her cup, head out and help Fauul finish the work.

CHAPTER SIXTEEN

After the morn meal all of them briefly sat on the porch. Jllon and Doube were about to head back into the village to bring out the team. Jllon was doing some last minute arrangements with Lauut as to how best use the workers shelter. The shelter was larger than the main unit since it had been built for a large number of workers. It consisted of a number of spaces. It had one large common meeting and relaxing space, a common food prep, and eating area, a common necessary space for the single workers and then a number of sleeping spaces. Included were two spaces for mated workers and their families.

These two spaces were a miniature version of the layout of the main shelter, but lacked the family space. These had their own necessary spaces, and two sleeping spaces. One for the mated and one for any whelps they may have had. There was also a food prep and eating area. While not as big or as well supplied as the common area it would work.

Since the two mated spaces were next to each other Jllon with the approval of Lauut decided that Jllon and his mate would occupy one of the mated spaces and the single females the other – allowing the rest of the team access to the rest of the unit. Again, because of the size, it would work out well. Then the two of them said their good byes for now and headed out back to the village.

"Interesting person that Jllon", Lauut commented. "I must say that he seems to think about everything. Plus he just doesn't seem to be bothered by someone bringing up something counter to what he was either saying or doing. A very rare quality if I must say so. It's no wonder he is the Head Keeper of the Past."

"Yes, I have to agree", Fauul said. "And I have to admit that I do like him a lot. He really thinks things through. I'm really looking forward to seeing who his mate is."

"Of course you are!" Lauma responded. "After all you are a male, and any pretty female will turn your face towards her."

"Now wait a minute here, that's not what I meant . . . I, after meeting him, was just curious as to who would be drawn to him."

Lauut watching the action between the two started laughing. "Ah yes, nothing like a female's jealousy to get those knives out, and to put a male in his place.

But I have to admit that I'm curious myself. I mean if you look at him he's not anyone special. You know like me he's just average in appearance. I know from talking with him that he is quite deep, thoughtful and cares about what happens to his people. But first you would have to get to know him. As you know physical attraction is usually the beginning, and sometimes the end of a relationship. So what was it that attracted this female to him?"

"Oh you too. Sure, I bet it's just because of what you said. Here you are defending him also. "I will never understand you males and this draw."

Looking at Lauma, Fauul asked. "Aren't you curious yourself? I mean from what Jllon said it seems that you would anticipate the meeting?"

Lauut then interjected, "Enough of this. Let's say that finding those objects seems to finally paying off for us. I mean we are being paid for the use of the workers shelter – something that for such a long time as been in disuse. From my talk with Jllon he said that they would probably be back here in about three to four days. So we need to go in and clean it out so that it is presentable to them when they arrive.

"Plus, other than the space I was living in, I don't know if everything functions in the other mated space, or the common space for that matter. So we need to work everything over in there – including the common facilities. As far as I know they haven't been used since we were whelps when our sires had thrown a gathering for the surrounding properties."

"I had forgotten about that gathering. I must have only been four or five turns old. I know that it was exciting. I never had seen so many people, and other whelps that we played with."

"Yeah, it was noisy and filled with excitement. I don't remember what it was for, but like you I had never seen so many people. Well enough of the reminiscing, we need to get the work done."

The next three days flew by and immediately after the zenith meal, as they were preparing to continue their normal routine, the dogs starting barking furiously. Curious, they entered the yard and looked in the direction of the barking and saw that the dogs were at the gate. In the distance they saw a large group of people approaching, and since they were already past the fork and heading for their gate it had to be the ones they had been waiting for. Calling the dogs back Lauut told the other two to keep the dogs in the yard and he would go to the gate and see if it was the right group and not someone who had become lost and was looking for another property.

The approaching group was still too far away to be able to identify anyone within it so with the dogs under control Lauut approached the gate. He noticed that as usual, Sadie lay at the feet of Lauma at the ready position. That dog was always going to be her protector. It had taken a while for the dog to accept that Fauul was now to be included in her pack. She also knew that this new one was the alpha male as Lauma was the alpha female. But now there seemed to be many additional humans she would have to deal with. Well until she found them to be harmless she would protect her pack members. So she lay at their feet in the "ready to attack position", if it became necessary.

The two of them watched as Lauut approached the gate. From their vantage point they watched as he stood by the gate watching as the group approached. There had yet been a change from him indicating that he recognized anyone. Turning to Fauul she said, "I would have thought that the group would be close enough for him to recognize someone. I think we better be prepared just in case they turn out to be one of the bandit groups. You do you have your knives?"

About the time she had finished her statement they saw a change in Lauut. He appeared to have relaxed and was now leaning on the gate. Shortly he raised his arm in greeting, unlocked the gate and opened it. "I guess it's always good to be prepared," Fauul commented. "If that had been a bandit group, I think we would have been in real trouble. Even with the dogs, I don't know if the three of us would have been enough to detour them."

"Fortunately none of the bandit groups seem brazen enough to attack a property. I think they realize that if they started doing that then eventually the countryside would rise up and eradicate them. So they stay away and are seen rarely. But, you never know . . ." with her voice trailing off, she was beginning to concentrate on the approaching group. "Hmm . . . bigger than I expected. But I guess I really didn't know what to expect."

"It looks about right to me. I mean you have to remember that not that long ago I was part of a mapping team. And while it was smaller than this group, we were not doing the kind of work they are."

Lauut turned around and signaled them that it was okay. He turned back around and started to talk with someone. Fauul recognized the gait of Doube and he relaxed. Yes this was the team they were expecting. Turning back to Lauma he said, "Let's get back over to the porch and call the dogs there. They will be approaching us shortly so we need to introduce them to the dogs so as to avoid anyone getting bit."

"No," Lauma replied. "I have a better idea; let's put them into the work shelter. It has a door they can't get through. Then once everything is a little more controlled we can let them get to know each other."

"Okay, but we better get moving."

They quickly called the dogs into the work shelter and closed the door, only leaving Sadie out. Knowing her dog, she knew that an immediate introduction would be necessary to prevent future incidents. The two of them plus the dog headed back to the porch just as the group was approaching the yard. Immediately Sadie started growling, but a quick hand and word from Lauma stopped her. It sure seemed like a lot of people. The property hadn't seen this amount of people around since that gathering so many turns ago.

She noticed that they had pack beasts that appeared to be loaded with their equipment. Immediately she noticed that the beasts were not as good as the ones they bred here, but still were good overall. She began to study the members of this team, and as she looked the team over she suddenly saw one of the most beautiful females she had ever seen. Even the work clothes she was wearing could not hide who or what she was. Yet it was obvious that it was something that didn't affect her. It was like it didn't exist, and she was no different than any other female.

This new revelation would take some getting used to. From her personal experience, not that it was that great, when one looked as this one did, the female was usually well into herself at the exclusion of anything else. It was very puzzling. Yes, she knew that she had been warned, and informed that this female was completely unaware of her natural beauty, but to actually see it and then realize that what she had been told was true was a shock.

Lauma suddenly realized that she had been staring and found that the one she had been staring at was now looking back at her, and smiling. Then she left the group and came over to her with her arms open offering a hug and said, "Hi, you must be Lauma. I'm Nouma, the mate of Jllon. When Jllon told me your name I thought with just one letter change we would have the same name. Then I laughed because had it been that way it would have caused all sorts of confusion. I think it will anyway but in that way it would have been worse."

Not quite knowing how to take this female, she hugged her back, smiled a little, and didn't say anything. Meanwhile the other two females with the team noticed Fauul and quickly said to each other, "Wow, do you see that big one there?" They laughed since they had said it to each other at the same time. "Yeah how could you miss him", Kaern commented. About this time Nouma returned and had just caught the end of the conversation.

"Ah I see that you have seen that big one. He is attractive isn't he?" Both Kaern and Suzzane had to agree. "Well, I suggest you look at that female that's on his left there . . ."

Looking over and seeing her they both asked why. Then smiling a knowing smile Nouma said, "Okay, let's just say that he is off limits period. That female is his mate, and if you want to survive this project I would stay away from him."

With a questioning look Kaern then asked, "Why? She doesn't look like much."

Laughing Nouma said, "Well keep thinking that way, I'll just come back later and pick up what's left of you after she has finished with you. I tell you now, just from my brief visit with her, she would be like a wild she beast protecting her whelps, and neither of you would have a chance."

Still unconvinced Kaern said, "If you say so, but she doesn't look so tough."

Again laughing Nouma said, "If that's the way you think, but before you do anything stupid I suggest you go talk to Doube about her. It just might change your mind and put it back where it should be. Besides I thought you and Jayson were seeing each other."

"Yeah, we were, but we found that we were not quite what each of us was looking for. So we are friends, but that's all. Are you sure? I mean he looks like he would be fun to be with."

"Oh, I'm quite sure. If you don't believe me, then later after we are all settled in here and all the introductions have been made, go talk to her, and of course bring up the subject of her mate. Then watch her eyes. Believe me you won't miss it."

At this moment Jllon got everyone's attention and with Lauut leading, headed off to the workers shelter where they would be staying. Of course they had let the dogs back out of the shelter so as not to be overwhelmed when they tried to enter. Once they had moved everything in and were set up then they would all meet back in the yard and more formal introductions would be made. And for this evening they would set up tables in the yard and everyone would eat there as if they were at a small gathering.

Jllon had suggested it. He felt that with the informality of a small gathering that the family would have an easier time getting to know the team members. Fauul and Lauut had commented quietly to each other, out of the hearing range of Lauma, that yes, Nouma was a very beautiful female, but did really seem to be unaware of it. And they could understand why the question had always been what had attracted Jllon and Nouma to each other. It really didn't matter and it was their right not to say anything about their personal life.

Suzzane, being from the outback in another region, and having grown up on a food producing property, was curious as to the differences between the operations. Since this property produced herd and pack beasts, and while they had used the work beasts on their property the beasts were only a part of the overall operation. Here they were the main concern. Still there were similarities. Thinking about it she thought. *I guess even though these are different doesn't mean that there aren't be many ways that the operations would be same.*

Still looking around during the informal gather that evening she was becoming impressed on both the condition and the age of everything here. Nothing here was new or even close to new. It all showed age and use. Still at the same time everything was neat, clean, and in good repair. It showed pride and a love of the land. Before joining the group she had walked around the yard, pens, and out-shelters and found that the same pride was everywhere. Even in the areas that would always be out of sight.

She started to study the beasts themselves and even though it was not her area of expertise, she again saw the same quality put forth in the breeding. She knew from what had been relayed to the team that this place had been operated by a brother and sister, and that a tragedy had happened in their past with the loss of their sires. Then a short time ago the sister had found a mate who would assist when he could, but that his field of work required his time away from the property. She had to admit from her initial impression that her mate was quite a catch.

Remembering her first view of the owners she knew that like Kaern her eyes were first drawn to this Fauul. But she did look at the other two, and immediately it was obvious that they were sister and brother. They could not have denied the relationship if they had wanted too. Again, and maybe because Fauul was standing there with them, they didn't appear to be anything out of the ordinary – average height, and average build, but showing the bodies of ones who work hard. She knew that she probably would be one that would be overlooked if Jllon's mate Nouma were around. There were few females that could compete with her on the physical level. Still she knew that she was pretty and was proud of what she had.

It was time to get back and join the gathering, but she had much to think about. Maybe it was time to really get to know these people. First impressions being important and her first impressions of the property were good. Smiling, she thought. *Now how are the personalities of these three?* She had been warned about Lauma, but wanted to find out for herself. Again smiling, she thought. *This might be fun.*

When she rejoined everyone she found that things were just starting. Kaern asked where she had been, and she replied that she had just been wondering around. Then Jllon called the team to be quiet and said, "As you know it was here that half of what started this project came from. This half was physical, something you could touch and look at. I have asked and received permission from the finder of these objects to have each one of you handle one. I think once you do, it will leave you with much the same impression that I have had. But I will not say what mine was, since it is important for each of you to draw your own conclusion. Anyway before I do this, I want to introduce the family and their hospitality that we are sharing." He first introduced Lauma, and followed by her brother Lauut. Pausing briefly he said, "To the females here I think you picked him out immediately . . ." This brought out a laugh from the team, because they remembered how at least the two females had reacted when they first saw Fauul. " . . . Anyway this is Fauul and he is the mate of Lauma. Again if any wants to know any more about his mate I suggest you talk to Doube. I think you will appreciate the story of their first meeting.

"I want all of us to get to know each other. I have a feeling that we will be here for quite a while. And I mean that truthfully, as I have had the opportunity to visit the location of the discovery. And unlike our work in the desert, this is going to be a much larger challenge. So enough of this, let's have the food brought forth and eat and mingle. On the morrow we will go to the site and begin our initial work. So enjoy the evening as it is the last of our down time, and now we must begin our working again." With a signal from him the camp managers brought out the food and everyone grabbed a plate and went to fill them and sit down to eat.

The three of them felt a little self-conscious being the guests of honor, so to speak – even though it was informal, to be singled out as they were, seemed to be a little bit embarrassing. Plus, other than Doube and Jllon, they knew no one here. For Lauma she was still trying to come to terms with Nouma. Nouma seemed to be very down to earth and completely ignorant of her beauty and the effect that it had on males. She was friendly and outgoing, and didn't appear to care about her status as the mate of the Head Keeper of the Past.

In fact on that particular subject it appeared that Jllon was unusual as well. He did not seem to be the type that allowed his position to go to his head. Like his mate he was open, friendly, outgoing and willing to listen to what anyone had to offer. It was a rare combination she was seeing here. Maybe, after being around the two of them, she would finally figure out why they were who they appeared to be. Suddenly she realized that in many ways, she probably was in a similar situation. Only here it was reversed. Her mate was one who continually attracted females, and she had seen it happen again today. While she was not ugly by any means she could not compete with the likes of Nouma. So how was it that Jllon wasn't jealous when his mate was out talking with other males? Was he that sure of their relationship? Or was there something else more subtle?

In her case, she found that it was easy to be jealous. She loved Fauul and knew that he truly loved her. After all, didn't he give up everything to be with her? Still, when females were attracted to him, she felt the jealousy rise unbidden, and could feel the fire flash within herself. She really needed to understand why. So maybe by talking with Jllon and Nouma she'd begin to understand.

Lauut couldn't believe that in a sense they were the guests of honor here. It was something that had never happened to him. He had seen it with others and wondered how it would feel, but thought with how things had always gone with him that he would never get the chance. At first he was surprised that Jllon would introduce them this way, and then felt embarrassed since it was only by accident the fire starters were found anyway. He had done nothing special, and truth be told, had done something really stupid. Well, the introductions had only lasted a moment anyway and he knew it was done so that the team members knew who the three of them were.

Again he knew why Jllon had insisted on having this small gathering. It was an easy way for both sides to get comfortable with each other. As the three of them had been around each other long enough to know one another, it would be the same with this team. So now that both would be around each other, it would be important to learn the boundaries each side required. Plus he knew with this many people around, there would be at least one or two whose personalities would clash. It was better to learn now and avoid a situation than have it happen later when it could become an issue.

Fauul, normally a people type person anyway, felt right at home with the small gathering. While it was not as large as some of the crowds from the township it still gave him the same feeling of energy and a little chaos. By walking around the group and listening in on a number of conversations and participating in none he was getting a sense of this group. Having been second in charge of a team himself he recognized the touch of the leader on the team, and that impressed him. Even if he had thought it so, by observing, he now had confirmation that Jllon was one of a rare breed of leaders who only lead because they are placed in the position. It was obvious to anyone wanting to find out the condition of the team. This team worked together well, and there was a comfort level that was there for all to see. This meant that Jllon had instilled respect among the team members, and in turn they respected his decisions – so different from Joellie and his self-indulgence on his abilities. He remembered that time after time he would have to work hard on keeping the team under control, because of some slight or complaint that Joellie would level at the team – mostly ill-advised and without tact. He would attack the team members which would leave them mad and on edge. What a difference a good leader made.

As he expected, eventually the two females from the team found him and cornered him for a short period of time. It was something he was used to. He truthfully worried how Lauma would take it. He was sure that these two had yet to talk with her. *Probably a mistake*, he thought. Since he knew that he was totally dedicated to Lauma there would be no problem from him. But he knew that where relationships were involved one did not know how the other would react. Smiling to himself he realized that probably in this case he did know.

Just as he thought it he saw Lauma approaching from the other side of the team. *This ought to be interesting,* he thought. The two females had their back to Lauma so they didn't see her approaching, but then heard her as she said, "Ah Fauul there you are. And who are your two friends, if I may ask?"

Laughing he said, "We haven't quite got that far, since they just accosted me. But from what Jllon told me I suspect that this one is Kaern." He pointed to the taller and darker of the two, and continued saying, "And she I believe is Suzzane. Do I have it right?"

Looking at the two Lauma said somewhat sarcastically, "Yes, a couple of learners out to learn . . . what? Oh I know that he is great on the eyes, and I know that he is easy to talk to. After all I am his mate, and other than some talking now and then, he is off limits to anything else you two may have had in mind."

Looking at her, the two females saw that fire in her eyes that they had been warned about. No doubt about it Nouma had stated the facts exactly as they were. This one would not be one to cross. She could and probably would be deadly. Nervous now the two giggled a little with Kaern saying, "Now please. We are doing only what Jllon has asked us to do. And that is to get to know the three of you. Is that okay? I mean if it is a problem then we can just avoid all of you."

Smiling, but with some acid in that smile she said, "I do hope that we all get to know each other. I just feel that it is necessary to lay down a few rules and since you are here because we have given permission, then you will live by those rules . . . and of course he is completely off limits to the two of you. I expect to be there if you need to talk with him. But since I know that is impossible, then I expect the two of you to understand that at those times I am not around him, *then* you deal with him as if I was."

Shaking his head Fauul said, "Now Lauma please. I suspect that they were just curious. I think you know quite well that there will be no problem here."

"You can bet on it, but I am making sure that they understand it. You . . . I have no problem with. You have proven to be exactly who you say you are. But these two are females and as one I know what traps they can lay for an unsuspecting male."

Again looking at Fauul and Lauma they saw that he was smiling, but where they were concerned she was not. Probably the best thing to do at this point was to just leave. But before they could figure out an exit Nouma joined them. "Good evening all", she said. Taking in the whole sight she already could see what had transpired and actually started laughing. As she did, it broke the tension that had been building and they all laughed a little. Looking at the three females there she knew who would have ended up as the alpha female here, and it wouldn't have been either of the ones from the team.

From the looks on their faces she again laughed and said, "See, what did I tell you? But I guess like all of us you had to find out for yourself. Didn't go talk with her first, did you?" Shaking her head she said, "I suspect if you had, then this confrontation wouldn't have happened, but by trying to see him before permission was granted, allowed the two of you to be put on notice. Am I right?"

Fauul, with his arms crossed, stood back and watched. While he had been dealing with the female sex most of his life he rarely got a chance to watch them work in this way. To him it was surprising how much they seemed to naturally know. How it seemed they could read each other's minds, and instantly know what the situation was. So being the observer here was a learning experience. Still, being that up until recently he had been single, he was now learning the differences when one was mated.

"Are you telling me that you warned them? Warned them about what?" Lauma asked.

"Why you Lauma," Nouma replied knowingly.

"Me? What did you tell them?"

"Simply that if they decided to mess with your male, and Fauul don't take that wrong, that they might as well be messing with a wild she beast protecting her territory. And if they decided to cross that line that in the end they would be the ones who would lose."

"Really? You said that? Am I like that?"

"Ah, Lauma you are a strong female, and one who could easily be in charge, but for the circumstances. And anytime your mate's name was stated I saw your reaction in your eyes. We females have a tendency to be more jealous of our males than they do of us. I know it can be both ways, but it seems to be stronger on our side. I don't know why. Maybe it has to do with who we are and what we represent. After all we are the ones who carry the next generation. And as such are putting much more into that generation than any male."

Silent for a moment she thought about what was said and had to admit that what was revealed was true. She hadn't realized that she was that obvious. "Okay, I probably over reacted. But like him, I am new at this . . . and to have found the one who I consider my life mate . . . I just couldn't stand losing him. I've already had that kind of tragedy in my life. I'm also beginning to understand my mother and her position much better now. I just wish she were here to be able to talk with. I have so much I would ask her now."

Suzzane and Kaern looked at each other with Suzzane asking, "Tragedy in your life, what are you talking about?"

Before Lauma could answer, Nouma said, "It's her call but if I may . . ." Looking at Lauma, Lauma nodded allowing her to continue. . . . "Part of what we do, Jllon and myself, are to know what we are dealing with before we enter into a situation. It is well known in the village, and had you asked you would have gotten the complete story there instead of the brief bit we told the team. Anyway you didn't and wouldn't, so here it is. When she was younger she and her brother lost their sires to a freak accident. I will say no more than that. If she wants to she can tell you the details. I do believe that this is one of the reasons for her strength now."

Lauma knew that it was common knowledge in the village, but hadn't realized that Nouma knew as much as she did. This female kept herself well informed. When she thought about it, it did make a lot of sense. The position that she was in required the two of them stay on top of what might be happening out in the real world. Of course the beauty this one had didn't hurt. Such beauty had a tendency to loosen the tongue of many a male.

Suzzane said, "Ouch! Being a farmer myself I know that there is always a chance of an accident. But to lose both at the same time . . . how ever did you survive such a thing?"

Fauul decided that it was time to back out and let the four of them work things out. He wanted to go see Doube and probably talk some more with Jllon. He was finding out more about him, and was finding himself drawn to him. Doube was right. He could easily be a friend with this male, and he suspected that before this was over that the two couples would end up close friends.

But as he went through the small group of people Doube was nowhere to be found. It really didn't surprise him, as Doube was not one to be around groups. He enjoyed his own company more than large groups of people. He saw that Jllon was in deep conversation with one of his team members and thought it better not to interrupt. He decided to grab a cup of hot beverage and go sit on the porch and observe for a while. He was on his second cup when he saw Lauma approaching him. Smiling he thought. *Okay let's see what has happened.* "So how'd it go?"

"Oh, okay I guess. When Nouma came over she kind of smoothed things out, and then all four of us just talked it out. By the way why did you leave?"

"Once the four of you started talking I figured it was time for me to bow out. Besides what started this was me and if you were going to include a discussion about me in your conversation then I figured it would be best if I wasn't there."

"Coward!"

"No, not really. I have yet to find a male who can defend himself against one determined female let alone four. Besides I suspect that the four of you were more comfortable being by yourselves than with me there anyway."

"Okay, I guess I will have to give you that, but it was a surprise when I turned back around and you were gone."

"That just shows how deep into the conversation you were, and something you need to think about here, and I understand very much where you are coming from, is that possessive streak. I became your mate because everything about you fits with who I am. You are not going to lose me to some other female. I have had to come to terms with the fact that nature made me attractive to females. At first I thought it was a good thing, but it can be a problem also. You've seen that yourself. They seem to just pick me out no matter where it is and must come closer to see if I am real. I've gotten used to it, and I hope that you will after a while."

"Yeah, that's true. I must admit it was the same with me when I first saw you. Even though at the time I did not know who you were and that you might possibly be a member of the bandits made my thoughts conflicted. And yes I know that I overreacted, but I just can't face the thought of you leaving or having another female take you away from me."

Hugging her he said, "I really believe that you should have no worry there. I know that the loss that you have suffered has kind of put you where you are now, and because of that I understand. Again we have been mated for less than a turn and we both cannot know each other as well as we will. So doubts and fears are probably quite natural."

Looking up they then saw Jllon and Nouma approaching them, Jllon asked, "Can we join you? The two of you look so comfortable there we just couldn't resist the idea that it would be nice to sit there with you."

"Sure, and we will go get you both a cup if you would like," Fauul said.

Nouma replied, "Now that would be wonderful. Do you sit here often?"

Smiling Lauma said, "Oh yes. It's always been kind of a tradition here. Once the work is completed and we've eaten, no matter the weather we come out here and sit and enjoy the evening before retiring. We have always had a nice view from here, and it has been a great place to unwind after a hard day's work."

"Well, looking around," Jllon said, "I can see that there is plenty of hard work, so having a place to relax is very important." They took the other two chairs and sat down. Once Fauul and Lauma had given them a cup they sat back down enjoying the company, comfort and view.

Nouma turned to them and said to Fauul, "I can understand the attraction they had to you. It kind of affected me too. But at the same time I knew the way your mate, Lauma would react. Anyway the two had been warned to come talk with you first Lauma, but by either accident or design they ran into you Fauul before they could talk with you Lauma. And as I predicted you were there instantly. So Fauul, why did you leave?"

Laughing he said, "Funny you should ask. Lauma just asked me the same thing, and I said that there's no way one male is going to be able to deal with four females. One is enough to outclass him and four would be impossible."

"Coward."

"No, and that's the exact word Lauma used. Just smart, besides it was a good time for the four of you to get to know each other and it was a good time for me to disappear and allow that to happen."

"You know Fauul, I understand completely. I really have never understood Nouma and her deep love for me, not that I don't return it. I feel very fortunate to have one such as her. We are great together, and I could never see another in my life. Yet, I know when to step away. Sometimes it's better to retreat gracefully then stay."

"You too?" Nouma asked.

Laughing he said, "Yeah me too. We males have learned that there is a time to stay and definitely a time to make a hasty withdrawal – especially if we want to stay around for another day."

"Oh really, I will have to remember that."

This started all of them laughing. They stayed there the remainder of the time and talked generally about whatever came to their minds. Both Lauma and Fauul knew that they would have a strong friendship with these two. And before they knew it the evening was done, and everyone was working on the clean-up and then heading off to bed. The next morn it would be the normal work for them, while the team that was living in the workers shelter, would be heading out to begin the initial survey of the proposed site. There they would set up their temporary shelters and according to a decision at that time decide whether to remain on site for a few days before returning to the more permanent shelter or just go from there each day.

As was their usual practice, the three of them were up at dawn to get the work finished at the pens, then come in and eat the morn meal before working on the "whatever planned projects" they had going. This morn Lauut headed out ahead of the other two. Lauma would be on the cooking detail at least for part of the day. So she would be joining them after they ate. Fauul would be out shortly and once the meal was finished would be going out with the team to help set up the mapping and to show Jllon how it worked.

Lauut liked to be out first in the morning air. Other than the bawling of the beasts it was quiet and peaceful. The air was usually cool and at times seemed to have a bite to it. It was the time he would do some of his thinking. But this morn it was different. As he approached the rails to the pens there was someone there leaning against them and looking at the beasts. Knowing that neither of the other two were out of the shelter yet it had to be someone from Jllon's team. Curious, he approached a little closer and saw from the shape that the person had to be one of the females.

A little surprised he quietly approached, but not so quietly as to surprise her. Once he was in hearing range he asked, "So what are you doing out here so early?"

Even though he had meant not to startle her he saw her jump, with her saying, "Oh! Sorry you made me jump there. I was in deep thought and didn't hear you. What was it you asked? Oh that's right . . . good question . . . haven't really figured that out myself but I think that once I was back on a property in the outback that it was bringing back memories of home."

"Home? Do you live on a similar property?"

"No . . . yes . . . well kind of. I grew up on a food producing property – really very different from this one. But we had working beasts, and, of course, a few herd beasts for milk and meat. I think hearing your beasts bawling just brought back those memories. It kind of put me back in that life. We, as you are here, were up early every day. There always seemed to be things that had to be done and it would take every minute of daylight to get those things done. So I found myself up early like I was back there. I thought I'd just come out to the pens here and do some thinking. And that's where you found me deep in thought and then surprised when you arrived."

Leaning on the rails next to her he said, "Let's see . . . you are . . . let me think here, yes you are Suzzane, am I right?"

Smiling she said, "Yes that is right and you are Lauma's brother."

"I guess she made an impression on you if I am just Lauma's brother."

Laughing she said, "Oh yes she left an impression. But I think after the four of us talked last night that in the end we all became friends. What can I say, her mate is very good looking, and it left Kaern and me wondering about him. So when we cornered him last night just to find out, your sister came in and let us knows where we stood."

Smiling Lauut replied, "That would be Lauma. She has always been strong and not afraid to speak what she thinks. I think you found that out. Anyway the two of them were almost instantly attracted to each other. Any who saw them could not deny they were meant to be together. Kind of what I saw with your boss Jllon and his mate Nouma."

"Yes, they are a great team, and very much in love with each other. You just never know what attracts one to another. Anyway, back to what we were originally talking about, I started to become homesick and thought I would come out here before we started and come to terms with it. But instead found myself drawn back to it instead."

"As you know this is a hard life, but not one I would trade. Fauul was a township whelp and couldn't understand the outback. But if you ask him now I think that he would tell you that even he prefers it here."

Laughing again she said, "I'd ask but don't know if I would be allowed to."

"Oh come on she's not that bad. In fact since you are now on a friendly basis with her, you will find that she will do anything, short of giving him up, for you."

"Probably true, and speaking of him, it looks like he just left the shelter. Guess I had better let you get to work, and it's probably time for me to go back any way. Nice talking with you Lauut . . . I'm sure we will have time to talk again in the future." She took his hand nodded to him turned and left heading back to the workman shelter.

He watched her until she was out of sight. He heard Fauul say, "So one of the females from the team was out here. What were the two of you talking about?" He smiled before continuing, "Of course if it was a private conversation I won't ask."

"No, no it wasn't a private conversation, but she has left me wondering what she plans to do."

"Now that sounds like trouble to me."

"Trouble? I don't understand what you mean?" He turned around and saw that Fauul was smiling at him. "Now what is that smile all about anyway?"

Laughing Fauul said, "Now anytime a female leaves a male curious, then it is time to watch out. Pursuit isn't far behind. And before you know it you are no longer single."

"Now wait a minute here, that's not what I meant. It's just she has some things in common with us, not you, but Lauma and myself."

"Sure, convince me. I can see you at one of the future major gathers now – you and that female joining as mates." He started laughing, "Yes, I can really see it now, and if there's anyone who should know this, I'm one who should."

Embarrassed by the direction Fauul was taking, Lauut said, "Okay brother-by-mate, enough, we're late on this work so let's get this done. I don't want to be late for the morn meal – especially since Lauma is fixing it."

Still smiling and continuing to tease Fauul said, "Okay by me . . . mate to be."

Disgusted and shaking his head, Lauut said, "Okay if you say so, but this still isn't getting the work done."

The two of them worked with the beasts until the sun begin to rise above the horizon and headed in for the morn meal. After they had washed up and entered into the shelter Fauul said, "I think your brother has found someone to pursue."

Not really listening closely to what he had said she replied, "That's nice . . . what? Lauut has found someone to pursue?" Then turning towards her brother she asked, "What's he talking about Lauut?"

"Oh he's just teasing me. He found me talking to one of the females who happened to have preceded me to the pens."

"Really, which one? I assume it wasn't Nouma."

Now having to tell his sister and then looking over at Fauul, he saw that Fauul was enjoying this. "Right, she wasn't Nouma."

"Okay brother, who was it?"

Shaking his head in disgust he said, "Okay, okay . . . it was Suzzane. I found that she comes from the outback also, and worked a food property. It seemed that coming back to a similar property has left her homesick."

"So that's all there was too it?"

"Yeah, that's all there was to it. Your mate here wants to make it into something more than what it is."

Again smiling at him Fauul said, "Yes and if I remember right you said you were curious about her. And from personal experience that is the beginning of the end of you being single."

Looking at Fauul Lauma asked, "So you are telling me that you have a problem being mated to me?"

Laughing at the look on her face he replied, "No not at all. I would have it no other way. I have found more than I have ever hoped for by being your mate. It is just your brother is on the outside looking in, and I have found, more times than not, that when one starts becoming curious about the opposite sex then things just start happening."

"Okay you two . . ." Lauma paused and asked, ". . . really? Are you saying that it all started with you being curious about me? Then she looked at the food, wanting to change the subject. "Oh . . . let's eat this food before it gets cold. There's a day's work waiting for us out there."

CHAPTER SEVENTEEN

The team, with Fauul, reached the site later that morn. In the next few days they all would be learning from Fauul. Jllon had been thinking heavily about what Fauul had asked him. He knew now with the way they had worked sites in the past that anyone who wanted to recreate the work they had done at a later time, would only be guessing. Thusly duplicating or confirming past work would be impossible. This new way would give anyone; at any time, the ability to go directly to the site and find exactly where something was recovered or where the excavations began and ended.

Turning to the team Jllon said, "Okay all, the next few days will be involved in mapping our work. Fauul asked me some pretty penetrating questions, and when I had no answers, presented a solution. Like when Doube gave me a way to roughly date our digs, what he will give us will allow us to accurately document our work and finds."

"Are telling us that the work we did in the desert, the drawings and sketches, and such wasn't good work?" Celt asked.

"No not at all. Let's say what we learn from Fauul will make our work and the results from that work even better. What I have been learning, this time around, is that it is important to bring other disciplines into our work. They complement what we do, and help confirm our results. What he gives us is a tool that will allow anyone at any time to see where something came from."

"You must understand that if you do not have a point from which to work from, then anything you do ends up only important to the ones who were there at the time of the dig. No one and I mean no one will be able to come back and find your work. It allows some to say that maybe what was found was not really that important. It is the overall area that can give credence and importance to your finds." Fauul looked over the team before continuing.

"So what I will show you, and have you do, will not only give you the ability to return, at a future time, to the exact spot of your work, but also allow you to see the complete picture of how the finds relate to each other – and maybe the importance of that relationship." Going over to one of the pack beasts that had brought out the team's equipment, Fauul removed a device that they all were unfamiliar with. "Okay before I get started I need for all of you to learn some terms. It is what we use when we map. Where the terms came from is unknown, but we, in our field, have always used them. It means that any that map anywhere on our planet use the same measurements. This brings a consistency to any map you would pick up.

Okay we use what is called a chain. A chain consists of sixty-six units. Each chain is the same length and has one hundred links. It cannot be stretched so that when extended it is always the same length. Eighty chains equal a walking unit. Each chain can be divided into four sections called rods. Ten square chains is a parcel of land, and six hundred forty parcels of land equal a section."

Setting up a tripod type device that had a plumb line hanging down the center he said, "Okay this is what we use to keep our work consistent. It is important that one establishes north and this tripod be level. This device allows us to not only plot a straight line but because it is level it allows us to track differences in elevation."

Taking out a long stick, he said, "To make this system work correctly, it takes a minimum of two people. It works better with more, since you can speed up the work. Anyway, one person works this tripod, and the other goes out a chain's length with the rod you see here. If you look at it you can see marks on it." Pointing he said, "This one here is at the same height as the tripod when it is set up. So when sighting along it where you see the marks either above or below that equal line you would know if you were going up or down in elevation.

"Now the first thing you would think, logically that if you see a line above that level point that you would have a rise in elevation, but in truth it is just the opposite. If you see above the level line that means the one holding the rod has lost elevation, and of course below would equate to a rise. So, even in this work you are doing, elevation is important. While it is more critical in my line of work it still is very important for yours. Once you work with this and understand it, then you will be able to not only mark a find's location, but also it approximate elevation from your established base or starting point – any questions?"

"Base point, what would that be?" Flar asked.

"For us it would be from established maps from the past. We are adding to them continually to try and map as much of this land as we can. Of course, this last major push was to bring most of the trails to maps. There still is much that is not on our maps yet. In your case it would be a place just outside of the planned area of interest. There you would set up a cairn or something similar so that anyone who came to this site would be able to locate the starting point."

"Makes sense", Flar said, followed by asking, "But why the north orientation?"

"Good question. If you look at any of the maps that have been made, you will notice that the top is always North. Like that cairn if you do not establish a base line and direction then all the work you do is worthless. By keeping it as mappers have done, eventually, your site could be overlaid with an existing map. Like the ability to reproduce your results, without a consistent direction established how good would your map be?"

"So let's see if I understand it here. If we just pick a random direction as a base line with no regard to direction, then anyone who attempted to orientate our findings with the map we created would only have the cairn as a point of reference. Since the map would have no directional reference it would be nearly impossible to make the map work. Is that about right?"

"Good summing of the facts. That is really the truth. Without either the starting point or a consistent base line in an established direction then all your work would be wasted."

"Okay, now that we understand the importance of this. I believe it now becomes obvious to us how such a method only improves our work and results," Jllon said. "Now Fauul, if you would demonstrate this for us, and you can show us how to use, what did you call it, ah the chain even for small areas, then we can get to work."

"So Jllon, where would you like to establish your cairn? My suggestion would be to put it a little outside of the area of interest. So that if that area expands that most likely the cairn will not have to be moved at a later time and invalidate everything you had done up to that time."

"Good question. This time it will be a little more difficult to establish our starting point." Looking around, Jllon continued, "So what do you think? You went with us and know just about as much as I do."

"In a sense, that's not true. Yes, I went with you to the location of the find, but I have no real knowledge of how you make your determinations."

"Okay, I think we need to include this steep hillside as a place of interest. So how about we establish our cairn at that campsite where Lauut set up before making his first trip. That's probably far enough out."

Nodding, Fauul said, "Probably a good choice. While it is a little distance from here, if something is found close then by establishing it there, there is little chance of having to move it later. Okay, I'll agree to that, now will all of you follow me back to that location." The team followed Fauul and Jllon back to where the initial camp had been located. "Okay now if you look closely at the tripod you will see that the legs are adjustable. Whoever thought of this must have been a genius. It makes it so much easier to level this."

With the plumb line down he set up the tripod and adjusted the legs until the plumb line was centered. He took the rod, and when it was closely inspected they found that it too was adjustable. Fauul brought the rod up to the tripod and set the height of the rod to be the same. Once this was established he pinned it in position so the rod would remain properly adjusted. From there he took out some sheets of data and from these he was able to establish how many days had passed since the winter solstice. With this information he looked at a second, which showed the degree the sun would be from its zenith position to either the north or south. He followed this by setting up a portable sundial which he also leveled.

Turning to the team he said, "As you can see there is much that goes into finding north. There is one more item that we use. Each of these methods is a check to confirm that we are as accurate as we can be. Now, as with the measurements we use, the origin of this device is unknown. It seems to have always been." Reaching into his travel bag he pulled out a small box, reverently opened the box, and removed a small circular device. "This is a compass. Again, on what it is that makes it work, I do not know, but it does. Now, unknown to most there are two norths. One is found with this device, and the other is known as true north. Now I am going to pass this around.

Please be very careful with it. They have always been with mappers. We cannot even say who made them. I have been told that presently we cannot."

Then passing the compass around he continued, "Between the sheets with the information on them and the compass we can then establish true north. Now once all of you have seen the compass please return it. I have only this one. Although there may be a possibility that your team could get one, I personally do not have an extra to give you. Okay, next, if you look at the head of the tripod you will see that it sits on a plate that again is adjustable. This will turn and then like the rod be pinned in place. Once you establish north then by turning the plate to face north this device is now ready to be used. Like much of your work you spend more time in the setup than in the actual use. Still it is worth the extra time since it makes the results accurate, and prevents one from having to waste time by repeating it." He grabbed the tripod from its place and said, "Now it is your turn. I will watch and make corrections where it needs to be made – Jllon you want to start?"

"Okay, but from what you said I will need an assistant, so Celt please join me. And the rest of you divide yourselves into teams of two. I have a feeling that he is going to want all of us to do this . . . and I agree." He nervously took the tripod and with the help of Celt attempted to set up the device. He had to admit that Fauul made it look easy, but he was finding it was not. Eventually the two of them got it level to the satisfaction of Fauul. Still finding true North turned out to be just as hard as getting that thing level.

Once everyone had a turn at setting up the tripod and establishing north it was time for the zenith meal. Jllon had to admit he now had a new appreciation for the cartographers. He knew that what they were being shown today would just scratch the surface of the knowledge necessary to do what they did. Again Fauul had made it look so simple and when they had tried found it not to be so. But Fauul was patient and eventually they all had seemed to grasp the setup. Still this was just the setup, and to be honest they had yet to use it. That would come this after zenith.

Because the camp had been set up close to where they were learning it was a simple and quick trip back to the training. "I said that two were the minimum needed to work this. But it can be worked better with three. That way you have one sighting, and two working the chain. Now if all would look at the head here you will see here a sighting structure. You see here a hole, and on the other side of that hole, a stretched line, followed by a second hole. The three together are used to line up the chain. Now this head will rotate, but like everything else about it you can lock it in position.

"The two members who are taking the chain out will take direction from the one who is sighting. The furthest out will have the rod, and when everything is aligned then the one who sights will have the one furthest out stand up the rod and the information will be written down. On the north-south line each chain is numbered with the rods lettered using small letters. The east-west line of each chain is lettered with large letters and the rods numbered. That way when one looks at a map one can instantly know the orientation.

Now, for this part of the exercise I want everyone to have a chance at both parts of the work. It is important to learn hand signals. As the further out you go the less likely you will be heard." He showed them some basic hand signals, and then got them to practice. Again he had them divide into teams and for the rest of the day they practiced. Before they knew it the sun was setting and it was time to head back in. While nothing had been done as far as setting up the dig, it still turned out to be a very good day. Jllon, with the new knowledge he had gained today realized that this addition to their work was almost as important as the work itself.

Part of the camp staff had remained at the worker shelter so that when they returned from the work area food would be ready. And as they had done at the other site, this staff would rotate. He found that he actually had a headache. *Guess I'm not used to thinking in this way,* he thought. Then he said to the team, "Okay everyone, I hope that you can see the importance of what we learned today. On the morrow we will begin the mapping of our proposed site. I think the two artists we have, Rasti and Wahlter will have their hands full on putting our maps together. One last thing that Fauul told me was how to set up a scale. I asked him to work with the two of you so that we can be consistent when we do the site map. Okay all, that's it for tonight. The rest of the time is yours. I would say that before we turn one spade on this site that we will be very busy for quite a while."

As predicted indeed it did take some time. In fact a cycle and one half passed before they had finished. This included the help of Fauul. Had he not been there, it probably would have run closer to three cycles. Yet at the end of the mapping they all felt relatively confident in their abilities. Still it was obvious they were entering summer. The days had warmed considerably, and also had lengthened. The surrounding vegetation was turning yellow and curing under the heat. Jllon privately was glad they were not in the desert at this time and wondered how the smaller team was faring there. But with no planned contact he was left with just his thoughts.

One of the interesting results he was seeing from the mapping was the work being done by the artists now appeared to be much more accurate. He began to wonder how they ever did any of their work without mapping. Still, without the knowledge, it was something that they thought wasn't needed. As of yet, because of this preliminary work, they had not returned to the underground, and the location of those ancient objects, so it was decided that on the morrow they would make their first excursion with the team into the cavern.

He had yet to decide if he was going to divide the team and have some work underground and others work here on the surface. Still not knowing how safe the tunnel was that led into the cavern he worried that it could collapse and trap anyone who happened to be down there at the time of the collapse. Turning towards Celt he said, "Celt, I think we are finally ready to go back down into the cavern. I know that none of us has had a lot of underground work, but I want you to take a couple of our best diggers and as we go down there on the morrow to inspect as best you can. I don't want a collapse, and since an earth shake recently opened this pathway into the cavern, I do not want another to close it.

"I think we should be looking at ways to improve the tunnel. There were a couple of really troublesome places, and Fauul would barely fit. So I think before we get serious on working down there we need to do whatever work is necessary to feel . . . well . . . at least a little safer down there."

"I haven't been down there so I don't know what to expect. But I will check with the diggers and see if any have had any experience in tunnels. What you are describing makes me more than a little nervous. I don't mind doing the work like we have in the past and in the desert, but the underground always brings fear to me."

"I guarantee it isn't my favorite place either. But what can we do? It was there the discovery was made, so it is one of the places we have to start. If you have any other suggestions I am more than open to them, believe me."

"Again, since I haven't seen the cavern yet, I have nothing to suggest. I guess we can only be as prepared as we can be and hope for the best."

"I guess that's true, and I do hope that we have prepared enough." Jllon turned and faced the rest of the team, he whistled to get their attention, sent them a hand signal to come to him, and waited for the team to assemble. The shadows at the site were beginning to stretch to the east as the sun began its descent, and once they were all with him he said, "I'm calling end of the work for this day a little early. I want everyone to get a good night's rest, as on the morrow we will be descending into underground. The plan is for everyone to go down, but not all at once. I want everyone to see what we are up against, and on the morrow night after we return to the shelters, we will discuss our options. Tonight we will split the team into two teams and all of the morrow will be involved strictly with the underground. One team will remain on the surface and the other will go underground. Then when the first one returns to the surface, the second team will descend. From my own brief experience down there, I know that by the time the second team re-emerges from the underground that our day will be done – any questions?" With none forthcoming he continued, "Alright let's head back."

The next day arrived quickly and the two teams were back at the site with Jllon leading the first team down. He got Lauut to come to take the second team down. Lauut would show up just before the zenith break. The plan was for the first team to enter at dawn and be back for the zenith meal, after which, the second team would then descend. Of course, all times were approximate, as they had no way to track their time once they left the surface. The torches would allow them an approximate guess though. Still with one member of each team having already gone down to the cavern it would at least make the trip down and back a little faster.

Taking one last look around before lighting his torch, Jllon said, "I guess that's it. We've planned as well as we can, and have as much in order as we can foresee. So let's go. See you around the zenith Celt." He lit the torch, signaled his team, and they entered into the tunnel.

As they descended into the tunnel Jllon had the team strengthen the marks that Lauut had originally placed. He also explained the system that Lauut had used so that if any were to become separated then by using the marks they could find their way out. Not much had changed since their last trip down, and their footprints from their last trip were still visible on the floor of the tunnel.

It was still hot and sticky, giving further credence to a hot spring being down in the main cavern somewhere. There had been plenty of time, had it been just trapped heat, for the heat to dissipate. They finally reached the apparent dead end. Here Jllon had them mark this area so that it would easily be recognized. Once they made the turn and entered the cavern again, he had them mark the entrance into the cavern very well. He knew from his last visit that once inside this looked no different than any of the many walls.

"Be careful while you are here. I was shown some areas where there are holes that seem to have no bottom. I want everyone to work in teams of no less than two. This trip we are going to survey the area carefully and attempt to mark the danger areas. So each team will light one torch and use the additional light to avoid these hidden traps – let's get to work. Flar, you're with me. I want the learners split with ones with more experience. Lastly, keep in sight of each other. This trip is to mark the danger spots. I want the artist that is with us, Rasti if you would, sketch as much of the area as you can. When we return to the surface you can turn over what you have accomplished to Wahlter, and he can continue your work. We only have a short time so let's get busy."

Seeing the ten of them break into groups Jllon led Flar over to the pile of debris where the fire starters had been found. "Okay Flar, if you look up you will see a hole. I think this debris is from that hole – probably was part of the roof at one time. Looking at the debris I think that the earth shake that opened the tunnel probably brought this portion of the roof down. As you can see the location of that hole is such that I can think of no way to get to it. In this area, my guess would be that it's around ten body lengths just to reach it, and we have nothing that can reach even close to that height."

"True, and unlike on the surface, we just can't build something up to it. Yes, I can see this will be a real problem. When you were down here the last time did any of you find anything additional in or around the debris pile?"

Shaking his head Jllon said, "No – while we didn't do a complete search, still it appears that the ones that Fauul and Lauut have are the only ones, we at least did a brief one."

Both looking up in the flickering light of the torch at the hole so far out of reach, Flar commented, "It sure is tantalizing, and it sure makes me curious. What's up there? Of course it could turn out to be nothing . . . still without being able to go there . . ." He just trailed off, leaving it unsaid.

"Yeah, I know. It does make the imagination kick in. And as in so many other places, in the end, it might be just another level to this cave complex and nothing else. But without being able to look . . . yeah." Looking at his torch Jllon had caught one of the warning flares, "Next time it will be time to leave here. So let's look around here and see if we can find anything."

Before they knew it the time was up and he signaled the team to meet with him and they headed back to the surface. When they finally emerged into the light the sun was approaching the zenith. "Well, I guess we hit that just about right. I wouldn't have believed that the torches were that accurate. But it seems that they are. Looking at himself he saw, as last time, he was covered in a light film of mud. His clothes were soaked from his sweat, and the breeze almost made him cold. "Guess we had better change. Let the two females go into the portable shelter first and then we males can go get into something dry.'

Celt was approaching asked, "Well, how was it?"

"Hot and humid, as if you can't tell." Looking around he located Rasti and said, "Hey Rasti, come here and bring your sketches. I want to show Celt where we were and the area I want him to look at."

Coming over to join them Rasti said, "Okay, give me a sec here. I want to make sure that the sketches didn't get damp from my sweat." He carefully unrolled his work and looked at it and said, "Good! Nothing got on the work. Okay, now I worked from the entrance into the cavern. See there, that's where you were." He pointed to an area on his drawing.

"You are good." Then looking at Celt he said, "What I would like your group to do is to start here where I was, and work back further in. Have Wahlter start his work right here. I would like to locate that hot spring so I know what we are dealing with. Watch your time closely and definitely watch out for those dangerous drops. We found a couple of more. Please have your team mark them well. I don't want any accidents from someone falling into one of them. I think eventually we will rope them off and then hang something off the ropes to identify the danger."

"Okay, sounds great." Looking up Celt said, "I think I just heard the call to eat, shall we?"

"Okay, I'll join you shortly. I need to get out of these dirty and wet clothes. Funny how you adjust to the temperature you're in. When I came out of there it felt cold out here, and I know it isn't."

The rest of the day went faster than expected, and when Celt and his team arrived back at camp just as dirty and wet as the first team had been, Jllon had them change into dry clothes. They packed up what they had and headed back to the workers shelter. After the meal in the evening they would have a meeting in the common room and discuss all that they had discovered in the cavern.

With everyone in the common space, Jllon said, "Okay everyone, let's open this up with your impressions."

Suzzane spoke up first saying, "Other than being scary, dirty, hot, and damp, well once I got used to it, the cavern itself was beautiful."

There was an agreement from the rest of the team. Jllon replying, "I can't disagree with that statement. It was all of that and more. Celt I'm sure that Lauut showed you the point where the roof collapsed, and its height. And the rest of you please think about it. The roof at that point seems to be very high and we need to find a way up to it. Not only up to it, but actually we need to get inside to that next level. At least the hole is large enough for someone to fit through, but still getting to that point is the problem." Looking around Jllon could see that the team hadn't a clue as to what could be done. The silence from them confirmed it also.

"I want for us to keep the team split while we are working that deep underground. So that if there is ever a problem that we will always have someone on the surface to get help or assist. We need to work on that tunnel and make it easier to navigate, and maybe look at propping a couple of areas up to make it safer. Does anyone here have any mining experience?"

Again the answer was no from the team. Shaking his head, Jllon said, "Too bad. We sure could have used some of that expertise. While some of our work has required shoring up walls and such this is the first time we have been so deep."

"How deep do you think we are when we are in that cavern?" asked Ehlie.

"I really have no idea. But there is a continual slope downward as you enter the tunnel and at times it gets steep. Anybody care to guess?"

About this time Fauul entered into the workers shelter and saw that a meeting was going on and had caught part of the question. "Could you repeat the question again for me?" Fauul asked.

"Oh, it was asked how far underground the cavern is," Jllon said.

"Well, I can't say accurately but can give a rough guess. One of the things we deal with in mapping, especially the trails is something called grade. It is important if the trail is going to have carts on it. If a grade is too steep then it is dangerous for carts to travel – whether these carts are people or beast drawn.

You have the solution right in what I have shown you." Taking a writing implement and something to write on he continued. "If we were to draw a level line here, and then let's say that these marks represent a number of chains of distance . . ." He drew a second sloping line down from the beginning point forming an angle. "Okay as you can see here we can now mark the same chain markings on this slope. With the tripod you used to lay out your map of the planned work area and the rod you can then count the marks from level on that rod for every chain that is marked. Hold on I'll get a rod so you can see it better." He left briefly leaving the team questioning how this all worked.

"Sorry about that, but I really had not planned on doing this . . . anyway each mark on this rod is the same distance as a link on the chain. So you should remember that there are one hundred links on a chain. This makes it easy to convert the change in elevation into a percent of grade."

"Percent of grade? I don't quite know what you are talking about," Jllon said.

Looking at Jllon Fauul continued, "Okay it really is simple math. If in one chain the change or drop is five links of the chain then in that one chain distance the grade is a five-percent downgrade from the beginning position."

"Oh, I think I've got it. So if, for example, if the difference were twenty-five links or one rod then the change would be twenty five percent. Is that right?"

"Exactly. So by plotting the drop into the cavern you can come up with a rough figure as to how far down you are. And that is one of the reasons it is so important to have your sighting device level."

"Fauul since you are here, one of the problems we are trying to overcome is finding a way up to that hole in the cavern. We haven't been able to come up with any way of getting up there. After all it is not very close to a wall so we cannot cut footholds into the wall, and it's really high."

"Haven't really thought about it, so right now I don't, but I will discuss it with Lauut and Lauma and maybe between the three of us we can come up with something. That's of course if you don't figure it out first."

"That's all we can ask, and thanks for explaining that to us."

"You're welcome. Almost forgot as to why I came in here. Lauut said that we are about to get a weather change. For the next few days it is going to be hot and dry. Plus we are going to get some of those strong easterly winds."

Celt asked, "How does he know that? When we were in the desert, the nomads warned us of the very thing. If they hadn't then there would have been more damage to our equipment than there were."

"I don't know really. But they, the nomads and Lauut, have lived with it all their lives. So maybe it's just something they unconsciously recognize."

"Thanks for the warning; I guess when we go back out on the morrow we had better make sure everything is tied down."

"Oh one last thing, please be very careful with fire. He said that until you see one of the wild fires here you have never experienced one. The final warning he wants to give is that if you see smoke on the horizon that seems to be coming in your direction pack up and come back here quickly. And he says very quickly – as fast as you can. Again he says that if you wait then you may find yourself trapped. These wild fires move so fast that there is nothing in nature that can outrun them."

"Warning taken. While I have never seen one of these wild fires here, I have experienced them up north. Still his description seems to make them appear to be a campfire. I guess I will have to see one to see how accurate his description is. It does seem impossible for a fire to move that fast."

"Yeah, I had the same reaction. But he assured me that he was not exaggerating at all. He says there has been times, in the past, that the smoke from these fires has covered the sky so thickly that the flyers roosted back in the trees thinking it was dusk, and with the smoke and ash so thick it was hard to breath."

"That almost sounds like the end of the world. I wonder if that was what it was like with that worldwide disaster happened. It had to be horrible."

"If indeed that is what happened, yes it would have been horrible. I guess if we have a chance to see one of these it may give us a first-hand feel of what it may have been like when that disaster happened."

"I hadn't thought about it that way," Jllon said, "but you're right."

Turning to leave Fauul said, "Sorry for interrupting here but I thought you needed to know."

"No apology needed. In fact you have given use more to work with, and for that we thank you."

As predicted, the winds began just before sunrise. While normally calm that time of the night there was always a slight down canyon breeze. First it became very quiet, and then the winds shifted. At first these winds were slight but as the time passed they picked up in strength. Eventually they were blowing hard enough to shake the shelter. Temperatures also rose, and the air felt very dry. The shift in winds and the shaking of the shelters woke all of them up, as it went from silence to noisy. The winds would blow steady then have a large gust come in and shake the shelters. At these times it felt as if a giant hand had grabbed the shelter and was shaking it with a determination to destroy it. While generally out of the east, it would vary its direction somewhat. Again anything outside that hadn't been put away was knocked over and would create another noise.

Finally giving up on any more sleep the team assembled blurry eyed in the common space. The sun wasn't even up yet, and with the heat generated from the winds it felt like it was mid-morn. It was now very obvious that it was heading to be tremendously hot day. "I guess if you live in paradise you have to have something to remind you that's it not that way all the time." One of the team members commented.

Thinking back they remembered commenting on how nice it was here in comparison to where they came from – temperatures mild, cool breezes, sunny most of the time, and no truly cold weather. It sure did seem like paradise. Now they were seeing some of the things that changed that view. "I wonder how often they get these winds?" Jayson asked.

"I really don't know, but I can say that I am finding that they are no fun at all", Kaern answered.

Eventually they had the morn meal and headed out to the work site. And as the day continued the winds increased in speed and it became almost impossible to be heard over them. One couldn't walk in a straight line, as the winds would gust, pushing one off balance. Anything that was loose would be picked up and blown away. One couldn't run and catch whatever was lost. Dirt, sand, and small pebbles were picked up and tossed in multiple directions at the whims of the wind. The temporary shelter they had set up was double staked, and even that wasn't good enough. The winds were destroying the shelter as the gusts would almost lay it flat.

The time spent was simply on trying to keep from losing anything and to prevent any destruction of their equipment. Their skins stung from the blown dirt and sand, and the heat was oppressive. Jllon, thinking about what Lauut had said about fires, began to understand how bad they might be. With this type of wind how could anyone stop such a fire? He couldn't even see how one could build a fire for cooking, and if you did, would the winds pick up your embers from that fire and start the nearby vegetation to burning?

Finally Jllon signaled the team to gather around him and said, "This is not working. I want everything tied down as well as it can be. Then we will simply head back and wait this out. I'm sure that there are some things we can do back there, and if nothing else help Lauut, Fauul, and Lauma around their place. We will come out here two or three times a day to make sure what we have here is still here. Okay, one more look around and then let's head back." He found that he had to yell just to be heard. He found that his skin actually stung, and his lips were cracked. Even when the wind was not blowing, which was rare, one's hair would stand up from the static in the air. It almost seemed that one might start a fire just from touching something. The shocks the team were experiencing were not only when they touched something made of metal, but found that it was also between each other. While humorous in the beginning, when it was discovered, it eventually became old and they tried to avoid each other. Then one would unconsciously do something they would normally do and receive a shock as a result.

On the third day, the winds, as evening approached, appeared to be dying, or at least slowing down. Once the sun set the winds started calming down, and every once in a while they would stop completely and it would be dead calm. They found that their ears were ringing, and the silence, after so much noise, was almost deafening. But as night approached the winds picked up again and they had one more uncomfortable night. Those winds wouldn't give up without a fight.

CHAPTER EIGHTEEN

That morn, three days later when they awoke, they felt a chill to the air, and instead of the howling winds there was a soft breeze. When they got up and dressed, all of them stepped outside briefly. With that chill they also felt the return of moisture. It was wonderful; the winds of the east were finally gone. Jllon standing next to Nouma asked idly, "I wonder how often they come around, and if three days is the normal length?"

Shaking her head, Nouma had no answer. Like him she was new to the area. It was something to ask Lauma that was for sure. Turning around at the sound of a closing door they both saw Lauut leaving the main shelter. Jllon seeing him signaled him that he would like a quick word. Lauut see the signal came over and joined them. "Good morn, to the two of you.

As you can see the weather has changed back to normal and it is a relief."

"Yes, and for the whole team I agree. But what we wanted to know, since you have lived all of your life here, is a little about these winds. This one that has just passed blew for three days, is that normal?"

"Actually yes, but this was a short one. They always seem to blow in series of threes."

"Threes? I don't know what you mean by that."

"Oh, three, six, nine, or twelve days – never had one last longer than twelve days, but fortunately these are rare. The three to six day winds are closer to normal if you can call these winds normal."

Nouma looking over at the pens saw one of the team leaning against the rails and realized it was Suzzane said, "Ah I see you have someone waiting for you over there."

Turning and looking down to the pens Lauut smiled, "Yes that is true. She, as you know comes from a farm. While quite different from this one there are enough similarities that it made her a little home sick. We've been doing a lot of talking and she has helped me a little. Normally this is my time to be by myself and do some thinking, but I don't mind the company."

Smiling, Nouma said, "Yes, I'm sure it is a nice change."

Excusing himself Lauut said, "I really must get to it. After these winds we have much to inspect and repair. I do hope everything survived out at your site." He left and went down to join Suzzane.

"I think we have a new relationship blooming," Nouma said.

"You really think so?" Jllon asked.

"Well if it isn't obvious to you then you are not looking too closely. I was wondering where she had been going after our evening meals here, and I had missed her a few times in the morn before we eat. After all, if you remember, you put the females under my care so I watch closely – although not so close as to intrude."

"I guess if it continues she could do much worse. From what I have seen here they have struggled, but you cannot deny the quality of their beasts. There is a lot of pride and hard work here and it shows."

When they finally reached the work site later that morn sure enough the winds had played games with all of their equipment. They spent the rest of the morn cleaning up and finding items that had been blown around. Overall, they had been lucky that there was very little damage. The temporary shelter though, had been completely destroyed. There was just enough left to put up a sunshade. Jllon decided that after the zenith meal that he would send a couple of the team members' back to the main shelter and pick up a replacement.

Taking a break from the cleanup he looked at one of the maps of the area they had created. Thinking about the approximate distance and the twists the tunnel made he was guessing that the cavern lay under the hill that was directly in front of them. Putting down the maps in a safe place he walked over to the edge of the large hill and really looked at it. When one first looked, it appeared to be no different than many others in the area, but on closer inspection there were many things about it that just appeared to be wrong. What was wrong, he just couldn't figure out. Continuing his walk around the hill he found that it extended quite far into the distance. Again, for whatever reason, there was little growth of any vegetation on it. Just some light grasses and nothing else. He could see that this maybe had been caused by the steep grade. The hill seemed to continue to shed dirt and small rocks all the time.

From his trip around the hill he found that there appeared to be no beast trails or any apparent way up its sides. As steep as it was and as loose as the soil appeared to be meant that the climb up to the top would not be easy. But his curiosity had been raised. He needed to get on top of this hill. From there he might possibly get a better idea of what was going on. Looking at the position of the sun in the sky and the growl of his stomach he realized that it was time to head back to camp and the zenith meal.

When he got back to the camp the meal was in the process of being served. At least things were getting back to normal after those winds. He remembered Celt telling him about them in the desert, but his description just did not come close to the actual winds. While he ate he was lost in thought. Suddenly he realized that someone had been asking him something and he hadn't heard a word they said. "What? Sorry, I was thinking."

"Really? I would never have guessed," Payle said. "Anyway what I asked is how many did you want to go back for the replacement shelter? Celt sent me here to find out."

"I'm sure he could have come up with a figure, but I think that we will need at least three of you – a beast handler, and two others. As you know those portable shelters are not light and I want to make sure that no one injures themselves from the weight. By the way, when you get back to Celt, tell him I'd like to talk with him."

"Sure thing boss." Payle left to report to Celt who was visible from where they were.

Returning to his thoughts again it took a moment to realize that someone was talking to him once again. Turning around he saw that Celt was standing there. "Sorry Celt, but I've been working on a problem and have been lost in thought."

"Well boss, I hope you found your way out."

"What? Oh I get it, lost and way out. Okay, anyway you probably could have come up with a number to send in for that shelter, but that's not why I wanted to talk with you. Do you know if any of the team has found an obvious way up that large hill over there?" He turned and pointed before continuing. "I don't know but to me something just doesn't look right, and I want to get on top of it, but so far have found no easy way up."

"So far no one's commented to me on finding a way up. In fact I don't think anyone really has thought about it since what was found was so far underground. I believe we have been trying to come up with a solution to get into that hole."

"Yeah that's probably true. I think that after zenith time until we head back in I'm going to try and find a way up. So if anyone needs me you will either find me attempting to find a way up or will be climbing that hill or if my luck holds be on top."

"Okay, but what is the plan for the rest of the day for the remainder of the team?"

"Really simple, just continue the cleanup and try and find some of the stuff that the winds blew into the surrounding countryside. I noticed that a couple of our closed containers that contained our notes had been broken open and apparently those notes were blown away. We really cannot afford to lose them, and once the new temporary shelter arrives to have everyone help in setting it up. One way or the other I will be back in camp here just before we leave to head back in. I really think that soon we will probably be spending a few days at a time here when we start the serious work."

"Yeah you're probably right. We lose too much time by making the trek each day from that workers shelter. Anyway, I'll make sure that the cleanup continues and will send a couple of people out to search for that missing stuff. The problem in my mind lies with the strength of those winds, and when those containers broke open. If it was near the end of the winds then we will probably get lucky, but if it was any earlier than that I doubt if we will ever find the notes."

"True, I really wouldn't want to have to reconstruct them," Jllon said. "So I do hope that it's closer to the end of the winds when it happened."

Finished with their conversation, Celt headed back to where he had come from and Jllon went back to thinking about how he was going to climb that hill. "Well just sitting here is not going to accomplish anything", Jllon said to himself. He got up and headed back to the hill and once again started walking around it and looking up.

Eventually he gave up on finding a path that led up the hill. Finally settling on an area where it appeared less steep, he started his climb. The soil was even looser than he expected and found that it was almost impossible to keep his balance. He also continued to lose forward progress and slide back down. This was going to really take a lot of physical strength to do this. Finally he found that by climbing at angles instead of straight up provided him the best solution.

Having to stop and catch his breath he found that more times than not he was having to use his hands and arms as much as his legs. *If we are going to work on top of this thing, I think we will have to cut our own trail. Otherwise it will take too much time and effort to reach the top.* Eventually he looked up and found that he was almost there, but at the same time seemed almost exhausted from the effort. Finding a place to sit to catch his breath, he found that he was sweating profusely and that his shirt was soaked. He was glad that he had remembered to bring water along. Fortunately there was a cool breeze out of the west and it helped cool him. Finally feeling a bit refreshed with his break he pushed on until he arrived on top.

The first thing to hit him was a very strong breeze, which almost chilled him because of his wet shirt. Quickly looking around he could find no place to get out of the winds. Again like most of the hill it was barren, and most surprising to him, almost flat. Walking completely around the top, it finally dawned on him what was wrong with the hill. While not perfectly so it appeared to be rectangular in its general shape, and normally, as far as he knew, such things were not seen in nature too often. It also changed direction a couple of times extending out, but more or less keeping to that general shape.

He found that he had a great view of the surrounding countryside from there, and then a second oddity hit him. This hill sat all by itself on an area that was relatively flat. Off in the distance he could see others and even there off to the west a couple of the areas just did not look natural to him. Of course, in both cases, this hill and the ones he saw in the distance, he could be fooled. The natural world was not his expertise, and there was none on his team other than Doube who was.

Again, from what he had learned on this project, first from Doube, and then from Fauul, he now thought it would be a good idea, in the future, to include such experts. That left him wondering how many different disciplines it would be smart to have with them. Looking at the position of the sun he knew that it was time to return to camp. He suspected that going down was not going to be easy either. He also found that his legs were shaking from the work of climbing in the difficult soil. Yes he probably would be muscle sore on the morrow.

Finally he reached the ground from the hill and found that his legs were really fatigued. But he was back on level ground and figured that he would be able to walk it out. Really, he had no choice, since they were returning to the permanent shelter. As he entered the camp area he found the team waiting for him and the new shelter had be erected and double anchored and placed so that it sat on the lee of where the strong east winds blew. "Okay I can see that I am the last to assemble, so let's head back. After we clean up and eat tonight I want a brief meeting in the common area so that I can relate to all of you what I have found and what we will probably be doing. So let's head back."

After the team had cleaned up and had eaten they converged on the common space to hear what Jllon had come up with. Jllon said, "Okay all, this will be brief. Now, as you know, we are attempting to enter that hole down in the cavern, and we will continue to try and do that. I feel that it is important. But not to waste all of our efforts in one area I want to rotate the team to both work under ground and to work on some digging. Today, again as you know, I tackled that hill. It was a tough climb, but that hill just bothered me. There was something about it that did not look right. Finally I decided that it was much too rectangular, and thought that maybe it is artificial.

"So the plan is for us to split the team as we did in the desert, and as one half works on the problem of entering the hole and the second half will start digging a trail up that hill. I found that the top is relatively flat, and surprisingly large. So the goal, simply stated, is to start digging at the top, move the dirt we dig down the trail we will create and then dump it away from the site. Because of this it will take longer, but for some reason I have a strong feeling that in the end it will be worth the extra trouble – more than that I cannot say.

So on the morrow I will have Celt take half the team back into the cavern and the other half with me will begin the construction of the trail on the hill. I know to make it safer we will also be reinforcing the tunnel in certain areas. I do not want to have any chance of an accident or a cave-in there. Now if there isn't anything else that's all I have." Looking around he saw that there was nothing that any of the team members wanted to bring up. He ended by saying, "Okay then . . . see you all early in the morn. Shortly we will be staying out there and only coming in after five or six days of work. But for now we will continue as it is." He left the group and decided to go outside for some air and probably go join the other three on their traditional "sitting on the porch" after a day's work was finished. Leaving the workers shelter, he saw that Lauut, Fauul, and Lauma were sitting there enjoying a little relaxation before calling it a night. "May I join you?" Jllon asked

"Of course, and you do not need to ask. You and Nouma are always welcome. You know that," Lauut answered.

"Thank you, but it is a courtesy and one I will always present. After all, it is only right to be invited and not to just assume. I suspect that Nouma will be joining us soon anyway. I know that she has found that this is a nice way to end the day. It sure is a great tradition you have created."

"Yeah I guess it is one – even though it was something that kind of happened naturally. We just found after the loss of our sires, that at the end of the day we were exhausted. So coming out here with something to drink and just relaxing was a great way to wind down. So as time went by it just became something we always would do."

"Yeah", Lauma added, "we found that if we didn't, we ended up missing it, and I found it to be one of my favorite things to do once everything was wrapped up for the day. And I think now that Fauul has been here a while that it is the same for him, right Fauul?"

"I must admit it is a great way to finish. Still there are others that are just as nice." Looking at Lauma he smiled and continued, "If you know what I mean."

Blushing a little and then trying to look a little angry, but not carrying it off successfully, said, "Yes there are other nice things; still I cannot deny that this is still one of my favorites." Then looking out in the yard and wanting to change the subject she said, "Oh look, you were right, here comes Nouma now."

Smiling, as he saw his mate approaching, Jllon said, "As I predicted, she has found this to be nice also." Then turning to her he said, "I see we both had the same idea. I actually only got here myself."

"I wondered where you went after leaving the common space and realized that this was the most likely spot. Like you, I have found it a nice way to finish. By the way Lauut how are you and Suzzane getting along?" She asked innocently.

Caught off guard he paused before he answered. He first looked over at Fauul and saw that he was smiling at him. Remembering how he had been teased he decided to be just non-committal. "Okay, I guess we've been talking and comparing the different ways things work between the farm she's from and this one where we deal mostly with the beasts."

"Common interests, makes sense to me." Nouma said, not pushing the subject. She knew that it was becoming more than that. But for now let it be what he wanted it to be.

For the next cycle the teams worked on making the trail up the hillside and reinforcing and opening areas within the tunnel leading to the cavern. In the cavern area they continued the explorations and found that the hot springs were located much deeper in the complex. As they explored the complex they found that it had many lower levels. Doube, upon inspecting these finds, concluded that the whole complex was volcanic in origin. Yet, with all this exploration they were no nearer on finding a way into the hole as they studied other possibilities but so far had found none.

This seemed to be the one major problem that they would have to solve – no simple solutions here.

Meanwhile, with the soils being as loose as they were, it had taken much longer to build a trail to the top. Everything seemed to be against finding any answer to the questions they had. Then the winds came again. Once again Lauut had warned them of the approach, and warned that from the feel in the air these would be much stronger than the last.

"Stronger than the last? You've got to be kidding right? I mean those winds almost tore everything we had out there apart." Jllon stated.

"No unfortunately I'm not. I think they will last even longer than the three days it did the last time. I suspect this will be a six-day wind, and from the feel of the air my guess is that it will be much drier also. Be very careful with fire out there, and one other suggestion put a couple of your team members on fire watch. We are later into summer now and things are very dry. So if there is a fire with these winds . . . well let's just say I hope it isn't close."

Thinking to himself, after he had left Lauut, he thought. *What else can happen?* While the desert dig had gone well from the beginning, it seemed that it was just the opposite for this one. So far the only finds had been the original ones that Lauut had found. The areas of interest had not allowed much work in the direction needed and now those winds again.

He relayed the information to the team, and when they went out the next day the first items to be worked was to insure the integrity of the temporary shelters. They all had experienced the winds and now knew what to expect. It was decided to take them down and to store the supplies inside the tunnel instead of risking the loss of another temporary shelter or any of the supplies and notes, which they had been fortunate and had recovered.

By the time the work was completed the winds began to arrive. First by the area becoming dead calm without any breeze at all, followed by slight breezes in the prevailing winds direction and then coming from the east. They all felt the air drying out with the temperature rising, and then the winds arrived. Again, at first, their speed wasn't too great, but in a short period of time they were at their fury. Anything spoken had to be yelled, and it was obvious that there would be little they could do at least above ground. So the decision for this day was to have the whole team other than the two they would leave on the surface for fire watch and safety, to work in the tunnel.

By using the torches for timing they emerged towards the end of the day to find the two looking far to the east and south. "What are you looking at?" Jllon asked.

Flar, who was one of the two on watch said, "Look way out there on the horizon." He pointed to the southeast saying, "I think that may be smoke, but I can't tell. I'm no expert. But the last thing I would expect in winds like this is clouds."

Looking in the direction that Flar pointed, Jllon said, "Yeah I see what you mean. It does look like a cloud. Let's get back to the shelters and see what Lauut has to say. I don't want to be caught out in the open if that is a fire."

Even though they were tired from the day's work there now was an impetus to get back. If indeed this was smoke it still was a long way out. But from the description that Lauut had given of past fires it might arrive here quickly.

As they came into the yard there was a smell of smoke in the air. They had their confirmation that this was a wild fire. At this moment it wasn't strong, and there was no smoke close to them, yet the smell permeated the air.

As the team entered the yard they saw the three of them by the main shelter. Immediately Lauut came over and met with Jllon. "It's what I feared. We seem to have a couple of these a turn and now you will get a chance to see one of them first hand. Once you do you will never forget."

"Are we in trouble?" Jllon asked. "Are we in the path of this thing? I mean I really don't know, and what should we be doing?"

"My guess, at this time is no we are not. It appears to be south of us at this moment. But we have to watch closely as a wind change would move it in our direction. We need to prepare for that possibility and that means to fill anything that will hold water, and to make sure there is nothing close by that can burn. I'm afraid that none of us are going to get much sleep tonight. We have to have fire watches all night. So let's set it up to be two at a time and the rest to get as much rest as possible.

"With the amount of people we have here we can divide the task up so that at least all have some sleep. Now, while we have some daylight left, let's see what still needs to be accomplished and then just do it. Have your camp managers put together some foods that can be eaten cold, and get some containers that each of you can carry water in.

"Fauul and I will be gone a little while. We need to drive the herd beasts back into the holding pens so they are out of danger. Lauma will be here to fill you in on any questions you may have. We really do not have a lot of time so we are going now. Ask her where anything you need can be found and while we have this daylight to clean anything around here that might burn. I do hope to see you just after dark. We should be back by then." He turned and left signaling Fauul to join him. The two of them headed out with the dogs to where the herd beasts were located.

Jllon left standing didn't know what to do for a moment, seeing Lauma standing on the porch he decided that she should lead them through what was coming. He had never experienced such as this and she had. That was enough for him. "Lauma, I want you to take charge of my team while your mate and brother are away. I am completely unfamiliar with what we are about to face, and I want someone who is experienced to lead."

With a shocked look on her face, she couldn't believe what she was hearing . . . *A male asking a female to lead? It was unheard of.* But now was not the time. She could understand why he had asked it of her. She wondered if the team would take orders from a female. Still there would be little time for speculation. "Okay, but are you sure I can count on the cooperation of your team? After all I'm a female, and our society doesn't allow such a thing."

"They will if I tell them too. They trust my judgement, and I have yet to do them wrong. Besides I think that once Lauut returns the two of you should run the operation until the two of you deem it safe. And right now he is not here and you are."

"Okay then, bring them out to the yard here and explain your reasons and I'll get things going. Hurry, if that wind does change it will get hot and nasty here quickly."

Turning around and looking, he could see that the sky to the south was covered heavily with smoke.

"Heck," he said, "just a short time ago we were wondering if that was just clouds and now there is no blue sky there at all." He quickly headed into the workers shelter and got the team and brought them out to the yard. "Okay all, I have no experience in what we may be about to face, so I have put Lauut and Lauma in charge of this emergency. Lauut with Fauul, have gone to bring in the herd beasts, so for now you will follow the orders of Lauma."

The team turned expectantly towards Lauma and awaited her orders. Lauma with her hands on her hips looked over the team, thought for a moment and said, "With these wild fires we never have any idea what they will do. The winds that push them are variable in the direction and because of their strength it can start fires a long ways ahead of the main fire. This is one the greatest dangers you will face with these. You could be attacking the main fire trying to protect something only to find yourself trapped between two fires.

"With the strength of these things all you can do is try and protect what you have. In the supply shelter there are many buckets. We will need to fill these, and along with them are some tools we have for firefighting. Our roofs are covered in a tar and sand combination to keep them waterproof. But even with the sand content that's in the tar they can and will catch fire and burn. So we need a number of the buckets filled and placed on the roof tops to have them ready in case one of the roofs catches fire.

"Understand this, and it's critical, there is no way that you will ever be able to outrun this fire. So we have a safe area where you will come to if it becomes impossible to protect what we have. It is better to survive this and rebuild than get yourself killed. If you notice, where we are standing, here in the main yard, there is nothing around you. Even the shelters are back from here. This is the safe area. It will get very uncomfortable, but you should survive. Do not, and I emphasize, *do not*, under any circumstances, play hero here. If you haven't experienced these fires you do not know what you are up against. There is nothing that can compare, in the north, to the speed and devastation that these fires can do.

"Both my brother and Fauul will be back soon. When they come back Lauut will show you how to use the tools. There will obviously be a fire watch all night, and we all will share in it. No less than two at a time, and while it would be easy to be drawn to watching the main fire, you must continue to look everywhere. As I have said, these fires throw stuff ahead of themselves and start other fires. It could be one of those other fires that might be the problem for us – any questions?"

There was a general shaking of the heads, with Kaern asking, "I've never seen anything like this. How long do they burn and how far do they go?"

"They burn extremely fast and as long as the wind is blowing the fire will continue to burn. And it only stops when it runs out of stuff to burn, and sometimes that's the ocean."

"And there's nothing you can do to stop them?" Kaern asked again.

"What do you think? You saw how fast it went from is it, to the sky being covered from the smoke of the fire. Take it from me if it came across our property it would be completely across it in, as you do time in the townships, minutes." She could see the reaction that brought from the team, and she continued, "We will probably be lucky on this one, and because of preparation we have been lucky in the past. This one probably will stay to the south, but I suspect it will get a little closer than I would like. So let's just do what we can, and wait. Okay let's get to it. Time is not our friend here."

They were finding it at times hard to hear what she had been saying. The wind was so strong that again it was difficult to keep standing in one place, and the small pebbles the wind was picking up continued to pelt them. They found their skin stinging from the contact of the blowing sand and small rocks. They all glanced nervously to the south and saw that now there was no blue sky at all. Instead it was dark and ominous. With every change in the direction of the wind they would smell the smoke. As the time passed the smell seemed to become stronger and the sun took on a yellow tinge. It wouldn't be long before it set, and they would be heading into darkness. Lauma led them over and handed out the buckets and showed them the permanent ladders that were attached to the shelters to allow quick access to the roofs. There were five buckets for each roof, and at least another fifteen that were to be filled and placed in strategic locations for easy access.

While they all were involved in the filling and placing of the buckets Lauma heard the approaching herd beasts. Soon they would be in the pens, and the dogs would remain with them there to keep them from trying to break out from panic. It was an old game for the dogs. Something they had done many times before.

It was soon dark. It seemed to become that way much earlier than normal. Still it was probably because of the smoke in the air. It appeared that it was going to cover the whole sky and blot out the sun as it set. And true to that vision the sun did enter the smoke and disappear – leaving a yellow-reddish hue touching everything – making everything appear to be quite unreal. With the fall of night when one looked into the far distance they saw the glow of the fire. It appeared to jump from one place to another. The air seemed to be filled with little yellow lights floating ahead and then where they set down to start another fire.

For the team it was a very uncomfortable night with little sleep. With that ever-changing wind came smoke pouring into the area where they were and with it came a gray-white ash that rained down on them continually. Even within the shelters the ash found its way in. The acrid smoke burned both the eyes and lungs, and at times making it hard to breathe. Then the winds would change and for a short period they would have fresh clean air only to have it disappear again.

If they had any doubt of the speed of the fire, as described by the family, that was now gone. It was quite obvious to any watching the moving fire that there was nothing on earth that could outrun it. And if briefly possible, they could, with new fires always starting ahead of it, run into the new blaze with no escape between the fires.

For them and their location the fire was still east and south of them. And the winds seemed to continue to blow out of the east and northeast, meaning that if it remained so that the fire would miss them. Suddenly the smell of smoke became stronger and then lay in on them, obliterating everything, and leaving them choking and unable to breathe. They fell to the ground trying to escape the enveloping smoke. In what seemed like an eternity before a wind change finally blew it away and they were able to once again breathe. Still with the howling wind it was impossible for one to hear another unless they yelled while standing next to each other. Hand signals seemed to be the only way to communicate. Running up to the main shelter Jllon saw Lauut standing on the porch and asked, "How long is this going to last? I mean I have never in my life experienced anything like this. You say you have these every turn?"

Taking a deep breath and with resignation Lauut said, "Yeah, every turn. But so far none has come close enough to cause us any loss. Still when one approaches this close, and really it's not very close, it reminds us as to why we keep the main area clean down to just dirt."

"Even with this intrusion of smoke and ash you are telling me that this thing out there isn't very close? It sure seems so."

"Yeah, believe me; if it was closer you would be feeling the heat from this thing. Now all we are receiving from it is the ash and a little of the smoke. So I think we are safe. But it would be easy to simply concentrate on this one. There always can be a second and because we're not paying attention it could come in and destroy everything and everyone."

"I hadn't thought of that. It's so easy to think that there only could be one at a time. But I guess when you really think about it why would that be so?"

"Exactly. We've seen three or four burn at the same time in the past. And sometimes they even come together and make an even larger fire. They are spectacular, and hauntingly beautiful, even as they destroy."

"Where are the other two?"

"Right now they are trying to get some sleep. It won't be long and Fauul will be here and I will try to get some sleep. From what I have seen you haven't gotten any sleep either and it's rather late. You should. If there is a wind change then there will be no opportunity at all. It will be a desperate struggle just to protect what we have, and you will only have a chance to rest when it's over."

"Do you think that will happen, a change in the wind I mean?"

"Don't know, but with these winds it could happen any time. That's why until you know for certain that the fire is past you and there is no chance for it to come back at you, you must have a continual fire watch. Right now, because of the conditions, it is difficult . . . near impossible to do so, but everyone who can rest should."

"Good advice, but you're right. This smoke, and it's really warm, and the gusting wind shakes and rattles the shelters, plus the ash added to the overall tension makes it near impossible to rest."

"Well, if that's so, then I suggest you get one of your camp managers to maintain a bunch of the hot beverage to keep everyone going, and to provide some cold meals that can be grabbed quickly. If this does happen and the fire turns on us, it will happen quickly and we will be very busy."

Taking his leave Jllon headed back over the workers shelter and passed on the information he had just received from Lauut, and went into his space with his mate laying on top of the bed fully dressed. "So Jllon what have you learned?" she asked quietly.

"We need to try and rest was one of the most important things he passed on, but admitted that it would be difficult to do. And if there is a wind shift it could bring the danger here. And if that happens, it will be crazy for a long time with no chance for any break or rest."

"So does he seem worried about it changing, the winds I mean?"

"Actually he seemed to be relaxed, well kind of. But he seems to be taking a wait-and-see type of attitude. I guess that comes from living with these things every turn. After all, it is a new experience for us. I thought I really knew what a wild fire was, but I am learning that I know nothing. There has been nothing to prepare me or us for this kind of wild fire. I cannot see how anything can survive such a thing. And how do you protect what you have if it comes your way?"

"I hope that we do not need to find out. Seeing it as it is, far away from us, is as close as I ever want to come."

"My sentiments exactly. This seems to be too close personally. And I know that it is far off. But watching this thing move, in the darkness, has made me realize that we cannot even come close to competing with nature when it rages like this. If this is any indication of what it's like when nature rages, and this is only a small part of this world. I get an inkling of what it must have felt like when that worldwide event happened those many thousands of turns in the past."

"I didn't think about that, but this scares me, and I am not afraid to say so. At least we have somewhere to go, but if our ancient ancestors, because what happened was everywhere, well it must have seemed more than hopeless that any would live."

"Yeah, it kind of gives one a new appreciation when you personally get a chance to experience something similar to what they must have."

"I've been lying here quite a while, but sleep just won't come. This is just awful. I think I'll get up for a while and go out to the common area and get something to drink and then come back – how about you?"

"Well, after what Lauut just told me, I think I will just lie down for a while. Even if sleep doesn't come I may be able to come close and anything will be better than nothing."

"Okay, then I won't be long and will come back and join you. Good luck." She arose and left the space going into the common space leaving Jllon alone.

To his surprise he found that he had fallen asleep, and even his mate whom he had never heard rejoin him had finally fallen asleep herself. He, in truth, had no idea how long, but he did not really feel refreshed. *Probably because there were so many strange noises and smells,* he thought. Carefully he got up not wanting to wake Nouma and quietly left their space and headed into the common space to see about half the team sitting around looking quite exhausted, and not talking at all. He figured he probably didn't look any better than the group sitting here. He went into the food prep area and got a cup of old hot beverage. It seemed strong enough to have leaped out of the cup and fight him. But maybe it was exactly what he needed. Looking around he saw that presently, there was no camp manager here, and figured that they were attempting to get some sleep also. One thing for sure, this time and event would remain in his memory maybe forever.

The smell of smoke still permeated the air, and there seemed to be a light blue haze within the shelter. With his beverage in his hand he opened the door and immediately had it grabbed out of his hand by the wind, which slammed the door into the side of the shelter. Shaking his head he wrestled with the door and managed to get it closed again. Immediately, once away from the lee of the shelter he was fighting the wind, but he wanted to get out into the open and see how the fire was doing. He stopped in awe. While only a short period of time had passed since he had slept, and remembering how he had seen the fire then, could not believe what he was seeing. This just could not be real. There was no way that anything could have moved that fast. Yet the evidence was there in front of his eyes. As he looked to the south, now from as far to the east as he could see to as far to the west was nothing but fire. How was it possible? It was shocking, how could anything survive such a conflagration?

Suddenly he realized that someone was standing next to him. Looking over he saw that Lauma had joined him. "Spectacular isn't it?" She commented.

"That's not quite the words I would have used, but yes."

"It's one of those things about living in paradise that is usually not known."

"Paradise? What do you mean by that?"

"Oh, when visitors come to the gathers they feel that with the way the weather is here that it must be paradise to live here. But now you get a chance to see the other side."

"Yeah, I kind of felt the same way. I mean the area seems to be so mild and it would be easy to live here. But I guess every place has something to make it a dangerous place to live."

"Yes, I guess that's true. Still you must admit that this area puts on quite a show when it shows its nasty side."

"You seem pretty calm Lauma, is there a reason?"

"Oh, I've lived through a number of these, and while they never become old, I've learned that you cannot let yourself get upset whenever one of these comes close. If I did, I suspect that eventually I would move out just to avoid them. But while they are wildly destructive, it really doesn't take too many turns before stuff grows back. It probably is just the way things are here, and I suspect it is the way things renew. I understand that where you are from that there are forests with large trees, and at times they burn also, but from your reaction, nothing to the scale of here. Still even in those forests things die, return to the earth and new things grow. Here it just happens much faster."

"That's an understatement! I never imagined that things could burn like this. Different subject, but how long until dawn I can't tell because of the smoke and the fire what time it is."

"Actually only a couple of hours off . . . This type of view will not be available to you once the sun comes up, as the daylight and smoke will hide the actual fire. The only thing that will truly be visible will be the smoke and every once in a while you will see the fire make a run. Right now the winds have held steady away from us and I'm hoping it remains that way. Soon the fire will have advanced enough that it will not be an immediate threat, and then we will be able to relax for a little while.

"But that will not be the end of the danger. You see the danger will only end when the fire burns itself out. You see if it is still burning when these winds die, then the prevailing winds will pick it up and push it back at us. Not at the same speed or intensity, but it still will be a danger."

"Really, I hadn't thought about that. I see I have much to learn about your area – especially if we are to be here for a while."

"Yeah, I guess it would be same if I came up to your area, other than that short time was up there with Fauul. Anyway, I'm going to go fix the morn meal for my two males, as I am the last on watch. So enjoy your view, and know for at least right now, you can do so without worrying too much about its danger." She left and headed back into the main shelter leaving him standing alone.

"Glad she can say that," he said to no one in particular. He did have to admit that the view was so unbelievable, and yes, he could see the beauty in its destruction.

As dawn approached, out in the distance, a sound reached them that sounded like a herd of beasts running by them. But not being able to imagine such a thing Jllon went to the main shelter and knocked. Lauut came to the door and asked, "How may I help you Jllon?" I know that this has been a tough day or so, but when nature becomes like this you kind of have to ride it out and hope that you're not her target."

"True, I must admit until I saw this wild fire, I was skeptical of how fast you said they would move. Well, I'm not skeptical any more. If anything you probably downplayed the real thing, and here I thought you were exaggerating. Anyway, what I wanted to ask is this; just a short time ago we heard what sounded like a large herd running way out in the distance. But thought that would be impossible, since there wouldn't be any beasts close to this thing if they could avoid it. So what was it we heard?"

"I guess I wouldn't have described it as such, but I can see how you would come up with that description. Actually what you heard was that wildfire passing us. It's much louder when you are closer. In fact it can be deafening. When they get this large, and thankfully it's not all the time, they create their own winds, sounds, and actually can create thunderstorms at the top of the columns of smoke.

"On another subject since you are here. I need to ask if we can take the team, once this thing is either out or safely away and go south to help any of the properties that may have been caught. Anytime we have one of these things pass, and once it is deemed safe, the community immediately sends out teams to check on the areas affected. It has always been difficult for us since for the longest time it was only Lauma and I. But right now you and your team are here, and your assistance would be greatly appreciated."

"Just say the word, and you can have the whole team." Shuddering at the thought of actually having been in the path of what he had just witnessed, he continued. "I can't see how anything would have survived such a thing. So you will have no problem from me."

"You know that one would think, with such fires, that absolutely everything in its path would burn. But that's not true. You will see places where the vegetation is heavy and one would have thought it was prime burning material for the fire, only to see it untouched. While everything around that area has burned so hot that there is nothing but white ash ankle deep. It just doesn't make sense, but that's the reality of it.

"As you know we try to prepare for these wild fires and as such our living shelters are cleared of anything burnable other than the shelters themselves. So if any were in the path they would have a chance of surviving, but as you can see it would be a small one. If the fire wants what you have it will take it."

"You make it sound like it's something living, making its decisions as to what to take or what to leave."

"I do make it sound that way don't I? Well wait until you get out into that burned area and see what your conclusion will be. Some of what you will see out there just doesn't make any sense. And while I do know it isn't a real living thing, some of what it does make it appear to be so."

About this time the sun began to rise, and as the light hit them once again the sky took on the yellow-red hue from the smoke that was in the air. From the initial report that came from Lauut about the time the winds would remain blowing, there was still two to three days left. Everything smelled of smoke, and the gray-white ash lay everywhere. The winds would pick it up and blow it out creating small whirls and as soon as it was blown away new ash replaced it. Again their skin was raw and red, their eyes continuing to burn and water from the irritation of the acrid smoke in the air and the ash being blown into them.

"How long before all of this is gone?" Jllon asked.

"What . . . The smoke and ash, the odors, or just being able to breathe good fresh air again?"

Laughing Jllon said, "Oh any or all of them I guess."

"Actually, now that the fire has passed us, we will start getting better air, although it won't be all of the time. There is still vegetation burning out there behind us. In fact today Fauul and I will be going out to see how close it came and if there is anything that needs to be done to prevent it from starting up behind us and putting us in danger."

"Are you telling me that even though the main fire has passed that the danger to you is not over?"

"That's exactly what I am telling you. You see while there is a main fire, there are also many smaller fires that were created by the main fire – I know I've said that – and just because it has passed don't mean that something that it left behind will not start burning and leave us in danger. A wind switch here could start something that has been smoldering, and once again, off it will go."

"Okay, I am beginning to understand. Tell you what; I think I will go with you if you would allow it. I need the knowledge of what we are facing . . . especially if this dig turns up anything. I know, if we are successful, we will probably be here many turns, and probably will have to face others like this one."

"I have no problem with you going. In fact another body helps. Just a thought, maybe you can bring some of your team along. The quicker we can do this the quicker we can prevent any new danger."

"Okay, I'll get the diggers from my team, and we will assist. I guess once we get out there you can show us what we need to look for and how to, what did you call it, protect the property."

"How soon can you have them assembled? I would like to get started as soon as we can. We need to be out there before the heat of the day helps the fire, in the areas where it has already passed, start again."

"I'll get them moving now. We haven't eaten yet, so once we are finished then we will meet you here in the yard. At that time you can explain what we should take with us and then we can go out."

"Sounds good to me . . . so I guess we will see you after your morn meal. As if it isn't obvious, expect to get very dirty from this."

Turning to go back inside the shelter Lauut retreated as Jllon headed over to the workers shelter. From just a simple question he ended up with much more.

After they had eaten the team assembled out in the yard. There waiting for them was Lauut and Fauul. Lauut led them over to the supply shelter and handed out tools that were similar to one they were used to working with, but still had differences. Lauut explained that these tools were specifically for firefighting and had been in existence for as long as any could remember.

They also had unusual names for each. Again, what each meant had been lost sometime in the past. For example there was a tool that looked as someone had attached a rake and a hoe together. Obviously it was much heavier and larger than what the individual components would have been. At once the advantage of this tool became obvious. With the one tool you could rake the materials you had cut all with the same tool. Plus, because of the strength of the tool, there was little chance that one would break it.

Then there was the one that looked like a single bit axe, but with a hook put on the tip. Another had what appeared to be a single bit axe head but on the backside a mattock side for grubbing. And the one they were most familiar, but were smaller. It was a shovel, but again different. Instead of rounded, it was pointed, and with its smaller scoop area and the size was easier to handle. The names attached to these tools were as they were shown to them, McLeod, brush hook, Pulaski, and female shovel. Weird names for sure, but it made it easy to remember the differences.

Lauut outfitted the team with a mix of these tools explaining that by having a certain mix they would form a crew that could construct a protection line close to where the fire was, and help prevent its further spread. He also stated that once they got out to the edge of the fire area that he would demonstrate how to make the combination of tools work so that they would be able to work the maximum amount of area in the minimum amount of time.

They left early mid-morn with the plan of being out the rest of the day. They took along food and drink since there was no plan on returning for a mid-day meal. That left the females responsible for taking care of the work at the property. Once again, because of her experience, Lauma was in charge of assigning duties to each of the females. They were to help her take care of the beasts, and since Suzzane had some experience with this kind of work she assigned the other learners to help her. Lauma and Nouma would form the other team, and between the two teams be able to accomplish what was ahead of them.

She sent the three younger females to go out and work with the penned herd beasts. It was the simpler of assignments, even though it was hard work. She and Nouma would work the normal assignments in and around the shelters. All of them would meet and put together a meal at the zenith. The wind was still blowing out of the east-northeast, but seemed to have lost some of its strength. Still, it was early, and most likely, as the day continued, and the sun heated up the earth, the wind would return to its earlier fury. At least, for the moment, there was something positive out of it as the fire had passed them early in the pre-dawn hours and had moved on. With the winds continuing in the present direction there was little chance that it would do any damage to them.

Lauma and Nouma entered into the shelter where the young ones and their mothers were kept, and once the door was closed, other than the bawling of the beasts, it had become quiet and they didn't have to physically fight the wind. "Whew, I'm glad to be out of that," Nouma stated. After a pause she continued.

"So, how often do you get these winds anyway? And how often fires like that one?"

"Oh I've never counted the amount of times in a turn we get the winds, but normally they seem to arrive in the summer and continue through the fall. There seems like there's times when one arrives and then ends and in a day or two another comes. As far as the fires like the one that just passed us, only a couple that I know of. I cannot say if other areas down here deal with them also, but my guess would be that they do. So for the region I really have no idea. It's just something you live with. I guess it's the price we pay for having the type of weather we have."

"Yeah, you do have wonderful weather. Where we are from it gets very cold and at times the snow is so deep that you are shelter bound. It surely can drive one crazy. I thought that this would be a wonderful place to live. But now I'm not so sure. Even though that wild fire wasn't very close, it scared me badly. Yet, you seem so calm, why is that?"

"I really don't know. Maybe because I know what to expect and while we haven't had one of these actually burn through the property, we have had a few that were close. You know like this one. Still it wasn't very close."

"Maybe that's it, anyway I have something I would like to talk with you about. But I must get your promise not to say anything until I'm sure. Do I have it?"

Smiling at Nouma, Lauma said in jest, "What is it about you township folks – always keeping secrets – first Jllon, and now you." Then seeing the serious look on Nouma's face said, "Sorry, I was only kidding. Of course you can have my promise. After all if we females cannot keep things from our males, then something is wrong."

Being silent for a moment, Nouma was trying to figure out how to say what she wanted. "Okay, I guess I'll just say it. I'm late."

With a questioning look Lauma asked, "Late? You weren't late, and as far as I knew there wasn't a time set to start this."

Almost laughing Nouma said, "No silly, not that kind of late, but late with my female cycle."

Catching her breath, and then hugging Nouma, she asked, "Really? Are you sure it's not because of the stress of what we are going through right now? Or maybe just a little off because of changes you have been dealing with?"

"Shaking her head Nouma said, "No, I don't think so. I'm one of those females that you can set time by. I am that regular. But I'm at least four days past, but I am still not sure, because, as you have said, we are going through some pretty stressful times."

"I'm glad that some of us are that regular. I am not that fortunate. I can vary from cycle to cycle so when it happens with me it will probably be the beginning sickness that lets me know that I may be carrying. You don't have any of that do you?"

Again shaking her head she said, "No, not yet. But again I may be completely wrong and things will start and I will be back to normal. Anyway, I just needed someone to talk to about it, and until I am sure one way or the other I wanted to be sure that it was just kept between us."

"Oh you have my promise on that." Then hugging her again she said, "Shall we finish up here and continue, and please keep me up to date. While I know that I deal with beasts all the time, I can still help you as this continues."

"I appreciate it, and since this would be my first, any assistance would be nice. Is there a good midwife in your village?"

"One of the best. Her mate is a healer, and she has been from a long line of females who have handled deliveries. So if you are and you are here long enough to go full term then you will be in excellent hands."

"Oh that's a relief. I wasn't sure what I could expect being this remote. Anyway, at this moment, I am not sure so all of this might turn out to be a good laugh in the end."

They returned to the work at hand and the day really flew by. Before they knew it the sun was setting, and the five of them worked to get a hot meal together for when the males returned from their work on fire line construction around the property. Soon, in the distance, they saw them approaching and from the way they were walking it was obvious they were very tired.

Lauma, watching both Nouma and Suzzane could see they were interested in seeing certain males in the group. Smiling Lauma thought. *She can say what she wants, but Suzzane is very interested in my brother.* She had to admit to herself that she was looking for Fauul, and fortunately with his size he was easy to pick out. Still they all looked similar because of the blackness of the soot and ash they were all covered in.

Jllon approaching hugged his mate said, "I think we all need to clean up before eating. I never realized how hard of work it is building a decent fire line. I must admit, it would be easy to just sit down, and never move again."

The team washed up, and then sat down and ate the food. There was very little conversation as they were just too tired. After eating they'd bathe and probably go to bed. On the morrow they would be heading south to see if any would need assistance. Once this was compete, then get back to what they were here for. But before heading that way, as was becoming a tradition for the both, Nouma and Jllon went over to the porch and sat down. Jllon speaking to Nouma again said, "I never realized how hard of work it is constructing a fire break. I don't know when I have felt so tired. It would be so easy just to sit here and not move . . ." He was silent for a moment.

Nouma said, "You just said that a short time ago."

"Really? As tired as I am my mind seems a little clouded also . . ."

Nouma looking over at him realized that he had drifted off while he was talking. Sighing to herself she shook him gently . . . "What? Oh, sorry I guess I fell to sleep there. Okay that settles it I'm going straight there. I'll see you in the morn." He, with effort, got up from the porch where the two of them had been sitting after eating, and getting cleaned up, headed into the workers shelter.

About this time Lauma came out and joined her on the porch, and said, "Well, Fauul has decided to sleep. It seems he can barely move. I have a feeling my brother worked them pretty hard, but I know from my own experience that that kind of work is not easy."

"Are you telling me that you have done it yourself?"

"Oh yes, what else would you expect? After all, it's been Lauut and me for such a long time. And when something like this happens we would have to do the work."

"Yeah, I guess that's right. But I never thought about it. So how long do you think they will be away to the south checking the other properties?"

"I suspect it will be around seven days. By then I think you will know whether it has been the stress that has caused your lateness or whether you are carrying. So if it turns out that you are, how do you feel about that?"

"Nervous . . . Then excited, followed by being worried . . . I mean there's so much emotion and thoughts that are going through my mind right now. I must admit it's something, as a female, that I've always looked forward to. But, now with the real possibility . . . it's such an unknown."

"I guess that's true . . . I mean with the beasts, I deal with it all the time. But when it becomes personal it takes on a whole new meaning. I felt that about being physical with Fauul. I help with the breeding of our beasts so I'm well aware of what was to happen. And personally, in some ways looked forward to it, the time it would be me, you know my turn. But at the same time . . . well as you said, it became very personal, and suddenly it did involve me. And when it becomes something so personal it's really scary. I mean, look, you suddenly find that you will taking something inside of you where you never had such a thing before."

"Yes, but when you think about bringing another life into the world, and you are completely responsible for everything they are and will become, it is even scarier, if that's the word, then having to face your mate for the first time that night of your mating ceremony. You know, like you just described – so many changes with this. I know it is the only way we can have the next generation, and females have been always doing this. I guess the males have the easier part. We end up investing so much more into our whelps than they ever do."

"That's true, but I think at least some of the males are quite aware of what we go through. Lauut told me of a conversation he had with Fauul and it was profound in its way. He basically said that females have their hands on eternity. That it is through them or us that the future is dependent upon, while they the males are more of the observers with no way to have that kind of influence, other than the obvious."

"I've never really thought about it. But when it's presented that way I can see how that can be so. I mean the males donate their part to create a new life. But it is us who must sacrifice our bodies and energy to bring that new life along. All the males can do is support us and watch."

The following seven days with the team away went quickly. The females had remained on the property to take care of the beasts and to keep everything as close to normal as they could. It had been decided that because of the primitive conditions the team would face they would keep it all males. This would be no place for a female to be isolated – leaving her vulnerable.

Nouma woke up on the seventh day, the day the team was to return, feeling a little queasy. Not sure what to attribute it to she arose, got dressed and headed over to the main shelter after taking care of the morning nature call. She just didn't feel right and couldn't really explain it. As she neared the door she smelled the cooking food and the hot beverage. Usually this was something that was so welcoming, but on this morn it made her nauseated, and she could tell that she was going to be sick.

Lauma had heard her approaching, and heard her stop. Coming to the door to see what was happening, she saw Nouma standing there and she appeared to be weaving a little, and her skin had pallor to it. Looking at her face she saw that it was white. Nouma put her hand to her mouth and had a surprised look on her face. She turned around and ran back to the workers shelter. Lauma wanted to follow but with the food cooking could not leave. Turning around to see if any of the other of the females had made an appearance yet, she saw they hadn't. Shrugging, she would have to wait. Going back inside she continued to prepare the food, and with her back to the door heard someone open it. Turning around she saw Suzzane coming in. She said, "Suzzane, before you sit down here can you go check on Nouma? She was coming across the yard, stopped and looked a little ill and quickly turned around and ran back to the shelter."

"Nouma? Oh yes, I'll go do that now." Suzzane immediately left and went to see what she could find out. As she went out of the door she saw Nouma leaving the workers shelter, but before she got very far turned around and went back inside. Curious as to what was happening with Nouma, Suzzane hurried back across the yard and entered into the shelter. Once inside she asked, "Nouma are you all right?" She then heard Nouma say, "I'm in the necessary space." This was followed by a retching sound. Not sure what to do Suzzane waited in the common space until Nouma made an appearance.

Suzzane looking at Nouma saw that she looked a little pale. "Are you sick?"

"I guess I might be. I awoke this morning feeling a little queasy, but thought I would be okay. But once I smelled our morn meal cooking it just set me off and I knew if I didn't get here quickly I would be throwing up out there in the yard. Then once the first episode was over I thought I was okay until I got outside and it hit me again."

"Is there anything I can do, and Lauma sent me over to check on you. She seemed very worried."

"Right now I feel okay, but I plan to take it easy. I am not sure if I want to try and smell that food again. I'm afraid that it might set me off again."

"So what do you want me to tell Lauma?"

"Oh I don't know. I think I will stay here for a little while though. I guess you can tell her that."

"Okay, I can do that." Then hesitating she asked, "Are you sure there isn't anything I can do?"

Nouma shaking her head said, "No not really. I think this will pass, and I will be okay. In fact I think I will just lie down for a little while. Oh you can tell her that once this passes that I will join all of you on the work. The team is supposed to be returning today, and even if I don't feel well, I can't wait for both the news they will bring and to see them safely back."

Reluctantly Suzzane left and went back to the main shelter to let Lauma know what had transpired with Nouma. Nouma returned to her area and did lie down for a short period of time. She must have fallen asleep because suddenly sitting right next to her was Lauma. She had some bread and something to drink. It looked to be a hot herbal drink of some kind. Lauma said, "I think we have the answer. Here eat this bread, and drink this. It will settle your stomach and I think you will begin to feel better."

"Answer? Answer to what?"

Smiling at her Lauma said "Oh the question you asked about seven or eight days ago. You know the one where you wondered if you were carrying or not. I think this is your answer. You have the morn sickness, and it is a sure sign that you are carrying. So I think you will need to have both this bread and this herbal drink close to you each morn for at least the first third. It will help settle that uneasy stomach. But, unfortunately, you will continue to throw up. There really isn't any way to avoid it. There's never been a good explanation as to why it's this way, but my personal idea has to do with a female carrying something that is not really a part of her. So your body has to make an adjustment, and this morn sickness is the signs that it is happening."

"If I have to face this for the first third, I surely am not going to feel any joy."

Laughing Lauma said, "You may be surprised. This is all new, as it will be for me when it happens. So each day will be a new adventure as both you and your body changes. I'm sure you are wondering how I know what I know. It simply is because I have helped the midwife and she has told me much that one should expect throughout the term, and being there at a birth is both scary and exhilarating. It's scary because you can see the pain the mother goes through during the birthing, but at the same time exhilarating because almost immediately the new mother seems to forget about all the pain, and wants to hold that new life closely to her. It really is an unbelievable sight."

"I guess I'll have to take your word for it. So this will settle my stomach? Will I be able to eat normally later?"

"Later as in the day, yes. Normally no . . . nothing will be normal for you from now on out. You will find yourself wanting to eat, and then have cravings for things that just don't make sense. When you have eaten the bread and drank this, I think you will find everything settling down, and then you can come over and believe it or not, nibble on the normal stuff and not have it force you to the necessary space. So I think I will see you shortly. If they return today I think you have some great news to tell your mate."

She remained in bed for a little longer eating the bread and drinking the herbal drink. Finding out that it really didn't have a bad taste at all. In fact she felt that she could really grow to like it. Then speaking to herself she said, "I guess I had better. I have a feeling I will be drinking a lot of this stuff for a while." Shortly the bread and drink did its magic and she found that indeed she did feel better. So reluctantly she got up and headed back over to the main shelter. Not sure that she wanted to smell any of the food or not. As she approached the shelter there was a lingering smell of the morn meal but found that it did not bother her this time. "That's a relief." She said quietly, and entered into the shelter finding that Lauma had left her some food for her to eat, knowing that with confirmation she was carrying, she would need to take care of herself. The others were already out and doing the morn work so she was by herself, and took time in eating. Even the normal hot beverage, which was one of the main smells that had set her stomach off this morn, didn't seem to have the same effect now, which was wonderful since it was one of her favorite drinks.

She was now beginning a new chapter in her life. While she could remember her mother carrying her brother before he was born, there never was much said. She seemed to remember, as her mother came closer to full term, that she seemed to tire easy, and seemed to be very uncomfortable. Still she remembered that her mother smiled much of the time, in anticipation of the new life she was carrying. It left her feeling completely inadequate. She knew next to nothing about what was coming for her and Jllon, or even how he would react to the news.

Finishing her meal she headed out to find Lauma and thank her. She did seem to know much, and she suspected it had a lot to do with living in the outback. In the townships one usually had help for just about anything one needed. But out here you learned to do for yourself. She now saw the strength and confidence that Lauma had and was envious of it. While, yes she had spent time in the outback with Jllon on some of the projects, it did not equate to the same as having lived there all one's life.

Hearing a noise over at the pens she headed that way and found Lauma finishing the clean-up of the pens and the beasts eating heartily and ignoring her completely. "Hey Lauma, what would you like me to do? I'm okay now, and thanks for leaving that food for me. I wasn't sure but that bread and drink did the trick and I was able to eat just like nothing happened."

Standing up and leaning on her rake, then pushing a strand of hair out of her eyes, she smiled and said, "Glad to hear that it did the trick. I'll make sure you have a good supply so that it can be there with you in the morns. But I must warn you, as if you haven't figured it out, throwing up will still continue. That stuff will just settle everything afterwards, letting you eat what you want. Anyway I am just about finished here. Why not go into that shelter there and see how the young beasts are doing and if we need to clean it up. I've sent the others down to the holding pens where the herd beasts are. This will probably be the last feeding we will do there. I believe I can release them and put them back out this after-zenith.

"Once the winds died and the westerly started again I've seen no smoke and I've been watching closely. So my guess is the fire burned itself out. But I always like to add a day or two just in case. If you notice there hasn't even been a smell of smoke . . . another good sign of the fire being out. Oh I do suspect that the team will be back just after the zenith meal, and I for one cannot wait to see them back here safe. Of course I do miss Fauul and cannot wait to see him again. I'm sure it's the same for you."

With a questioning look she asked, "I'm waiting for Fauul? Why would I do that? He's your mate, not mine."

Laughing Lauma said, "Now come on you're not that dense, or that stupid. You're kidding right? I know you must be eager to see Jllon. You two have been together much longer than Fauul and me."

"I'm sorry, but having this confirmed for me today has left me not myself, and as far as Jllon goes I have mixed feelings. Yes I miss him terribly, but I just do not know how he will take the news."

"Oh I wouldn't worry about that too much. From what I know of your mate he will probably become even more caring of you." Then smiling she continued, "And if he isn't then he will have to answer first to me, and then the rest of the females here. We will set him straight."

The rest of the morn went quickly and before they knew it the sun was directly overhead announcing it was time for the zenith meal. Nouma found that her appetite was starting to increase even now. This was a surprise since she knew that the new life growing inside her was barely beginning. Neither of the other females was aware as of yet, and until it was known by Jllon her mate, only she and Lauma knew the truth.

Lauma said to them after the meal, "Okay this will be all we need to do. All of us will go out and release the heard beasts. And with the dogs, we will drive them back out to the area where they were located before the fire. This will probably take us enough time that when we've finished that we will need to prepare for the team's return. Because all of the camp managers and assistants went, we will all go to the food prep area in the workers shelter and as a team put together a meal for them. I'm sure they will be tired, and while they are eating I'm sure they will let us know what they found. So let's get to it."

With all of them and the dogs, the herd beasts moved easily. It was as if they were aware they were returning to familiar ground and was eager to get there. Lauma knew that once they were clear of the holding pens that there would be much cleanup that needed to be done. You couldn't hold that many beasts in that small of an area without a mess being made. But that was for another day. The one thing about living like this was that there was always work waiting to be done.

They finally arrived back at the main shelter smelling of the beasts. Lauma said, "I don't know about you but I think I'll take a quick bath. Smelling of those herd beasts is not my idea of a great scent. See you all in a few." She headed into the main shelter. Turning she saw that the others agreed with her and headed into the workers shelter for some freshening up.

Feeling clean and in some clean clothes she entered into the workers shelter and saw the others already in the food prep area starting to put together a meal. "Ah, I see, this time I am the late one. Okay what would you like me to do?"

It took a while but they eventually had a large meal put together. It was decided to set up the tables out in the yard as they had for the small gather Jllon had asked for when they first met each other. And it was none too soon. As they finished setting the tables and bringing out the cool beverages they could see the team approaching from the south. Smiling Lauma picked out Fauul. His height made it easy, but she couldn't see Lauut her brother. Then looking towards the back she saw both Lauut and Jllon together. She felt relief roll off her. She hadn't even realized she had been carrying the tension or worry.

Finally they were all in the yard and Jllon, looking tired said, "What a wonderful surprise – all you beautiful females and a hot meal waiting. What more could a group of tired, hungry and dirty males ask for?" He laughed before continuing, "Since you have prepared this for us, I guess we should wash up and come eat this bounty before it gets cold."

Looking around he saw that the rest agreed. The males quickly washed up and came over sat down and began eating the meal, Lauma with Fauul, Nouma with Jllon, and Suzzane sitting with Lauut. Jllon looking at Nouma could see both reluctance and an excitement in her eyes. Curious, he asked, "Is there something wrong?"

Nervously she shook her head, and said, "No, no nothing wrong. In fact I suspect everything is right at this moment."

"Okay if you say so. It's just, well I am seeing conflicting thoughts in your eyes – that's all."

"You have been gone, and I have been worrying about you . . . am I allowed to do that?"

Shaking his head and somewhat confused he said, "Of course, and I have been worried about you and that everything back here was going okay. You are very important to me."

"I'm sorry. I didn't mean to sound that way, but I do have something I want to tell you later when we are alone. Can you wait that long? Besides we, the five of us, would like to know what you found. We've been stuck here without any news as to what if anything happened."

"Sure I can wait, and yes that's true. We have lived it, but all of you know nothing of what we found. So once we finish eating I will relate to you what we discovered. That way the rest of the team can clean up properly and again, I suspect, call it finished for today. On the morrow we have to get back to the project. We have lost enough time as it is."

Nodding she said, "Yes that works fine. I think Lauma will allow us to go to the main shelter and then you can bring us up to date."

After the meal and clean up Jllon related, to the females who had remained behind, what they had found and how they had helped. It turned out that there were three properties that had been in the path of the fire. Two had lost some out-shelters but other than that they had escaped. The third was the property where they grew the trees with the wood used in the torches. Over half of the trees had been burned. The owners had no idea if they would recover or not. Fortunately, they had a new planting ready to go in at the beginning of winter, so while the loss was devastating, they should recover. Again, for them, it was only the trees that were damaged. None of the shelters were touched. So the team helped with the clean-up at the three properties, including helping dig out some of the trees that would not recover. And yes, to their surprise, while walking through the burned area there were many places that did not burn. As had been pointed out to them before they had ever been inside such a burned area, there was just no explanation as to why. Many times they saw prime burning stuff with evidence of high heat by what had burned next to the unburned, and not a leaf scorched. It was like islands of green on a black ocean.

Jllon said that he needed to get a good bath and excused himself leaving them there by themselves. They had to admit that overall the other properties had been lucky to have survived such a fire. But since they lived in the area the people had been prepared. The stories that Jllon related from those who had faced the fire directly made them all glad that it had missed them. Then Nouma, Suzzane, Ehlie, and Kaern said their good-byes and headed over to the workers shelter.

Nouma entering the space where she and Jllon were living saw that he had finished his bath and was relaxing in one of the chairs that were there. "Okay, my special one, we are alone. And I have related to you, and the others of our adventures. Now you can let me know what was so important that it could only be told when we were by ourselves."

Again smiling a nervous smile, since she really had no way to know how he would react to the news she was giving him, she said, "I've thought of a number of ways of telling you, but . . . I just haven't found any easy way."

Interrupting he asked with concern in his voice, "Is there anything wrong?"

"Wrong? No, but this is something that will change who we are . . ."

"What could change who we are? Are we not mates? And I have no desire to ever lose you. You have always been special to me and I for one will never understand your choice in me, but that is not for me to know. Just understand whatever it is, we can do this together."

Again smiling a little she continued, "I'm glad to hear you say that. Since what I am wanting to tell you was because we did it together." Taking a deep breath and signaling him not to say anything she continued. "I am carrying."

"Carrying? Carrying what? I don't see anything in your hands?"

Then laughing at his misunderstanding she said, "No not that kind of carrying. We are going to be sires."

For a brief moment he was silent. Then he asked, "You mean that we will have a new life coming into ours? When did you find out? How do you know?" Before she could answer any of the many questions he got up and hugged and kissed her deeply, and asked, "Does it matter? I know that it has been something on your mind for many turns. And I know that much of what we do has not helped. I must admit that this is life changing." Then shaking his head and smiling he said, "Wow, sires . . . what a responsibility. Who else knows?"

"Just Lauma and actually she confirmed it for me. I had thought it might have been so since my female cycle was late. But because of what has been happening, it might have been for other reasons. But today . . . this morn to be exact, it was confirmed. I started having the morn sickness. I am told I will be facing this for my first third, and then it will go away. I was so afraid that it would bother you since that it happened now."

"As if we have some control over when it happens. I know that the future for us will be more difficult, more complicated, now that we will have a whelp in our lives, but even with all the chaos this one will bring, I think we will appreciate it." Then smiling at her tenderly he said, "I have a feeling it will not be our last."

They stayed together in an embrace with her head on his chest for the longest time. Then she looked up into his eyes. "I truly had no idea how you would take this news, but thought it might be like this."

"You are my world, how else would you expect me to be? Come on now, even though I'm tired, I think being physical tonight would be a great thing. Even if it's just so we can be so very close. After all being that close to you is something I always look forward to."

"I hope you think so in my last third. I won't be so pretty, and will be large in areas I have never been. And I'm sure I won't feel like I am desirable either."

"Don't ever let it bother you. No matter what is going on, you will always be desirable to me." He kissed her softly on her forehead, rubbed her shoulders and again hugged and kissed her.

"You don't understand how it is with us," Nouma said. "You see we can never be sure of how long our significant other may be with us. So much of what we are seems to be based on how we look and act. And, when we leave our roles as lovers and companions, and enter into the world of motherhood . . . well, let's just say, it changes everything. So if I seem to have doubts it's because of this and what I have observed.

"I know that you are a very loving and giving person. It shows in how you care for not only me but also everyone you come in contact with. And I really love that about you. But now we are coming to the biggest and hardest change we will ever face, and I do not want to lose you or what we have. I'm sorry if I feel this way, but truthfully I can't help it."

"How can I remove those doubts and fears? I didn't become your mate just so that someday I would just turn around and leave. I became a part of you until the end of our time, whatever or whenever that might be. I'm not allowed to see our future, but I do hope that you are in that future always. Yes, I know that what we are facing is the biggest change ever, and yes you will become a mother. But isn't that the way it is supposed to be? Our sires faced the same dilemmas when they had us, but they are still with each other.

"I find that the ones who are unfortunate enough not to be able to produce their own whelps are the most unhappy and unfulfilled. I know that you possibly think that I do not have room in my heart for another. Yet from what I have heard, when my sires spoke, and I suspect it's the same with yours, was simply that as each new whelp arrived, their love expanded to include them. I believe it will be no different for us."

Then not being able to hold back the tears, she cried. It was both for the unknown future, and the love her mate was showing her at this moment – making her both happy and sad at the same time. She felt him hold her close as the tears flowed and finally stopped. "I'm sorry. I have been told that during this time that I will be much more emotional so please be patient." Then she wiped away her tears and looked up into his eyes giving him a slight smile. "I thank you for your encouragement, and your promises. I know being who I am that I probably will continue to need your help."

"You know all you have to do is ask . . . still I'm sure that many times you will not. So I will have to depend on you to let me know somehow you need me. However or whatever that need may be. Soon, a different subject here, since you are saying that you have this morn sickness, why not stays here with Lauma. She seems to know something about what is happening with you, and once she and you are sure it is okay then you can join us back out at the site. I would feel so much better knowing you are safe and with someone who would know if there were signs of trouble with your carrying."

"I'd rather be with you, you know that. But I also know that there is no one on the team who could handle any problems I might have, so it's a good idea. Still I would like to think on it. I just might decide the risk is worth it."

"To lose you because of some unforeseen complication and not having someone there that would help . . . I just don't know how I'd live with myself. So please give it some serious, and I mean very serious consideration. Once you have a passing mark from Lauma or the midwife then I would be much less worried. Do I have your promise?"

Nodding slightly she said, "Yes, you have my promise. Although if I stay I will be worrying about you all the time, since this site is so different than any that we have worked before."

"The plan right now, is to stay out there five days and then come back in for two. That way there will be a break for everybody, and it will give us time for some real quality closeness and conversation. As you have so aptly pointed out our lives are changing."

"Okay, I'll give it, as you say, some serious thought, but it seems to me that tonight you were wanting to get physical . . . shall we?"

He awoke the next morning with her side of the bed empty. He heard her in the necessary space, and yes he could hear her throwing up. Thinking to himself he thought. *I'm glad I'm not a female. I don't know if I could handle being sick each morning for as long as she said she will be. I'll have to remember to ask Lauma why it seems to work that way, as I'm sure at this point Nouma doesn't know.*

She eventually came back into the sleeping space. She was eating some bread. "Lauma told me that this would help settle my stomach. She also has given me an herbal drink. I've got water heating for that now. I don't know how it works, but it does. Although it appears that I am still going to throw up at least once a morning anyway. No fun, but I guess one can get used to almost anything."

"Does it really work?"

"Well, it did yesterday. I found myself throwing up several times, but once I ate the bread and drank the herbal drink everything settled down and I was fine for the rest of the day." Then smiling she continued, "I must say that last night was one of the best times we've had in bed. It was absolutely wonderful. I do wish they would always be that way, but I do know it doesn't work that way."

Laughing he said, "Yeah it was rather nice wasn't it. And I have to agree if it was that way all the time then we probably would never see the light of day."

Then smiling rather impishly at him she said, "Once my stomach settles down, why don't you join me for a bath before you start your week. I think it would be a nice way to say goodbye before you head out."

"So you've decided to stay. Great, and of course I will join you in your saying goodbye for my five days away – wouldn't miss it for anything."

Later Jllon joined the team in the common area and said that Nouma would not be joining them for now and that she was having some problems and would be with Lauma so she could be monitored for a while. He knew that the announcement of her carrying would be hers to make when she was ready. He would make a quick stop at the main shelter where he knew they had been up since dawn. He needed to let Lauma know that Nouma would be staying here until they agreed it was safe and there were no complications.

* * *

There seemed to be a change and he couldn't explain it. But it was as if the natural world had been testing them. Up to the time of the fire it seemed that everything they tried on solving the puzzles they were facing failed. Now that they were approved by these apparent tests, things and solutions became clear.

He put two members of the team on the solving of entering the hole in the cavern. The rest of the team worked on removing the soils on top of that hill. Time really flew by and the hard work started showing results. After removing approximately a body length in soil from the top of that strange hill, the color changed to dark. They were entering into that layer that had been identified by Doube as from the time of the great disaster – at least that was what they were calling it.

After another body length of digging into this soil something was starting to be exposed. Here they slowed the digging and was careful. Whatever they were uncovering it was definitely artificial. At first it appeared to be a metal strip that seemed to extend the full length of the hilltop. Then they located a second and then a third strip. There was a little distance between these strips and all were metal. They appeared to all have some type of protective coating except in the one area where the team had damaged it slightly when they had struck it by accident.

Once located, these three strips gave them a working point and carefully they dug and worked the dark soil that was around them. It was difficult work as some of this soil seemed almost as hard as rock. Excitement was rising as they continued the digging. Slowly they were exposing a framework that seemed to be covered in a dark glass. Miracles of miracles, not one piece of this mysterious glass was broken. The framework was huge. Still what its purpose was again was a complete mystery.

What could this dark glass provide? It didn't cover anything and at the same time one was not able to look through it. Was it for decoration? Yet its orientation was more to the south. This meant that it would receive more sunlight – why? But one thing became obvious to them . . . this had to be the second confirmed found site of the *ones before*. Those mysterious ancient ancestors had been here also. How many places on this world did they inhabit?

The cycles began to fly by, and though Nouma had never officially stated she was carrying, no one could deny that fact. She was beginning to show, and had a glow that seemed to be with females who were carrying. She was left at the workers shelter to help with the information that was brought back when the team returned on the two days. She found herself peaceful within, and had no explanation for it. She would find herself smiling and again found no reason for it either. Everything just seemed right with both Jllon and herself.

Then came the news, only for her ears that Lauma was now carrying. As she was having the early signs of the morn sickness which was her first proof. "Look what you did Nouma", Lauma would teasingly say. "You just had to get yourself this way, and now I've ended up following you." Then she would laugh. Nouma had asked if Fauul was aware yet, and was informed not yet. That would be for later when she was sure all was okay. She did not want to worry him as of yet. She had said that there would be plenty of time for worry later.

The other thing she had noticed by being here all the time, was that when the two days of the team being at the workers shelter, that Suzzane and Lauut were spending almost all their time together. It was quite obvious to her that there would probably be a request for pursuit soon – even if it wasn't obvious to the two of them. Jllon would tell her of their progress and was quite excited with what had been found so far. Even though, overall, it was less than what had been found in the desert. Still the potential was there for greater finds.

CHAPTER TWENTY

Jllon got word that they finally were able to anchor a rope ladder to the hole they had been trying to get into. He went with Celt down the tunnel to the cavern. The team had decided since these finds were because of what he had gleaned, and had led them successfully to the greatest discoveries of their time that he should be the first to enter that hole.

Above, on top of the hill the framed glass had almost been completely uncovered, but the bases had yet to be located. So how or what they were anchored to was unknown. It had taken almost a full cycle to uncover these glass frames to the point where they were now. Still to finally be able to enter that hole in the collapsed ceiling might finally provide some answers. When he and Celt finally reached the location he saw Flar, Jayson, and Payle waiting for him, and smiling. "It was decided among us that you and only you have the right to climb this up and into that space," Flar stated. "You are our leader and have not as of yet led us wrong."

Smiling Jllon asked, "Now are you sure that's the reason? I mean there might be something dangerous up there, and by having me find out it leaves the rest of you safe."

Laughing at the comment Flar asked, "Now would we do something like that?"

Looking around at the group there and smiling in a humorous way he continued, "I don't know Flar, but I do thank you for the opportunity to be the first, but, after all, you three did the work of finally getting this thing up there. Shouldn't it be you instead?"

"Yeah we thought about it, and we almost went up inside. I have to admit that we have all climbed it far enough to make sure it would hold our weight and peeked inside. But we didn't take a torch up with us so we really couldn't see anything. It was perfectly black in there. So we decided that you should have the privilege of entering it and once you did, we'd pass a torch up to you so that once inside, you could light it with one of those fire starters and see what really is there."

"Okay, I accept. Hand me one of those ropes so I can throw an end back down, and you can tie a torch to it once I get inside."

Payle handed him a coiled rope, which Jllon threw over his shoulder, and started climbing the ladder up into that dark hole. When he reached the entrance he had to pause to figure out what he could grab onto to pull himself inside. As they had stated, it was pitch black, he couldn't see anything. Looking down he saw them looking up at him in anticipation.

Feeling around he touched nothing but a solid cold flat surface. It seemed to be much cooler here than in the lower cavern where he had just left. Finally gathering his courage he moved his hands to the ledge and hoisted himself up and into the darkness. Sitting on the ledge with one foot on the ladder for safety he dropped the rope down so that they could tie the torch and he then pull it up. He was worried that the ledge he was sitting on was not strong enough to support him. Unfortunately, if that was the case, not only would he fall, but the ladder would join him.

So carefully he pulled up the torch and then tied the rope around his waist, and even though the rope ladder could fall, at the moment it was the only thing he could attach the other end to − not the ideal solution, but he had no other at this moment. At least until he got the torch lit, then something else might reveal itself. He took out the fire starter that he had borrowed from Lauut and carefully lit the torch.

At first, when it flared, he was blinded by the brightness of the light. Slowly his eyes adjusted and he looked around. He found himself in a medium size space that seemed to be similar to a mercantile – *a mercantile, really*? Curious, he pulled himself back from the hole and stood up. Once standing he tested the floor for strength, finding it safe, untied the rope. Turning around he called down to the waiting members and said, "Hey, all of you, there's room for all of you up here. Come on up! You are not going to believe what this is."

"Are you sure that you want all of us up there? Shouldn't one of us stay here?" Celt asked.

Looking around the space again and then again testing the floor and finding it satisfactory he looked back down to the four of them and said, "No, I think it's safe for all of us up here. And there seems to be plenty of room for all of us also. Once you reach the top of the ladder I'll help you up."

He saw they were discussing something; he saw Celt shrug and turn and was the first to climb the rope ladder. Jllon made sure that it remained anchored. He didn't need any of them falling at this point and become injured. It would be a very difficult trip out of the cavern carrying someone who had been injured. Eventually he reached the top and took Jllon's hand and entered into the space. Like Jllon before him, he looked around in awe at what he saw.

Turning, he saw that Jllon was helping the next person enter, and soon all five of them were in this space. Looking over what appeared to be a counter of some kind they saw a large sign on the back wall that stated "The Tobacco Shop". Looking in another direction it appeared that there was a doorway and a glass wall. But all they saw were their reflections and nothing beyond.

Like in the desert, the door appeared to be locked and for now there was plenty to hold their interest within this space. Turning around Jllon noticed that close to the hole lay a broken display case. And around on the floor area lay more of the fire starters. Apparently, when the last earth shake had happened – the one that opened the tunnel, and probably caused the collapse of the floor – the case had been damaged, had spilled its contents and some had landed in the area below of what had become the hole that they saw from below.

Celt remained close to the door area while the rest headed back towards what must have been a supply area within the mercantile. They commented that other than the strange items they were seeing that this could be any of the many mercantiles that existed now. On what they thought might be the back wall there was a sign stating "Cigarettes, Cigars, and Tobacco from Around the World". Not really knowing what any of this was they got together and started discussing what this might have been.

Again, like in the desert, they refrained from touching anything. Since this place was of the great past, there was no guarantee that anything they touched would remain whole. Then in a voice that was subdued and full of awe, Celt said, "Ah Jllon . . . ah Flar, Payle, all of you come here. I don't believe what I am seeing. Hurry! This is unbelievable!" Jllon, still holding the torch started approaching Celt, with Celt continuing, "Leave the torch where it won't do any damage then come here."

He found a safe place on the floor that allowed the rest to join him with the four approaching Celt and before their eyes something was happening beyond that glass wall. But how could that be? Maybe it was just a trick of the eyes. Maybe their eyes had finally adjusted to the gloom that surrounded them. But no, it did appear that the area outside was becoming light – like the sun rising at dawn. Then to their shock the area they were in lit up and they all jumped. It seemed to be almost as bright as day here and the torch appeared to be dim in comparison. "What just happened?" Jllon asked in surprise.

Looking around at each other they saw the same shocked look in each other's faces. All had their mouths open in complete surprise and shock. What was this, and how was it accomplished? Turning around and looking again at the glass wall they saw a large . . . no, that wasn't an accurate description at all. The space they could see through the smoky glass could have held a small village. They suddenly realized that all of them had been holding their breath, as if breathing would destroy what they were seeing. It sent chills up and down their spines. Nothing in their time or lives had prepared them for the sight that was now before them. Finally Jllon, in a whisper said, "I don't know what happened, but . . . I thought our find in the desert was the best we would do . . . I . . . I'm sorry, I am completely at a loss for words here."

He walked up to the door that led into this lighted area and studied it for a moment and found a similar mechanism to the door they opened in the desert. He turned it and heard a satisfying click and found that the door opened, but unlike the other one when he pushed on it nothing happened. Having expected it to swing like the other he lost his balance when it did not happen. Instead, he found that it slid to the side on a path built into the floor and top of the frame. While the door did not retract completely it was open enough to allow them to squeeze by and enter the main area. Again, another shock awaited them. Immediately when they entered this area they looked up and saw that there were at least three levels above them. Everywhere they looked there were mercantiles. There had to be at least a hundred of them. How was it that such as this could exist? Then they saw a large banner hanging from the heights above stating *"You have entered the first Mall in America that is completely Solar and LED!"*

What was solar, and what the heck was LED? They felt as if the gods in the great fictional stories had descended upon them and revealed the wonders that had always been beyond their reach. Nothing, absolutely nothing, and that included the discoveries in the desert had prepared them for this discovery. They found themselves whispering to themselves and walking softly, unconsciously thinking that if they made a noise that it would break the spell and they would wake up and find it had only been a dream. They also found that none of them were talking with each other. Each lost in their own world of awe and shock.

Turning around to the rest Jllon said in a subdued voice, "I think that we should go get the rest of the team so that they can experience this. Plus I think that Lauut, Lauma, Nouma, and Fauul should also have a chance to see this. After all, if it hadn't been for them, we would never have known. Payle, Celt please go and get the rest of the team and bring them here. We will be here doing some minor exploring. We are not going to enter any of these places . . ."

Suddenly a sound interrupted his comments and they all thought they heard music – but it nothing like they had ever heard. Before the music really started they heard a voice stating that this song was a real oldie going back to before the millennium. The date of the release of the song is 1977, a time when your grandparents were still in high school. The voice stated, "This is from the group Kansas, and their hit, Dust in the Wind." Looking around trying to find the source they were completely unsuccessful. It just seemed to be coming from everywhere. With the place empty it had a tendency to echo giving it an eerie sound.

This once again brought complete silence to the small group. If the area lighting up was overwhelming, this was beyond comprehension. They kept expecting to see someone just show up and laugh and say they were responsible. Yet, this was an impossibility, as this place had been buried for thousands of turns. No one even knew of its existence, so how could any be here?

Again awe struck, and back to whispering they continued to listen to the music coming out of nowhere, and everywhere, Jllon motioned to the two and said, "Just go get the rest of the team. We will be right here waiting." Turning around he saw what looked like a sitting area and he pointed and again said, "We will be right over there."

When Celt and Payle emerged from the tunnel into the daylight they found the team just finishing the zenith meal and preparing to head back to the digging. "Hey!" Yelled Celt, "We need you all to come with us. There has been a discovery and Jllon wants all of you to see it for yourselves." Then smiling and shaking his head he continued, "In truth you will not believe what you are about to see, and don't ask any questions. It's just better that you see it for yourselves."

Following Celt and Payle the team entered the tunnel and then the cavern. To their surprise, a light shown down through the hole in the roof – seeing it sent a slight fear running through the group. How could it be that a place that was nothing but darkness suddenly became bright as day? There was a slight murmuring and questioning. Hearing it Celt said, as he smiled, "You've seen nothing yet. Just wait. Now here is what you must do . . ."

He explained that Payle would be the first up, and once up would assist them through the hole and direct them to where Jllon and the rest awaited them. Celt would be the last up.

Meanwhile Jllon and the two that was still with him were exploring the ground floor, but staying close to the meeting point. Jllon returned and watched for the arrival of the rest of the team. The first one he saw was Juri who, as he had appeared, to be in awe of what he was seeing.

Smiling and waving at him Jllon said, "Spectacular isn't it? I can see that you are having the same reaction as we did. Just come over and sit on one of these benches until we have everybody here. And before you ask, no, I have no idea where that voice or music is coming from." Looking past him he could see that the others were starting to file into the large space. By the tentative move made by each, as they first experienced this sight, it continued to humble him.

He had thought, while out in the desert that they had lost so much, and at the time thinking how far ahead these ancients were in comparison to where they were today. Now, with this discovery, it made the desert discovery seem minor. Here were advances that almost seemed as if magic had been the creator. When all of the team had arrived and was standing around him in a hushed reverence he said, "I believe that saying something profound now would be what is to be expected, but like you, I am completely at loss. This is so far beyond anything I could have imagined or even dreamed. There is nothing here I understand. I don't even understand what that banner is talking about, and yet the ones who read this in their time did.

"I do not know what we will find here, but from where we entered, my guess would be that all entryways would be locked. Unlike our find in the desert where we found a way around the ancients, here it will be harder to do. We know because of the passing of time that much of what is here is very fragile. So initially look, study, and try and understand, but do not touch. We do not know what will survive our touch. I have to admit that just being here where our ancient ancestors walked sends chills down my spine.

"For the rest of our time here today we will just walk and explore this ground floor area. I want each of you to write down your impressions and ideas of what you see here. After all, once again, we are a part of a history and even though I suspect that much of what we say and write will be changed to fit what our offspring want, but for us it still will help us come up with an overall idea of this place." Pausing a moment and taking a deep breath Jllon said, "Okay, let's do it."

He saw, as he had been, that rest still seemed subdued and in awe with just the size of the interior. In the desert finding the shelter of the flyer was something they had no capability of constructing presently. Here, this shelter made that one look like a small shelter or out-shelter. How had the ancients accomplished such construction? Were they so numerous that these, what did that banner say, *malls*, exist everywhere? Or were there just a few here and there because of the resources necessary to create such a thing? He thought that he had questions with their discoveries in the desert. Now he knew that he was only starting. This brought forth so many more, and it, in a way, made him proud to be a descendant of these *ones before.*

There was dust of time everywhere, and each step they made left their footprints there. Like a pristine snowfall unmarked they were now disturbing and leaving their own marks changing it forever. He stopped in his tracks. He suddenly realized that once again, of the knowledge they had lost and that this place could possibly bring some of it back to them. Still he wasn't sure, as the distance between what they knew now, and what their ancient ancestors knew, was great. So great in fact that it might take many generations for them to even learn what was here.

Listening he heard the exclamations made by the team as they saw something else. He could see them coming together and discussing what they saw. This was life changing. Not really paying attention he continued walking, deep in thought, when something grabbed his attention. Looking ahead he saw the team, every one of them, standing in front of one of the mercantiles.

Curious, he joined them and again joined them in silence. He was shocked into silence with what he saw. How was this even possible? Turning and watching the members of the team he could see the same disbelief in their eyes. Yet here it was right before them. They were actually seeing their ancient ancestors. Before them, on the other side of the large pane of glass, sat a number of large flat panels – most were dark, a couple showed some flickering lights, but this one had moving images. They were transfixed by what they were seeing. It seemed these ancients were above their world flying in the darkness of the stars, working on something artificial that was also located there. Words would flash across the panel stating that the history of space exploration was available here produced by the Discovery Channel.

Suddenly he felt dizzy and had to sit down. If what they were seeing here was real, their ancestors had even conquered, at least a part of . . . what did they call it . . . space. If they had advanced to this point and still came close to complete extinction what chance did they have if something similar happened in their present time?

Looking at some of these other flickering panels he saw that one suddenly began to produce images like the one they had been watching. Words flashed saying "*From the Military Channel*", and then he saw flyers like he had never seen. These had nothing on the front and looked so much different. In awe he watched as these moved across at speeds he couldn't believe were real. The images only lasted a short time and then the panel went dark. Whatever made it work had quit. He needed to get away from the team and be by himself. After all, if someone had come along and told him about what he was seeing, he would have called that person a liar. In the short time that they had been inside they had learned more than all the time shown in their own records and all the time they had spent studying the finds in the desert. What other secrets did this place hide?

Seeing what he had just witnessed was almost enough to make a grown male cry. What a world these ancients must have lived in, and in a moment of time, had been destroyed, buried, and lost. He knew that he would never be the same person as the one who first entered here. He, again lost in thought, started walking down the corridors and was subconsciously looking at the different mercantiles, but really not seeing them. He stopped and thought. *Wait a minute there, what was that one?* Turning back he looked through the glass front and saw books. Not just a few, but even though it was hard to see, it looked like hundreds. Excited, he realized that this could be the richest part of the find. Here, they might be able to discover that lost knowledge. Even with his excitement he knew that with the time that had passed these books could fall apart if touched. He went to the entryway and as expected found it locked.

Continuing his introspection and walk he found covered carts in the middle of the corridors and then an area that had another banner above stating "*Food Court*". Seeing this he thought. *They even had meals here. Life sure must have been much easier then. Still I might be naive in thinking this. After all, I am only reacting to what I have seen and I really have no facts to back up such a conclusion.*

He went to one of the tables located there and found that once again it was made of some artificial substance. Sitting in one of the chairs he stared out at nothing, becoming lost in thought. Suddenly he realized that someone had asked him a question. "What? Sorry, I am just overwhelmed here. I feel like a whelp that has been given the permission to enter the mysterious world of our sires."

"Yeah, I know what you mean. Really all I asked was can I join you here? This place is almost scary," Flar stated. "This is so far beyond anything in our world it almost seems unreal."

"Yeah, that's an understatement. I wonder where Doube is? I'm sure he would like to see this. Anyway, on the morrow we will get the rest from the property. They have to see this, and I know Nouma will want to. Fortunately she isn't so far along that she cannot join us."

"Tell you what, I'll grab Suzzane and we'll head back now and go back to the shelters and inform them. That way they can prepare and be here on the morrow early. I'm sure Suzzane would want to see that Lauut anyway and this is an excuse to have that happen."

"Great idea – I was thinking of sending someone on the morrow, but your idea makes much more sense. Yeah go ahead. We will be spending the night in camp. There is much work ahead of us all so let's enjoy this while we can."

"Okay then, I will see you on the morrow with the others." Flar got up and went to find Suzzane and head back. Jllon hoped that there would be no more failures in the equipment that had existed since this place had been buried. He was amazed that any of it worked after all this time. Of course he had no idea how any of it worked anyway. Still with the amount of time that had passed he felt fortunate to have at least some of it function. He knew that it could fail at any moment, and did expect it to do just that. After all he had seen that happen already.

It was pushing dusk when Flar and Suzzane entered the yard. They saw all four sitting on the porch enjoying a rest after the day's work. Seeing Fauul rise, they waved in recognition. "Don't get up; we will be with you in a moment," Flar said. "But we both need to take a quick trip to the necessary space. We have some very important news for you, so will see you in a moment."

"Is there a problem? Did something happen to one of the team or to Jllon?" Nouma asked worriedly.

Smiling even though he knew it was not light enough for them to see it he said, "No, nothing like that. But Jllon did send us back. Now give us a minute and we will be with you." At this point he and Suzzane headed into the workers shelter and were gone from their sight.

The four of them looked at each other wondering what this was all about. None of the team was due to be back for another two days. Lauut asked, to no one in particular, "So I wonder what's this all about?"

"I don't know about you, but before we barrage them with questions, I think we should at least get them some food and something to drink. You both know that it is a distance from there to here and they had to be walking during the meal time." Lauma said, and paused a moment before continuing, "Fauul lets go put something together for them." She got up and Fauul followed her back into the main shelter. Then Nouma and Lauut looked at each other and decided to help. It would be faster if all of them were involved.

"That's a relief." Suzzane said, "I thought my bladder was going to explode. I guess I drank too much liquid before we left. Shall we go out and see them?"

"Yeah, it is funny how, as the pressure builds that one cannot even think straight. Nature calls always seem to take priority over anything else." They exited the workers shelter and found no one across on the porch. "Where did everybody go?" He asked.

"Wait . . . I think I hear voices inside." Then listening closer she said, "Yes, I am almost sure they are all inside the main shelter."

The two of them headed over and as they approached could hear the voices inside. Flar yelling out said, "Okay, now you surprised us, can we come in?"

"Yeah" Lauma replied, "come on in. We are putting some food on for you since we figured that you haven't eaten yet."

Realizing that this was true and they were hungry from the skipped meal they entered and found the table set for them and the four of them sitting around the table waiting. Suzzane said, "Wow, I've never been the guest of honor anywhere. This makes me feel that it's that way, and it looks delicious, thank you so very much."

"Enough talking for now, sit and eat", Lauut said.

"Don't have to say anything to me twice. Call me anything you want but don't call me late to a meal." Flar said. They sat down and started filling their plates. "Are you sure any of you don't want anything else? I know that you ate earlier, but I never had a problem coming back later for more."

They shook their heads in the negative, and Fauul said, "This time of night we just enjoy the hot beverage, and sometimes a sweet snack. We are comfortably full. Now we are going to retire to the family space, so when you finish you can join us there. As you can guess we are full of questions as to why you are here. But it would not be polite to interrupt you while you are putting food into your mouths."

Suzzane looking up from her plate of food had to swallow what she had in her mouth and said, "Thank you, we won't be long. After all this is very good, and I know that I will empty this plate quickly."

"When you do, bring in a cup of the hot beverage with you. It's a great way to relax and pass the time. I have found since I have been here that it really is something I look forward to." Fauul said and then he continued, "Once you come in we can decide whether we want to go back out or just stay here to hear what news you are bringing to us. So once again, see you shortly."

Leaving the two of them at the table the four retired to the family space, and waited for them to finish and to join them. Nouma asked, "I wonder what has brought them back? At least they confirmed that no one was hurt, so that's a relief. Maybe they need to get something?"

"Well we can speculate all we want, but with no facts we are just grabbing at straws of hay in the wind. So anything we ask or guess will probably be wrong anyway." Lauut commented, "But I have to admit for me it was wonderful to see Suzzane again."

Lauma smiling knowingly said, "And you continue to tell us she is only a friend. Right . . . convince me."

About this time the two entered the space with Suzzane leading. Immediately she sought out Lauut, and to Lauma said, "I heard that. And on that subject, I will only say that we are friends, and becoming a little closer as time passes."

"Well, both of you can continue in that vein if you want to, but for the rest of us it is kind of obvious where this is heading. Anyway enough on embarrassing my brother, which is only fair, anyway what is it that brought the two of you here at this time?"

Suzzane looking over at Flar said, "I'll let him tell you. After all he is one of the higher ups in the team and I think he deserves the right, Flar?"

"First of all I think sitting here where it's comfortable is fine with us. So after we are finished if you want to go out to the porch we can." Looking at Lauut Flar continued, "If you hadn't found those fire starters then the chain of events that led us here would probably never have happened. So our find in the desert would never have happened and then coming here would never have happened, and as such we would never have known what has been here for a very long time."

Looking questionably at Flar, Lauut asked, "What are you talking about? You seem to be talking in circles here."

Smiling Flar continued, "I needed for you to know that it was the combination of information from the mapping team that Fauul was on and the objects you found that brought about our work and us to here."

"Right we were aware of that. Jllon had explained this when he made us promise to keep silent about your work here." Then suddenly he had an inkling that something had been found. There was a surprised look on his face as he came to this conclusion.

Flar almost laughed when he saw the look, "I see you have figured it out."

The other three turned to Lauut and asked, "What have you figured out?"

"I think they have found something here on the property, is that right Flar?"

Nodding in agreement he said, "That, in truth, is an understatement. We thought the find in the desert was a find of a lifetime, but what was uncovered here makes that appear to be nothing."

"How could discovering the *ones before* be almost nothing?" Fauul asked.

"Oh, discovering the *ones before*, our ancient sires was important – life changing to be exact. Once we found they had existed and what they seemed to be capable of forever changed us. But you see it was only a teaser. That hill turns out not to be a hill at all, but a covered shelter from the same time as our discoveries in the desert."

"The whole hill? Lauut exclaimed. "Come on, we can't make a shelter near that size. And from what you have said the one is the desert was greater than any we can do now. So I'm guessing that this shelter could only be a small part of that hill, right?"

"I am not asking you to believe it or not. Jllon has sent us here to get all of you, and you too Nouma, he said that it would be safe, and go see for yourself. He wanted for us to get here tonight so that you can prepare and be ready to leave after your morn work. I'm not going to say any more than that, other than be prepared for a life-changing event. When you are ready, on the morrow, we will lead you back and into that shelter. I suspect that we will either meet Jllon and the team on the outside, but I really think they will be inside." At this point Flar shut up, and no matter how hard they tried they couldn't get any more information out of him. All he would say was that they would have to see for themselves and draw their own conclusions. He did not want to spoil any first impressions. Finally they just gave up, and then Lauut and Suzzane went outside to the porch to be alone for a short period of time. The rest remained in the family space giving them the privacy they wanted.

The next morn they were up with the dawn. The plan was simple, push through the work and be done with it before the morn meal. Then once they had eaten to have Flar and Suzzane lead them back to the site.

Meanwhile, unknown to them, in the village after his morn meal, Doube prepared to return to the property. He had two days before gone to the village to pick up supplies and any correspondence that may have been there. He went down to the yards and picked up the pack beast followed by going to the mercantile where he packed the supplies that they needed. Plus, they had set up with Franc, to be a place for the runners to leave any correspondence.

Finally on the trail long before mid-morn he headed out, pushed and made the main shelter between zenith and the early to mid-zenith. Expecting to see someone there he was completely surprised that shelters appeared to be empty. Looking around he thought maybe they had gone out to handle the herds, but, where was Nouma? She was nowhere to be found either. Other than the dogs it was silent. What happened?

Not knowing, he unloaded the supplies from the pack beast and put the beast in the pens so that it would have water, be safe, and not wander off. After doing a second closer search and again finding nothing amiss, other than it being empty, he headed out to the camp figuring he would find someone there, and if not at least part of the team working that hill.

While Doube was at the main complex, the six of them reached the camp, and it was empty. Nouma, thinking that they were going to the hill, started off in that direction, but Flar stopped her and said, "No not in that direction, we've got to go into the tunnel."

"Into the tunnel!" exclaimed Lauma. "I'm sorry, but I have been down there once, and if truth be spoken here it was enough for me. I know that we found stuff down there, but the trip down was tough, and I have to admit I was never comfortable there."

Suzzane and Flar looked at each other and then at Lauma with Flar saying, "Things have changed since last time you were down there. We've worked hard on making it easier to get into and out of. Plus we reinforced it in areas we thought were weak – actually did some digging, and now you can walk all the way down to the caverns. No more crawling or climbing . .

. well at least on the trip down to the cavern. Plus we have oil lamps, so the entire distance is lit."

"You've done all of that? Wow your team has been busy." Then looking at the hill she saw a reflection of sunlight off of what appeared to be glass. "What's that up there?" She asked pointing.

"We really don't know, but it was on top of that hill. Anyway, we have yet to get to the base of those things. So are you ready to go now? I promise you it will be well worth the trip."

With some trepidation she said, "Yeah, I guess so, anyway, lead on. I have Fauul to lean on if it bothers me too much."

Looking at his mate he laughed and said, "And who do I get to lean on if I get scared?"

Seeing the humor in his eyes she replied, "My brother, except I think you would knock him over since you are so much bigger than he."

With their permission Flar signaled them to follow him and they headed over to and down into the tunnel. And to her surprise it was as he said. While the lighting was not perfect, it did an adequate job and the path down, while not totally worked over, was much easier to navigate. Before they knew it they were in the cavern and Lauma said, "That seemed much quicker than I remember, and you were right Flar it was much easier this time. Sorry I doubted you."

They looked across the cavern and saw what appeared to be a bright light shining out of the hole in the ceiling. Fauul turning to Flar asked what they were all curious about. After all such light was unexpected. "Flar, where's that light coming from? From what I saw on the surface your team hasn't made that much progress to expose this to the sunlight."

"You are so right, we haven't. Let's just say this is part of what you have to see. I wish there was an easier way up from here, but all of you will have to climb that rope ladder. Eventually we will have something better but for now this works and it is safe. Don't worry Nouma we will have Fauul below to catch you if you slip.

Now Lauut and Lauma, since it was your discovery that started this investigation, I want you two to go up first. Suzzane will follow you. When you get up to the top wait for her and she will lead you from there. Once the three of you are safely up then I'll go followed by you Nouma so that I can help you up at the top and again with Fauul there at the bottom to protect you and what you are carrying if you fall. Once you are up there then Fauul will follow and at that point I will lead you out of the space up there. Okay, all of you got it? Good, then let's do it."

Everything went without a hitch and finally when Fauul entered the space and the bright light that seemed to envelop the enclosed space surprised him.

But what was even more unbelievable was the amount of light entering through the partially open door. Flar with Nouma behind him, headed through that door, and once through Nouma immediately caught her breath and stopped. Curious, Fauul squeezed through the narrow opening and found he was reacting in exactly the same way. Nothing had ever prepared him for this sight. Immediately he felt small and out of place. It was like he didn't belong here, and where was that sound coming from and just the sheer size, just so much hitting his senses at once. It was completely overwhelming. Looking out in the center he saw Jllon with Lauut and Lauma and carefully headed over in their direction to join them. He took Nouma's hand and led her as she seemed to be frozen to that spot since she had entered the space.

About this time Doube was closing in on the camp expecting to find some of the team members, but just like the shelters it was silent. There was nothing but flyers making sounds. He had tried to see the hill from the distance but was unsuccessful. So once he confirmed that the camp was empty he headed for the hill. Then once there he found the very same thing – no one. It was eerie. People just don't disappear so completely. There had been no sign of any problems or struggles, or anything that said something happened. So where were they?

He really hadn't been tracking when he came here, since he had expected to find the team. Now he started looking around for any sign that would help explain what was going on. As he cast about and circling the camp he finally found fresh tracks heading towards the tunnel. *Ah, something I didn't think about. Maybe they have found something.* Sure enough as he approached the tunnel entrance he found most of the teams' footprints leading into the tunnel. He descended to the cavern and found the rope ladder and like the rest was surprised by the amount of light coming from that hole. He climbed the ladder and entered into the space and was blinded briefly. He saw the partially open door and went through it and like the rest immediately stopped.

Again, like the rest, he was completely unprepared for what he saw. Eventually once he got over the feeling of being overwhelmed he located the team out in the middle of the space and headed towards them. Immediately he recognized Fauul and saw he was talking with Jllon. Shortly he joined them, waiting patiently until the two quit talking and said, "You know all of you had me worried. I came back to the main shelters and no one was there. Then I thought, well maybe you were out taking care of the herds, but that didn't account for Nouma. Then I thought, well maybe she came to the camp to see you Jllon, but the camp was empty and there was no one working the hill. It was as if someone or something had come along and taken all of you. It was at that point I started tracking and found all of your tracks leading down into the tunnel, and now I have found you here, whatever this place is."

"I'm sorry about that Doube; I forgot that you were due back today. The excitement of finding this kind of overwhelmed all of us, Jllon replied. "This kind of makes our finds in the desert small."

"Small wouldn't describe it. I suspect you could put many of those large shelters we found out there in here and still have room. I am guessing that this is from the *ones before* also?"

"No doubt about it. When we were digging on the hill we ran into that change in soil that identifies the time period. It appears that the hill we are excavating is actually this shelter that was completely covered by that incident. It was completely sealed and I suspect that even the air became stale. It wasn't until that floor collapsed and that tunnel opened up that any air got into this place. It's the only explanation that I can come up with that explains the condition we have found it in. My guess is that even that cavern was the result of that event . . . and before you ask, no, I cannot explain the voices, music, and the light. I think this banner here has something to do with how this works, but I don't understand what any of it means. See it says something about being the first mall that is completely solar and LED. I haven't a clue what solar or LED is. My guess is there has to be at least a hundred mercantiles in here. We haven't started counting them or even going to the upper areas yet. Everything is locked, and I have asked everyone to not touch anything yet. I'm sure that with the age of this place that much of what was has broken down, fallen apart, or returned to dust.

Now that you are here, I want you and the four of you to follow me. I have something to show you that will make you think that these ancients were like gods of the myths. You know those ones we knew never existed but were used to create fantastic stories." He led them down the corridor to one of the mercantiles and in front again the glass sat a flat panel, and it had people moving on it.

The five again were frozen by what they saw. They couldn't even come up with words to describe it. Turning questionably to Jllon, Jllon said, "I know it's unbelievable, but I think this is something they are using to sell something. We have watched this a lot, and there are a number of short stories and writing describing what you are seeing. It goes for quite a while and then repeats. I think we are the first to ever see what the *ones before* looked like. If you look, there are others of these here. When we were first here this one had something on it also, but it stopped working. So my guess is that very little of whatever this is will still work. Of course, understanding it is well beyond any of us."

Again other than the way the ancients dressed it would be nearly impossible to tell them from any of the present day. At this point Jllon told them to wander around and stay on the bottom floor, but to look at everything that they could. He also said the obvious, that they would be here for a long, long time. Once he was finished they all broke up and started to walk the corridors as they suspected their ancient ancestors once did. It almost seemed to send chills down their spines knowing that only time separated them from those who had come before them.

Fauul and Lauma walked together trying to understand it all. Why had it been that they, as a people, had been so advanced, only to be knocked back to almost nothing? They had felt that in many ways they had advanced a long ways from where their own history said was their beginnings. Still here was proof that they had barely begun the climb back. Like Jllon they found the food court area and went to the table and chair area and sat down and talked for a long time.

In many ways they almost felt that they had to whisper as they were so overwhelmed by what was here. This was special to them, but from what they saw, it was something that the common person could go to at any time they felt the urge to do so. Fauul even stated that he felt that this area would hold everyone that lived in the township he had grown up in. And if one thought about that banner one could only conclude that there were others such as this.

They finally got up and continued to wander, looking into the glass fronts just as their distant ancestors probably had. It seemed as if it went on forever and everywhere one looked were places selling. So much of what they were seeing was strange – they having no explanation or idea what much of what they were seeing was. Finally making the loop on the ground floor she curious, went to what appeared to be the entrance to this mall. At this time the entrance was dark and covered on the outside with that dark soil that marked the time of the disaster. Then turning and looking across the area she saw a similar area there.

Between and on her right was a large metal panel, with the corridor to her left. She wondered if there was anything of importance behind that metal panel. Walking up to it and tapping it she felt it flex a little and rattle with her tapping. Then turning around she saw a small pillar like structure. The only problem lay in the fact that a pillar normally supported but this was only about two body lengths in height. Leading Fauul over to it she suddenly became excited. "Fauul look at this! It looks like a listing and location of all the mercantiles that are here!"

Lost in his own thought, he said. "What . . . a list? What are you talking about? A list for what . . . sorry, this place has left me thinking, and sad."

"I know what you mean. This place shows us what we have lost. Where would we have been if this disaster hadn't happened? Anyway, look here, this seems to be a list of what is here and where they are located . . ." Pointing at the dusty glass covered drawing she continued. ". . . See, it even shows you where you are located."

Looking closely at what she had found he was becoming excited. "I wonder if Jllon or any of the team has seen this? Let's go find him and see." They both headed out to find Jllon. But he or any of the team wasn't located where they had met when they first entered the mall. "I bet they have moved to that food court area. There's enough room there by moving some of those tables and chairs to establish a base to work from," Fauul said. "And it's sort of in the center also."

They headed down between the mercantiles and to the food court area, and just as he had concluded Jllon and the team were there discussing something. "Jllon . . ." Lauma called, "Jllon, we've found something that might be important."

Looking up questioningly he asked, "What could be so important? I mean all we are doing is finding something important here."

"Okay maybe that was a bad choice of words," she said smiling, "Anyway I want to ask if any of you have found a listing of what is here?"

Standing and looking at her seriously he said, "No, why do you ask? I mean we have only been here for close to a day, so how would we have created a list by now?"

Almost laughing she said, "Because you won't have to create one. It seems whoever built this place was smart enough to put together a map of what is here and to list the different mercantiles and where they were located."

"Really? Where is this list located?"

"Just follow us and we'll show you." Heading back, Lauma and Fauul took him to the pillar. "See, I went to what I thought was the entrance to this place and saw the same across over there. Then I saw this in-between and came to look at it. See, it lists everything here, and even where you are inside here."

"My gosh, you're right, this is a great find, and my will it help."

"Of course I'm right. And we females are very good at being right, more than you males want to admit." She said smiling. She still was unhappy with the position of females in the present society, but knew that with males like Jllon and yes her mate Fauul out there that changes were coming. She just liked to remind him, and of course her mate, now and then, that her views had not changed even if she had become a mate.

She had yet to inform her mate that he was to be a sire soon so thought while she had them off guard a little it was time to inform him. "Oh by the way Fauul I think that Jllon's mate started a small epidemic here."

"Are telling me she's sick?" Both Fauul and Jllon asked.

Laughing she said, "No not that kind. As you both know she is carrying and is nearing the end of her second third. Well, mate of mine I'm carrying myself and am early in my first third. So you and I will be sires soon."

At first Fauul was at a loss for words. Then laughing and picking her up and swinging her around followed by hugging and kissing her he said, "What a surprise this is. Wow, I really did not expect this."

"I think that when one is intimate one can only expect that eventually this is the result. And I think you have to admit that we have been very active that way." Looking at Fauul she could see that even he could blush. The laughing as she remembered all the times he had made her blush, she said in a triumphant voice, "Yes, even you can be embarrassed!"

....

As the time passed Jllon sent a correspondence to the council telling them to release the information on the desert discovery. The main portion being left out was the location. The information spread like a wildfire throughout the known world, and as is in so many cases, once a discovery is made others began to be found. He resigned his position as Head Keeper of the Past, and devoted all his time and energies to the work at the second site. There was much to excite, but at the same time there were many troubling aspects also discovered. It had a tendency to make him cautious. While their ancient ancestors had advanced in so many areas, they appeared in many others to be behind them in the present time.

In the present, while there were still crime and bandit groups, there were no wars. Yet, it seemed from what had been discovered that wars were common, and many died from the fighting, disease, and starvation. It seemed that the race from which they had descended was violent. And they had created weapons to enhance that violence. When reading of these wars it depressed him tremendously. Yet even in this, there seemed to be a brief light showing that change might have come.

But before any could be made that would have significantly changed their ancient descendants that worldwide disaster almost wiped them completely off this world. It left him wondering what he should reveal and what should be left buried. Still he realized that once a box is opened, it is nearly impossible to close it again. He learned that many of the terms they used in their daily speech came out of the disaster. Words like *shelter* and *hot beverage* for example. As he had thought, it was the mercantiles that sold books that brought them the most important information. He found wonders beyond any thoughts he had ever had known.

The team returned home after finishing the dig. Once completed, they had uncovered the, as they found in the ancient's vocabulary, building, or structure. Doube continued to scout, and ended finding a mate, who like him, loved this type of life. His sister also found a mate, and they worked the property with Doube coming to assist when needed. On the site a shelter was constructed where slowly but surely they began to understand what was here. It became a place of study, and many came to learn from the ancients. Jllon and Nouma ended having five whelps, with the oldest and youngest being female. While Fauul and Lauma had eight whelps, four males and four females, the oldest being a male, they too ended up building on the property. Lauut and Suzzane did become mates and they ended with four whelps all male. Lauut and Suzzane were able to take the best of what each knew and create a property the produced both beasts and vegetation type food. It became an example of what was possible, again with cooperation, instead of keeping the secrets within a family or group.

With the discoveries throughout the world a picture was slowly forming of what the world was like before the near extinction of what they learned had been called mankind. They learned that unlike the present where they used the lunar cycles and the summer and winter solstice to determine the turns around their sun, the ancients used something called months. While this method of tracking time had been lost, they were surprised to find that they still tracked the time of the day in a similar method. So some things changed and some remained the same.

In the end the three families continued to grow closer and the once remote village became an important center of learning, and an important place in their history. Even though it was not the first discovery, the one that identified the ancients as real, it was the one that revealed them completely. Their daily lives, the way they lived, the way they were transported, what the world had been like, and that in the end, they the present generation, were truly their descendants.

Still mysteries remained and one had to do with those fire starters that had been discovered. On the bottom were five letters that formed a nonsense word and the only thing anybody could figure is that it had to be the name of the artist or the one who created these things. And those letters were Z I P P O.

And so it is asked is this the End or is it truly the Beginning?

ABOUT THE AUTHOR

Storytelling and writing has always been F.D. Brant's passion, but responsibilities took preference. And because of those responsibilities it took retiring to allow those passions to come to fruition. Since retiring he has written 9 books, and maintains a weekly eclectic blog, Words in the Wind.

Growing up in the backcountry he learned the appreciation of "doing things for yourself". Because it was impossible to call in someone to repair anything one either did it themselves or went without. This led to the appreciation of the natural world, and the daily struggles that one faced as nature threw problems at the family that had to be overcome, leading to confidence and self-sufficiency. This led to the strong characters that populate his stories and books. And his female protagonists are strong willed and confident – something that he saw in both in his mother and sister.